ONE CUP OF CHEMISTRY

DESTINATION WEDDING TRILOGY BOOK 1

THE WAY TO A WOMAN'S HEART SERIES

SHERI TYLER

For Tom Roberts—

Your passion for R&B, sparked by your love of James Booker, and your unwavering dedication to pursuing a career you truly love have been nothing short of inspiring. Thank you for showing me what it means to follow your rhythm in life.

And for you, my reader—

Your laughter, your love for these stories, and your unwavering support are the heart of everything I create. Thank you for being the chemistry that makes this journey so extraordinary.

BIBLIOGRAPHY

Contemporary Romances
By Sheri Tyler
The Way to a Woman's Heart series - the **Coming Home** trilogy
Slow Simmer
Here's the Scoop
From Bitter to Sweet

The Way to a Woman's Heart series - the **Destination Wedding** trilogy
One Cup of Chemistry
Say Cheese
Kebabs and Kisses

Historical romances
By Sheridan Jeane

Gambling On a Scoundrel

Secrets and Seduction series:
* *Lady Cecilia Is Cordially Disinvited for Christmas*
*(only available via Sheridan's VIP club)
It Takes a Spy…
Lady Catherine's Secret
Once Upon a Spy
My Lady, My Spy
Along Came a Spy

Duke By Dawn (Novella, part of the anthology *Dukes All Night Long*)
Coming August 2025

The Rose and the Spy - a Victorian-era Romantic Suspense trilogy
Coming 2026
Whispers and Spies
The Spy In Disguise
A Spy For All Seasons

1

A PRIVATE AIRPORT

Grayson

The problem with being the best man at your sister's wedding is that you can't exactly skip the event—even if the maid of honor has a knack for tying your stomach in knots every time she's near.

Not that I actually would.

Driving to a private airfield just outside Pittsburgh, I expected something closer to a James Bond setup—sleek lounges, valets with impeccable posture, maybe a few secret agents lurking in the shadows. Instead, I found a few modest hangars, a control tower that looked like it belonged in an '80s action movie, and a runway that had seen one too many summers. Maybe all private airfields were like this, but "private airfield" had definitely oversold it.

Pulling into the lot, my trusty Toyota Camry stood out like a sore thumb amid a sea of gleaming BMWs and Audis. For a moment, I debated stashing it in the employee parking area, where a few well-worn beaters huddled like kindred spirits. But where was the fun in that? My car had character. Besides, I didn't need a flashy ride to prove my worth. In my world, it wasn't about what you drove; it was about what you knew. Results trumped appearances every time—though Dad would've seen it differently.

I grabbed my bag and went in search of the wedding party. Silence reigned inside the hangar. There was an open space toward the back as big as theater stage, inspiring me. I pulled up *My Girl* on my cell phone and propped it against a crate. Mara's wedding was already a logistical minefield, but leave it to Mom to make things even more interesting with her grand surprise: a choreographed dance routine during the reception.

"It'll be fun," Mom had said over the phone last week. "Trust me, everyone will love it—especially Mara!"

She wasn't wrong. Mara would be over the moon. Me? I was already imagining the moment I tripped over my own feet in front of the entire guest list.

I tapped my foot to the music, easing into the groove…exactly the way I was supposed to get drawn into it at the start of the number. The way Mom had planned it, she and my younger twin sisters, Rachael and Aubrey would carry the load, and I'd be there to add comedy—and make the three of them look good. My goofs were supposed to be part of the routine.

I glanced around the hangar. Empty. Perfect. No one needed to see me butcher basic choreography.

Picking up the phone again, I pressed "repeat" on the song and took my spot on the concrete floor. One-two-three, spin. My shoes squeaked against the smooth concrete as I pivoted, wobbling slightly but managing to recover. Sort of.

"Okay," I muttered to myself. "Not terrible. Let's try that again."

I stumbled on the next step, catching myself before I went tripping over my own feet. Not exactly graceful, but progress. At least Mom's choreography didn't require the precision of Bob Fosse. Baby steps, I reminded myself.

The problem wasn't the combos—they were simple enough, a mix of spins and shuffles Mom had drilled into me over video calls. The problem was me. This kind of dancing had once come naturally, but not anymore. Too many years since I'd abandoned music and dance in favor of science and research. I wasn't coordinated or flashy like my mom and sisters. I was functional at best.

My mind kept flashing forward to the reception, where Mara would probably beam while I tripped over my feet in front of a hundred amused wedding guests. Great memories in the making. Dad? He'd be disappointed in me no matter how I performed... either because I'd made a fool of myself by not being polished enough, or because I'd put too much time and energy into practicing instead of focusing on my floundering career.

Dad always saw dancing and the other arts as a waste of time, as if science was the only thing worth excelling at. I never understood how Mom put up with him. Maybe it was because he treated her differently—or maybe she just learned to tune him out. No doubt he'd be judging me at the reception, calculating every misstep like it was a failed experiment.

I narrowed my focus, suddenly more determined to master this. And then something clicked. It wasn't perfect, but I hit a step in sync with the music and took off from there. For a moment, I wasn't thinking about work or wedding logistics. I was just... having fun.

It had been years since I'd danced like this, and even longer since I'd allowed myself to enjoy something so unmeasurable, so unproductive. It stirred something in me—a feeling I thought I'd stamped out long ago.

My focus locked on hitting the next step, my mind blocking out everything else—until Courtney's voice cut through the air like a record scratch.

"Grayson Stellar," she said, her voice laced with amusement. "For a college professor, you look damned good on the dance floor."

I froze mid-spin, my footing faltering. She was leaning casually against the wing of a small airplane, arms crossed, her smirk firmly in place.

"Didn't anyone teach you to stomp your feet when you sneak

up on someone?" I asked, quickly pausing the music and shoving my phone into my pocket.

"Hangar floors aren't exactly designed for stealth," she said, stepping closer. "Relax, I'm not here to critique. Although…" Her gaze flicked to my feet. "That spin could use some work."

"That's why I'm in here."

"Honestly, you're… surprisingly good," she said, her smirk softening for just a moment. "You might even steal the show at the reception." Then that smirk snapped right back into place. "It's nice to see Mara managed to pry you out of your lab for the weekend."

"And miss her wedding? Not a chance."

Courtney laughed, the sound warm and easy. "Mara's looking for you. She's out by the plane, scheming with Ford."

I ushered her forward. "Lead the way." The small pocket of calm I'd carved out evaporated as I followed Courtney. My nerves shifted gears. Dancing in front of a crowd was one thing; navigating this destination wedding might be another dance entirely.

As we exited the hangar, Mara immediately spotted us. "Grayson!" she called, waving us over. "About time you got here. Ford and I were betting on whether you'd blame traffic or coffee for being late."

I grinned. "Traffic. Always traffic. That's my story, and I'm sticking to it."

She smirked. "Noted. Anyway, Ford's got the grand plan," she said, gesturing to his clipboard.

Courtney took in the clipboard with raised eyebrows. "You're scaring me with that thing. Are we flying to a wedding or planning an invasion?"

"Both," Ford deadpanned, gripping his clipboard like it held the plans to storm a castle.

Mara grabbed Courtney's arm. "Come on, I need to grab the charger from the car. You're coming with me."

Courtney shot me an amused look as she followed Mara. "Try not to break anything while we're gone," she teased.

Ford grinned, his clipboard firmly in hand, radiating the confidence of a man who'd just won a Best Director award. "Grayson! Glad you made it. We've got things running smoother than a film set."

"Glad to be here," I said, clapping him on the shoulder. "Need anything from your best man? Luggage handling, moral support, maybe a foot rub?"

Ford chuckled. "Just help me get everything on board. This jet's a loaner from a friend—don't let the glam fool you. We do our own luggage handling."

As I followed him toward the plane, I gestured toward the jet's polished exterior. "So, I take it this whole setup is for the wedding party? You and your brother sure know how to travel in style."

Ford nodded. "Yep, just the core group on this flight. Two brides, two grooms, your parents, and the wedding entourage. Turks and Caicos weddings don't plan themselves, you know. The rest of the guests are flying commercial or private."

"Two weddings, one ceremony," I said, shaking my head, "and enough logistics to make NASA jealous. Did Mara have to do much arm twisting with Sonya?"

Ford grinned. "You know your sister. When Sonya and Max got engaged, Mara said, 'Why not share the day?' And here we are."

I laughed. "Share the day? Sounds like something Mara would say after taking over all the planning."

"And don't forget," Ford added, "she somehow convinced Sonya that a destination wedding was low-maintenance. The real miracle was getting my brother to go along with this extravaganza. Max likes to keep things low-key."

I raised an eyebrow. "Extravaganza? How many guests are we talking here?"

Ford smirked. "Enough to make the hotel staff start breaking out the champagne early. Mara and Sonya are calling it an 'intimate extravaganza,' whatever that means. I think it's their way of saying it's going to be both over-the-top and exclusive."

At least he'd said *intimate*. "I assume that still means plenty of drama and excitement," I said, half-joking.

"Let's hope not," Ford replied, grinning. "Don't worry. As best man, you'll get a front-row seat to all the chaos. Hope you're ready."

As I loaded the last bag onto the jet, Mara approached, her blue-dyed ponytail swishing with determination, Courtney by her side. She pointed a finger between Courtney and me like she was addressing unruly children.

"Just so we're clear," she said, "you two workaholics are officially off duty. No labs, no research, no breakthrough talk. I mean it. This is a wedding, not a conference. Got it? I've seen each of you dive into medical breakthroughs at the drop of a hat," Mara said, narrowing her eyes. "Putting you together is a recipe for disaster. I'm not letting you turn my wedding into a think tank."

I raised my hands in surrender. "No work talk. Got it. But if you think that means I won't embarrass you with my toast, think again."

Mara grinned. "Toast away, big brother. Just save the science lecture for Monday."

I rolled my eyes, but my mind was already spinning. Between the dance, the toast, and Courtney being part of the wedding party, this weekend was shaping up to be more of a high-stakes performance than I'd signed up for.

TAKING OFF TO NEW HEIGHTS

Courtney

The wind betrayed me.

One gust, perfectly timed, and my summery skirt billowed up like I was reenacting Marilyn Monroe's iconic scene in *The Seven Year Itch*. My emerald green panties? Front and center.

I slapped my offending skirt down so hard I probably bruised my thighs, praying no one noticed, but a low, far-too-amused voice cut through the tarmac's noise.

"Nice choice, Gillette," he said, his smirk betraying him. "Very… vibrant."

I whirled to face Grayson Stellar—all six-foot-two inches of infuriating charm and confidence. He wasn't the type to let anything slide. Of course, he looked annoyingly put together, his blue button-front shirt trim enough to prove he hadn't indulged in airport snacks—and patterned with tiny white fish skeletons that somehow managed to mock me, like even his fashion choices were in on the joke.

Mortification flared hot in my cheeks—a frequent hazard of being a redhead—but I forced out a laugh. What were my options? Hide under a plane wing or own it. "Glad you approve," I said. "Green is the new black, you know."

Grayson grinned and headed up the Gulfstream's stairs. To my credit, I managed to walk away with my head high, even if my dignity was limping behind me.

Inside the hangar, Mara approached me, her blue-tipped ponytail swinging. "What happened out there? You look like you just faced a firing squad."

"Nothing," I said too quickly. "Grayson's just… here. And helpful."

Mara raised an eyebrow, the corners of her mouth twitching. "Helpful and hot, you mean?"

"Mara!" I yelped, my face heating again.

"What? He's my brother, not my blind spot. He's objectively attractive, and you've clearly noticed."

"Not this again," I groaned, side-eyeing her. "Why are we talking about my love life?"

"Because you don't have one," she teased, grinning before her tone softened. "But seriously, how are you holding up? You like your new digs?"

I shrugged. "Peace, quiet, and an alarm clock that doubles as a jet engine."

Mara snorted. "Sounds idyllic."

"It's not the worst," I said with a shrug. "The rent's decent, and it's close to work, so I can't complain too much. But between the noise, the workload, and this self-imposed dating hiatus post-breakup, the past few months have been… less than idyllic."

Her expression softened. "Richard, right? Mr. TED Talk and LinkedIn?"

"That's the one." I sighed. "Every conversation was a résumé competition. And when I won that award last spring? He disappeared faster than a New York cab in a rainstorm. His ego couldn't handle it."

"Good riddance," she said firmly. "Honestly, he always seemed more in love with his accomplishments than you. You deserve better."

"Well, I'm not exactly holding auditions," I said with a shrug.

"Right now, it's just me, my lab, and old episodes of *The Great British Baking Show*. Who needs romance when you've got lemon drizzle cake and Paul Hollywood's skeptical eyebrow?"

Mara grinned. "You just need a little push. Or maybe someone to whisk you off your feet—kind of like Ford did with me."

Before I could reply, my phone buzzed. A glance at the screen showed a message from Pete in IT: **"Unusual access attempts on the lab server. Investigating. Will update."** My brows knit together. It wasn't unheard of, but the timing was suspicious since I was about to leave the country.

Mara peeked over my shoulder, her curiosity uncontainable. "Work already? Weren't you paying attention earlier? I implemented a strict no-work-talk rule this weekend."

"It's probably just a glitch," I said, pocketing my phone. "Cyber-gremlins."

Mara raised an eyebrow. "Well, keep the gremlins in their cage. No work, remember? This weekend, you're Courtney the Maid of Honor, not Courtney the Scientist."

She nudged me forward, and we ascended the jet's stairs. Inside, the luxury of Ford and Max's borrowed jet was something straight out of a billionaire's wish list—wide leather seats, chilled champagne, and an unusual seating arrangement designed to encourage conversation. Two front-facing armchairs near the cockpit, already claimed by the parents, were flanked by arcs of seats that faced each other down the center, like someone decided a flying living room was the height of sophistication.

Emma, Ford's twelve-year-old niece, was already at the snack bar like it was an all-you-can-eat buffet...which it sort of was. Officially, she was on the plane with her guardians, Sonya and Max, but she clearly had no intention of waiting for permission to dive into the chocolate truffles. "Where's the caviar?" she asked innocently, popping a truffle into her mouth.

"Already finished it," Ford replied without missing a beat, lounging in one of the oversized chairs like a king surveying his kingdom.

As I claimed a seat, Grayson slid into the one next to mine, annoyingly unruffled. "Now, *this* is how the other half lives."

"Pretty posh" I agreed, glancing at Ford and Max as I set my laptop bag down and sank into the plush leather.

Takeoff took place faster than I would have guessed, and we were in the air without much fanfare.

When the pilot told us it was safe to move around the cabin, Emma straightened, her eyes widening with purpose. "Wait here. Aunt Mara and I have a surprise."

Before anyone could question her, she and Mara darted to the back of the plane, disappearing behind a partition. There was a brief scuffling sound, followed by an exaggerated "Shh!" and what I could've sworn was a bark.

By the time Emma stepped into the aisle holding Zephyr's leash, the plane was practically vibrating with energy. It wasn't the engines—it was Emma's determination and the dog's obvious delight.

"Dum-da-dum, dum-da-dum," she sang as she paraded Zephyr, now dressed in a tiny tuxedo with a perfectly straight bow tie.

I couldn't stop grinning. The absurd cuteness was too much. "Is he auditioning for the royal wedding?"

Zephyr paused in the aisle and barked, as if to answer. The plane erupted in laughter.

"This," Mara announced, sweeping an arm like a showman, "is our ring bearer. He's taking his responsibilities very seriously."

Grayson and Mara's mom just smiled faintly, shaking her head like someone resigned to her children's antics. From his seat across from her, their father's disapproving gaze occasionally flicked toward us, lingering on Grayson with subtle disapproval. Not at the tuxedoed dog—no, that would've made too much sense.

The look was a quieter kind of judgment, the kind that simmered under the surface and stuck. Grayson slouched just a fraction under it, the easy smile on his face thinning ever so slightly, like he'd forgotten how to hold it up.

Grayson, clearly ready for a distraction, turned his attention to me with a grin that could've doubled as a dare. "What do you think, Courtney? Can we count on Zephyr to be a reliable ring bearer?"

I gave a snort of laughter as I glanced doubtfully at the little dog, who now sat regally at Emma's feet as if he hadn't caused a scene at all. "I don't know… he looks pretty confident. I haven't seen that level of focus since my college chess days—and I still found ways to lose."

Grayson's eyebrows shot up. "Chess tournaments? You?"

"Don't read too much into it," I warned.

"That's unexpected," he replied, leaning back with a look that told me he wouldn't let it go. "Are you ranked? How often do you play in tournaments?"

I huffed out a laugh. "Never. I haven't been in a competition since college." I hesitated, the words teetering on the edge before I gave in. "I set chess aside for work."

The confession felt oddly raw… like something I shouldn't have admitted in front of Grayson, of all people.

He was Mara's brother—off-limits despite her awkward comment earlier. And yet, there was something about him, something that made me forget he was supposed to be nothing more than a colleague. Maybe it was the way he looked at me, like he actually saw past the polished version I tried to project.

I hated that he saw this crack in my armor. Worse, I hated how much I wanted him to.

"You set it aside, huh?" His tone softened, and the usual edge in his voice faded. It caught me off guard. He seemed to get it, really get it. And it made me wonder how much he'd had to leave behind, too.

"I get it," he added after a beat. "Sometimes it feels like the things you leave behind don't even miss you."

Mara glanced toward the front of the plane, then at her phone.

"Dad just gave Zephyr his first thumbs up," she announced, holding up her phone as evidence. "The social media post practically wrote itself."

I glanced over with mock shock. "Did he? Or did your dad's finger just twitch?"

"Hard to say," Mara replied with a grin. "Either way, Zephyr's on track for favorite child."

Laughter rippled through the cabin, but Grayson's gaze drifted to the front of the plane, where his father sat apart, half-hidden behind a newspaper. For just a second, the easy smile slipped, replaced by something heavier—an instinctive flicker of hope for approval that would never come.

Grayson's smirk turned competitive. "Speaking of favorites..." He swiped the phone out of her hand with an easy, practiced motion that said this wasn't the first time he'd stolen her thunder. "How'd you manage to get internet at ten-thousand feet? This has to be sorcery."

Mara grinned. "It's called flying on a private jet. Unlimited Wi-Fi is one of the perks."

"Clearly, I've been doing life wrong," Grayson said, shaking his head as he handed back the phone. His smirk stayed in place, but I caught his eyes flick toward the front of the plane. "Next stop: favorite child status for me. Zephyr, you're going down." He let out a low chuckle, but his attention lingered briefly on his father. I could see it now—the unspoken tug-of-war between wanting approval and being tired of needing it. It was a look I knew too well.

3

MILE-HIGH CHEMISTRY

GRAYSON

Courtney was impossible to ignore, which was good since looking at her drove all thoughts of my dad's impossible expectations from my mind.

It wasn't just because her flowing skirt reminded me of that glimpse of emerald green panties, but because she had a way of turning every conversation into an exchange of wits. And I couldn't help but enjoy sparring with her.

"Let me guess," I said, leaning back in my seat, arms crossed. "You traded chess tournaments for late-night lab reports."

Her gaze flicked toward me, wary, as if deciding whether I was teasing or prying. "Something like that. When you're trying to cure cancer, hobbies tend to feel… irrelevant."

"Or optional," I added. I didn't mean it as judgment. It just came out sounding like I knew exactly what she meant. Because I did.

Her eyebrow lifted. "You? The professor who's never late to a lecture and probably wins 'best teacher' awards for fun? Please."

I snorted, shaking my head. "You think that just happens? Publish or perish is the name of the academic game. If I'm not at the lab, I'm at home reading the latest research and staring at a screen until my eyes feel like they're melting. It's a great look."

She laughed—softly, but there was recognition in it. "Sounds familiar. I'm big on 'obsessive midnight research' myself."

Ford, sprawled lazily in his seat like he'd orchestrated the whole trip, chimed in without missing a beat. "Workaholics, the both of you. Is there a support group for that? 'Hi, I'm Ford, and I'm surrounded by overachievers.'"

"When spoken by a Sundance award winning director, that comment carries less weight." I smirked, but something about Ford's joke struck a little close to home. I glanced at Courtney again, taking in the faint crease in her brow. She didn't look like someone who knew how to slow down. Just like me.

"When's the last time you did something that wasn't work?" I asked.

Courtney opened her mouth, then froze—like the answer was there but refused to cooperate. I didn't blame her. I didn't have an answer for that one either.

"Today?" she finally said, clearly reaching, and I smirked.

Before I could press further, Sinan—who I'd almost forgotten was there—closed his medical journal with a soft thump. For someone as unassuming as Ford and Max's brother-in-law, he had a talent for commanding attention without raising his voice. Tall, calm, and perpetually put together, he looked more like the neurosurgeon he was than the other best man in this double wedding chaos we were flying into.

"All work and no play," Sinan said, his tone so mild it bordered on conversational, but his gaze pinned us both in place. "You two sound like you're trying to win a match nobody's playing. When's the last time you did something just for fun?"

Courtney shrugged. "Fun is… subjective."

I snorted. "Subjective? What does that even mean?"

"It means I find joy in being productive."

"You find joy in chasing breakthroughs at work," I countered. "Admit it, seeing the pieces click together gives you a rush."

Her lips twitched, almost a smile. "Guilty. But at least it's a productive kind of fun."

Before she could continue, Sinan stepped in. "As a neurosurgeon, I've seen burnout firsthand," he said, the calm in his voice making his words hit harder. "You're both on the same dangerous path. Brilliance needs room to breathe, or you'll burn out completely. Then what?"

"Creative expression," I muttered. I shot a quick glance toward Dad, who sat at the front, oblivious. My comment wasn't sarcasm —well, not entirely—but it still earned me a sharp look from Sinan.

"Exactly," he replied, unruffled. "Recharge your brain. Pick up an old hobby. Learn goat yoga, if that's your thing. When's the last time you pursued a hobby or interest that wasn't about work?"

I didn't answer right away. My instinct was to deflect—to throw out a joke, maybe some vague excuse—but instead, I heard myself say, "I used to play piano. R and B. Ragtime. Scott Joplin. I was obsessed for a while." The admission sat there like a surprise, even to me. My voice had softened without my permission, and I wasn't sure I liked that.

Courtney started studying me like I'd just sprouted a second head. "Piano?" she echoed.

I didn't look at her. Instead, I spread my hands and glanced at them, then shrugged. "I haven't touched a keyboard in years."

It was a small truth, but one that carried more weight than I wanted to admit.

Sinan nodded and shifted his focus to Courtney, who suddenly looked like she wanted to vanish. "And you?"

She squirmed, her voice quieter now. "I used to bake. Birthday cakes, after school snacks...Mommy Julie taught me. My mom's mom. And I played in chess tournaments in college. But life happens, and certain distractions get left behind."

"Distractions?" Sinan repeated, arching a brow. "You mean joy?"

"It's just baking," she muttered, looking anywhere but at me. "Nothing I couldn't pick up at a bakery. And I was never going to be a grandmaster."

"That's not the point," Sinan said. "The point is balance. You're both brilliant, but brilliance needs room to breathe. Consider this an experiment in happiness. Do something for yourself."

An experiment in happiness. The phrase shouldn't have worked, but it did.

"What, like a creative pact?" I asked, half joking but curious to see what Courtney would say.

"Exactly," Sinan said, clearly satisfied.

I turned toward her with a small, lopsided grin. "Well? Are you in?"

"What am I agreeing to?" she shot back, cautious.

"You bake something when we get back to Pittsburgh," I said, smirking. "Something worthy of this experiment."

Her eyes narrowed, but the smile tugging at her lips gave her away. "Fine. I'll bake a proper cake. Something challenging that would make my grandmother proud."

Something about the way she said that hit me, though I wasn't sure why. I didn't let it linger. "And I'll play the piano, which also means buying one," I said, more to myself than to her.

It was ridiculous—a silly mid-flight pact made on a private jet over the Atlantic. But as I leaned back in my seat, watching her scratch Zephyr behind the ears with surprising gentleness, I wondered if maybe—just maybe—there was something to it.

Because for the first time in a long time, the idea of doing something just for the sake of it didn't seem so impossible.

4

FLIRTING AND FLYING HIGH

COURTNEY

The plane settled into a steady hum. The earlier chaos of Zephyr's tuxedo debut had died down, Ford had finally given up on trying to out-charm the dog, and Mara was absorbed in her wedding magazine, flipping through pages so worn I was surprised they didn't fall apart.

Grayson, though, was staring out one of the windows. Quiet. Too quiet.

I nudged his foot gently, pulling him back from wherever he'd disappeared to. "Lost in thought?"

He blinked, like I'd jolted him out of a fog. "What?"

"You've been brooding for ten minutes straight. Should I be concerned?"

He let out a soft laugh, unconvincing. "I don't brood."

"Whatever helps you sleep at night."

A ghost of a smile tugged at his lips, but he didn't argue. Instead, he turned back to the window, clouds glowing faintly in the fading light.

"I thought I should tell you—I was up for the Cates Foundation job," he said abruptly, the words tumbling out like he'd ripped off a bandage.

The air shifted around us, jolting me upright. "Wait. *My* job?"

Grayson turned to me, his expression neutral, though the tension in his jaw betrayed him. "Yeah. Same position. Congratulations, by the way."

My stomach dropped as I stared at him, searching his face. "I... I didn't know."

"It's not a big deal," he replied quickly, too quickly. "You deserved it. Your research is a better match for what they needed."

My heart twisted because I could tell he meant it. And somehow, that made it worse. I knew how much it stung to pour yourself into something, only to come up short.

"What about your research?" I asked carefully.

Grayson's gaze slid back to the window, his shoulders sinking ever so slightly. "It's complicated. AI is catching up to my cancer cell identification faster than I can pivot, and my dad's already convinced I should've gone into cardiac surgery. 'Real medicine,' as he calls it."

The flatness in his voice tugged at something deep in my chest.

He shifted slightly, his voice softening. "Actually, someone with MedcoVax asked about you the other day—mentioned your work. I told them your success wasn't surprising. You've made an impression on the field."

I blinked, caught off guard. "MedcoVax?"

"Yeah." His mouth quirked in a faint smile, his tone light. "I think it's just proof Cates made the right choice."

The compliment was so earnest it left me momentarily speechless. My instinct to deflect faltered under the weight of his sincerity.

"Well," I said finally, "it's nice when those late nights in the lab pay off with results that get noticed."

Grayson's smile widened slightly, though his gaze flickered briefly toward the front of the plane, where his dad sat behind his newspaper. "Trust me, people notice. He hasn't said a word to me this entire flight. Pretty obvious he thinks Zephyr's tuxedo is a bigger achievement than anything I've done lately."

I tried to smile at his attempt to make light of it, but the words were too raw to be funny. My parents might've been emotionally absent, but at least they'd never pressured me to be something I wasn't.

"My parents were hands-off," I admitted after a pause, surprising myself with the confession. "Too hands-off, honestly. My brothers and I had to figure things out ourselves. I had freedom and a home, but nothing else. I don't think they even knew what I wanted to do with my life until I'd already done it."

Grayson turned his attention to me, his expression softening. "That sounds…"

"Lonely?" I offered. "Yeah. It was. In a different way, I guess. At least I had my grandparents They were the best."

He didn't argue or try to one-up me with his own story. Instead, he nodded faintly. "Life still brought us both here, though. Same plane. Same double wedding."

"Same burnout," I added with a small smile, trying to lighten the mood.

The corner of his mouth lifted, but it didn't quite reach his eyes.

Before either of us could say more, Ford leaned forward. "Two brilliant cancer researchers, both griping about burnout? This flight is officially a think tank on overwork."

Laughter rippled through the cabin as he raised his drink in a toast. "To Courtney and Grayson—the only two people here who need a vacation more than I do!"

The others joined in with scattered applause and laughter, the noise warm and light, breaking the earlier tension.

I snuck a glance at Grayson. His shoulders tensed as every head turned toward us. Dr. Stellar's paper rustled, just slightly, and though I couldn't see his expression, I didn't need to. The disapproval in his posture said it all.

Grayson's neutral smile reappeared, but I caught the flicker of something else in his eyes. A grimace, there and gone.

Ford popped the can open with a celebratory fizz, breaking the moment. Across the aisle, Mara and her new niece Emma were deep in debate about Zephyr's outfit—bow tie versus top hat. Their laughter rippled through the cabin, warm and grounding, but my focus stayed on Grayson.

He sat stiffly, tension lingering in his posture, and his gaze flicked—just briefly—toward the front of the plane, where his dad sat behind a newspaper. The silence between us felt heavier than the hum of the engines.

I nudged his foot again, softer this time. "Take the compliment," I said, keeping my voice low. "It won't kill you. Promise."

His lips twitched, but he didn't quite meet my eyes. "Noted," he said after a beat, the word cautious, like he wasn't sure how to hold it.

Before I could respond, Zephyr trotted into the aisle, tuxedo slightly askew, and hopped onto my lap with the confidence of someone who'd just claimed their throne. I scratched behind his ears, and he let out a happy huff, his tail thumping gently against my leg.

Grayson leaned closer, his smirk sliding back into place. "Don't think I've forgotten about that cake."

I tilted my head, giving him a sidelong glance. "What, you don't think I can handle a baking challenge?"

"Oh, I'm sure you can," he replied, his tone deliberately casual. "I just want to see what you come up with. No shortcuts."

"Sounds suspiciously like a dare."

"Call it what you want," he said with a shrug. "You're still baking."

I smirked, refusing to let him win this round. "Fine. But you'd better start practicing the piano. No excuses."

His smile lingered, softer now, not the quick-witted shield he used like armor. "Deal."

Zephyr let out a huff, as if sealing the pact himself. The cabin's chatter filled the space around us, but for the first time, Grayson's shoulders relaxed, and the weight behind his earlier tension seemed to ease.

And for once, I didn't overthink it. I let the moment stand—a silly promise forged mid-flight, surrounded by laughter, warmth, and the comfort of being with people who felt like family.

Sometimes, it wasn't about planning every step. Sometimes, it was enough to just be.

5

ON THE BEACH

GRAYSON

Sunlight poured across Grace Bay Beach, the turquoise waves lapping lazily against the shore. I crouched near a growing sand-castle, patting a turret into shape while Mara sculpted a makeshift moat with a seashell. Sand clung to her sapphire-tipped nails as she worked, her usual sharp focus softened by the whimsical task.

"You're going to have to pry Ford off that call if you want him at the rehearsal on time," I said, smirking as I adjusted one of the castle's walls.

Mara huffed, brushing sand off her hands. "He's lucky I love him. And that he's directing *Ghost*. Otherwise, I'd toss his Assistant Film Editor's number straight into the ocean and drag him out here to the beach for some pre-rehearsal downtime."

I laughed, but my attention snagged on two figures approaching from the resort—Courtney and her friend Rose. Courtney's emerald-green swimsuit caught the sunlight as she strode across the sand, her cover-up drifting behind her. My stomach clenched. She had a way of effortlessly drawing every eye, mine included. I forced my gaze back to my castle, smoothing a lopsided corner.

Courtney was stunning, and our chemistry was undeniable.

Team Desire was all in, claiming the connection was like a perfectly balanced chemical reaction—sharp, full of energy, and completely irresistible. She was clever, funny, and intriguing—all the things that lit up my scientific curiosity and more.

But then Team Practicality cleared its throat. A weekend fling? Not likely. That kind of arrangement would unravel fast—too many variables, too much risk for entanglement. I wasn't built for fleeting connections, and Courtney deserved more than that.

Plus, she was Mara's best friend, which came with its own set of complications. And my schedule? Let's just say it was bursting at the seams. It would already be a stretch to add in those piano lessons that were supposed to help clear my head.

"Oh, look," Mara teased, elbowing me. "Your competition's here. You should probably go hide."

"Not funny," I muttered, irritated she'd poked at that tender spot. Losing the Cates Foundation position to her had been disappointing, sure, but she'd earned it, no question. What chafed the most was Dad turning it into yet another notch in his ongoing tally of my failures.

"Space for two?" Courtney asked as they reached us, motioning to the empty chairs nearby.

"Always," I replied, gesturing to the spot. Her voice had this lilting confidence, and the way she smiled made me feel like she was looking forward to spending time with me. But my heart sank when she and Rose glanced at the ocean instead.

"We'll be back," Courtney said, her smile brief but somehow still disarming. Her eyes lingered on mine for half a beat longer than necessary, enough to make me wonder if I imagined it.

I nodded, masking my disappointment. "Enjoy."

As Courtney and Rose jogged toward the water, Mara stood, brushing sand off her legs. "Come on, big brother, time to walk. This castle's not going anywhere."

We strolled along the shoreline, the warm water licking at our feet. Mara bent to pick up a shell, holding it up to the light before skipping it across the surface. The calm water of the bay let it bounce twice before sinking.

"Nice form," I said, trying my own hand at it. My shell skidded once before vanishing.

"Gray, it's a tropical beach. Brooding is illegal here," Mara said, smirking. "Alright, spill. Is this about Courtney, Dad, or work?"

"All of the above." I sighed, running a hand through my hair. "Work's... complicated. Ever since AI started identifying cancer cells better than I can, that groundbreaking research that launched my career has become obsolete. It's frustrating, disappointing, and honestly, a little terrifying. I keep trying to chart a new path—something that will reignite the passion I used to have—but nothing feels right. And school's about to start. I've got grad students to manage, a teaching schedule that's already overflowing, and an article due in three weeks. Publish or perish, right?"

Mara tilted her head, concern creeping into her expression. "That's rough. But you're still one of the smartest people I know. You'll figure it out. Sometimes, the best ideas come when you take a step back and let yourself breathe. Relax a little, Gray. You're on a beach, not in a lab."

"Breathe, huh?" I gestured to the horizon. "Does breathing include chasing seagulls and staring at the waves?"

She smirked. "Today, stick with staring. You're not allowed to injure yourself right before my wedding."

I shrugged. "Dad doesn't see it that way. To him, 'relaxing' is just an excuse for failure. Losing out on the Cates job just added fuel to his whole 'you're falling behind' speech, and now he's doubling down on the 'nose to the grindstone' routine."

Mara sighed heavily, stopping to scoop up another shell. "He's impossible, I know. He's always pushed you the hardest because he sees so much of himself in you. But Gray, you've got to set boundaries with him. I did, and now he's... tolerable."

"Yeah, well, not all of us are Mara the Magnificent," I said, smirking. "How's juggling the comic shop, the game company, and the movie going? All on top of planning a destination double wedding? You really make it look easy."

Her confident façade cracked slightly. "I'm not keeping up with the dailies for *Ghost*. I've missed weeks. Ford's being patient, but… I haven't even reviewed the script changes, and I'm terrified the movie's drifting from Chance's vision. *Ghost* was his dream, you know? He poured everything into it, and I'm scared I'm letting him down."

I frowned. "That's not good. The whole family's counting on you to protect Chance's legacy. You need to keep his vision on track."

"I know," she said softly. "But between the wedding, the company, and everything else, I've… dropped the ball. I can't believe I managed to pull off this double wedding."

"You aren't married yet," I quipped, letting the joke linger just long enough before I shifted. "But seriously, I get it. You're swamped," I said, turning her words over. "Let's not wave the white flag just yet. How about this: what if I help you?"

Her eyebrows shot up, suspicion and curiosity colliding. "Help with what, exactly?"

"The movie," I said, the weight of the offer sinking in as soon as the words left my mouth. Where would I find the bandwidth? But *Ghost*? That was Chance's legacy. For family, you found the space. Somehow.

Before she could reply, a seagull swooped down, aiming for the bag of snacks Mara had tucked under her arm. She shrieked, flailing her arms as though she could intimidate the bird through sheer indignation. When that didn't work, she grabbed a handful of sand and hurled it with the precision of someone who'd had years of practice slinging jellybeans at her siblings.

The bird flapped off with an indignant squawk, and Mara spun toward me, her face a mix of triumph and exasperation. "You saw that, right? Nature is literally out to get me."

I bit back a laugh. "Clearly, the seagull union has declared you public enemy number one."

She jabbed a finger at me. "You joke, but this is personal."

I finally let myself laugh, the tension breaking like a wave. The whole scene felt absurdly fitting—unexpected challenges swooping in when we were least prepared, demanding snacks we didn't have the energy to give.

"Nature's a menace," I said, laughing as Mara brushed sand off her hands.

"You're not wrong," she said, grinning. Then her expression sobered. "Gray, you're drowning in your own stuff. You can't add mine on top."

"I'll manage," I replied firmly. "*Ghost* is too important to let slide. If you're falling behind, I can help catch you up."

Her eyes narrowed, studying me. "You're serious, aren't you?"

"I'm serious," I said. "We'll make it work."

Mara sighed, then scooped up a handful of sand and tossed it lightly at my shoulder. "Fine. But if you regret it, don't say I didn't warn you."

I brushed the sand off, chuckling. "Noted."

We turned back toward the beach chairs, Courtney's laughter carrying on the breeze as she and Rose floated in the gentle waves. For a moment, I let myself wonder what it would be like to join her—to let go of practicality and dive headfirst into the unknown. To feel the cool water against my skin, to hear her laugh up close rather than from a distance. But then the thought tangled itself in reality: the demands waiting for me back on shore, the responsibilities that felt heavier with each passing day. Could I ever truly step away from all that, even for just one moment?

But then, my father's voice echoed in my mind: *You had every advantage, Grayson. If you don't stay sharp, someone else will take your place.*

The moment passed, and I shook off the thought. "Come on," I said to Mara. "We've got a wedding rehearsal to attend."

As we left the beach, Courtney's laughter followed me, a melody I forced myself to ignore.

6

REHEARSAL AND REJECTION

Courtney

I caught sight of Grayson and Mara leaving the beach. She turned and waved at us, while he stared off into the distance, his expression unreadable—a far cry from the warmth he'd shown me twenty minutes ago. One moment he seemed drawn to me; the next, it was as if I'd drifted out with the tide.

The image of him lounging next to his sandcastle flashed in my mind: lean muscles, easy confidence, a heat in his gaze that told me attraction wasn't the issue. Maybe it was the whole "we competed for the same Cates Foundation position and I won" thing. I'd learned before how messy mixing rivalry and romance could be, and I wasn't eager to revisit that particular disaster.

As we settled into our chairs, Rose whipped out a glossy magazine while I tried to shake the thought. Why did ambition so often feel like a game of tug-of-war in relationships? I loved competition, but not when ego got tangled in the ropes. Finding someone who saw ambition as a team sport? That felt as likely as finding a soufflé recipe that didn't deflate.

Rose smirked, looking up from her magazine. "Saw Grayson eyeing you earlier. Like a kid sizing up the last cookie on the plate."

I rolled my eyes but smirked. "Oh, was he now? The question is, does he prefer standard chocolate chip or my unique coconut surprise?"

She laughed, leaning closer with a conspiratorial grin. "Or maybe you should just take him for a spin and find out if he's your dream ride."

"If only dating were that simple," I said. "Hey there, handsome! Got anti-lock brakes? How's your rear suspension?'"

"Honestly, wouldn't it be great if it were?" she teased. "You could pick up a Maserati of a man—zero to breathless in under four seconds."

I laughed. "Please, with my luck, I'd get the used car special. Spare tire, fuel guzzler, needs constant maintenance."

Rose grinned. "I'm stealing that line for my next book. But seriously, sounds like you're already talking yourself out of it."

I shrugged. "Maybe I am. He's smart, gorgeous, checks a lot of boxes. But he's Mara's brother, and apparently I stole his dream job. Getting involved with him would feel like signing up for a slow-motion car crash."

Rose raised an eyebrow. "Or maybe you're just overthinking it?"

"Probably," I admitted. "But bruising his ego isn't a great starting point, and my track record with competitive types speaks for itself. Entertaining? Maybe. Worth repeating? Not so much."

Rose shrugged, setting her magazine aside. "Fair enough. But you deserve a Maserati. If Grayson isn't it, keep moving. Someone else will be."

My phone buzzed, reminding me of the time. "Duty calls. Time to shower and get ready for the rehearsal dinner." I slipped on my beach cover-up.

Rose sighed dramatically. "I'll stay here until the tide sweeps me away."

"Your cheeks are looking rosy," I said with a grin.

She groaned. "Another rose joke? Really?"

I shrugged. "Couldn't resist. You must hear enough to stock a flower shop. Do they ever get old?"

She laughed. "I add them to my 'Flower File' for rough days. Always good for a laugh."

***

Forty-five minutes later, shampooed and dressed, I tried to focus on the night ahead. But thoughts of Grayson kept sneaking in, those piercing green eyes taking up more mental real estate than I wanted to admit.

Grayson was Mara's brother, which put him firmly in 'off-limits' territory. Besides, there was that competitive streak I'd seen when he mentioned the Cates Foundation job. The last thing I needed was another relationship that felt like a game with ever-shifting rules. Richard had taught me that lesson too well.

No, getting involved with Grayson would be like diving into an experiment with too many unknown variables and a high risk of explosive results. Better to focus on what I could control and avoid unnecessary complications. After all, I had enough on my plate without adding another helping of trouble and sending things spilling off the edges.

Decision made. I mentally filed Grayson under "Not an Option" and resolved to enjoy this weekend without any added drama.

Stepping into the hallway, I took a deep breath, letting the fresh air clear away any residual thoughts of Grayson.

The wedding venue was straight out of a bridal magazine—tinkling water features, artfully arranged tropical blooms, and the kind of curated elegance that felt more like a set than reality. I wound through it all, zeroing in on the door labeled "Bride."

To my surprise, I was the first to arrive. The room oozed sophistication: an ornate mirror framed in gold, director-style chairs labeled "Bride" and "Maid of Honor" in each bride's signature color, a pristine white sofa, and a glass-fronted fridge stocked with sparkling water, champagne, and organic iced tea.

I was debating what to drink when Mara and Sonya breezed in like stars hitting a red carpet, which, of course, they basically were with all the celebrities who'd be attending.

"You're early?" Mara's eyes sparkled approvingly. "You're the Nick Fury of this bridal party, assembling the team for the ultimate showdown."

I grinned, catching her wink. "Every superhero squad needs a strong support team."

Sonya's gaze swept the room with the intense focus of someone who'd misplaced the rings. Light caught in her chestnut hair, giving her a look of determined elegance. "Where's my sister? How can we have a rehearsal if my maid of honor's gone AWOL?"

Right on cue, Kendra burst through the door, her wavy brown hair tousled and a look of pure frustration on her face. "There's sand in my shoe," she announced, lifting one foot as if it had committed a personal offense.

With a dramatic sigh, she whipped off the offending footwear, whacking it against the doorframe in a desperate attempt to banish every last grain. "Why didn't I bring sandals? Is formal footwear worth this level of sacrifice? Sand hurts."

Sonya chuckled, her earlier tension dissolving. "It's a wedding, not a royal gala. Go barefoot if you want."

Kendra's face lit up like she'd been released from an ancient form of torture. "You are officially the best sister ever."

Mara, the picture of calm determination, took charge. "Alright, team. Tomorrow, we're meeting here two hours before the 'I dos.' Maids of honor, you're our crisis managers. Anyone mentioning bad omens or rain is getting escorted out. We're keeping this wedding stress-free."

Sonya nodded, all business. "Seriously, please play defense for us. Treat any stressors like villains in a romance novel—keep them far, far away."

I shot them both a confident nod. "Roger that. Emotional bouncer, reporting for duty."

The door swung open, and Emma burst in, Zephyr's leash in hand. "Make way, people! The junior bridesmaid has arrived!" She beelined for the director's chair labeled "Junior Bridesmaid" and plopped down with a huge grin. "Oh my gosh, this chair and I are soulmates. Can I take it home?"

Sonya chuckled. "Nice try, kid. And good luck cramming it into your carry-on. We had the private jet for the trip out, but we're flying coach on the way back."

Meanwhile, Zephyr lapped delicately from a pink water bowl that looked straight out of a luxury pet spa.

Emma scrunched her face in mock indignation. "The universe clearly has it out for me, making me go back to coach with the commoners."

Sonya sighed with exaggerated drama. "One flight on a private jet, and she's already too good for the rest of us."

Emma shrugged, undeterred. "I promise not to let it go to my head. I'll stay grounded... like, uh, something very grounded."

A gentle knock interrupted our banter. A round-faced woman in a flowing sundress entered, warm eyes scanning the room. "I'm Tandy, your wedding coordinator. The men are ready, so we can start the rehearsal. And, before you ask, the flowers at the altar are from a wedding we had earlier today. We'll replace them with your flowers in your colors tomorrow."

"Sounds good. We're all here," Mara said. "Let's get crack-a-lackin'.

Tandy gave a bright smile. "Alright. Let's get started! Junior bridesmaid, you and Zephyr are with me to lead the way to the wedding arbor."

Emma sprang to her feet, tugging on Zephyr's leash. "Come on, Zephyr, it's showtime!"

As I stepped out the door, my breath hitched. There he was—Grayson. Our eyes locked for a beat, then he turned away, his expression unreadable as he shifted his attention to his father. Dr. Stellar—Grayson and Mara's dad—stood slightly apart from the bustling crowd, looking faintly out of place among the younger group.

A confusing pang tightened in my chest, hot and unwelcome at this second brushoff. Was Grayson deliberately keeping his distance? Fine. I wanted distance, too. Right?

Mommy Julie's voice echoed in my mind: *Good manners are the best armor for awkward situations.* So, I squared my shoulders, pasted on a smile so polite you could frame it, and resolved to handle this with grace. Perfectly, distantly, politely pleasant—easy enough.

Tandy lined us up, and I was arm-in-arm with Grayson, the man who managed to set off every nerve in my body just by existing. His arm was warm, solid under my hand—a grounding presence that, irritatingly, made my pulse race. I glanced up at him, but he stayed focused on Tandy, listening to her directions like she was about to reveal the meaning of life. Meanwhile, I was hyperaware of every heartbeat pounding in the silence between us.

We followed Tandy to a secluded path near the beach, framed by tall grasses that rustled softly in the breeze, creating the illusion of privacy. Ahead stretched a weathered boardwalk bordered with seashells, sand dollars, and starfish, with splashes of soft pink flowers. The whole setup looked like a mermaid's dream wedding. Beyond the boardwalk, the beach lay quiet and serene, waves brushing the sand in gentle whispers as the setting sun cast everything in a golden glow. It was almost annoyingly romantic.

For a split second, I wavered. Was I jumping the gun, dismissing whatever this was between us? But I shook it off, chuckling inwardly. If this setting got any more poetic, the sand might morph into rose petals. Still, I wasn't about to let a picturesque view dictate my decisions.

"Wait here, you two," Tandy said, gesturing toward us. "I'll signal when it's your turn. Emma, let's go—Zephyr's ready for his big moment!" And with that, Grayson and I were left in a bubble of quiet that felt heavier than the humid island air.

The silence stretched until Grayson cleared his throat. He

looked at me, oddly formal, like he was delivering a company memo. "We need to clear the air. I think you're incredible—smart, funny, beautiful. You set my head spinning on the flight here."

I blinked, caught off guard.

"But anything more? Even a fling?" He shook his head, offering a weak, apologetic smile. "I just don't think it's a good idea. You're one of Mara's best friends. And I'm juggling research dead-ends, a mountain of grad students, Chance's movie script revisions—my life's one big game of advanced Tetris, and I'm struggling. Let's just say I'm not meeting the high bar that's been set for me lately. And you? With that new job, you've got to be just as busy, if not busier. So…friend zone?"

The words hung in the air like a poorly timed punchline.

Heat rose to my cheeks, the preemptive dumping bruising my ego more than I wanted to admit. Logic had been telling me the same thing, but hearing it from him felt like someone tossing cold water on me. I'd been chanting the "keep it casual" mantra all afternoon, but somehow, his words landed like a gut punch. Was the connection I'd felt just wishful thinking?

Annoyance flared. Had he really just yanked the decision out from under me?

I forced my chin up and met his gaze, searching for hesitation or regret. Nothing. His usual easy posture was gone, replaced by an irritating stiffness. Even his cologne, that warm mix of spices and woods, grated on me now.

"Well, Grayson, as it happens, I came to the same conclusion." I kept my tone light, masking the sting. Why did this feel like he was dumping me when we hadn't even started? And why, for the love of everything, did he pick this moment?

Seriously? Here? Now? Moments before we walk down the aisle together?

Then it hit me. He'd just given me the "it's not you, it's me" speech—before we'd even gotten together. The irony was rich, even for me.

I was seconds away from letting loose on him when Tandy's

voice cut through the tension. "Courtney, Grayson, you're up! Time to head down the aisle!"

Clearly, the universe had a flair for timing. I swallowed down my snarky comment. This wasn't the moment for an emotional showdown, but oh, it was coming. With every step down the aisle, I felt like we were a mismatched comedy duo, complete with exaggerated fake smiles and a cane yanking us offstage. The whole scene around us practically sang of romance, while Grayson and I shuffled along like reluctant actors in a farce.

Ahead, the arbor loomed, a gorgeous arrangement of sea-weathered wood adorned with fabrics in soft shades that billowed gently in the breeze. Bright pops of hibiscus, frangipani, and orchids punctuated the scene, their colors glowing in the golden light of dusk.

"As Mara and Ford's maid of honor and best man, you two will take your spots on the left side of the arbor," Tandy directed, pulling me back to the task at hand. "Emma, as junior bridesmaid for both couples, you'll be front and center. When the brides arrive, you can stand to the right, where Sonya and Max will be."

She then waved over the other best man and maid of honor, Sinan and Kendra, who moved down the aisle to stand on the opposite side of the arbor—our mirror image.

"Everyone keeping up? Any questions?" Tandy asked.

Oh, I had questions—like why Grayson couldn't look me in the eye and why he looked like he'd swallowed a mouthful of broken glass instead of just saying a simple "Let's be friends." But I kept my mouth shut, only managing a nod.

"Alright," Tandy said, "let's bring in our brides."

Mara appeared first, stepping onto the boardwalk like a burst of color in her dress adorned with oversized red poppies. By her side was Dr. Stellar, her and Grayson's dad, who looked a mix of proud and overwhelmed, eyes fixed just beyond the driftwood arbor as though mentally fast-forwarding through the ceremony.

When they reached the arbor, Tandy nodded at Dr. Stellar, who made a beeline for his seat beside his wife, giving Mara a moment to catch her breath and step up to Ford.

"Sonya, it's your turn," Tandy called out.

Sonya stepped onto the boardwalk in a gauzy white summer dress, barefoot, her whole look managing to be both island-casual and effortlessly elegant. With her mother gone and her father "kind of an ass," as she put it, Sonya walked solo, her blonde hair catching the light as she moved, almost like she was floating down the path.

At the arbor, Max reached for her hand, their fingers intertwining naturally, their shared glance so full of unspoken things it made me want to look away.

"Alright, everyone," Tandy's voice cut through the moment, "I'll be standing in as the minister for today. Just to confirm, Mara and Ford are up first with their vows, followed by Sonya and Max?"

The couples nodded, exchanging quick looks of mutual excitement.

"Great. Now, how are we handling the rings? Simultaneous exchange or separately for each couple?" Tandy looked to both couples for the plan.

After a quick huddle, it was decided: they'd exchange rings separately, just before the vows.

"Perfect," Tandy said, turning to me. "Courtney, you'll need to hold Mara's bouquet for her."

I accepted the imaginary bouquet she handed me.

"Best man, you're up next," Tandy continued. "Rings, please."

"Actually, Zephyr's handling the rings for me and Ford," Mara chimed in.

Tandy's eyebrows shot up. "Well, that's... new. And you want him to bring them down the aisle at this point in the ceremony? Alright then, who's on Zephyr duty?"

"That would be Kincaid," Mara said, nodding toward my youngest brother.

Kincaid stepped forward, his easygoing grin firmly in place. He'd eloped just last month, much to the surprise of the family, but it hadn't slowed him down. With his usual laid-back charm, he crouched to rub Zephyr's head, earning a happy wag from our furry ring bearer.

Emma handed Zephyr's leash over to Kincaid, who gave her a mock salute before leading Zephyr to the head of the boardwalk, ready for his big moment. It was classic Kincaid—reliable in his own way but never making a fuss about it.

At Tandy's signal, Kincaid unclipped the leash, and at Mara's call Zephyr trotted down the aisle like a pro, tail high, ready to deliver the rings.

Grayson pulled the actual ring box from his pocket and dropped to one knee, pretending to retrieve the rings from Zephyr's collar. As he stood, his grip on the box slipped, and it tumbled toward the sand.

Mara gasped as Grayson lunged to catch it, missed, and sent it flying into the air. With a mischievous grin, he tapped it up with his heel, juggling it briefly before catching it with a flourish. Finally, he presented it to Ford with a wink.

"Grayson! You nearly gave me a heart attack!" Mara scolded, reaching across Ford to give Grayson a backhanded smack on the arm. "Lose our wedding rings with one of your 'funny' stunts, and I swear I'll skin you alive."

"Hey, sorry!" His eyes sparkled with amusement. "If it's any consolation, I really did drop it. I just added the juggling bit to lighten the mood."

Mara crossed her arms, unimpressed. "Well, it didn't work. I wasn't laughing. What if the box popped open and sent the rings flying?"

Meanwhile, Kincaid stepped up, holding out a dog treat to lure Zephyr back. He crouched again, leash in hand, his easy grin never wavering as Zephyr happily trotted over for his reward. Kincaid reattached the leash, gave Zephyr a pat, and said, "Show's over, buddy. Back to being a good boy."

When it was Sinan's turn to hand over the rings for Max and Sonya, he executed a flawless bow, passed the rings to Tandy, and then turned to give Grayson a smirk. "See? That's how it's done."

"Boring," Grayson shot back. "Style points matter."

Tandy, the picture of calm, got us back on track. "I understand you've written your own vows?"

Mara looked a bit hesitant. Her nod turned into a side-to-side wobble, prompting a raised eyebrow from Tandy.

"Mine aren't exactly...finished," Mara admitted. "I kept putting it off, and now here we are, the day before the wedding, and I'm, um, slightly freaking out."

Ford grinned. "Just promise to love, honor, and obey me till death do us part, and I'll be good."

Mara shot him a look of mock horror. "Obey? Big nope on that one. I'll definitely write something better."

"Just trying to help," Ford said, hands up in surrender.

"Those two are perfect for each other," I muttered under my breath, shaking my head with a smirk. "He tells the worst dad jokes, and she loves playing his straight man."

Grayson, overhearing, leaned in. "Right? What are the odds those two would meet, let alone fall in love? Million to one?"

I gave him a quick, narrowed look, but tamped down my irritation. This wasn't the time or place for a showdown.

Tandy brought us back to focus. "After Max and Sonya's kiss, the minister will announce each couple, and we'll head into the recessional. First Mara and Ford, then Sonya and Max."

She gestured at Emma. "Junior bridesmaid goes next, then Courtney and Grayson, and finally, Kendra and Sinan."

"Quick and easy," Kendra chimed in. "Just how I like it."

"Now, that's a shame," Sinan murmured.

Kendra smirked. "Oh, don't worry—I make exceptions for special occasions."

Tandy didn't bat an eye. "Any questions? Now's the time to ask."

Silence. Tandy nodded, clearly pleased. "Alright! We'll run the recessional one more time, then everyone can head to the poolside venue for the rehearsal dinner. But before we do, let's take a second to celebrate—just us. On the count of three, I want to hear the loudest cheer you've got, like you're at the happiest place on earth!"

She counted down. "One, two, three!"

The whole group erupted into cheers. For a moment, the stress and tension melted away, replaced by pure joy and excitement. Even Grayson's antics faded into the background as I let myself enjoy the laughter and celebration.

After one more run-through, Tandy announced, "You're ready. This wedding is going to be perfect, thanks to each and every one of you. Now, off to the rehearsal dinner. It's just down the beach next to the giant chess set. You can't miss it."

"Giant chess set?" I repeated, the words pulling me out of my thoughts. It had been too long since I'd played, and the possibility soothed me. I glanced at Grayson, who was already watching me with that familiar, knowing smirk.

"Figured you'd want to check it out," he said, his voice low, meant just for me.

I narrowed my eyes, irritated that he'd predicted me so well, the hum of conversation from the rest of the group making our exchange feel oddly private. "Oh? And why's that?"

"You did mention you used to compete," he replied with a shrug. "Unless, of course, you're afraid I might actually be good at it."

I crossed my arms, the spark of irritation rekindling. "You're assuming I'd waste my time playing against someone who just friend-zoned me."

Grayson chuckled, the sound drawing my focus entirely to him. "Friends can play chess. And who knows, maybe I'll surprise you."

"Doubtful." The words came out sharper than I intended, but I couldn't stop the competitive streak taking over. "But fine. Let's see if you can back up all this talk."

"Game on," he said, his grin widening.

As we followed the others toward the dinner, my frustration began to ebb. The rest of the wedding party chatted and joked ahead of us, their voices blending into the background. Maybe he wasn't wrong. Friends could play chess, and this felt like the kind of distraction I could use right now.

7

CHECKMATE

GRAYSON

I stood with Ford, watching the last of the guests trickle toward the rehearsal dinner. As he relayed some story from shooting *Ghost*, a sharp shriek and a splash cut him off. Our heads snapped toward the pool just as two soaked figures emerged, sputtering.

Ford squinted, then barked a laugh. "Figures my brother, the stuntman, would end up fully clothed in the water."

"Not one for subtlety," I muttered. Sinan rushed over to help. Normally Dad would've jumped in to show off his medical prowess, but tonight he stood off to the side, arms crossed, frown deepening. A "showdown with the new sheriff" vibe flickered in the air, but maybe Sinan's efficiency would keep Dad too busy to grill me about my losing the Cates Foundation job.

Before I could dwell on it, Sinan strolled over, drying his hands on a spare towel.

"How's Rose?" Ford asked.

"She's fine—just a bit drenched," he said with a quick grin. "Sean's dramatic dive wasn't my recommended rescue method."

Ford clapped Sinan's shoulder in thanks. "He's the king of

well-timed heroics. Now let's grab some food before the party descends on the buffet."

The breeze carried the scent of seafood and tropical flowers. I filled a plate with ceviche and conch fritters, trying to match Ford's laid-back energy. But my gaze kept straying across the pool, where Courtney stood with a soaking-wet Rose. She was hard to ignore. My "just friends" tactic felt shakier by the second.

Dad's glare hadn't softened—he seemed irritated that Sinan, not he, had been the problem-solver tonight.

Sinan turned to me mid-bite. "By the way, Max gave me my best man gift. Did Ford give you yours?"

"Nope." I glanced at Ford, raising an eyebrow.

"Glad you asked," Ford said, eyes twinkling. "Your best-man gift is a year of cooking classes at Dante's restaurant, Not a Yacht Club. Men only, and the women get to sample the results. Dante even flew out to bake the wedding cakes this weekend."

I tried not to grimace at the time commitment, but Ford just smirked. "Relax. It's fun, and you'll eat well."

"Well, I hope you're prepared to get feedback from Mara," I said, gesturing toward her across the pool. "You know she's got opinions—and she's not shy about sharing them."

Ford's gaze followed mine, softening as he watched her laugh with a group of guests. "She's always had that spark, hasn't she?"

"Dimmed for a while after we lost Chance," I admitted, my voice lowering. "But it's back now. Growing up together, they were unstoppable—always laughing, no grudges. I miss that."

Ford nodded. "She helped me heal after I lost my own sister last year. Sometimes I catch that same look in her eyes—missing Chance, but stronger for it." From across the pool, their eyes locked in a way that seemed to pull the world into focus, the laughter and chatter around them fading into a distant hum.

Admiration mingled with a pang of longing in me. Maybe that kind of closeness—that magnetic connection—was what I'd been missing all along.

Ford stood suddenly, crossing the distance to her with a

purpose that left no doubt. Mara rose to meet him, her movements unhurried yet certain, as if the space between them had been calling her the whole night. When they met at one end of the pool, the air around them shimmered with an unspoken energy, the kind that tugged at everyone watching and demanded attention.

When their lips met, it wasn't just a kiss—it was the crescendo of a symphony, the kind of moment that made everything else seem small. Their love radiated outward, warm and undeniable, stirring something deep in me that I hadn't felt in years. It wasn't envy—it was hope. Hope for something just as raw, just as real.

My gaze drifted, unbidden, to Courtney. She stood a few feet away, her head tilted slightly as if catching the same wavelength I was. Her eyes found mine, locking on with a quiet intensity that sent a jolt straight to my chest. Maybe I'd written her off too soon, stuffed her into the "not possible" category without giving us a chance. My mind might reject the idea, but my heart? It was already ahead of me, pulling me toward her like gravity.

She tilted her head in challenge, then nodded toward the giant chess set on the beach. One silent dare. I shot her a quick grin. How could I resist?

A few minutes later, we left the reception's music and laughter behind for the flicker of tiki torches and a bit of competition. Courtney found two wine glasses while I grabbed a bottle from a nearby cart—what's a friendly showdown without flair?

And just like that, it was game on.

The chess set was enormous, the pieces towering like they had opinions about our skills. The pawns stood at child height, the tiki torches casting long shadows over a board as big as my bedroom. It was the perfect backdrop for a romantic subplot, though I reminded myself that's not what we were here for.

A seagull perched on the black queen, eyeing us with a snaggle-beaked glare. "Think he's here to give me pointers?" I asked.

Courtney smirked. "Looks like he's already decided you're a lost cause. Don't take it personally."

The sea breeze teased her auburn hair, and the green fabric of her dress caught the light just enough to make her look like a chess-playing siren. She ran her fingers over a small silver and white cancer-awareness charm on her necklace, her expression thoughtful before she met my gaze. "Your move," she said, her tone teasing.

I moved a pawn, grinning. "Hope you're ready for this."

"Ready to win? Always." She watched as I maneuvered the oversized pieces, feigning concern. "Careful. These things look heavy. Don't hurt yourself."

"Consider me your humble chess-piece wrangler for the evening."

"Why, thank you, kind sir," she said with a laugh. "Tonight, I'll happily let you take on the heavy lifting., but don't think that means I'll go easy on you."

The game unfolded with a mix of banter and strategic intensity. Our feathered referee shifted from the queen to a bishop, silently judging my every move. When Courtney captured my queen and sealed her victory, I tipped over my king with a loud thump. "Well, that's it. Got any advice for a struggling knight?"

Courtney grinned, her laugh warm and infectious. "Ask the seagull. He might finally relent and offer some tips."

I eyed the bird, deadpan. "Nothing? Not even a wing-flap of encouragement? Figures," I muttered with a shrug. "He's clearly on your side."

Round two began, and as we played, the conversation drifted to work. She shared more about her team's recent breakthrough, while I talked about two new post-doc students I'd be working with. "One of them is diving into new methods for analyzing research data, which, frankly, I'm thrilled about. There's something exhilarating about finding hidden gems in data."

Courtney's eyes sparkled with shared enthusiasm. "Exactly! It's like panning for gold. That's what got me on my current research path—I stumbled across an intriguing virus in a dataset, and it just clicked." She shrugged with a grin. "What can I say? Data nerds, unite."

I laughed. "One of my current students, Joaquin, is all about independent verification and validation. Not my favorite subject —it feels like Big Brother monitoring researchers—but considering recent scandals, I get the need for it."

When she won again—faster this time—I laughed, shaking my head. "You're ruthless."

"Just observant," she replied. "Patterns are everything. Miss a few, and it's game over."

Our snaggle-beaked referee seemed wholly unimpressed with my losing streak. "I get the feeling our feathered friend expected better from me."

She looked at the bird, smirking. "Maybe he's just giving you the bird."

We both burst into laughter, the tension between us loosening.

"Those chess patterns. Can you teach me to spot them like you do?" I asked, swallowing my pride.

Her eyes lit up. "Gladly. Ready to lose again?"

By the third round, I was learning, albeit slowly. She coached me through the logic of a few moves, her explanations animated and full of wit. For the first time, chess felt more intriguing than frustrating.

"Checkmate," she said finally, with a grin as wide as the beach.

My gaze narrowed as I surveyed the board, realizing I'd been trapped yet again. I raised my hands in mock defeat, then studied the board, hoping to find a way out. When I looked back, her confident grin had me chuckling. "Alright, Ms. Chess Virtuoso, enlighten me. What would you do in my shoes? There has to be a way out of this."

She folded her arms, amused. "Want the hard truth? You're up chess creek without a pawn, my friend."

"So it's not that I'm missing the winning move... it's that it doesn't even exist," I said, meeting her gaze with a mix of resignation and admiration. "Would you mind showing me where I went wrong?"

She lit up, guiding me through the sequence of moves that had led to my downfall. Watching her move around the board with such confidence was both humbling and mesmerizing. "Do you always think several moves ahead?"

As she looked up, a smile teased her lips, and I had a sudden moment of clarity. Why was I relegating this incredible woman to the friend zone? She was all of it—intellectually stimulating, endlessly intriguing, and absolutely captivating.

"Always, but it's mostly about spotting patterns," she explained, a playful glint in her eye. "Right now, your options are... well, not great."

Doesn't it always come down to patterns?

"Teach you, I will, my Padawan," she teased in a sing-song voice. That radiant smile was all the encouragement I needed.

I set up the board and we spent the next half-hour buried in strategy. For the first time, chess actually felt intriguing—maybe because the whole game was wrapped up in her animated explanations and infectious enthusiasm. I was captivated, both by the game and by her.

Finally, I sighed dramatically, glancing from the board to her. "Well, you've got me beat again. Probably a good thing we didn't bet on this."

Halfway through, she paused, a mischievous grin tugging at her lips. "Ever heard of strip chess? Lose a piece, lose a piece of clothing."

My pulse quickened. Was this a joke or a signal? "Sounds dangerous," I replied, leaning in just enough to keep things playful. "Though I'd be at a disadvantage. You'd have me down to my socks in no time."

"Then maybe we'd better stick to the basics," she teased, her eyes sparkling with mischief.

The tension between us shifted, electric and undeniable. Her gaze held mine, a challenge in them. I felt the magnetic pull between us, and I started to lean in, sure that this was about to be one of those kiss-moments—the kind that novels are written about.

"Courtney!" Mara's voice cut through the air like a crash cymbal, jolting us apart.

Even the seagull flapped its wings in what felt like protest as Mara hurried toward us, her expression a mix of relief and urgency. "I've been looking everywhere for you. I need your help with my vows!" she exclaimed. Dropping to her knees in the sand, she clasped her hands dramatically. "Obi-Wan Kenobi, you're my only hope!"

Courtney sighed, clearly torn, before slipping seamlessly into character. "Ah, Princess Leia, your distress call has been received. I'll assist however I can."

8

LOVE, SAND, AND SNAGGLE-TOOTHED SEAGULLS

COURTNEY

Stepping into Mara's hotel room, I barely had time to close the door before Zephyr bounded toward me, tail wagging in overdrive. He was adorable, but after I picked him up and his tongue started assaulting my ear, I quickly set him down, preferring my eardrum unwashed.

Mara plopped onto the bed, arms and legs splayed, and let out a dramatic sigh. "I can't do this. I've been wrestling with these vows for weeks, and everything sounds like it belongs on the reject pile of a greeting-card company."

Finally, something I could tackle. Academic presentations were one thing; wedding vows, though, had to be simpler—right?

"Show me what you've got so far," I offered, scanning the room's stylish décor as if it held some vow-writing inspiration.

Mara groaned, like someone asked to rewrite her entire thesis the night before it was due—which, in a way, she essentially was. "Please, no. They're all disasters. I need a full reset. Blank slate."

"Alright, let's see what we can do." I settled into an armchair. Zephyr hopped up beside me, his tail thumping as I rubbed behind his ears. "What turned Ford from 'that guy at Dante's restaurant' into 'the one'?"

A genuine smile broke through her frustration. Zephyr took his cue to abandon me and snuggle beside her instead. "Ford decided the way to my heart was through my stomach. He'd show up with these incredible meals he'd cooked, like a romance ninja. I was on a dating hiatus, so we started as friends—and before I knew it, bam. Emotional entanglement."

I laughed, swept up in the sweetness of her story. Then it hit me—had Grayson been subtly deploying his charm tonight? Friend-zoning me one moment, then hitting me with his wit and intellect the next? I was starting to wonder if resistance really was futile. Our almost-kiss definitely hadn't felt like "just friends" behavior.

"I remember watching it unfold. You were the queen of mixed signals. Ford's a great catch—how did you manage to hold off for so long?"

Mara shrugged. "Just stubborn, I guess." She looked at Zephyr, who rolled over, gazing up at her with abject love. "What do you think, Zephy? Am I stubborn?"

Zephyr wisely opted for silence.

I chuckled. "He's a vault. Your secrets are safe with him."

"At least I finally took the plunge," she sighed. "Sometimes, great risk comes with great reward."

Her words hit home, needling at my carefully built walls. Was I too wary to let myself fall for Grayson? Maybe he felt the same.

I shook off the thought, turning back to her wedding vow dilemma. "You're not stubborn, you're determined. You shape the people around you, Ford included. You are absolutely a force."

A spark of confidence lit her face. "You and Grayson are kind of the same—driven, laser-focused. I always suspected you'd click. Seeing you two earlier? Who knows? Maybe sparks will fly."

I nearly choked. "I thought we agreed not to talk about my love life. Are you actually giving me the go-ahead to date your brother?"

She gave me a playful wink. "Life's a buffet, Courtney. Don't skip the prime rib." Then she resumed typing, a grin hinting at mischief.

I sank back into the armchair, feeling my cheeks warm. Bullet point one on my "Reasons Not to Date Grayson" list? Gone, like steam off a hot sidewalk. But in the back of my mind, a faint caution light still flickered, a reminder that impulsiveness didn't always pay off.

Her typing slowed, and she looked up with a laser-focused gaze. "In the lab, you take risks all the time—one experiment fails, you adjust and try again. Isn't love worth the same risk?"

I swallowed hard. "I guess I'm more fearless around test tubes than people." When had failure become an omen in love but just part of the process in science?

Mara resumed her typing, a mischievous grin tugging at her lips. "You're a lifesaver. My vows were clogged up, and you, my friend, are the creative laxative I desperately needed."

I cringed at the metaphor but grinned at her twinkling eyes. Taking the hint, I slipped out with my own thoughts swirling. Had Grayson's near-kiss been inevitable? And did I really want to fight it?

***

The next day blurred by in a whirl of final touches and photo ops. Our calm book club brunch had been the eye of the storm before Tandy and her glam squad started rotating us through hair and makeup sessions. The moments leading up to the ceremony blurred.

Meanwhile, the guys had spent the day on a carefree island adventure with a a carefree energy that made me a little envious. Still, the camaraderie with Mara, Ford, and Sonya's families was worth every hectic minute. Our junior bridesmaid, Emma, was practically vibrating with excitement.

I finally caught sight of Grayson as I left the bridal suite. Sun-kissed and wearing a crisp tux, he looked like a cover model for a summer wedding brochure. Our eyes locked, and my pulse stuttered. Before I could move toward him, his dad intercepted him, something terse passing between them. Grayson's gaze flicked to me apologetically as he hurried off.

Tandy had no time for second-guessing—she lined us up for the processional like a drill instructor. When it was our turn, my hand found Grayson's arm, a jolt of anticipation racing through me. We stepped onto the aisle, the sound of waves and the murmur of guests fading into a gentle hush.

A flash of recognition almost made me stumble. In the crowd sat Chris Pitt and Kim Curry—Hollywood royalty—and a few seats down, Margot Robbie and Charlize Theron. Who else was out there? Maybe I was better off not knowing.

My sympathy for Mara soared; she'd had to pen vows with that star-studded audience in mind. No pressure.

I took a steadying breath, letting the sound of the waves ground me as the rest of the wedding party made their way down the aisle.

Everything looked picture-perfect: the sky clear, the floral arch stunning, and the brides radiant, as though hand-painted for a fairytale, the guests eagerly awaiting the vows.

Right on cue, my brother Kincaid sauntered to the aisle, Zephyr trotting proudly by his side—a tuxedoed heartbreaker in miniature. Kincaid unclipped the leash, setting free our four-legged ring bearer. Zephyr, a purple pillow proudly tied around his neck, strutted down the aisle like he owned the place.

A seagull swooped in a moment later, landing just above the altar with the confidence of a seasoned wedding crasher. Zephyr's head jerked upward, his entire body going stock-still.

I clenched the silky fabric of my dress. "Don't you dare," I muttered, hoping to ward off a catastrophe.

Zephyr, predictable as ever, dared.

He launched himself at the floral arch, barking like the avenging hound of justice he clearly thought he was. Mara bent to corral him, her fingers outstretched, but Zephyr zigged left, dodged right, skillfully avoiding capture all while yapping incessantly. The pillow around his neck bounced like a purple buoy.

Gasps rippled through the guests as phones rose into the air to document what was quickly becoming the most chaotic—and entertaining—ceremony of the year.

Next to me, Grayson sprang forward to help, because of course he did, which meant I also moved to help—because I'm apparently incapable of staying out of trouble. In my haste, I collided straight into him, a tangle of limbs and silk and sand.

For a split second, as we tipped sideways, I thought, *No, no, no, he's going to crush me like a pancake.*

Then—boom.

The sand cushioned our fall, and Grayson narrowly avoided flattening me, instead landing sprawled between my legs with my dress tangled around his face like a rogue silk parachute. Around us, gasps gave way to laughter and even applause—yes, applause —because, of course, this Hollywood crowd would treat our mishap like an expertly choreographed stunt crafted solely for their entertainment.

Someone hollered, "And the award for best supporting role goes to...!"

Chris Pitt, of course. I could've clocked him with a shoe.

I tried to scramble up, but my sand-colored dress—a slinky, silky menace—had other plans. Grayson turned his head, his voice muffled through an unfortunate veil of fabric that had firmly cocooned his face—which also explained why my dress felt like it was trying to suffocate me.

"Stop flailing," he muttered, far too calm for someone being attacked by couture. "I'm searching for the hidden escape hatch in your dress."

In my frantic attempt to free us both, my knee shot up— straight into his nose.

"Gah!" Grayson yelped, jerking back. "Am I trying to escape your dress, or are you trying to kill me?"

"Oh, you're hilarious," I deadpanned, yanking the fabric off his face like I was ripping open a gift I didn't ask for. "Move before we end up on *TMZ* or *Here's the Scoop*—headline: *Best Man Suffocated by Maid of Honor's Killer Dress.*"

He blinked, eyes watering as he gingerly touched his nose. "I think I preferred the suffocation."

Meanwhile, Zephyr, emboldened by Mara's obvious failure to apprehend him, was in peak frenzy mode, yapping at the suspiciously familiar snaggle-beaked seagull like he was the hero of a Disney movie.

Mara's mother—who, up until now, had been the picture of wedding decorum—shot to her feet, shrieking, "Stop that dog! Someone grab that pillow! The rings are in there!" She pointed an accusatory finger at the bird. "Shoo!"

Mara's dad leapt to his feet like a man half his age but promptly caught his foot on the aisle runner, pitching forward with a startled "Oof!" and landing hard on his knees.

"Not you, Thad!" Mara's mom wailed, hands flying to her pearls as if she'd witnessed a tragedy. "Let one of the young people chase him down!"

The snaggle-beaked seagull, not one for stage fright, tilted its head and flapped its wings with theatrical disdain, as if to say, *Yes, people, this is happening. I orchestrated it all.*

Grayson finally helped me to my feet, sand spilling from my skirt in a cascade of humiliation. "Thank you for that cartoonish rescue," I muttered, brushing grit off my elbow.

"You're welcome," he replied, his voice laced with amusement as he brushed a stray patch of sand from his sleeve. "By the way, your dress could use some brushing off."

I glanced down and groaned. "Brushing off? It's practically a sand dune. I could open a beachside concession stand." How had I managed to get sand *down there*?

Mara finally let out a shriek and kicked off her heels, marching barefoot down the steps in full bridal battle mode, intent on capturing Zephyr, who was racing back and forth in front of the altar like a dog obsessed. Kincaid, God bless him, zigzagged after him like he was chasing a fumbled football.

The snaggle-beaked seagull, apparently fed up with the entire debacle, gave one final flap of its wings—sending a stray petal fluttering onto Mara's mom—before soaring toward the ocean.

Zephyr bolted past the altar after his nemesis, clearly believing he could sprout wings. Mara let out a yelp as he tore past her and dashed after him, unintentionally flinging sand on Grayson and me as she flew by. Not to be outdone, Kincaid sprinted after them both, quickly overtaking Mara.

The crowd was in full-on chaos now—laughter, cheering, someone starting a slow clap. Chris Pitt leaned over in his chair, cupped his hands around his mouth, and yelled, "Zephyr! I believe in you!" earning a theatrical groan from Mara's mom, who threw her hands skyward. "Why are you encouraging this madness?"

Finally, with a heroic dive that would've made the NFL proud, Kincaid leaped across the sand, gently tackling Zephyr mid-sprint. Mara stopped running and threw her hands in the air, half-victory, half-resignation, while the guests erupted into cheers.

I glanced at Grayson as he dusted the last bits of sand from his jacket. "Think we'll ever recover from that level of secondhand embarrassment?"

"Probably not." He said with a grin. "But I'll remember it forever. Weddings should be memorable, right?"

Zephyr, having vanquished his foe, barked triumphantly and showered Kincaid's face with enthusiastic licks. I couldn't help it—I burst out laughing, and soon the whole wedding party joined in, making us sound like a chorus of demented seagulls.

Chris Pitt crouched, patting his legs and calling, "Hey, Zephyr, come here!" Zephyr, instantly on alert, wriggled free from Kincaid's arms and raced toward Chris, tail wagging like a fanboy meeting a Hollywood icon.

"If you think you've got this miniature wedding tornado under control, he's all yours," Kincaid said, handing over the leash and leaving Zephyr settled between Chris and Kim, who looked ridiculously pleased with the solution.

"Just keep him, right there, that's all I ask," Mara's dad added.

As the commotion died down, Grayson and I reclaimed our spots. "Entertaining as that was," he said, a teasing lilt in his voice, "I think we're lucky Zephyr and his seagull buddy didn't resort to bloodshed."

"Small miracles." I grinned, watching Mara shake out her veil and slip on her heels before stepping back onto the altar, looking endearingly disheveled. Poor woman. This wedding was one for the books.

Meeting her halfway, I brushed sand off her dress and readjusted her veil. "Just roll with it. Everyone's laughing; you're in the clear. Besides, thanks to Zephyr, you're off the hook for anything else that could go wrong. It's all they'll be talking about."

Mara's tension visibly eased, her eyes softening with relief. "You always know exactly what to say to keep me from a meltdown."

Back at the altar, Tandy appeared like a bridal fairy godmother, seamlessly steering the ceremony back on track. She leaned in, whispering, "The rings? Please tell me they survived that chaos."

Grayson's eyes sparkled with mischief as he produced a small blue velvet box. "Luckily, I didn't trust our star ring bearer with the real deal," he said, handing it to Ford with a flourish.

Ford let out a relieved chuckle as he took the box. "Grayson, you're a lifesaver."

I leaned slightly toward Grayson, lowering my voice so only he could hear. "That seagull looked awfully familiar, didn't it?"

He smirked, matching my hushed tone. "Same bird, same snaggle-beak. I'd recognize that schemer anywhere."

The minister, barely holding back a smile, shook his head. "Ah, weddings with pets and children—always a wild card." He adjusted his posture, his tone turning reverent as he continued, "Now, if we may refocus on the love and commitment that brought us all here today…"

As the sun cast a warm, ethereal glow over Mara's veil, she

took a steadying breath, her hands clasping Ford's as if anchoring her to the moment. She raised her voice just enough for the gathered crowd to hear clearly, her tone carrying a mix of humor and sincerity. "Ford, standing here, ready to bare my soul in front of everyone—especially after Zephyr's, uh, comedic interlude—is a little intimidating. But holding your hands, looking into your eyes? It centers me. I never expected to find someone who fills all my gaps and rounds out my edges. It sounds cheesy, but you make me feel complete."

Ford gazed back, eyes brimming with love, as if willing her every ounce of courage.

She flashed a quick look my way, her eyes sparking with both joy and a touch of mischief, a silent handoff as if to say, *Your turn's coming.* And then, back to Ford, her world narrowed to just him. "I'm extraordinarily lucky," she continued, her voice soft but sure. "Lucky you ducked into my store that rainy day. Lucky you kept trying, even when I shut you down. Lucky you gave me your friendship and slowly built something I didn't realize I was missing. And luckiest of all, that you tore down every barrier I'd ever put around my heart."

The lump in my throat swelled, blurring my vision. Her words cut deep, unearthing emotions I'd neatly buried. I blinked back tears, but they had other plans.

"I love you, Ford Ross. For today, and for every tomorrow we get together."

That did it. I couldn't stop the tears streaming down my face. In a desperate swipe to salvage my mascara, I lifted Mara's bouquet to cover my attempt at damage control. Why didn't wedding dresses come with pockets for tissues?

Grayson's eyes caught mine, filled with a gentleness that eased the tidal wave inside me. Silently, he pressed something into my hand—a tissue. "You okay?" he whispered, voice warm with concern.

My heart did a little hop-skip, expanding in ways I wasn't sure it should. Dabbing at my eyes, I shot him a grateful smile. "That was devastatingly beautiful," I murmured, still dazed. Had he anticipated this moment, ready with that tissue just for me? Ignoring Grayson was getting trickier by the second, but I'd shelve that problem for later.

For now, I needed to compose myself—especially since Sonya and Max were up next, and my tear ducts had proven themselves more than willing to take on an encore performance.

As the sun dipped, bathing the ceremony in a warm, tangerine glow, I clung to my last shreds of self-control. When the newly-weds finally made their way back up the aisle, I let out an enormous sigh of relief. Emma followed, then Grayson and I, with Sinan and Kendra bringing up the rear.

Grayson's arm beneath mine was steady, a grounding warmth that felt oddly natural. It was a good arm—solid, supportive, one I could maybe, possibly, very easily get used to. But as we reached the end of the aisle, I pulled away, slipping back to reality. Being that close to Grayson felt like standing on the edge of something exciting and terrifying. And yet... that almost-kiss last night, a kiss we'd only narrowly missed, lingered between us.

Now what? Do I risk it all for the chance of something real with Grayson? Or would that send my life spinning off its carefully charted course? The safe play was to keep my distance. But since when did "safe" equate to "fulfilling"?

I stole a glance at Mara, radiating confidence and joy by Ford's side, so clearly in her element. Was love about throwing caution to the wind or laying down bricks one by one? Maybe Mara had been right all along. Maybe, in the grand scheme of things, great risk did bring great reward.

9

BEYOND THE BEACH WEDDING

GRAYSON

The sun dipped below the horizon, setting the sky ablaze in fiery hues as the photographer captured every picture-perfect moment. Once our formal photos were finally done, we groomsmen were dismissed, leaving Mara, Sonya, Courtney, Kendra, and Emma to bask in their own spotlight shots.

As I wandered down the sandy path toward the reception, the scene shifted into something out of a dream. Twinkling fairy lights and lanterns cast a warm glow, laughter floated on the breeze, and a string quartet played a melody that felt like magic. You'd think celebrating love on a beach would lift my spirits, but Dad's sharp words earlier clung to me like smoke after a fire.

"Trivialities," he'd muttered after overhearing the dance rehearsal plans. "Playing around instead of focusing on real goals. You probably think I'm being hard on you, but this is a pivotal time in your career." His tone had been sharp enough to cut through the day's joy, a reminder of why relaxing never came easy. I'd barely managed to shut him up before Ford showed up—he'd have ruined the surprise, and my sisters would've gone ballistic.

The music pulled me closer to the reception area, where the

festivities were on hold, waiting for the brides and grooms to arrive. Just as I neared the head table, Tandy materialized beside me, her timing as impeccable as ever.

"You're seated next to Courtney," she said with a grin. "Place cards are set—you can't miss it."

As if summoned by her words, Courtney appeared, radiant in a flowing sand-colored gown that caught the torchlight like it was designed just for her. Our eyes met, and she smiled—a warm, genuine smile that made looking away impossible.

"Together again," I said, pulling out her chair. "At this rate, people might start talking."

She raised a curious eyebrow as she settled in, her shoulder brushing my hand. The jolt that small touch sent through me was almost embarrassing.

"Seated at the head table? Guess we're moving up in the world," she said, her tone light but her eyes sparking with humor. "What's next—preparing our Nobel acceptance speeches?"

Her words drew a laugh from me, but it was her presence that hit harder. In that moment, something clicked. Courtney wasn't just my sister's brilliant friend or a respected colleague. She challenged me, intrigued me, and somehow, in the middle of this wedding, she was making me realize what I'd been missing.

This night wasn't just about Mara and Ford's happily-ever-after—it was a wake-up call. And Courtney? She might be the answer, if I just gave this a chance.

Was Courtney feeling the same pull, or was this a one-sided equation? Every glance her way amplified my interest. The way her hair was elegantly pinned revealed the graceful curve of her neck—a detail that made my heart rate spike like data points on a breakthrough graph.

As if sensing my thoughts, she turned to me with a soft sigh. "You know, there're a lot of unspoken variables between us," she said, her eyes meeting mine. "We've got undeniable chemistry, but you put up some serious barriers with that friend-zone speech. Are we going to address the elephant in the room or keep pretending it's not there?"

I paused, choosing my words carefully. "Honestly? My brain's been working overtime, listing every reason why diving into something with you could complicate things. We're both swamped with work, and you're one of Mara's closest friends. But then there's this other part of me that's tired of overthinking and ready to just... go for it."

Her lips quirked into a tentative smile. "So, what? You're flip-flopping again?"

"I think it's time to stop overanalyzing and start testing the hypothesis," I said, the corner of my mouth lifting. "Passing on something amazing just because it's inconvenient? That's not how real discoveries are made."

She studied me as she tilted her head, thinking. "You know our lives are already chaotic—research, teaching, families, our new hobbies. But maybe... maybe you're right. Maybe we should give this a shot."

Relief swept through me like a breath of fresh air. "Exactly. We're problem solvers, right? Hypothesize, test, analyze. We can figure this out."

Her eyes sparkled, a mix of excitement and determination. "So, a relationship. As a collaborative project?"

"Precisely," I said, grinning. "One with that looks extremely promising."

She let out a soft laugh. "Well then, Dr. Stellar, it looks like we've got some groundbreaking research ahead of us. Let's put *us* to the test tonight."

Before I could respond, applause erupted from the crowd as the newlyweds made their grand entrance. I stood, joining in the celebration, but my thoughts remained fixed on Courtney. "Looks like the main event has arrived," I said, catching her eye.

She leaned closer to me, her smile now fully blossomed. "Funny. I thought the main event already started."

Night had fallen, and the stars above glimmered like scattered diamonds against the deep velvet sky. The brides and grooms took their places down from us at the head table, their laughter mingling with the gentle murmur of the ocean. Around us, fairy lights twinkled from the nearby trees, their soft glow adding a touch of magic to the scene. It was the kind of moment that belonged in a storybook—or, knowing Ford, a movie pitch.

The moment arrived for my best man speech, and I rose without hesitation. Years of teaching lecture halls packed with students had left me unfazed by public speaking. I started strong, balancing sincerity with just enough humor to keep the mood light and ensure all eyes stayed on Ford and Mara. Stories about their quirks and compromises—his obsessive need to direct everything, her ironclad belief that "graphic novels are literature"—earned easy laughs. The applause that followed felt natural, almost effortless, and Ford clapped me on the back as I returned to my seat.

"Smooth as silk," he said, his grin as wide as the ocean behind us. "Thanks for making us sound like romance royalty."

"You're welcome," I replied, matching his grin. "Though if this were a movie, you'd need a way bigger twist."

Ford laughed, but as I sat back down, a new kind of tension wound tight in my chest. The speech? That had been the easy part. What came next—stepping out of my comfort zone and risking something real with Courtney—felt infinitely more daunting.

"Well done," Courtney said softly, leaning just close enough for her words to carry over the applause. Her shoulder brushed mine, the brief contact sparking a jolt of awareness. "You made that look easy. I don't think I could've pulled it off with *this* crowd."

I glanced at her, a flicker of amusement breaking through my nerves. "They're all either family or strangers. The trick is not caring too much about impressing either."

She lifted her eyebrows and glanced out at all the guests, then her lips twitched in a small, almost-smile. "Not your run-of-the-mill strangers, but okay. Color me impressed."

Mara leaned closer, fixing us with a sharp gaze. "Alright, you two. Something's up. I'm sensing… a shift in the Force here. Don't leave me hanging—what's going on? You've leveled up or something, right?"

Courtney's eyes widened, clearly caught off guard, and she shot me a look that practically screamed for backup. Trying to play it cool, I leaned in with what I hoped was a convincingly casual smile. "Mara, you've been playing way too many video games. Courtney and I? We're just two perfectly platonic allies on the same side quest. No romance perks, no secret character boosts."

Mara snorted, her skepticism palpable. "Oh, please. I know relationship tension when I see it, and you two are practically a cutscene away from a major plot twist. So, spill it: are we looking at 'will-they-won't-they' or are you two gearing up for a full-on 'I choose you' confession scene?"

I blinked and glanced at Courtney, who seemed to be thoroughly enjoying my predicament. She leaned in, a mischievous spark in her eye. "Yeah, Grayson. Answer your sister."

I froze, scrambling for a response. What exactly did Mara expect me to say here? Sure, we'd agreed to give this a shot, but not only hadn't we worked out any details, we hadn't even kissed! Luckily, Mom appeared with impeccable timing, wearing a look of pure undercover-agent stealth.

"Grayson, could I borrow you for a sec? We need to discuss the quantum mechanics of the Macarena or some such." She winked, and I couldn't have been more grateful.

I sprang up, seizing my exit strategy.

"Don't think I'll forget that non-answer!" Mara called after me as I followed Mom to a quiet spot behind the sea grass. The DJ had taken over as the string quartet packed up, and Mom turned to me, her eyes twinkling.

"Alright, showtime," she said. "You practiced with your sisters earlier today—how're you feeling?"

I shrugged, thinking back to the whirlwind rehearsal in my twin sisters' hotel room and my own private practice session on a lonely stretch of beach earlier today. While the rest of the men in the wedding party were exploring the islands and soaking in the view, I'd been stepping through the sequence like a madman, trying to hammer it into muscle memory. "I won't say I'll be perfect, but I didn't trip over my own feet today, so… progress?"

She smiled, giving my arm a reassuring squeeze. "You've got rhythm, Grayson. Trust yourself. This is supposed to be fun."

The twins, Rachael and Aubrey, joined us, practically glowing with excitement. "One last group practice for that tricky combo," Rachael insisted, all drill-sergeant precision.

We breezed through the moves as I synched with each step. To my relief, everything came together with only a few minor missteps, perfect for my "clumsy sibling" role.

Mom's eyes gleamed with pride. "Be yourselves. You three are gonna shine."

Then Aubrey stilled, her eyes going wide. "Oh my gosh—Chris Pitt is here," she whispered, barely containing her excitement. She nodded toward the crowd. "Right over there."

I followed her gaze and spotted the guy from the ceremony—the one who'd held Zephyr.

"Shhh!" Rachael nudged her, casting a swift, cautionary glance at me. She shook her head at Aubrey, who looked appropriately chastised but still buzzed with excitement. Then Rachael turned to me, lowering her voice. "Don't let him being here throw you off your game. Just… stay focused, alright?"

"Wait, who's Chris Pitt?" I asked, blinking at them, trying to make sense of their sudden concern. "Am I supposed to know this guy?"

My twin sisters exchanged a look, one part amused, one part exasperated, but before they could answer, Tandy's voice rose above the crowd as she stepped up to the mic.

"Alright, everyone, if we could have your attention, please!" Tandy's commanding tone quieted the guests, smoothly preparing everyone for the next part of the evening. The familiar opening chords of *My Girl* began to fill the air.

With no time to unravel the mystery of Chris Pitt and why he might "rattle" me, I took a steadying breath, refocused, and stepped onto the dance floor. Leaning fully into my role as comic relief, I gave my best flailing attempt, flopping my limbs like a malfunctioning marionette while my mom and sisters danced circles around me with effortless grace.

Laughter erupted, filling the air like music. But beneath the laughter and the ridiculous steps, I felt it—that quiet pull. The way the bass and melody threaded through the noise, reaching a part of me I didn't often acknowledge. Even when I wasn't *listening*, music always seemed to find me. It was steady, grounding, and impossible to ignore—and my feet seemed to recognize it.

I caught Courtney grinning, eyes bright and encouraging, and I couldn't help but let the rhythm guide me a little more. My flailing turned to something resembling actual dancing—nothing fancy, but enough to remind me how music always seemed to draw something out of me, whether I liked it or not.

The song transitioned seamlessly into Bruno Mars' *Marry You*, and I leaned into my over-the-top instincts with an exaggerated spin. Naturally, I wobbled straight into Sinan.

Sinan caught me with a steady hand, saving us both from disaster.

"Nice catch, Spider-Man," I quipped, still catching my breath.

"With great power comes great reflexes," he shot back, grinning.

The laughter swelled again, but this time, the music was in my bones, letting me relax into the moment.

We struck our final pose just as the song ended, and the applause was deafening—a wall of sound more exhilarating than I'd imagined. I caught Courtney's eye, her face glowing with joy and a spark of something else that made my pulse quicken.

As we gathered for a family hug, Aubrey whispered, "You stole the show, Grayson."

Rachael stepped back, her grin wide. "You nailed it! They couldn't get enough."

Mara joined us, looking both astonished and delighted. "Seriously, you guys. That was incredible. I had no idea you had something like that planned."

The moment was pure joy—family, celebration, and maybe a hint of something more. A wave of nostalgia hit, pulling me back to simpler days in Mom's community theater productions, when I'd reveled in the spotlight. She'd once suggested I try out for the middle school musical—a suggestion I'd stubbornly refused. Then there'd been the piano. I'd played with passion until advanced biology and Dad's relentless expectations took over.

Bittersweet as it was, the memory sparked a moment of clarity. Had I left the arts behind just to keep Dad happy? The applause reminded me of something I hadn't felt in years—the thrill of doing something just because it felt good. Maybe it was time to reclaim that part of myself. Maybe even make room for people who added color to my world, like Courtney.

Mara slipped away to rejoin Ford, and Courtney appeared by my side, pulling me into a hug. "Grayson, I had no idea! You're like a one-man comedy show meets dance troupe. Seriously, I knew your sisters were talented, but you—brains, beauty, and jazz hands?"

I laughed. "Mom had me jazz-handing before I could walk. It's been years, but this was fun."

The lightness I was feeling evaporated when I caught sight of Dad weaving through the crowd, zeroing in on me like a homing beacon. Instantly, the air felt heavier, a tension threading through the festive hum, as if the stage had been set for an inevitable showdown. I knew the look on his face—it was his "I'm not mad, just disappointed" mask that somehow cut ten times deeper.

Stepping forward to intercept him, I positioned myself away from Courtney and the others. The last thing I needed was for them to hear whatever thinly veiled critique Dad would deliver under the guise of polite praise.

"Grayson, you and your sisters certainly… entertained," my father remarked, his tone laced with a subtle edge. "Let's just hope this performance doesn't end up on social media. Your university might not find it as 'amusing' as this crowd does."

The words landed like surgical strikes, as precise as a scalpel. Right on cue.

Before I could even process a response, Courtney's fingers slipped from mine, and she turned to Dad, unflinching. He shifted his gaze to her, extending a businesslike hand. "Good to see you, Courtney. Congratulations on securing the position with the Cates Foundation."

My stomach churned. Why bring that up now? Was this his version of a well-timed jab?

Courtney shook his hand, her face lighting up with genuine excitement. "Thank you, Dr. Stellar. It's a dream opportunity, really."

Dad didn't miss a beat. "Grayson felt the same way," he said, his voice a shade too smooth. "It's unfortunate he wasn't selected. They must've chosen the more… qualified candidate."

My jaw clenched as I glanced at my mom and sisters, their faces a mix of sympathy and irritation. Dad's remark had been perfectly timed, a backhanded compliment that stung like a slap. Still, was my sister's wedding really the time to call him out?

Before I could let my temper take over on Mara's big day, Courtney's hand found mine again, its warmth grounding me. And just like that, his attempt to chip away at my self-worth lost its sting. Instead, it kindled a flame—not for my own pride, but for Courtney's. Using her success as a prop to highlight my supposed failings? That wouldn't fly, not today.

Just as I was about to speak, Courtney turned to my father, her expression frosty enough to freeze over the beach. "Dr. Stellar," she began, her voice calm but cutting, "Grayson's talent isn't up for debate. My selection by Cates wasn't about competition—it was about finding the right fit. And there's no trophy for belittling family, especially not today." She smiled, razor-sharp, then turned to me. "Now, if you'll excuse us, Grayson promised me a dance."

Her words sliced through the tension like a clean breeze, leaving no room for argument. Taking her cue, I offered my arm, and she slid hers through mine, leading us toward the dance floor.

"Not that I'm complaining, but I don't remember signing up for dance duty," I teased as we wove through the crowd.

She tilted her head, a hint of a smile on her lips. "Call it a tactical retreat. Plus, I might have a thing for waltzing with over-achievers."

"High stakes, high rewards," I said, her words landing deeper than I expected. "But sometimes the best rewards aren't the ones you're chasing."

Her eyes softened, glinting with something unspoken. "Mara said the same thing last night—'With great risks come great rewards.'"

I grinned as the music swelled. "Ready to test that theory?"

She raised a brow, daring me. "Lead the way."

WHAT LIES BENEATH

COURTNEY

Coming off the dance floor next to Grayson, I felt like I'd stepped out of my everyday life and into something brighter. In that moment, lab reports and research deadlines seemed miles away. I let myself bask in the novelty of it all.

A sharp squeal of feedback suddenly broke the spell as Dante —chef, restaurateur, and wedding cake maestro—took the mic. "Alright, folks, brace yourselves: it's time for the double wedding cake reveal!" He waved grandly at a curtained area, working the crowd like a pro.

Guests clustered around, buzzing with excitement. With a theatrical flourish, Dante yanked back the curtain, and the group gasped in unison.

Mara's delighted squeal cut through everything. "Wonder Woman as my cake topper? That's perfect!" She beamed at the miniature superhero bride poised beside a tuxedoed groom—tiny figures capturing every detail, down to the Amazonian tiara.

Ford slid an arm around Mara, grinning. "So I'm your Superman tonight?"

Mara laughed. "Wrong DC reference, Ross. Wonder Woman's

main man was Steve Trevor, a mortal pilot—though yes, you're still my hero."

A blur of pink rushed by—Emma—heading straight for the second cake. Her eyes went huge as she realized what she was seeing. "Aunt Sonya? Uncle Max?" she whispered, excitement and awe colliding.

Sonya and Max joined her, warmth glowing in their smiles. Sonya's voice shook a little. "Do you like it, Emma?"

I followed Emma's gaze to the other cake. Alongside the bride and groom stood a mini Emma—a family united in sugar and frosting. After losing so much, this moment felt even more poignant.

Emma flung her arms around Sonya and Max. "I love it!"

Max's expression softened. "We'll always be together."

"And we're here for you, forever and a day," Sonya added gently.

My chest tightened, and I blinked against the sudden sting of tears. "I wasn't prepared for an emotional rollercoaster," and Grayson, always tuned in, slipped a tissue into my hand.

I glanced up at him, a bit stunned by his thoughtfulness, and saw a tenderness in his eyes that went straight to my heart.

"They make a beautiful family," he said quietly.

"That they do," I agreed, dabbing at my eyes.

Silverware chimed as everyone dug into slices. When Grayson offered me a bite of Mara's chocolate cake from his fork, the chocolate dissolved like velvet on my tongue. "Incredible," I murmured.

I eyed Sonya and Max's vibrant tropical cake, its glazed fruit shining like jewels. "What flavor is that one?"

"Pineapple, coconut, and orange," somebody chimed in.

Grayson snagged a slice and guided me to a quieter corner. The fruity explosion of pineapple and orange melted into each bite, making me think unexpectedly of my research. The fruit chunks, the cake structure—my brain flipped into science mode.

He noticed. "I can see those gears turning—what are you dreaming up over there?"

I grinned, realizing I must have been staring off into space. "This reminds me of my research. If the fruit chunks represent the rogue cancer cells, I'm designing a virus that targets them without ruining the whole cake."

"Only you," he teased. "From wedding cake to cancer research in three seconds flat. Never change, Courtney."

"It's how my brain works. Precise targeting, like defusing a bomb." My excitement grew. "Imagine applying that concept to viral therapy."

His eyes lit up. "Speaking of precision, did you catch that new peptide article? Nature's GPS for cancer cells."

I brightened. "Heard about it, haven't read it. Send me the link?"

He smirked. "When you get your Nobel, don't forget to thank the messenger."

"I'll open with it," I joked, then exhaled. "But maybe we should enjoy the night and talk shop another day?"

"Deal." He took another bite of cake. "Ford gave me cooking lessons at Dante's as a best man gift. Between that and my piano lessons, my schedule's jam-packed. When can we squeeze in real dates?"

"Cooking lessons? My brothers take those classes too!" I said, amused. "Conner is the manager and co-owner of Dante's restaurant." I hesitated, wondering how long we'd be able to make time for any sort of relationship, then did a quick mental tally of my overstuffed planner. "Saturdays, maybe Tuesdays—unless it's my book club night."

"Works for me." He took my hand, his gaze warm. "But tonight..." His gaze flicked to my lips. "I think we should make the most of it. Maybe do something tomorrow, too."

Reality hit. "Actually, I'm leaving for Florence at dawn. Planes, planes, and more planes—here to Charlotte, then Heathrow to Florence. Perks of island life: no direct flights." It hadn't seemed like a big deal when I booked it, but now? Leaving so soon felt like a cruel joke.

His face fell in exaggerated despair. "Say it isn't so." Kissing my hand, he grinned. "Guess we have to cram all our romance into one night."

My heart thumped at his playful intensity. "Challenge accepted."

The wedding crowd erupted into laughter when Mara prepared for the bouquet toss. Grayson drew me aside, slipping an arm around my waist. "Shall we continue our evening?" he asked, his voice warm and inviting.

I slipped off my heels, hooking them with a finger. "Mara's going to give me so much grief for skipping this, but I'm in. Lead the way, Prince Charming."

We wandered along the shoreline, pale moonlight dancing on the water. Grayson bent to pick something from the sand. "Sea glass," he announced, holding up a smooth, blue fragment.

"It's so pretty."

"A rare find," he said, placing it in my hand. "Once debris, but after being polished by the ocean, it became something beautiful. A reminder that even turbulent experiences can create something beautiful."

I slid it into the only place I had free—my bra—earning a bemused smirk from him. Despite the swirl of responsibilities and my looming trip, the moment felt perfect.

He brushed a thumb across my cheek. "You realize we've covered everything tonight from cake to peptides. You fascinate me."

My breath caught. "You're easy to fascinate."

He stepped closer, lowering his voice. "Not usually."

The weight of work and responsibility fell away, replaced by a thrill that had me blurting out a confession I'd been holding back. "It's both thrilling and terribly unfair to discuss science with someone who's so… completely engaged."

"Oh?" His gaze held mine, his voice low and teasing.

"You're curious," I said, feeling my pulse quicken. "You don't just nod along. You dive in, fully immersed. And on top of it, you're breathtakingly handsome. Ever since this trip began, I've been fighting the urge to grab you and kiss you."

My confession hung between us, and my heart pounded as though it had just placed a winning bet. His smile spread slow and delighted. "Breathtakingly handsome, huh?"

"Unfortunately, yes," I murmured. "You should really tone that down."

He edged closer, gaze intent. "I could say the same about you."

My eyes darted to his, the air sparking with tension. "We could keep talking," I teased softly, "but I'd rather—"

"Me too," he murmured, leaning in.

Our lips met in a heady rush of chemistry and warmth, a silent acknowledgment of the unspoken pull between us. It was urgent and sweet all at once, like we both knew time was short but refused to waste another second.

My hands slipped from his chest to his lapels, gripping the silky fabric, pulling him closer. I wanted to erase any lingering distance, to dissolve until we were one—no lines, no barriers.

The night air brushed my skin, but Grayson's warmth chased away the faint chill. The kiss was fast and urgent, a delicious frenzy ignited by anticipation that had simmered too long. We kissed like we were racing against time, pouring every unspoken feeling into this one intoxicating moment.

Then he slowed, pulling back just enough to study my face. His gaze was intense, almost reverent, and his thumb brushed my upper lip with a gentleness that tempered the fire between us. It wasn't just a kiss—it was a promise, a shared secret, and the start of something we could no longer deny.

I couldn't resist. I nipped at his thumb, following it up with a quick, playful lick.

His lips curled into a knowing grin. "Ah, she bites."

"Only if you enjoy that sort of thing," I teased.

He chuckled, "As long as you don't make it a blood sport—or leave visible marks I'll struggle to explain."

I grinned, leaning in slightly. "Duly noted."

His eyes sparkled, alive with something I couldn't quite define. "You're an incredibly clever woman." He took my hand, guiding me effortlessly toward a nearby lounge chair nestled in a sandy alcove next to some palm trees.

As we settled in, our breath hung suspended in the heavy air. Salty ocean air filled my lungs, mingling with the spicy, musky scent of Grayson. All I could do was lose myself in this moment. Was this—could this really be happening?

He lifted his hand and the back of it grazed my breast, causing my nipples to harden. I inhaled shakily, wanting more. The fabric between us suddenly became a barrier that frustrated me.

I let my hand glide over his waist, tracing the contours of his frame through the fine fabric of his tuxedo shirt. The enticing warmth of his body radiated through the material, sending an electric thrill up my spine. He caught my gaze, a slow, deliberate smile curving his lips, and then reached for my hand. With a gentle tug, he pulled me to my feet.

His hands lingered at my waist, steadying me for a beat before sliding up to the zipper of my dress. His touch was both delicate and purposeful, sending shivers of anticipation down my spine as he slid down the zipper. I glanced around, making sure we couldn't be seen by prying eyes, but our spot was a secluded one. Relieved, I tugged off his black tuxedo jacket, tossing it aside, the world around us dissolving into nothing but this moment.

As my dress fell away, the sea glass slipped from its temporary nest and dropped to the sand. With a swift movement, Grayson snatched it up and tucked it into his pocket. "For safekeeping," he murmured, his words simple yet filled with unspoken promise. He removed his jacket and tossed it onto the chair.

Accompanied by the sound of gentle waves and swaying grass, Grayson pulled me close, the world narrowing to just us. I melted into him, tilting my head back as his lips brushed my neck.

Shivers of delight chased away my remaining awareness of the world beyond, leaving only the heat of my growing desire.

His hands slid down my body, sending my heart into overdrive.

I opened my eyes to find him staring at my breasts. He cupped one, teasing my nipple with his thumb. When I gasped, he dipped his head and suckled, nipping slightly before moving to the other breast.

I grabbed fistfuls of his short, wavy hair, its texture as intoxicating as his scent, and pulled him closer. God, but this was perfect.

He lifted his head, his gaze sweeping over me, leaving nothing unseen with my standing in my tiny thong. The gentle ocean breeze flirted with my exposed skin, its caress electrifying, but it wasn't what I wanted. I wanted him. I wanted Grayson's touch.

I pressed my body against his, and the proof of his arousal pressed into my belly. His length was startling and rock solid.

He gave a moan and pressed his fingers into my hips, pulling me closer.

I stripped away his shirt, revealing that well-muscled chest I'd glimpsed on the beach. But I wanted to see more, to experience all of this man. I instantly stripped away his pants and boxers, but before I set them aside he pulled a foil packet from his pants pocket.

I glanced at the small square and gave a playful smile. "Thinking a few moves ahead, I see. Those chess lessons paid off in unexpected ways."

We both chuckled, and then he rolled the condom in place.

We wrapped ourselves around each other, arms, lips, chests touching. He felt amazing. Hard and smooth and warm and supple. Perfect.

He slid his hands over my body, touching me everywhere and setting me on fire as the water of the bay lapped rhythmically against the shore, setting the tempo for each touch and sigh. I was fire and water. Sky and ocean. Logic and lust.

The instant my fingers met his cock, a quick, sharp breath escaped his lips. It was neither a sigh nor a moan, but a whisper of sound that told me how deeply my touch affected him.

He dropped his head back and closed his eyes, an expression of pure bliss on his face. He pulsed in my hand, and as I stroked him, I watched closely to gauge his reaction.

The man looked absolutely flawless. Radiating joy. Aroused and filled with an intense energy.

His eyes snapped open, seeking mine, their smoldering intensity reflecting the desire that churned within me.

We wobbled slightly on the soft sand, the unsteady footing mirroring the thrilling uncertainty of our newfound intimacy. Grayson steadied us, guiding me toward a tall palm tree. Its trunk, smooth and reassuring, curved just enough to cradle my back as I leaned against it. The contrast of bark against my bare skin grounded me, my feet sinking into the cool sand for balance. The mingling scents of salt air and tropical foliage swirled around us, cocooning us in the moment, as if the world had shrunk to just this one perfect space.

Grayson grabbed both my wrists and lifted them over my head and pressing them against the tree, then slid his free hand down to touch my most sensitive spot, teasing me. His touch was so sudden, so perfect, that I gasped in a mixture of delight and surprise.

He tapped, then flicked, then stroked—all while watching my face. Gauging my every reaction. Testing and teasing and learning my body.

Everything he did felt good. Felt amazing. That tapping thing —that was new. New and wonderful. My pussy was definitely taking notice.

He gazed at me with an intensity that overwhelmed me. A scientist observing—gathering data—fascinated with learning everything about me.

I wanted to touch him, but something about giving him

control over my body this way was erotic. Yes, I could break free, but did I want to?

Not in the least.

By the time his finger finally slid inside me, I was in a frenzy of want. This was good, yes, but I wanted more. Needed more. Desperately.

"Grayson, please," I managed to say through the haze of desire. God, I hated talking during sex. It pulled me out of the moment. I wanted to *feel*, not talk. *Act*, not think.

"You want me inside you?" he asked. Pressing. Teasing. Coaxing.

"Please," was all I could manage to say. The word came out in a whimper.

He lowered my hands and placed them on his shoulders, and an instant later his cock slid between my legs, nestling near my opening.

Pressed up agains the tree, I wrapped one leg around his waist and guided him to my entrance. When he finally—finally— pressed into me, we let out simultaneous gasps of pleasure.

He nuzzled my neck and cupped my ass, lifting me off my feet. I wrapped both legs around him, locking my ankles behind him as he pressed me against the palm tree. Thrusting. Thrusting.

I dug my hands into his hair. Suddenly his mouth left my neck and was on mine again. The taste of salt on his lips, salt from my own skin, as if he'd been kissed by the ocean itself, made me want to devour him.

I sucked gently on his tongue, on his lips. It was almost as though our bodies had melded and become a single entity.

A moment later, I pressed my tongue deeper into his mouth. He let out a moan as he gently sucked on it. That throaty vibration did something to me, and I tightened my legs around his waist.

He changed the rhythm of his thrusts slightly, adding a bit of a rotation to his hips.

Damn, but that was good.

I sighed my approval.

A moment later, I felt the soles of my feet go hot.

That was an incredibly auspicious sign. When my feet got hot like this, it usually indicated the onset of an orgasm—one that was nothing short of breathtakingly spectacular.

"Grayson," I breathed. "Oh, my stars, Grayson."

"Can you come for me now?" he asked, his tone both sexy and coaxing.

"Now—" was all I could manage before my body clenched around his cock. I gave a moan of such deep and fulfilling satisfaction that I didn't even recognize the sounds as my own.

And he kept thrusting. Oh yes, he kept thrusting. It was perfect. My orgasm seemed to keep going on, and on. Just as I thought it had to be over, he pressed into me again, keeping me at that pinnacle of sensation. How long had this been going on? A minute?

Two?

Could a person die from too long an orgasm?

Did I care?

This would be one hell of a way to go.

Finally, the waves slowed, then faded, letting me know my epic orgasm was finally at an end. Trembling, I unhooked my ankles and let one foot drop to the sand. My wet-noodle of a leg wouldn't hold my weight, and I tilted sideways against the palm tree, nearly pulling Grayson over with me.

We were still joined, my leg still wrapped around his waist, and Grayson steadied me, pulling me closer and pressing deeper into me. This new angle sent a fresh wave of arousal careening through me.

God. This orgasm wasn't quite done.

Grayson's thrusts changed again, becoming deeper and slower. A moment later his body stiffened as he drove into me one last time.

Oh. My. God.

Was this even happening? My very core seemed to implode as

the mother of all orgasms swept through me, all but incapacitating me.

My entire body trembled. I could barely move. Barley stand. Thankfully I was pressed against the tree; otherwise I'm certain I would have crumpled to the sand.

As he withdrew, more little tremors wracked my body. Aftershocks of that orgasm. It was as though my body couldn't quite let go of it.

"Are you okay?" he asked.

"I—holy hell. What did you just do to me?"

He gave a slow, sultry smile. "I've never had a reaction quite like this before."

"Just give me a minute. I've never had an orgasm quite like this before."

His smirk evolved into a radiant smile that seemed to illuminate his entire face. "For me too. It was nothing short of spectacular." He pressed closer to kiss me. Even as he pulled back, a satisfied smile clung to his lips.

"Okay, I think I can stand on my own two feet now," I said, loosening my grip on his broad shoulders.

He stepped back, giving me room to breathe. I hunched over, my palms pressing against my knees as I caught my breath. "Wow, that was... intense."

Grayson shot me a quick grin. "How about a quick dip in the bay to cool off?"

I peered out from our secluded, palm-shrouded haven. "Aren't you worried someone might see us?"

He glanced around the deserted beach. "Just a sliver of moon tonight. It's dark on this end of the beach, and we've been alone this whole time. I think we're safe."

"What about towels?" I asked, considering the logistical nightmare of putting snug fitting clothes on a wet body. "Getting dressed when you're damp is like wrestling with a waterlogged octopus."

Grayson lifted a finger in a "hold on" gesture, then jogged

down the empty beach, all bareass naked and unfazed by it. He returned within a minute, arms loaded with plush, white towels. "Scored these from the hotel cabana," he said, grinning as he draped them over a nearby chair.

He extended his hand toward me, palm open and inviting. For a heartbeat, I hesitated, caught in indecision. Then, with a thrill of daring, I grasped his hand. We raced into the bay's gentle surf, our laughter echoing in the night air as if we were kids again, carefree and untamed.

The water enveloped us in its refreshing embrace. It was cool, but far from chilly—a welcome contrast to my heated skin. Grayson led me deeper until we were submerged, the water lapping our shoulders.

"I assumed the ocean here would be more... turbulent," I observed, watching the delicate waves ripple around us. "I expected crashing waves, not this serene lull."

He chuckled, a low sound that vibrated through the water between us. "You and me both. I had body surfing on my mind earlier today. Went out with the guys to look for some action. We found some great waves on one of the nearby islands, but the beaches were rocky, and navigating them felt like an obstacle course."

Below the water, I slid my hand down his front, stopping just as I reached the curls of hair past his belly button, and gave him a mock-scowl. "You should register that thing as a deadly weapon. You nearly killed me with it."

His admirable cock, which had gone to sleep after doing its duty, gave a twitch.

"Oh, no, no, no," I said, scooting away warily. "You can't tell me you're ready for round two already. I haven't fully recovered yet from our wild beach sex."

His cock brushed my thigh, seeming to disagree. It was just plain obstinate.

"We could try it in a bed this time." He raised his eyebrows endearingly.

To my surprise, my body reacted to his suggestion with a sudden flare of lust that quickened my heartbeat. "So, what you're saying is, we should turn this into an experiment? I'm noticing a trend here. You're big on experimentation." A quality I was currently enjoying.

Grayson's eyes twinkled as he rubbed his chin, pretending to mull over my suggestion. "Well, you did raise an interesting point. It's entirely possible that the location skewed the results. For all we know, bedroom sex will be of the run-of-the-mill variety."

I pretended to consider the idea. "I hadn't thought of that. It's distinctly possible. That happens to have been my *first* beach-sex."

He raised his eyebrows in surprise. "Then we should gather more data, don't you think?"

Gather more data? My heart gave a little lurch. He was such a perfectly perfect nerd. He even used sexy science-speak on me.

"You sure know how to sweet-talk a woman," I teased, letting my words linger like the warm water lapping at my skin. I stepped out of the bay, the cool evening breeze brushing over me, leaving a pleasant contrast to the lingering warmth of the water. Droplets streamed down my legs as I cast a quick glance back at Grayson.

He'd followed me out, and now he stood close, watching me with a soft, amused smile that made my pulse race.

I gave him an impish grin and trailed a fingernail across his chest. "Let's get to work gathering that data," I added, then reached down and snatched up one of the towels.

11

DAWNING REALIZATIONS

GRAYSON

The sun had barely peeked above the horizon, draping the room in warm, peachy hues when my eyes opened to find Courtney nestled against my chest. The dawn turned her into a masterpiece, the kind that might spark a Louvre bidding war. After our beachside adventure, we'd ended up in her room, knowing she had an absurdly long, twenty-two-hour travel marathon to Florence first thing. I held still, content to savor the quiet, just watching her breathe.

Last night had been amazing. We'd clicked, not just our personalities, but in the bedroom as well. Maybe this thing between us could actually work. But just as I started settling into a Courtney-induced high, that little internal to-do list of mine chimed in, reminding me of my real-life responsibilities—the students, the commitments, the ever-mounting pressure to find that breakout research topic. Could I really afford to let myself get blissfully distracted?

The soft chime of Courtney's alarm punctuated the morning calm. With a graceful stretch, she rolled over, her eyes catching mine as she smiled, groggy but radiant. "Hey, you."

"Hey, yourself," I murmured, leaning in to steal a good-morning kiss.

She blocked me with a hand, eyes twinkling. "Nice try, but I need to freshen up first."

She slipped out of bed, gloriously naked, her perfect ass giving the slightest jiggle as she disappeared into the bathroom. I stayed behind for a moment, marveling at the absurdly high success rate of this entire getaway. When it was my turn, I followed her lead, brushing my teeth with my finger and her toothpaste before stepping back into the room. She was already in full-on packing mode, wrapped in a silky blue robe that looked like it had been conjured specifically for this moment. Meanwhile, I stood there, still completely naked, feeling both ridiculous and entirely unapologetic.

"Last night was amazing," she said, dropping a shirt into her suitcase and crossing back toward me, her eyes gleaming.

"Mutual," I replied, thinking of our impromptu beachside escapade. "Except maybe for the sand."

"Oh, right. The rogue grains," she laughed. "Venturing into uncharted territories even the mapmakers don't dare label."

I grinned. "Our unscheduled exfoliation session—one beachside amenity the resort's brochures conveniently forget to mention."

Her laughter softened, but a sigh escaped as she glanced at her half-packed suitcase. "Leaving today feels like a crime. One more day here would be heaven."

My heart did a hopeful leap, and words slipped out before my brain caught up. "Any chance you could reschedule?"

She shook her head, her expression tinged with wistfulness even as her gaze lingered on my bare body. "I wish. But I've got a panel tomorrow afternoon in Florence, and I'm already cutting it close."

"What's the panel about?"

She paused, folding a dress. "Challenges in inter-pharmaceutical collaboration. Back at my last job, we spent months developing a protocol only for the lawyers to shoot it down." She shook her head, a wry smile forming. "I could practically hear them shouting 'liability!' in their sleep." Her hands moved as she spoke, and despite the frustration in her words, there was a flicker of passion behind them. "At least the science held up, but still—it's one of those lessons you don't forget."

"Still impressive that you even attempted it."

"Thanks," she said, shrugging. "Learned a lot, but I hope I never have to deal with lawyers and their roadblocks again."

I scanned the room, itching to be helpful. "Need a hand packing?"

Her eyes softened. "Sweet of you to offer, but if you help, I'll just end up missing something."

"Should I head back to my room, then?"

She shook her head. "No, stay. I'm not ready to say goodbye yet either."

I settled on the bed, watching her gather her things. She moved with the ease of someone who'd done this a hundred times but still took pleasure in each movement, each item she tucked away. When she bent to retrieve something, her ass in the air and her hair spilled forward catching the morning light, she made me me forget every coherent thought in my head.

Catching my stare, she glanced over her shoulder, a mischievous glint in her eyes. "Cat got your tongue, Grayson?"

"Hardly," I said, my gaze still fixed. "If I had to pick a word, it'd be 'perfection.'"

She laughed, her eyes sparkling. "Dr. Stellar, living up to your name, I see."

"And to think, I got to hold every breathtaking inch of you all night." I grinned, savoring the memory. "You made me a very happy man."

Her laughter filled the room, a melody I wanted on repeat. But I reeled it in, my practical side taking the reins. "Do you have a ride to the airport all set?"

She nodded. "Emma's flying back with Zephyr and her grandfather, Don Ross. We're all sharing a cab."

"Good call. Max and Sonya need some quality honeymoon time to themselves."

"Exactly. Emma was the one who suggested it. She told them she'd just be a third wheel and would rather spend time with her friends back home. Don offered to have her stay with him since he's heading back early to oversee Ford's movie—he's producing it, after all."

For a moment, I thought about the film adaptation of my brother's comic and made a mental note to coordinate with Don when I got back.

"I need to shower." She disappeared into the bathroom, leaving me to dress in silence. I buttoned last night's white tuxedo shirt slowly, intent on staying long enough for a proper goodbye. The faint scent of coconut and florals wafted into the room—a tender whisper of her essence.

When she emerged, *something* came with her. A shift, intangible yet undeniable, lingered in the air. I couldn't place it at first, not with her standing there, her slinky robe slipping just enough to offer a teasing glimpse of those perfect breasts. The air between us felt charged, heavy with unspoken words and something else I couldn't quite name.

She was about to fly away from me, and suddenly, all I could think about was seeing her again. I mentally flipped through my calendar. "When do you get back?"

"Next Saturday." She smiled hesitantly.

"Well, wouldn't you know it? My Saturday is as open as a twenty-four-hour diner. How about I pick you up from the airport?"

Her smile faltered, and she glanced down at her suitcase before looking back at me. "Grayson, I've been thinking. Are you sure we should even be doing this? I mean, with everything we both have going on, doesn't it feel like we're setting ourselves up for failure?"

The question hit like a curveball direct to the center of my chest, but I kept my voice steady. "I know we're both busy, but isn't that the point? We make time for what matters. And I think this—us—could matter."

She hesitated, her fingers brushing the edge of her suitcase. "I don't want to disappoint you. Or myself. What is there simply isn't enough time in our schedules? What if we can't make it work?"

I stepped closer, my voice soft but resolute. "Or what if we can? What if this is exactly what we need? We won't know unless we try."

Her eyes searched mine, as though testing the sincerity of my words. Slowly, a small smile tugged at her lips. "Okay," she said, her voice quiet but sure. "Pick me up at the airport. I'll text you the details."

Relief coursed through me, but I kept it simple. "Deal. I'll be there." I paused, letting the moment settle before adding, "Holding the world's most ridiculous sign."

Her smile widened, this time with a glimmer of hope that matched mine. I could already picture the sign I'd bring to baggage claim—something outrageous, like Dr. Gillette's Personal Chauffeur. Yeah, I'd be that guy. And for her, I had the feeling it would be worth every bit of effort.

As Courtney disappeared into the bathroom with her clothes, I reached for my tuxedo jacket, slipping it on with practiced ease. When she reemerged, she looked effortlessly stunning, her hair falling in soft waves around her face.

"You clean up nicely," she teased, her gaze trailing over my ensemble. A playful smile tugged at her lips. "That five o'clock shadow adds a certain rugged charm. Very... James Bond-morning-after chic."

I rubbed a hand over my emerging stubble. "Thinking of growing a beard. What do you think?"

She stepped closer, looping her arms around my neck. "The rugged gentleman look suits you," she mused. "But honestly, it's not just the look—it's the man wearing it. You're undeniably hot, Dr. Stellar."

I pulled her gently into my arms, our lips meeting in a kiss that asked, *Are we really doing this?* and answered itself with, *Maybe we should.* Each soft press and retreat carried a question and a promise, filling spaces we hadn't realized were there. But as the moment began to stretch and heat, she pulled back with a playful sigh, her eyes holding a flicker of something between resolve and hesitation.

"If we keep this up, I'll miss my flight," she said, her voice low and amused.

I stepped back, a soft smile on my face, and gestured toward the door. "We can hit pause for now. Saturday's not that far off."

Her lips curved into a tentative smile, a mix of uncertainty and hope. "We'll see how it goes," she said softly, as if testing the words aloud.

"One step at a time," I agreed, letting the moment settle. Offering my arm, I added, "Shall I escort you downstairs, or is my current 007 look too much for daylight operations? Wouldn't want to pique Emma's curiosity."

"Oh, there's no doubt she'd interrogate you," Courtney laughed.

I reached down to extend the handle of her suitcase, then held the door open as she wheeled her life for the next week through the doorway. As she passed, she leaned in for one last, swift kiss, her lips brushing mine like a fleeting promise, before heading down the hall with a determined stride.

Once the door clicked shut, I surveyed the room—a space still humming with the echoes of laughter and shared moments. Spotting my tuxedo jacket draped over a chair, I picked it up. That's when a glint of silver caught my eye near the foot of the night-stand. Bending down, I found her cancer awareness necklace—the silver and white ribbon loop pendant she often wore.

I turned the pendant over in my palm, its smooth edges catching the light. Courtney had a way of leaving her mark, intentional or not. She'd seen the messy parts of my life—flaws, family drama, the works—and hadn't flinched.

I glanced toward the door, knowing I should take the necklace to her immediately. But the idea of walking into the hotel lobby, still in my tuxedo, invited far too many questions from Emma. No doubt she'd start with a pointed "Nice outfit, Uncle Grayson," and end with a half-joking interrogation I wasn't ready for.

I slipped the necklace into my pocket, the cool metal pressing into my palm. It wasn't a resolution, not yet—just a quiet reminder that some things were worth the risk. Her smile lingered in my mind as I stood in the stillness of the room. One step at a time—that was all we could promise. Maybe it would be enough.

1 2

THE SKEPTIC, THE SCIENTIST, AND THE SISTER

COURTNEY

Florence, Italy

The email arrived as I was arranging my notes, a last-minute review before heading downstairs to the Florence conference center. At first, I thought it was another update from the event organizers—a schedule change or a speaker's event. But when I saw the sender's name, my stomach dropped.

Subject: Let's Reconnect

Courtney,

I know it's been a long time. I probably shouldn't have fallen out of touch, but I wasn't sure what to say to you. I think it's time for you to meet Adele—your sister. She's been asking for years. She wants to get to know you. I hope you'll consider reaching out.

Take care,

Your Father

The words stared back at me, stark and clinical. Twelve years of silence, distilled into a handful of sentences, none of them offering even a hint of warmth. *Take Care, Your Father.* Not even *love.* Typical. And then there was *Adele—your sister.* The phrase felt like a brick to the chest, heavy and jarring. I didn't even know where to start with that.

I hovered over the delete button, my fingers shaking slightly. One click, and the email would vanish into the digital ether where it belonged. My father, master of guilt and timing, knew exactly when to strike. Of course, this wasn't about him. He'd made that abundantly clear with "*She* wants to get to know you." A sentence so loaded, it could've tipped the scales in a courtroom drama. Not a word suggesting he wanted to reconnect too.

I tapped it, relegating it to the trash.

Suddenly, the weekend in Turks and Caicos felt like a fading dream compared to this reality.

Striding through the serpentine hallways of the conference center moments later, I tried to shake off the lingering tension. The air whispered secrets of ages past, cool and reverent, while antique chandeliers cast flirty glints of light across frescoed ceilings. I had bigger things to focus on—like my presentation and the sea of scholarly stares awaiting me.

But as I approached the room, I found myself retrieving the email from my trash folder, my thumb hesitating before swiping it back into my inbox. *Adele—your sister.* The words wafted through my mind like a lingering scent I couldn't ignore.

"Dr. Gillette!" A cheerful voice broke through my distraction. A volunteer popped up beside me, practically radiating energy. "I'm Alex, your timekeeper." He beamed like he'd just won a prize.

"Nice to meet you, Alex," I replied, gripping my notes like a lifeline. "Think we could wrap up five minutes early for Q&A? Just give me a sign when I need to wind down."

He nodded, glancing at the crowd already filling the seats. "Looks like you've got a full house. First time this room's been packed."

Focus, Courtney, I told myself as I stepped inside the grand room, its frescoed ceilings and ornate carvings a Renaissance masterpiece in their own right. Presentation first, long-lost sister later.

The sight of the rapidly filling seats buoyed my spirits, adding a spark of excitement to the faint scent of designer cologne in the air.

I turned to the screen where my PowerPoint glowed in neon contrast against the ancient walls. A digital-age presentation plastered over Renaissance frescoes—like something straight out of *Back to the Future.*

Then, in the front row, the unmistakable—and unwelcome— face of that guy from MedcoVax appeared, the doubter from my Tuesday panel, sitting front and center with a "prove me wrong" look plastered on his face. It was as if he'd come specifically to rain on my breakthrough parade.

I took a deep breath and let my showtime instincts kick in. "The results of our testing are promising," I announced, my voice bouncing around the room. "Our goal is to program a virus to make the patient's immune system go after the cancer cells like a guided missile."

A hand shot up. My heart sank—it was Mr. MedcoVax, naturally. I'd barely started, and he was already poised to fire off objections like we were on a game show.

"I'll take questions at the end," I said, smiling just enough to suggest *hold your horses.* He kept his hand hovering, but I refused to let him derail me. I turned back to the slides, explaining the science with a confidence honed over countless hours and caffeine fixes.

As the presentation wrapped, I opened the floor for questions, and hands shot up around the room. Ignoring MedcoVax, I chose a woman in the front row who looked genuinely interested, not like she was plotting my scientific takedown.

"Targeting lung cancer cells is especially challenging. Why not target ones that are easier to distinguish from healthy ones?" she asked, her tone thoughtful.

"Great question." I smiled, grounding myself. "Lung cancer

cells are masters of disguise. Imagine a haystack with some needles—both good and bad—and we're trying to pull out just the bad ones. We're borrowing techniques from those who've cracked similar puzzles in esophageal cancer. We're aiming to outsmart lung cancer's camouflage game."

The audience buzzed with a new energy, but the MedcoVax guy was determined to seize the spotlight. He stood abruptly, his smile too sharp to feel genuine, his polished demeanor almost unnerving. "This all sounds impressive," he began, his tone laced with condescension, "but where's the substance? You're talking in metaphors without giving any hard data. Are you sure you're not overselling an underdeveloped theory?"

The room hushed, and that dreaded warm flush crept up my neck. It wasn't the challenge itself that rattled me; I'd faced tougher scrutiny from peer reviewers. It was something about him—the smoothness of his delivery, the way his eyes lingered on me as if searching for cracks. I couldn't put my finger on it, but his questions felt less like genuine skepticism and more like a calculated attempt to undermine me.

So much for just answering questions. But I wasn't about to lose my cool over one loud skeptic.

"Thank you for your... enthusiastic skepticism," I replied, forcing calm into my voice and meeting his gaze evenly. "Our research isn't just some castle in the sky. While we're deep in the experimental weeds, we're also piecing together a puzzle solidly anchored in data. What I can share is that we're rigorously testing our techniques as we proceed, and so far, the results are promising. Since our work has yet to be published, I hope you'll understand why I can't provide specifics just yet."

His smile didn't falter, but there was a glint in his eyes that sent another ripple of unease through me. "Of course," he said smoothly, "but the devil's in the details, isn't it? Promising results only mean something when they can be replicated. And until then, this is just another unproven hypothesis." His gaze swept the room, his voice carrying a subtle undertone that made me feel like he was addressing the audience rather than me—as if he was trying to plant seeds of doubt.

I resisted the urge to clench my fists. This wasn't a genuine discussion—it was a performance, carefully crafted to make me appear unprepared. Or worse, to manipulate me into divulging more about my research than I was ready to share.

I forced a smile, letting a note of humor creep into my tone. "That's the beauty of science—skepticism drives us to do better. But I'd caution you against mistaking our early findings for empty theories. We're building this foundation carefully and deliberately, knowing the stakes couldn't be higher."

The audience stirred, a few murmurs of approval breaking the tension. Shifting my voice to something lighter, I added, "And yes, before anyone asks, I've logged more hours in the lab than at home. I've spent so much time at the Cates Foundation, my coffee cup is considering applying for residency."

That earned a smattering of laughter, easing the room, and Alex signaled for the wrap-up. I finished with a confident lift in my tone. "The complexities of cancer require bold, calculated risks. My team won't stop until we've changed the game."

Applause filled the room, sweet relief after all that back-and-forth, and I stepped down, feeling a satisfying mix of triumph and adrenaline. But as I glanced toward the MedcoVax guy, his expression didn't match the rest of the room's energy. He was clapping, but there was something in his eyes—a cool, assessing look that felt wrong, like he was cataloging me for some future use.

It wasn't just the skepticism that had set me on edge. There was something about him I couldn't shake, something that lingered long after I stepped away from the podium.

Once outside, Florence greeted me with its sculpted beauty, whispering reassurances to my overstressed mind: "Breathe, you've done well. Now, let the charm of Florence revive you."

After a quick walk, I claimed a table at a little café in the *Piazza della Signoria*, feeling like I'd scored prime real estate. In record time, I managed to order a glass of Chianti, ricotta-stuffed ravioli in truffle sauce, and a slice of carrot cake, then sat back to take in this beautiful piazza.

I breathed in the mingling scents of espresso and fresh bread surrounding me, letting the tension of the week unravel. My thoughts drifted to Grayson, and a warmth settled in me. Sure, he wasn't here in Florence, but his smile and those mischievous eyes might as well have been sitting across from me.

This moment of relaxation seemed to be doing the trick, allowing me a mental reset. The ravioli arrived, every bite a creamy, earthy symphony. And the carrot cake? A masterpiece, with hints of fig and orange zest that practically danced on my taste buds. I made a note to try baking it myself—and maybe share the results with Grayson to prove I was following through on his baking challenge. The thought made me grin.

My phone chimed.

Kincaid: Is a safari theme with crossbred animals for the nursery too… much? Lianna says it's "too many weird animals." I was thinking of adding a Zebraloo.

Me: What's a Zebraloo? Sounds like a smoothie flavor.

Kincaid: Zebra meets kangaroo. Obvs. Thinking of adding a Zedonk and a Ligur for balance.

Me: Balance? This nursery is starting to sound like a Dr. Seuss fever dream.

Kincaid: Harsh. Ligurs are majestic.

Me: I'm just saying… you might want to reconsider. Might as well toss in a unicorn at this point.

Kincaid: Fine. Zebraloo & Friends are benched. But this isn't over. I'm saving this for a birthday party.

Family decorating crisis averted. I set my phone down with a quiet chuckle, imagining Lianna's long-suffering expression as Kincaid pitched his next "creative" idea.

But the lightness faded quickly. *Your sister.* The words from my father's email crept into my thoughts, unwelcome and insistent. The message, now back in my inbox, with a weight impossible to ignore. My chest tightened, the unresolved questions pressing at the edges of my mind.

Not now. I glanced around the piazza, recentering myself. This was my time, not his.

I turned my focus back to the square, letting the sights anchor me. The Palazzo Vecchio stood like a medieval sentinel, and Neptune, his bronze entourage delightfully chaotic, presided over the fountain with fierce dignity. The piazza was an open-air museum, every cobblestone steeped in history and splendor. Slowly, the knot in my chest loosened, and the vibrant pulse of Florence reclaimed my attention.

Finishing my cake, I paid and wandered toward the replica of Michelangelo's *David*, drawn to its timeless, ethereal perfection. His marble form stood proud, daring the world to find a flaw. But my mind drifted to Grayson—no marble statue, but a living, breathing masterpiece. His muscles weren't carved by an artist but built by dedication, strength, and purpose. Yet, for all his grandeur, what I craved wasn't perfection. It was warmth, unpredictability, and the messy beauty of human connection.

I drifted over to the Fountain of Neptune. Fenced-off barriers kept people from getting too close, but there he stood—Neptune, the mythic god of water, presiding over his realm from a sea-chariot. His aquatic entourage of sea horses, satyrs, and river gods decorated the basin in various shades of weathered bronze and green patina. Unlike *David*, their expressions were a chaotic medley of joy, almost grotesque in their animated enthusiasm. They seemed flawed, real—alive in a way that *David's* perfect features could never be.

My phone buzzed, pulling me back.

Kitty: How was the presentation? Did you knock em dead?

Me: They're still reeling. Everyone's jealous of our amazing, hardworking team. Thanks for everything you do!

Kitty: 💕

Later, back in my hotel room, Florence's skyline shimmered in the fading light, the city glowing as dusk settled in. Just as I began to unwind, my phone buzzed again. Without thinking, I answered the video call, and there he was—Grayson, filling my screen with a smile that made the thousands of miles between us disappear in an instant.

"Hey, you." I grinned, feeling as giddy as a teenager.

"Hey, you." His smile was like a warm embrace across the miles. "Miss me?"

I rolled my eyes with a laugh. "Funny you should ask. I was literally about to call you."

His eyes sparkled with that knowing look. "Then I saved you the trouble. I keep thinking about you."

"I like hearing that. I'm having the same problem. It's distracting." I sighed. "You're distracting."

"Mutual distractions," he mused, his voice smooth as silk.

"So, any ideas for resolving this little conundrum?" I challenged, biting my lip.

"Oh, I've got a few. But I'd need you here for the full report," he replied, eyes gleaming with mischief.

I shook my head, smiling. "You're incorrigible."

"Better keep me that way," he said with a grin. "So, fill me in—how's Florence?"

"Oh, you know. Just the usual: sightseeing, saving the world from cancer—the works." I kept my tone light as I recapped the conference, carefully glossing over the tense showdown with the guy from MedcoVax. Still, it struck me how easy it was to talk to

Grayson about it all. He wasn't just listening; he got it. It was nice to share my day with someone who understood the jargon and the stress—and who also happened to make my heart race a little.

As I spoke, my thoughts wandered to the email from my dad. I decided against bringing it up. It was too fresh, too raw, and besides, things were too new between us to weigh them down with that kind of drama just yet. This moment with Grayson wasn't the right time to unpack that kind of emotional baggage.

"What about you?" I asked, steering the conversation back toward safer ground.

"Buried in class prep and coordinating with Ford's dad to get a copy of the *Ghost* script. You know, nothing too thrilling," he said, brushing it off with a shrug.

"Yeah, 'nothing thrilling'—says the guy whose brother's comic is going Hollywood." I laughed. "You're one of a kind, Professor."

"Glad you noticed," he murmured. "Just wait until I pick you up next Saturday. I've already got a sign planned."

"Oh, really? What's it say?" I asked, intrigued.

He smirked. "You'll have to wait and see."

"Fine, I'll be patient. But it better be good."

His expression softened. "You look gorgeous like that."

I cocked my head. "Like what?"

"Lying on the bed, your hair tumbled around you. Gazing up at me on your phone screen. I like seeing you that way. It gives me ideas." He shot me a sexy grin.

I grinned back, more certain of my feelings now. "And I like the way you're looking at me. Like you're dying to kiss me."

"I am. I keep thinking about that last kiss before you left. We need to do that again—make everything else fade away for a little while."

I sighed. "That sounds like heaven, especially after a day like today."

"What would you do if I kissed you right now?"

"I'd pull you closer and make sure you didn't forget how good we are together." My cheeks had to be turning pink... I could feel the heat in them. Suddenly, this felt very real.

"Being with you is impossible to forget."

At his words, I felt a tug in my chest—part excitement, part hesitation. Was it too soon to feel this close? But then there was something about the way he looked at me, like I mattered in a way that wasn't overwhelming but steady. It was hard not to lean into that feeling, just for a little while.

"Guess that means we'll just have to make the most of that airport reunion," he said, his voice carrying just enough promise to make my pulse quicken.

"Well, Dr. Stellar," I said, arching a brow, "I think we can arrange that."

As I ended the call, doubt flickered. Had I made a promise I wasn't ready to keep? For now, I chose to hold onto the possibility —a tentative step toward something worth exploring.

13

REDISCOVERING HARMONY

Grayson

Morning light streamed through my kitchen window as my coffee grinder whirred away, the Guatemalan beans promising a hint of chocolate and a smoky edge. I breathed in the aroma, still replaying Courtney's laughter in my head from last night's video call. A screenshot of her was my new wallpaper on my phone screen, a reminder of how she brightened my day more than any perfect brew.

I set the French press to steep, ignoring the nagging voice in my head that sounded like Dad: *Don't get distracted. Get back to work.* Today, I dismissed that voice. I kept remembering how, back in my teens, I'd protest his rigid plans by learning every James Booker riff I could find. Booker's music had been my sanctuary—until I dropped piano altogether.

My phone buzzed with a text from Courtney:

> Courtney: That guy who grilled me at the conference? Turns out he's a big deal. Should I make amends?

My thumbs flew before I could second-guess it:

> Me: Apologize? No way. You handled him like a pro. If he's that big, he can take it. You owe him nothing. Not even a comma.

> Courtney: That's what I hoped you'd say.

Satisfied she wasn't letting that critic derail her, I scrolled to the number for Eddie's Emporium. My thumb hovered over "Call." If I was going to reclaim my love for piano, I needed the right equipment.

"Eddie's Emporium of Melody and Mayhem, Eddie speaking," came the gravelly greeting, his voice like a vintage vinyl record with a few scratches but all the heart. It felt right, like I was about to crack open a new chapter.

"Hey, Eddie. Grayson here. I'm looking to rekindle my old romance with the piano and need a solid keyboard."

His laugh rumbled like a bass line. "A new set of keys, huh? You want something that'll keep up with your fingers or make you work for it?"

I grinned. "Something that can hold its own as I grow."

It felt good, deciding I wasn't going to sideline my music anymore. Sinan, Courtney, and Mara had nudged me in this direction, and I was done ignoring it. *No risk, no reward,* I thought, hearing their chorus echo in my head.

Twenty minutes later, I stepped into Eddie's shop—a cozy den lined with guitars, keyboards, and brass instruments. A faint metallic scent lingered.

"That's valve oil," Eddie explained when I asked, his eyes crinkling. "Part of the shop's soul."

As we moved toward the keyboards, I confessed, "Back when I played, I was big into jazz—James Booker was my idol. His style —mixing heartbreak and joy—was unmatched."

Eddie's grin widened. "Ah, Booker—now there was a guy who could make the piano weep and dance in the same song. You're chasing a rare groove there. Taught Harry Connick Jr. half his tricks. Ever seen that documentary on him? *Bayou Maharajah?"*

I shook my head. "Worth a watch?"

He grinned. "It'll blow your mind. By the way, if you're serious, you'll need lessons. Carter's the best in town." Handing me a card, he said, "Tell him I sent you. He'll have you channeling Booker before you know it."

I left with a keyboard and bench loaded in my trunk, feeling like I'd opened a new door. Driving home, I let myself imagine more than just writing a research article alone at midnight. An image of me with Courtney, hanging out together, me playing a Booker tune while she danced around the kitchen—it struck a chord. A simple vision, but it felt like the balance I'd been missing.

Back home, I set up my new keyboard and dropped onto the bench. In my head, I'd imagined picking up right where I'd left off years ago. Reality wasn't so kind—my fingers fumbled, producing clunky chords I barely recognized. Still, for once, I didn't mind. Even the wrong notes felt like a reclaiming of something I'd lost.

Dad's voice crept into my thoughts, sharp as ever. *Spreading yourself too thin again, Grayson?*

I pushed his commentary aside. This wasn't about him, or my CV, or anything else. It was about letting music back into my life. Testing the waters, I played a few more measures, each one a small victory over my own doubts.

I dug out Eddie's business card and called Carter. By the time I hung up, I'd booked my first online lesson—no turning back. Maybe it'd be messy, balancing research, students, romance, and music. But it felt right. And that was enough to get me started.

Night draped Sewickley in a soft glow as I pulled into the nearly empty lot of *Not a Yacht Club,* Dante's restaurant. The wide windows overlooked the Ohio River, the water reflecting the lights from the bridge. Maybe a little time here—cooking, laughing—would clear my head and help me figure out how to juggle everything: Ford's script, my research, piano lessons, and now Courtney.

In the nearly empty parking lot, I spotted Don Ross, Ford's dad, stepping out of his sleek Audi. He looked every bit the lead in a high-stakes crime thriller, clutching a sealed manila envelope like it held the secrets to the universe.

"Glad we can do this face-to-face," he said, handing me the envelope. "Leak this script, and we're talking millions in losses."

"No pressure," I quipped, tucking it safely into my jacket. "I'll keep it in my home office—nobody else sees it."

He nodded once, businesslike. "Thank you. And watch your grad students; you never know who's tempted by a Hollywood payday."

Inside, the warm scent of roasted garlic and onions pulled me in, a welcoming contrast to the antiseptic tang of my lab. Kincaid waved from across the room, and Dante—the multi-talented wedding cake guru—greeted me like an old friend. "Grayson! Good to see you again! Feels like just yesterday we were sipping margaritas in Turks and Caicos."

"I think it was day before yesterday," I joked, recalling sunlit beaches. "Ford said these classes are a must. Besides, Courtney's flying home Saturday—I'm hoping to surprise her with something better than my usual grilled cheese."

Dante raised his eyebrows and grinned. "Perfect timing. We're usually a Tuesday night gig, but I shifted this week's class to Wednesday since we were closed today. I just got back from Turks and Caicos." He turned to a tall figure approaching us. "Meet Conner—Courtney's brother and unofficial guardian; Kincaid's here too, so you're basically entering the lions' den."

Conner studied me, green eyes sharp—so much like Courtney's, but with an edge. I managed a relaxed handshake.

"So you're the guy keeping my sister on her toes," he said evenly.

"I try," I replied, holding his gaze. "I'm picking her up from the airport on Saturday."

His stance eased, though his voice stayed cautious. "She deserves someone decent. Don't screw it up."

I kept my smile in place, mentally checking off another sibling test.

Kincaid ambled over with a friendly grin. "Welcome to the chaos. But nothing will ever beat the image of Zephyr going full lunatic at Mara's wedding, chasing a seagull."

I smirked, nodding toward him. "Great tackle. You've got moves."

Kincaid laughed. "Next time, someone else can chase him."

Before we could continue, Dante clapped his hands, commanding the room like a maestro.

"All right, my cooking Padawans—tonight's lesson: Italian meatballs. I've prepped marinara for a head start. Tip: if you're short on time, never underestimate store-bought sauce plus a splash of wine or roasted garlic. Magic."

As we lined up at the cooking stations, Sinan claimed the spot next to me. Seeing another familiar face felt good. We started chopping onions and mixing spices, bantering about the wedding chaos.

"I noticed you and Courtney vanished partway through the wedding reception," Sinan commented, arching one eyebrow.

I grinned, memories of being on that moonlit beach with Courtney rushing back. "We indulged in an impromptu geology lesson. Very educational."

"Geology lesson, huh? Is that what the kids are calling make-out sessions these days?" Sinan nudged my shoulder. "Careful—her brothers will sniff out your intentions. They're protective like that."

"I already got the Conner talk," I said, rolling my eyes. "What about you? How are you and Sonya's sister Kendra getting along?"

He shook his head. "We're just friends. It's complicated."

We formed our meatballs—rows of uniform spheres. "Look at these beauties," I said, admiring them.

"To the oven!" Sinan announced, whisking the trays away.

As I started cleaning up our station, a sudden metallic crash echoed across the kitchen. I turned to see Kincaid staring down at a culinary disaster—a mess of meatballs scattered across the floor in a splatter of pink that dotted his pants and shoes.

"Well, hell," Conner said, surveying the scene with an arched brow. "It's like a meatball massacre in here."

Kincaid looked down at the mess, shaking his head. "Maybe they were trying to make a break for it?"

I couldn't help but grin. "No worries. You can share custody of ours. Those guys won't try to escape after they see the gory consequences."

Dante chuckled as he set the oven timer. "And now, we practice the fine art of patience."

Conner stepped closer, handing me a glass of Cabernet, his gaze lingering on me longer than necessary. The edge in his tone was gone, but his eyes still carried a silent warning. He wasn't letting his guard down, not entirely.

"Hope you've got more than just jokes to bring to the table," Conner said, the words casual, but the weight behind them unmistakable.

I met his gaze evenly, raising my glass in a quiet toast. "Good food, good company, and keeping Courtney's brothers happy. That's the goal."

Kincaid raised his glass with a smirk, breaking the tension. "To good food and forging friendships, no matter how many meatballs hit the floor."

Conner finally took a sip, his posture relaxing just a fraction, but the moment wasn't lost on me. Winning him over was going to take more than charm and one night of Italian cooking. "I hear you got my sister onto the dance floor at the wedding. Good to hear she's unwinding."

I shrugged casually. "She a fun dance partner. Guess you never know what'll happen when the music's right."

Conner's gaze narrowed, but he said nothing.

"She had a great time," I said, recalling her enthusiasm. "Maybe she just needed the right partner."

Kincaid nudged Conner with his elbow. "Hey, if Courtney's happy, that's good enough for me."

Apparently, earning the Courtney seal of approval from Conner involved more hoops than I'd expected, but at least I hadn't been handed a questionnaire… yet.

Conner's frown deepened, but Kincaid chuckled. "Relax, Conner. Mara vouches for him."

Finally, Dante retrieved our golden-brown meatballs from the oven, plating them with pasta and marinara. "Bon appétit, gents." As we dug in, the kitchen hummed with laughter, shared triumph, and just enough wariness from Conner to keep me on my toes.

Despite the undercurrent of tension that came with Courtney's brothers sizing me up, I felt something settle inside. Maybe this was the camaraderie I'd needed. A night with new friends, good food, and a reminder that life had room for more than just work.

Still, as talk turned to everyone else's weekend plans, I realized my phone remained silent. Courtney was in Florence, and I wouldn't see her until Saturday. The missing puzzle piece nagged at me, reminding me that even surrounded by people, a part of me was elsewhere—waiting for her.

<hr>

BACK AT HOME, I set the *Ghost* script next to a stack of research papers. My gaze wandered to the corner of the room where my new keyboard gleamed. The itch to play something—anything— pulled at me, too strong to ignore.

This keyboard wasn't simply a creative outlet; it was a promise to let both logic and creativity play lead roles in my life. I sat down, resting my fingers lightly on the keys.

For a moment, I hesitated, Dad's voice creeping in like an unwelcome specter. *Music? That's a hobby. Not a real career.* He'd said it when I was fourteen, his tone dismissive, like the notes I loved meant nothing because they couldn't be quantified or published in a peer-reviewed journal.

But as I pressed down on the first chord, I countered that thought, feeling its weight lose ground. Maybe a "real career" shouldn't feel like a prison. Maybe life was meant to have a little play, a little rhythm that didn't follow someone else's script.

The tentative chord echoed through the room—soft, unsteady, but mine. Another note followed, then another, until a melody began to form. My fingers stumbled at first, like an old machine sputtering to life, but the notes soon found their footing, flowing in a way I hadn't felt in years.

Music had always been my reset button, the one thing that could untangle thoughts too messy for words.

The soft melody filled the room, chasing away the hum of my father's judgments. Whatever came next—work, music, her—I could make space for it all. Life wasn't a solo act or a choice between passions. It was about finding harmony, one note at a time.

And for the first time in a long while, that felt possible.

14

TUSCAN TEMPTATIONS

COURTNEY

Florence, Italy

After a whirlwind day that felt like a nonstop rush, I was craving a slice of normalcy—something steady, like the rhythm of my research back home or the easy camaraderie of my team, who could make even tedious lab days feel worthwhile. The symposium had been a mix of highs and lows, with my presentation as the clear highlight—a peak greeted by applause that still echoed faintly in my mind. But even with that sense of accomplishment, my father's email lingered in the back of my mind. Twelve years of silence, and now a single message. He could wait. I wasn't ready to deal with it yet.

But the day hadn't been all rousing applause. Enter Mr. Doom-and-Gloom from MedcoVax, the one who'd appointed himself as my unofficial fact-checker at the symposium. I told myself his skepticism was valid—essential, even. People had come to conferences like this before and pitched ideas in bad faith, presenting wishful thinking as groundbreaking science. His challenges were the kind that kept our field honest, and in a way, I understood why some people flocked to him. But separating his critiques of my research from what felt like thinly veiled attacks on me as a person? That was proving harder than I wanted to admit.

There was something beneath his polished exterior that set my nerves on edge, like static buzzing just out of reach. His smile never quite reached his eyes, and his questions carried a sharpness that felt less like genuine curiosity and more like an attempt to poke holes in an effort to discredit me. I couldn't quite pin it down, but his presence left a ripple of unease that I couldn't shake. Was it simple sexism? Maybe. Or maybe it was something more insidious, cloaked in professionalism but dangerous to ignore.

Or maybe I was overthinking it and the man was simply obnoxious.

Dodging him had become a quiet mission. I'd catch sight of his entourage—sycophants orbiting him like satellites—across the room, and I'd pivot, taking the scenic route to my destination. Whatever it took to avoid his notice.

Despite the shadow he cast, the day had its bright spots. The highlight? A video call with my team back in Pittsburgh. Their faces lit up the screen, reminding me of why I did this work. We celebrated our latest breakthrough on the cancer-fighting virus project—progress that felt like a beacon of hope in an otherwise chaotic world.

"Courtney!" Andrew's voice boomed through the tiny speaker as his pale face and blond hair momentarily filled the screen, his grin infectious. "How's Florence treating you? Are you drowning in espresso and stunning architecture yet?"

"Mostly just espresso," I admitted, leaning closer to the camera. "And a few pointed questions from MedcoVax's resident pessimist. But the espresso's been worth it."

"That guy again?" Mercy chimed in, her eyebrow arching just enough to convey her signature mix of skepticism and sass. "Tell me he didn't bring up that tired data reproducibility debate."

"Oh, he did. And then some." I rolled my eyes dramatically.

"MedcoVax is a big deal, right?" our intern Roz asked. "Maybe you should try to stay on his good side."

"Or avoid him, which is my plan. But enough about him. Let's talk about you guys. Did you run the viral interference test?"

Kitty, seated next to Mercy, held up a whiteboard with an enthusiastic doodle of a virus wearing a superhero cape. "Not only did we run it, but we crushed it. Results are looking solid, and we're prepping the next phase."

"Kitty's underselling it," Andrew added, leaning into the frame. "Courtney, look at this—Line C is showing a threefold reduction in replication time compared to the others. Threefold. That kind of efficiency is launching it to the top of the list."

The pride in their voices filled my chest with warmth. "That's incredible. Sounds like we might have a winner. I just wish I'd been there."

"You're here now," Mercy said, her tone softer than usual. "And we're keeping everything steady until you get back. Just don't come home expecting us to adopt those Italian 'la dolce vita' work hours. We've got a system."

We signed off, and my phone buzzed with a text. A message from one of my brothers lit up the screen.

Conner: Some "foodie influencer" left a review complaining our live music overshadowed the Caesar salad. How do I overshadow lettuce?!

Me: Maybe use iceberg next time—less overshadow-able?

Conner: Ha. New policy: All salads must be accompanied by mime performances only.

I chuckled, shaking my head. Conner's dry humor always had a way of turning complaints into comedy gold.

The lighthearted moment helped dispel some of the lingering tension from earlier. As I was about to tuck my phone away, it buzzed again—this time, Maria, my favorite Florentine scientist-turned-baker and kindred spirit in the art of work-life imbalance. Our friendship had been forged five years ago over post-symposium wine, solidified by a late-night debate about the perfect cake-to-icing ratio. Since then, every reunion had been a celebration of science and questionable baking skills.

> Maria: How about dinner at my place? We'll keep it light, then tackle some Tuscan baking. Ever made cantucci?

A grin tugged at the corners of my mouth. *Cantucci*—Italy's take on biscotti—had defeated me more times than I cared to admit. My past attempts had resulted in dubious creations that could double as paperweights. Maria knew this, of course, and her offer felt like the perfect antidote to a long day.

> Me: I'd love to! Cooking with you sounds like the perfect way to cap off the symposium.

Maria's apartment was as welcoming as the woman herself—a blend of Tuscan charm and cozy elegance. Exposed brick walls, wooden beams, and warm, earthy tones greeted me, along with the faint scent of rosemary and something sweet.

"Welcome," Maria greeted, her round figure radiating confidence as she pinned back her dark hair. Her brown eyes sparkled with cheerful warmth, instantly putting me at ease.

Her kitchen was a Tuscan dream—cool marble counters, rustic wooden shelves, and an explosion of carefully curated ingredients lined up like the periodic table of baking: flour, baking powder, eggs, almonds, and sugar. The essential building blocks of magic.

"Eat first, bake later," she declared, pointing to a platter of prosciutto and pecorino. "Trust me, if we don't, the dough won't survive us."

I plucked a paper-thin slice of prosciutto, savoring the salty, smoky richness. The platter disappeared faster than either of us would admit, and Maria slid the empty dish aside with a flourish.

"Your presentation yesterday," she began, turning to wash her hands, "was nothing short of brilliant. Really, a triumph."

"Thank you. I needed to hear that after facing down the guy from MedcoVax. He was like a black hole of joy, just sucking all the positivity out of the room."

Maria tossed me a knowing look as she handed over the recipe card. "Ignore the rainclouds. They're fleeting. Focus on your spark; it's what makes your work matter."

I smiled, but her words struck deeper than she probably realized. My spark—my creativity, the synergy with my team—wasn't just a strength; it was something I guarded fiercely. "It's been an overwhelming couple of days," I admitted, shifting the recipe card in my hands. "Between the conference, an email from my dad, and… well, I met someone."

Maria's hands paused over the sugar jar as she raised an eyebrow. "Someone? And who might that be?"

"Grayson Stellar. Professor at Pitt. Brilliant, annoyingly charming, and not at all what I expected." I shrugged, trying to play it cool. "It's new, but he's… intriguing."

Maria's lips curved, though her sharp gaze lingered on me. "Intriguing? That sounds serious. What's he like?"

"Cute, kind, intelligent, great to talk to." I shrugged. "It's all still new. But, what about you? Anyone new in your life these days?"

She waved me off with a laugh. "We're talking about you, not me. So, this Grayson—does he know what he's getting into?"

I laughed softly, though her words struck a chord. "He might be starting to."

Maria tilted her head, scooping flour into a measuring cup. "There's something bothering you though. Not that cute professor —something else. I can tell something's eating at you. Is it that email you mentioned?"

With a sigh, I admitted, "Yesterday, my father emailed me for the first time in twelve years."

Maria froze, her hand hovering over the almonds. "That's a long time. And now he decides to reach out? He must want something. What did he say?"

The words felt strange as I said them aloud. "He wants me to meet his daughter. My half-sister. She's twelve."

Maria studied me, her expression softening. "And what do you want to do?"

"I don't know." I twisted the recipe card in my hands. "I'm feeling pressured to make a decision, but I don't even know where to start. How would this even work?"

Maria resumed measuring almonds, her movements unhurried. "Then don't rush. If he's waited this long, he can wait a little longer. Sometimes, the best decisions come when we let things rest for a while—like dough." She smiled, her voice steady. "You'll know when the timing is right."

Her baking metaphor earned a small laugh, but her words lingered as we began mixing the *cantucci*. As I sifted the flour, watching it cascade softly into the bowl, I let myself breathe. I brushed a fingertip along the rim of the sieve, catching the light, velvety powder.

Life whispered to me, soft and insistent: there's more than one way to find happiness. Maybe I didn't need to chase perfection all the time. Maybe detours, like a new sister or Turks and Caicos or this spontaneous baking session—or even the captivating presence of Grayson—weren't distractions after all. Maybe they were the pieces I'd been missing, the ones that could make my perfectly organized life feel whole.

With the ease of a lifelong baker, Maria guided me through each step. As we mixed and kneaded, she shifted the conversation. "So, Grayson Stellar? Tell me more about him. What's he like?"

"He's… amazing. It's all still new, but there's something about him. He makes me feel seen in a way I haven't felt in a long time."

Maria's grin was the kind you only get from someone rooting for your love story. "Ah, the new romance phase. Full of promise and possibilities, yes?"

I laughed, but it came out a little uneven. "It's more than that. It's like... he sees through all the noise. My ambition, my work—it's a huge part of who I am, but sometimes I feel like it pushes people away. With Grayson, it's different. I can talk about science with him, really talk, and he gets it. He doesn't just nod along or change the subject; he adds to the conversation, challenges me in the best ways. And that's terrifying, because what if I let him in and it's too much? Or worse, not enough?"

Maria placed a hand on mine, her expression soft but steady. "That's the risk, isn't it? The question is whether or not you're willing to take a chance."

I glanced at her, my hands hesitating over the mixing bowl. Maria had always been my voice of reason, the one who reminded me to slow down. Five years ago, she'd pulled me out of a spiral after a failed project by showing up with a bottle of wine and a ridiculous plan to bake croissants from scratch. They'd turned out lopsided and over-baked, but I remembered how much I'd laughed that night. Maria had a way of making even my failures feel like victories.

Maria's words lingered as I shaped the dough. "That's the thing," I said, the words coming out slower than I intended. "I've spent so much of my life taking care of everyone else—my brothers, my team, my work. Letting someone into that world, letting myself lean on them, feels... complicated." Was that why I hadn't replied to my dad's email? Because letting Adele in felt less like connection and more like taking on another responsibility?

Maria's voice was steady and warm. "Complicated isn't bad. It's honest. Real"

I slid the *cantucci* dough into Maria's vintage oven, sealing it with a satisfying clunk. "Phase one: complete," I declared, feeling a tiny thrill of accomplishment.

My phone buzzed on the counter, and Grayson's name lit up the screen. A small smile tugged at my lips.

> Grayson: Looking forward to picking you up from the airport. How's Italy?

I snapped a quick photo of the dough in the oven and sent it back. I could imagine his reaction: eyebrows vaulting skyward, eyes lighting up.

> Me: Trying not to burn down the Renaissance. You'll get the full report when I see you—possibly with snacks.

Maria caught my grin and raised an eyebrow. "Grayson?"

I nodded, slipping my phone into my pocket. "The one and only."

As we removed the *cantucci* from the oven, the kitchen filled with the scent of almonds, citrus, and that unmistakable warmth that feels like home. Maria poured decaf coffee as we sliced the golden loaves into perfect little pieces.

My first bite was heavenly—crunchy but not hard, with just the right hint of sweetness. "This," I said, holding up a piece, "is a triumph." I whipped out my phone and snapped a selfie of the two of us and our gorgeous golden *cantucci*.

Maria smiled, sliding a small jar of Florentine honey across the counter. "Try it with this. Trust me, it's transformative."

I drizzled the honey over the *cantucci* and took another bite. She was right—perfection.

As I packed up a box to bring home, Maria handed me a jar of honey with a wink. "For Grayson, in case your *cantucci* don't survive the flight."

15

HOMECOMING

Grayson

Pittsburgh International Airport

I stepped out of my car in short-term parking, adjusting my sunglasses and tilting the brim of my chauffeur-style hat. Nothing said "welcome home" like a bit of flair.

I spotted Courtney near the baggage carousel, engrossed in her phone. Right on cue, mine buzzed.

> Courtney: I'm here.

> Me: Look behind you.

She turned, her eyes landing on the sign I held aloft: **Dr. Gillette.** Her grin spread wide as she made a beeline toward me.

"You're incorrigible."

"What? You don't have a thing for limo drivers? I thought we might tick off some secret fantasy."

She plucked the sunglasses off my face, her expression softening. "There you are."

Her kiss was unhurried, savoring the moment. When we broke

apart, she handed back the sunglasses, her smile turning wry. "These work for the chauffeur look, but I want to see your eyes."

"Fair enough." I leaned closer, lowering my voice. "I see why they call you Dr. Gillette: you cut straight through me."

She groaned, half amused, half exasperated. "Tell me you didn't spend the whole day working on that line."

As her laptop bag slipped from her shoulder, I caught it just before it hit the ground. "What's in here? Rocks?"

"Close—laptop, cables, survival gear."

I held up the sign. "Should I change this to **Dr. Over-prepared**?"

She snorted. "Laugh all you want, but my 'over-preparation' has saved the day more than once."

"I believe it."

Her suitcase appeared on the carousel, and I grabbed it before she could.

"Much appreciated. I've been up since dawn, but with the time difference, that's basically midnight Pittsburgh time."

"Long day," I said as we walked toward the car. "Good thing your chauffeur's here to whisk you away."

She rattled off her address, and I loaded her bags into the trunk. As we climbed in, she paused, inhaling deeply. "Is it just me, or does it smell like an Italian restaurant in here?"

I shrugged. "Figured you'd be starving, so I cooked dinner. Selfishly motivated—I'd rather have you to myself than waste time at a restaurant."

Her laugh was soft, her eyes warm. "This is you being selfish? What does selfless look like?"

"No idea. I'm not the selfless type," I teased, though the words lingered uncomfortably. I'd always prided myself on knowing what I wanted and going for it. But did that make me selfish? And worse, would Courtney eventually see it that way? I pushed the thought aside.

The drive to her townhouse took less than ten minutes. As she unlocked her front door, I grabbed her suitcase. Inside, the space was dominated by a stack of cardboard boxes in the corner of the living room. The place had that temporary, in-progress vibe, still waiting to feel like home.

A plane roared overhead as I opened my mouth to speak, drowning me out. I raised my voice. "Airport living—it has its drawbacks. Anyway, I'll drop your bag here and bring in the food. The 'new move' vibe? Surprisingly chic. It reads 'adventurous scientist in transition.'"

She shook her head, her sigh heavy. "More like 'overworked scientist, too busy to unpack.' Honestly, I'm wondering if moving here was a mistake. The planes, the boxes… it's all so much more work than I'd thought. Staying put in Sewickley might've saved me some sanity."

Her composure cracked, just a little, as she glanced at the boxes. Courtney didn't do chaos—this limbo had to be driving her nuts. But those boxes told another story, too: she was building something new. Maybe that meant she could make space for me.

"Why don't you take a shower?" I offered, shifting gears. "By the time you're back, dinner will be ready—and maybe I'll find the elusive box labeled *kitchen*."

She blinked, startled, then pleased, gratitude flickering in her expression. She kissed me lightly before heading upstairs, past a box labeled *Lab Stuff* and another labeled *Books—Heavy!* The unfinished space felt like a quiet reminder that some things could stay incomplete for now.

The kitchen, already unpacked and organized, hinted at her priorities. As the shower hummed upstairs, I warmed dinner and set the table, overthinking the arrangement.

Then my phone buzzed on the counter. Joaquin's name lit up the screen.

> Joaquin: Hey, Dr. Stellar. Just got the grant proposal back—kicked back for corrections. They need it resubmitted by Monday midnight. If we don't fix it, we lose the funding. Can we meet tonight?

I stared at the message, the weight of it pressing down hard. This wasn't just about Joaquin; the grant was tied to my lab's budget for the year. Without it, several projects—including the one I'd been pushing forward for months—might stall indefinitely. Normally, I'd dive in, rearranging everything to make time. But tonight?

My eyes drifted toward the stairs. Courtney was here, in the middle of building something new in her life. I wanted to be part of that—not just an afterthought squeezed between grant deadlines and academic chaos.

I typed a response, my fingers hesitating over the keys.

> Me: Can't tonight. Let's meet Sunday afternoon. I'll carve out time then.

As soon as I hit send, doubt gnawed at me. Was this irresponsible? I'd worked for years to establish my credibility—not just as a researcher, but as someone my department could depend on. Prioritizing Courtney over something I'd usually consider non-negotiable felt unsettling, even reckless.

The scent of garlic and parmesan pulled me back, grounding me. Maybe this was the real problem: always chasing the next accomplishment, always carrying the weight of everyone else's expectations. Letting someone else share the load, just this once, wouldn't be the end of the world.

That thought reminded me. Reaching into my pocket, I pulled out the necklace she'd left behind in the hotel room, its delicate silver and white pendant glinting faintly. I set it beside her plate. Even when she didn't realize it, I had her back.

Footsteps on the stairs broke through my thoughts. I turned, wine bottle in hand, just as Courtney appeared. Damp hair swept back, her simple blue dress clung to her curves, managing to look both effortless and stunning. The faint scent of coconut drifted through the air—her body wash—pulling me straight back to

Turks and Caicos. She held a small brown paper bag, but it was her soft smile that snagged my attention.

"Watch out!" she called, darting forward as the wine I was pouring sloshed dangerously close to the rim of the glass.

Too late. I steadied the bottle, but a crimson streak was already spreading across the counter.

"Sorry about that," I said, grabbing paper towels. "Guess I got distracted."

"Distracted, huh?" she teased, settling into a chair and placing the bag on the table. Her gaze dropped to the necklace beside her plate, and her eyes widened as she picked it up.

"I thought I'd lost this!" Her voice softened, warm and grateful, as her gaze flicked up to meet mine. "Thank you."

"You left it in the room," I said with a shrug. "You wear it a lot, so I figured it meant something."

"It does," she murmured, her fingers brushing the pendant like it was something fragile. "It's a reminder of my grandmother." Her expression softened, quiet vulnerability flickering across her face before she tilted her head and smiled. "Guess I'm lucky my unofficial chauffeur is so thorough."

"Only the best for Dr. Gillette," I quipped, setting a glass of wine in front of her.

Her smile faltered as she turned the necklace over in her hands. A shadow passed through her expression, her focus drifting somewhere far off.

"You okay?" I asked, leaning casually against the counter, my tone easy.

She hesitated, her fingers brushing the pendant. "It's just... family. It's been on my mind the past few days, and I needed to get it out." Her gaze dropped to the table. "Dads. They're... complicated, aren't they?"

"Dads?" I echoed. The unexpected turn in the conversation hung in the air.

She nodded faintly, her posture tightening. "They have this way of shaping how we see ourselves. For better or worse." Her eyes lifted, meeting mine with a searching, almost hesitant smile. "You seem to carry a lot when it comes to yours. How do you handle that?"

The question caught me off guard, balanced between curiosity and something more personal. She wasn't prying, but it felt sharp —like she was asking for advice I wasn't sure I had.

I forced a grin, aiming to lighten the moment. "My dad's a tough crowd. If I cured cancer, he'd probably ask why I didn't solve world hunger while I was at it."

Her lips quirked upward, though her gaze stayed steady on mine, soft yet unrelenting. "It's just... your dad seems pretty rigid."

It wasn't criticism, but I couldn't shake the feeling I'd been seen a little too clearly. The bluesy strains of Dr. John's *Right Place, Wrong Time* floated softly from my Bluetooth speaker, adding an almost ironic beat to the moment.

"Was it that obvious?"

"Well, that conversation between you two at the wedding—it was charged, like this wasn't your first round."

"You're not wrong," I admitted, shifting my shoulders as if to shake off the weight. "I've learned to roll with it, to ignore his jabs. It's easier than confronting old... stuff."

She nodded slowly, her fingers gliding along the stem of her wine glass. "I guess I've been thinking about my dad too," she said finally, her voice quieter. "Trying to figure out how to deal with him. But I still need time to think."

"Whenever you're ready, I'm here," I said gently. "If you want to talk, vent, or just bounce ideas off me, I'll listen."

Her lips curved into a small, grateful smile. "Thanks. I might take you up on that."

The tension eased as her stomach growled loudly, breaking the moment. Her eyes widened. "Oops. Sorry about that."

"Eat," I said, sliding plates of pasta and meatballs onto the table. As Bill Withers' *Lovely Day* started playing, the kitchen seemed to glow. Dimmed lights, the aroma of garlic and parmesan, and Courtney's laughter—it was almost too perfect.

"R&B music, Italian bread, and a romaine salad?" She arched an eyebrow over her wineglass. "Your first-date skills are off the charts."

"Technically, this isn't our first date."

"Right. We kind of skipped the dating part and jumped straight to this." A faint blush rose to her cheeks, but she pivoted smoothly. "How was your week?"

"Not bad. Sinan's advice about 'refilling the well' stuck with me. I bought a keyboard and signed up for piano lessons. I'm finally bringing music back into my life."

Her face lit up. "That's incredible! I guess we both took a step. You with your keyboard, me with my *cantucci*. Baking yesterday reminded me how much I love it. Next up might be a cake— something ambitious."

"Do I get a slice of this ambitious cake?"

She grinned. "Only if it's edible. Otherwise, you'll just have to enjoy the concept of my culinary genius."

"Hard to imagine anything less than perfection from you," I teased. "You're practically a wizard in the lab. How different could a kitchen be?"

She laughed, her eyes sparkling. "Don't be so sure. Excellence in the biology lab doesn't always translate to the kitchen. I have the charred cookies and collapsed soufflés to prove it."

"Really? Labs and kitchens are basically cousins—precision, timing, chemistry. What's the problem?"

She shook her head. "Beats me. It's like the universe conspires against me every time I bake. Butter doesn't cooperate, cakes refuse to rise. It's chaos." She sipped her wine, then glanced at me. "How about you? Have classes started yet?"

"Not till next week. Right now, it's the calm before the storm— just getting everything in place."

Her brows rose with curiosity. "How's that doctoral student of yours? Joaquin, right? Did you let him switch to that independent verification focus?"

I blinked, surprised she remembered. "You have a great memory. Yeah, I let him switch. At the end of the day, it's his career. I can guide him, but he has to live with his choices."

She nodded thoughtfully. "You're more than just a professor—you're a mentor. A man of many talents," she added with a sly smile. "Speaking of which, what's the latest with *Ghost*?"

I leaned back, a relaxed grin on my face. "Don practically made me sign in blood to keep the script under lock and key. You'd think he'd handed over nuclear codes."

She laughed. "Corporate espionage in Hollywood? Wild. At Cates, we worry about with it too, but I never thought about it with movie scripts."

"It's everywhere," I said. "Hackers and IP thieves are getting smarter, and if you're not careful, it can cost more than just money."

Her tone shifted, more serious. "At Cates, it's a constant balancing act—keeping research secure but accessible. We're a nonprofit. If our breakthroughs end up locked behind patents or tied up with expensive pharmaceuticals, it defeats the whole point."

Admiration flickered through me. "That's a noble goal. It's not just big players who lose—it's the everyday people. IP theft costs jobs, even livelihoods."

She raised her glass. "Here's to finding the balance between protecting and sharing."

I clinked mine to hers. "To the delicate dance of life."

Her gaze lingered for a moment before she glanced at the brown bag on the counter. With a spark of mischief, she crossed the room and opened it, pulling out a bakery box. Lifting the lid with a flourish, she revealed a jar of golden honey and *cantucci* biscuits.

"I brought us a treat," she said, her voice light, though her gaze searched mine.

"*Cantucci* and honey? Straight from Italy?"

She nodded, her eyes sparkling with excitement, the warmth of her smile bridging the space between us. Her hand lingered near the jar, as though she were debating her next move. "An authentic Italian touch to cap off an already perfect evening." A playful smile tugged at her lips. "It's like they were made to complement your meatballs."

"You never cease to amaze me," I said softly, noting the sudden intensity in her gaze.

Courtney stepped closer, her eyes locking on mine. Her smile held steady, but there was a weight to it, like she was balancing between daring and vulnerability. "I aim to please," she said, her voice dipping to a sultry whisper. But the quick rise and fall of her breath gave her away—she wasn't as sure of herself as she wanted to seem. "And right now, I'd like to focus entirely on you."

A thrill surged through me, but I noticed the way her fingers brushed the edge of the honey jar before she took a deliberate step forward. "Did you have something particular in mind?" I asked, my voice calm but curious, careful not to break the moment.

Her grin widened, though a flicker of nervous energy shimmered beneath it. She leaned in, close enough to leave me wanting more, the scent of her coconut body wash pulling me in. "If you want to find out," she said, playful yet daring, "you'll have to follow me upstairs to my bedroom."

She turned and started up the stairs, her playful smile a siren song. I followed without hesitation, my gaze zeroing in on the hypnotic sway of her hips. She knew exactly what she was doing —or at least wanted me to think she did—and I was more than happy to play along.

In her bedroom, she placed the box of *cantucci* and the jar of honey on the nightstand with deliberate care, as though setting the stage for a performance. Her gaze shifted between the treats and the bed, her expression turning mock-serious. "As much as I love these biscuits, I can already picture us brushing crumbs out of the sheets. Not exactly romantic."

I chuckled, leaning casually against the doorframe. "Agreed. There's a fine line between indulgent and inconvenient."

Her eyes lit with a wicked gleam as she unscrewed the lid of the honey jar. "Well, the honey should be far less problematic, don't you think?"

My pulse kicked up, her words laced with layers of meaning. Closing the distance between us, I said, "I'd say the only problem we're likely to face is running out."

She held up the jar, tilting it so the golden liquid caught the soft light in the room. "Then I suppose we'll just have to savor every drop."

Our eyes met, the air between us crackling like the charged moment before a lightning strike. "Savoring sounds like an excellent plan," I murmured, my voice low and unsteady.

She placed the jar back on the nightstand and stepped closer. Our lips met, and the world narrowed to just her—her taste, her warmth, her presence. It was almost too much. But when her touch pulled me back, the moment left no room for doubt.

She pulled back, her lips brushing mine in a tease, then reached for the honey again. Dipping her finger into the jar, she swirled it slowly before painting her lips with a shimmering layer. Her eyes locked on mine, the deliberate motion making my breath hitch. A flicker of heat raced through me, my pulse pounding in anticipation. She was daring me, challenging me to close the distance again, and for a moment, all I could do was marvel at how effortlessly she unraveled me.

"Your move," she whispered, her voice rich and velvety, as she leaned in, her honeyed lips a hair's breadth away from mine.

The scent of honey mixed with the warmth of her skin left me dazed. I held back, letting the tension build between us like the crescendo of a symphony. When our lips finally met, it wasn't just a kiss—it was a collision. Honey and heat, sweetness and fire, all blended into one unforgettable moment.

When we broke apart, her lips curved into a mischievous

smile. "I've got an idea," she said, grabbing my hand and pulling me toward the edge of the bed.

She dipped her fingers back into the honey, this time letting it drizzle in a golden ribbon over her skin. "How do you feel about getting creative?"

I raised an eyebrow, my pulse quickening as a thousand thoughts raced through my head. "Creative, huh? I like the sound of that."

Her grin deepened as she unbuttoned my shirt, her honey-drenched fingers leaving a warm, sticky trail down my chest. "The idea is simple," she said, her voice dropping to a sultry whisper. "We explore all the possibilities of this honey."

The room seemed to hum with energy, the air between us charged with heat and anticipation. "Possibilities?" I echoed, my voice low and roughened by the moment.

"Oh, the possibilities are endless," she said, her tone full of promise.

And just like that, I knew I was in for an evening of experimentation I'd never forget.

16

COURTNEY'S BAKING FIASCO

COURTNEY

One week later

The ingredients for my carrot and fig cake, inspired by my trip to Italy, were lined up like contestants on a reality cooking show. I punched in the oven's temperature and murmured, "May the odds be ever in your flavor." Surely this recipe was easier than some of the *Great British Baking Show's* elaborate creations.

Grayson would be here in an hour, just in time to sprinkle his charm on the cream cheese frosting and enjoy the fruits of my labor. As Mommy Julie always said, baking is like love—best shared.

The warm scent of vanilla transported me back to days in the kitchen with my mother and grandmother. Mom, the eternal recipe rebel, would have declared, "No eggs? Toss in another banana!" Or worse, she would have dashed off to the store for eggs, gotten distracted, and forgotten why she'd gone out. But Mommy Julie, the steady hand, always guided us through the mess like a culinary Yoda.

Mommy Julie had known what I only realized later: Mom wasn't just absentminded; she lived in a perpetual state of organized chaos that the rest of us had to manage. My older brother and I became the calm in her storm, the ones who kept the fridge stocked, the bills paid, the noise down.

As I grated carrots, my thoughts drifted further, brushing against the edges of memories I didn't often visit. Had Dad left because he couldn't handle the chaos? Whatever reason, he'd ghosted us after the divorce, disappearing for over a year. When he'd finally resurfaced, it was to ask me to babysit my six-month-old half-sister I hadn't even known existed so he and his new wife could vacation—during my final exam week, no less. I'd declined, and he'd vanished again. Typical, even if it was painful. He'd barely been present in my life growing up, so his absence wasn't particularly noteworthy.

Dad's email last week had stirred something I wasn't ready to face. At twelve, Adele would be old enough to bake with me, but the thought terrified me. Would she be a recipe rebel like Mom and my brother Conner, steady and deliberate like Kincaid, or cooly detached like Christopher and Dad? Besides, letting her in might mean letting him in too, and I wasn't sure I could survive being a footnote in his life again. His attention had always been a double-edged sword, cutting deepest when it disappeared. What if Adele took after him and ghosted me after I let her into my heart? It had been almost two weeks since dad had sent that email, and I still hadn't replied. Why did my brain freeze up whenever I tried to craft a reply?

I shook my head. Today wasn't the time for family drama. Today was about cake, Grayson, and new, sweeter memories.

Focus, Courtney. Sifting flour—easy-peasy. Except... where was the sifter? After rummaging through a few cabinets, I finally unearthed it, feeling like a pirate with a chest of gold. But parchment paper? That was another story. It was probably buried in some yet-to-be-discovered corner, a casualty of my just-moved-in chaos. It wasn't disorganization—it was simply not knowing where things had decided to hide themselves in my shiny, new kitchen.

"Maybe this is why my baking has been going wrong lately," I muttered, finally lining the pans with triumph. On to grating carrots—until my grater decided to vanish too. Exasperated, I grabbed the food processor.

"Alright, Plan B," I said, anthropomorphizing the appliance like it was an understudy eagerly awaiting its big break. "Time to shine."

As I fed carrots through the chute, my phone buzzed. A welcome distraction.

Andrew: Feast your eyes on this marvel of science!

Me: lol. You can't possibly mean another picture of your forgotten lunch.

The image appeared. Not a sandwich. A cell. I pinch-zoomed, my heart rate spiking. Was this what I thought it was?

Me: Is this the Holy Grail of cellular biology I'm looking at?

Andrew: Dramatic much? But yes. Nobel Prize, here we come! Our pretty little virus destroyed the cancer cell.

Me: Easy, cowboy. Let's focus on eradicating cancer first. Nobel can wait.

My hands were shaking as I set my phone down, my thoughts buzzing faster than the food processor. This was groundbreaking. All I wanted to do was rush off to the lab to see this for myself. I glanced at my watch. Grayson was due any minute, and I still had a cake to bake, cool, and frost. Otherwise, I'd have another gooey disaster on my hands—a lesson I'd learned the hard way back in high school. Besides. Work would still be there tomorrow.

Focus, Court. Cake first. Science later.

I grinned at the thought of Grayson marveling at both the cake and our scientific breakthrough. Ah, the perks of dating a fellow cancer researcher—he'd understand just how momentous this was. But first, I had to conquer this cake.

With newfound determination, I poured the aromatic batter into the pans. Three layers promised a dessert as complicated as my relationship status. Into the oven they went. Timer set.

The fig and orange filling was next. Zesting oranges felt like bottling sunshine, bright and invigorating. Cooking the figs, however, dragged on. Note to self: next time, cheat with store-bought jam.

Ding! The oven's cheerful chime snapped me back. Armed with potholders, I opened the door, anticipation fizzing through me.

But the sight inside stopped me cold.

Flat. Completely, unbelievably flat. The cakes had all the elevation of pancakes but none of the charm. I pulled one out, jabbing a knife into the center. Goo clung to the blade, mocking my efforts.

What had gone wrong? My cake was officially a disaster.

This was the price of distraction—my thoughts spinning from Adele and Grayson to the groundbreaking cell photo, all while navigating my crowded kitchen. Baking was supposed to be therapeutic, but I'd treated it like a side hustle. Spreading myself too thin was a recipe for disaster, quite literally.

Between unpacking, work demands, and grappling with my dad's email, I wasn't sure I had room to add a relationship. And yet, the thought of Grayson—his steady presence, his easy laugh—was impossible to ignore. Could I really make this work, or was I setting us both up for disappointment?

The doorbell rang, pulling me from my spiral. Speak of the devil.

I swung open the door, skipping hellos. "Are you early?"

"Bad timing? Should I make a U-turn?" Grayson quipped, one eyebrow arched.

I winced. "Sorry." Leaning in, I kissed his cheek. "I botched the cake."

His exaggerated horror made me laugh. "Not the cake! Say it isn't so." With a flourish, he revealed a bottle of wine. "I even brought this to pair with it."

Despite the disaster, my heart did a happy little shimmy. "You're a gem. Come witness the crime scene."

Grayson stepped inside, surveying the chaos with a low whistle. "It's like the blooper reel of a cooking show."

"I wish they aired the bloopers. I could use tips on what not to do." I gestured to the mess of dishes and rogue flour streaks. "The recipe was a beast."

He smirked. "Did the cake commit treason and refuse to rise?"

I chuckled. "Pretty much."

"How about this—I'll wash, you solve the cake mystery."

His offer caught me off guard, easing my tension. "You'd really do that?"

"Absolutely," he said, rolling up his sleeves.

As he tackled the dishes, I skimmed the recipe again. There it was—a metric conversion I'd overlooked. My eyes landed on the untouched box of baking soda.

"Aha," I muttered. "User error. Baking soda was MIA."

Grayson glanced over his shoulder as he cleared the counters with practiced efficiency. "That's the rising stuff, right?"

I blinked. "Since when do you know anything about baking?"

His innocent expression was maddeningly smooth. "Who said I didn't?"

I replayed our conversations, realizing he'd never claimed to be clueless about baking. My cheeks warmed. "Oh no. I stereotyped you, didn't I? That's so unfair—especially since I hate when people do that to me."

"Don't worry," he teased, rinsing a bowl. "I'll survive. Besides, I like proving people wrong."

Another thing we had in common. I glanced around. The chaos of flour and sugar had vanished, dishes stacked neatly in the sink or dishwasher. "How did you do that so fast? You're like a domestic ninja." I gestured to the now-pristine kitchen. "I might have to keep you around."

He chuckled, drying his hands. "Living alone has its perks. I've had plenty of practice cleaning up after myself."

Unable to resist, I wrapped my arms around him and kissed him, savoring the warm, spicy scent of his cologne. "Having you around is definitely growing on me. Feel free to be my domestic superhero anytime."

"A tempting offer," he murmured, his tone warm and playful. "So, what's my reward for this unpaid labor?"

"Ah, but if there's a reward, it's not unpaid, is it?"

He grinned, his eyes glinting. "*Touché.* But being with you is reward enough. Let's keep that our little secret, shall we? Don't want it spoiling our haggling over future chores."

His smile was unfairly heart-stealing. Future chores? It sounded good, like a promise I didn't know I'd wanted.

"I've got an idea." My gaze flicked to the fig and orange filling cooling on the stove. "Are you a fan of brie?"

"A fan?" He looked scandalized. "I practically worship at brie's creamy altar."

"Good. I've got a small wheel. How about I bake it and pair it with the jam and that wine you brought?"

"Sounds like a masterpiece." His eyes twinkled, lighting up at the suggestion.

Before I could move, Grayson drew me close, his lips finding mine in one fluid motion. The rest of the world disappeared—no failed cakes, no counters—just the citrusy warmth of his kiss and the heady mix of his cologne and orange zest.

When he pulled back, his voice was teasing. "You taste like oranges."

"And now you do, too." I slipped free from his hold, determined to focus on the brie. "Give me ten minutes, and this combo will blow your mind."

The spark in his eyes made it hard to break away, but my simmering fig and orange jam wasn't so forgiving. With a reluctant sigh, I prepped the brie while he found wine glasses. Before long, we fell into an easy rhythm—his rinsing, my loading—a seamless teamwork that felt more intimate than it should.

When the timer dinged, I pulled the brie from the oven and crowned it with the gleaming fig and orange jam. Golden and shining, it looked like a triumphant recovery from my earlier disaster.

"*Voila,*" I said, presenting the plate with mock grandeur.

"From the ashes of my failed cake rises the phoenix of baked brie."

His lips twitched into a grin. "A culinary redemption arc. I love it."

Leaving my phone abandoned on the counter—it could buzz all night for all I cared—I carried the brie to the patio. The cool air, earthy forest scents, and rustling leaves created a peaceful backdrop.

Grayson took his first bite, his eyes lighting up. "This is incredible," he said through a mouthful.

"And to think," I teased, "this was the consolation prize."

"Imagine how great the cake will be when you nail it."

I relaxed back in my chair. "I'll pencil in another baking day. For now, let's enjoy this."

He glanced at the trees silhouetted against the fading light. "Your view here is amazing. Peaceful."

"It's a sanctuary," I said. "Sure, there's the occasional plane, but the forest, the deer at dusk—it's like living in a nature documentary."

He turned back to me, his expression soft. "You have a gift for finding beauty in imperfection. When life hands you lemons—or, in this case, a fallen cake—you make something amazing. That's rare."

The compliment warmed me, equal parts pride and discomfort. "Perfection's overrated. Sometimes you have to ruin a cake to discover a perfect new cheese plate."

He laughed, the sound easy and warm, as if it belonged in this setting.

For the first time in what felt like forever, I wasn't thinking about work deadlines, unpacking, or what my dad's email might mean. Grayson's presence made the chaos in my life feel manageable. Maybe that's what I'd been missing—someone who didn't just add to my life but helped balance it.

"Distractions come and go," I said, breaking the silence. "But knowing what deserves your full focus? That's the real challenge."

Grayson's gaze sharpened with curiosity. "So, what could possibly distract you enough to derail your noble cake-making mission?"

Grinning, I darted inside to grab my phone. When I returned, I handed it to him, barely containing my excitement. "This."

He leaned in, taking the phone. "What am I looking at?"

"That," I said, pride threading through my voice, "is a cancer cell our engineered virus is successfully attacking. You're looking at cellular demolition."

He pinched and zoomed, studying the image with his usual intensity. "This is groundbreaking," he murmured. "No wonder your cake didn't stand a chance."

"Fair trade," I said with a shrug. "Want the quick science breakdown?"

"Always." His focus stayed on the image.

I launched into it, my words tumbling out. "Our engineered virus relies on essential factors unique to cancer cells. It can't replicate in healthy cells, so there's less risk of collateral damage. We're also stabilizing its genetic makeup to avoid mutations that could throw off its targeting. And when it's done? It self-destructs. Like a superhero vanishing into the night."

Grayson leaned back, setting the phone down, his thoughtful expression deepening. That little furrow appeared between his brows—the one that always made me want to smooth it with my fingers. "I read an article recently," he said. "It was about self-correcting mechanisms in viral genomes. It's titled 'Restriction Enzymes and Proofreading.' Think of it as a built-in spellchecker that fixes replication errors. It could be a game-changer for what you're doing."

My heart flipped. "You'll send it to me?"

"Of course. Anything to help your superhero virus save the day."

I leaned in closer, resting my chin on my hand. "You just earned yourself a spot as my favorite research collaborator."

He grinned. "Good to know there are perks to dating a fellow scientist."

"Ah, so we're officially 'dating' now?" I teased, arching a brow.

His eyes sparkled with mischief. "Well, you said it first. But yeah, I like the sound of that. And it's nice to know our relationship isn't just about, you know, the obvious. We've got research, too."

I smirked, leaning into the playful tone. "Oh, so that's what defines 'us'? Research?"

He leaned closer, his voice dipping into a conspiratorial whisper. "We're all about two brilliant minds teaming up to create something greater than the sum of our parts."

I let his words hang between us, my smile softening. "Is that so?"

"Absolutely," he said, his grin tilting into something warmer. "And speaking of teaming up…" His tone shifted, suggestive, as he met my gaze.

Heat crept into my cheeks, anticipation mingling with a flicker of vulnerability. Suddenly, this felt real—like something more than just a passing connection.

He winked, his grin endearing. "Now that we're officially dating, how about an equally official date? No staying in. No lab talk. Just us."

His words landed with a weight that thrilled me. For someone who was used to orchestrating chaos and navigating endless deadlines, the simplicity of "us" felt like an experiment worth diving into. "I'd like that."

He tilted his head, his gaze steady, teasing yet warm. "We're not your typical couple."

"Definitely not," I said, a mix of nerves and excitement bubbling up as the word *couple* settled in my mind. We were stepping into something new, something exhilarating and just a little uncharted.

He leaned in closer, his tone soft but sincere. "Courtney, I have a confession."

My pulse quickened. "What's that?"

His pause was deliberate, his timing perfect. "I've never been on a first date with someone who challenges me as much as you do. Honestly, I feel the pressure to plan something exceptional."

A thrill shot through me, his words as grounding as they were exhilarating. If this was how it felt to start something with him, I couldn't wait for more. "In that case, maybe we should dial back the pressure and go for something more conventional," I said, my voice light but resolute. "Dinner at a nice restaurant?"

His smile widened, lighting up his face. "So it's a date?"

"Yes," I said, the word solid and sure. "It's a date."

17

FINDING LOVE IN THE TIME OF CANCER

Grayson
Friday

> Me: Hypothetical question: If someone accidentally drills a hole in the wrong spot…like, say, right through a shelf into the sheet music behind it…how would you fix that?

> Kincaid: Hypothetical, huh? Wood filler, matching paint, and a silent prayer. Or call me—I charge extra for musician-related catastrophes.

> Me: Good to know. Hypothetically, I might have to call soon. Reorganizing my "keyboard corner" turned into a fiasco.

One week later, I found myself sitting across from Courtney at a table draped in crisp white linen, fresh as a new lab notebook. She looked stunning—an emerald-green dress catching the soft candlelight, her auburn hair framing a smile that made my pulse skip.

"Why are you staring at me like that?" she asked, her lips curving into a teasing smile.

"Just admiring the most beautiful woman in the room," I replied, the words slipping out before I could overthink them.

She flushed but didn't look away. "Careful, Dr. Grayson. Flattery might just get you dessert later."

"Duly noted," I said, returning her grin.

The restaurant captured Pittsburgh charm in miniature: local artwork in bold abstracts, a jazz pianist in the corner playing quietly, and just enough ambient chatter to make our little table feel intimate. Perfect for the first truly "normal" date Courtney and I had shared—no weddings, no drama, just us.

But even with the romantic glow of the place, my thoughts lingered on the rough department meeting I'd sat through earlier. The pressure to find a new research direction kept buzzing in my mind, almost as irritating as the off-kilter shelf in my home office I'd tried to "fix" for my piano books—some of which now had accidental ventilation holes. Not my finest moment.

"Still feeling guilty about that bookshelf fiasco?" Courtney asked after we placed our orders. Her brow lifted, a playful glint in her eye. "You never said how bad it really got."

I let out a rueful chuckle. "Let's just say I tested your brother's theory that an electric drill plus overconfidence equals home-renovation horror. I was reorganizing my 'music corner'—big idea, poor execution."

Courtney laughed softly. "At least you can hide the damage with a few large books, right?"

"Or a standing lamp. Possibly a potted plant," I said. "I'm basically juggling a million things at once: mini home projects, academic deadlines, and, oh yeah, this new relationship I don't want to mess up."

Her gaze warmed. "That last one better rank high on your priority list."

I reached across to brush my fingertips over hers. "It does."

As much as I wanted to soak in the moment, the weight of my stalled research tugged at me. Losing the Cates Foundation position had been a blow, and watching new AI developments outpace my old methods felt like treading water in an endless ocean.

I explained my professional dilemma to Courtney, and she leaned in, genuine interest lighting her face. "Maybe it's not about finding the perfect plan. Maybe it's about giving yourself permission to explore."

I swirled my wine. "You make it sound easy."

"It can be," she said. "Think about breakthroughs in the lab and focus on the process instead of the outcome. We test, fail, test again. Why should your career be any different?"

A mirthless laugh slipped out. "My dad never saw it that way. His motto is 'If it fails once, it's a waste of time.' But real progress is trial and error."

Courtney nodded, a calm assurance in her expression. "You know that logically—just apply it emotionally."

Her words settled over me, a gentle nudge quieting the usual roar in my head.

Our entrées arrived: seared scallops over spinach, plated like a piece of art. Courtney breathed in their aroma with obvious delight. "This is almost too pretty to eat."

"Almost," I teased, watching her slice off her first bite. She shut her eyes in bliss, and I couldn't help but smile.

Conversation bounced from cancer research to a long-ago collapsed soufflé attempt—she recounted the fiasco with comedic flair, making me nearly topple my water glass with laughter.

Before we could browse the dessert menu, the scent of molten chocolate wafted by. That was all the prompting Courtney needed. She zoned in like a pastry detective.

"Chocolate soufflé," she announced. "That's it. I have to conquer the art of soufflé next—after I perfect my fig-and-orange carrot cake."

I cocked an eyebrow. "That's the Everest of desserts. High risk, high reward."

She gave a determined little nod. "I refuse to let one botched soufflé define me. I have grit, Dr. Grayson."

"Yes, you do," I said with a playful wink. "Count me in for taste-testing."

The waiter returned with our soufflé in all its puffed, sugary glory. Courtney took the first spoonful, eyes closing in reverence. I tried a bite, and chocolate nirvana spread over my tongue.

"If you can replicate this at home," I said, "I'll nominate you for the city's top chef award."

Her smirk showed no sign of modesty. "You'd be my co-author, obviously."

"Obviously," I echoed, fighting a grin.

As the sugar high set in, Courtney glanced around the softly lit restaurant, her voice dropping. "This feels like a bubble of normalcy. No deadlines, no lab meltdown. How do we hold on to times like this?"

I tapped my fingers on the table—an unconscious habit I'd picked up again since returning to the piano. "That's where music helps me, ironically. It's the one place I don't have to be perfect. I can let go, follow the notes."

She listened, brow arching. "So maybe that mindset can bleed into your research? Less about orchestrating the end result, more about exploring the patterns."

"Good point," I said, nodding slowly. "It's exactly what I do in music—try a chord progression, mess up, try again. No shame in the process. So why not do that with my job, too?"

A comfortable lull followed. Then I tossed out an idea. "You know, maybe we should treat our relationship the same way—an experiment, with metrics. See how it affects our work, our stress levels."

She paused mid-bite, spoon aloft. "A love experiment?"

"Exactly," I said, leaning closer. "We set parameters: over the next three months we measure if seeing each other improves our focus or if it's a glorious trainwreck. We can track intangible stuff, too—like how often we feel truly alive in a day."

She shot me a fond, exasperated look. "So love by the numbers, huh? We do have a thing for experimentation." Her smile grew, the tension in her expression easing. "The only part I refuse to quantify is kissing," she insisted. "Data or no data, that's strictly for fun."

"Agreed. And our baseline can start the day before we flew to Turks and Caicos," I suggested.

Her eyes sparkled at the memory. "That's perfect." She hesitated a moment, looking doubtful. "This is all subjective though."

"Admitted, but emotions are, by definition, subjective," I countered. "Besides, if the experiment goes off the rails—like drilling the wrong hole in a bookshelf—" I gave a sheepish shrug. "We'll patch it up. No big deal."

Courtney laughed, a warm, rich sound. "Deal. But keep the power tools far away from my emotional well-being."

We fell into an easy rhythm, phones out, typing quick notes: "stress levels before date vs. after," "number of bright ideas gleaned from coffee + romance," "chocolate soufflé correlation." It was whimsical, maybe a little silly, but it felt right. A structured way to embrace unpredictability.

Courtney glanced up from her phone, eyes shining. "Mixing science and emotions could go terribly wrong."

"Or," I said, capturing her hand across the table, "it could be the most groundbreaking discovery of our lives."

18

BAKED IN CHEMISTRY

COURTNEY
Saturday

> Kincaid: I just texted Lianna to say I'm "renovating the baby." Auto-correct is a menace.

> Me: snort I hope Lianna's sense of humor is still intact.

> Kincaid: She responded with "Better give her granite countertops. Our baby deserves the best." We're all good…for now.

Just over a week—180 hours, not that I was counting—had passed since Grayson and I turned our budding relationship into a full-on science experiment, complete with metrics and expectations. While daily Zoom calls kept the spark alive, they couldn't replace the real thing. Twice this week, we'd made plans only to cancel—me drowning in lab work, him in a race to the finish line with grant deadlines. But today? We'd finally made it happen.

The doorbell chimed, but Grayson didn't wait. He stepped inside, grocery bag swinging like he already belonged here.

"Hey, Dr. Gillette," he said, setting the bag on the counter alongside the tools I'd already assembled. "Ready to turn this kitchen into a delicious experiment?"

I tied my apron, grinning. "I'm hoping today's cake fares better than the last one. No pressure, but my culinary reputation is on the line."

"Tell me what to do. I'm at your command."

I sifted flour into a mixing bowl while Grayson picked up the long-handled spatula I'd planned to use for frosting and began twirling it like a sword, a devilish grin spreading across his face.

"I've never seen someone so excited about a spatula. Should I be worried?" I asked, one hand on my hip but unable to hide my smile.

"Some tools inspire… indecent ideas," he teased, raising it like a fencer's foil.

With one swift motion, he swatted my bottom. I shrieked, wagging a finger at him. "Kitchen tools are *not* toys, and they definitely don't belong in the bedroom."

His grin turned wicked. "Your phrasing suggests there might be other toys you'd entertain."

A delicious thrill ran through me, but I kept my tone firm. "Not now, Dr. Stellar. Cake first, mischief later. I refuse to get side-tracked again."

"Fine," he relented with a mock sigh. "But I'm holding you to a rain check."

"Deal," I said, snapping the lid off a jar of cinnamon. Its warm, heady aroma mixed with the citrusy zest Grayson grated, filling the kitchen with a symphony of scents. I mentally added *"Olfactory Delights: Bonus Points"* to our new list of metrics.

Grayson read aloud from the recipe card while I measured and stirred. The batter came together effortlessly, our rhythm seamless. I glanced at him zesting another orange, his concentration intense.

"You know, baking is a lot like our work," I said. "It's all about precision and chemistry."

He grinned. "And just like research, the best breakthroughs come from unexpected combinations."

"Exactly," I said, smiling. "A little chaos, some experimentation—it's where the magic happens."

His eyes lit up. "Speaking of breakthroughs, I was reading this article about sugar's role in cancer cells. Turns out, they thrive on it—like it's their favorite fuel. Some researchers are exploring ways to use that against them."

Perking up, I jumped onto his geek train. *Intellectual Stimulation: 10/10.* "No kidding? So, we could weaponize their sugar addiction? I'm imagining desserts that fight back."

His eyes gleamed, the idea clearly taking shape. "Cancer-Crushing Crème Brûlée. Tumor-Taming Tiramisu. We could turn molecular gastronomy into a weapon of mass eradication."

I laughed, charmed by the ridiculous brilliance of it. "Don't forget Leukemia-Liquidating Lemon Bars! A dessert revolution."

Grayson tapped his chin, striking a dramatic pose. "Courtney, this isn't just baking—it's the future of medicine. Nobel Prizes await, in both culinary arts and oncology."

Sliding the pans into the oven, I grinned. "I always knew my baking obsession was more than an excuse to indulge. Look at us, solving the world's problems one carrot cake at a time."

"Don't you wish curing cancer could be that simple?"

"Every day," I said, pouring fig jam into a saucepan and adding his orange zest. Steam unfurled, swirling into an intoxicating cloud of sweetness and citrus.

We kept tossing around ideas, each more outlandish than the last, riding the wave of creativity. "This is kind of great, isn't it?" Grayson said, his tone softer now. "Us. Brainstorming, seeing where ideas take us.

The jam gently bubbled as I stirred, the warmth of his words blending seamlessly with the air around us. "It is," I said, matching his tone. "The best things usually start this way—just a spark and a little curiosity."

"By the way, how much time is left on the cake timer?"

Grayson leaned over to check the display above the oven. "This conversation almost made me forget they're baking."

As if on cue, the timer chimed, punctuating his words with perfect timing. Grayson stepped back, giving me room. I opened the oven, the rush of heat carrying the rich aroma of warm spices and sugar.

Holding my breath, I pulled out the cake pans. "Perfection." I gave a sign of relief, setting them on the counter with exaggerated care.

Grayson leaned closer, inspecting them with mock seriousness. "Perfectly golden. A model bake. Paul Hollywood would be proud."

I laughed, shaking my head. "I have to say, there's something uniquely satisfying about nailing this after my last disaster."

"And to think," he teased, his grin soft and playful, "all it took was a little focus, teamwork, some sugar, and maybe a touch of genius."

"We're not done yet," I reminded him. "We still have to pull off the filling, the cream cheese frosting, and the fancy toppings."

About half an hour later, I delicately placed the first layer on a cake plate. With the precision of a surgeon, I piped a ring of cream cheese frosting around the top edge, creating a barrier for the fig and orange filling. After filling it, I layered on the second cake. That's when I spotted a disaster in the making—a minuscule breach in the frosting wall, allowing some filling to stage a stealthy escape.

"I got it," Grayson said, grabbing the pastry bag and squirting some to dam the hole. With an intense focus that I bet would make his cardiovascular surgeon father jealous, he examined his handiwork and used a paper towel to gently remove the filling that had oozed out. "Looks like the repair is holding. Problem solved."

"Wow," I said, watching him with a mixture of awe and amusement. "The focus, the precision. Should I scrub in for the next procedure, Dr. Stellar?"

"Please do, Dr. Gillette. You can take it from here."

I hip-checked him to one side, took his place in front of the cake, and placed the third layer on top. Luckily the frosting dam didn't spring a leak this time. I made a mental note about enhanced teamwork on my mental relationship spreadsheet.

"Now for the frosting," I said, spreading it smoothly over the cake in no time. With the pastry bag, I piped dozens of delicate stars along the edge, then reached for the candied ginger slices and carefully arranged them in the center, forming a flower. A final flourish with the pastry bag added a decorative center, completing the design.

Grayson shook his head in wonder as he pulled out his phone and took a picture. I posed, pastry bag in hand.

"It looks perfect," he said, tucking his phone back into his pocket. "Like it's straight from a high-end bakery."

"Just as long as it tastes perfect, too."

"Only one way to find out." Grayson grabbed two plates from the cabinet, his expression eager.

I collected two forks and a large knife from the drawer and headed toward the dining area. "Let's eat it at the table," I called over my shoulder. Setting everything down, I lit the candles for ambiance. Perfect. I turned to retrieve the cake and—bam—ran straight into Grayson.

And the cake he was carrying.

"*No. No, no, no.*" The words escaped in a horrified whisper as the plate wobbled in his hands. In slow motion, the cake pitched forward like it was auditioning for a disaster film.

In a panic, I lunged for it, only for my hand to smack into Grayson's arm. The cake did a pirouette worthy of a prima ballerina and landed—*splaaaat*—against my chest.

For a moment, there was silence. Total, awkward, frosting-dripping silence.

I stood frozen, clutching what remained of the cake, now firmly adhered to my chest. Fig and orange filling oozed down my cleavage, cream cheese frosting smeared across my torso like a culinary war wound. At first I leaned over to cradle it in my arms and try to salvage it, but the whole thing broke into wet pieces that plopped onto the floor.

Grayson's eyes were wide, his face a kaleidoscope of emotions: shock, regret, and—because he couldn't help himself—a twitch of suppressed laughter.

"Courtney..." His voice was thick with effort as he fought to maintain composure. "I—I don't know how to say this, but... you wear that cake beautifully."

I stared at him, incredulous. "You think this is funny?"

"Funny?" His lips twitched, and then it happened. He laughed. A deep, unrepentant laugh that filled the room. "I think it's hilarious."

That did it. I grabbed a fistful of frosting from my chest and smacked it squarely across his face. "How's that for hilarious?"

Grayson froze, frosting dripping from his nose. Slowly, he wiped a finger across his cheek and inspected it like a scientist analyzing evidence. "Well played, Dr. Gillette. But you just declared war."

Before I could react, he grabbed a glob of frosting from my shirt and smeared it onto my forehead with surgical precision. "First strike: effective and highly satisfying."

"Grayson!" I gasped, ducking away. "This is not how you win a girl over."

"Oh no?" His grin was pure mischief. "Because I think I'm doing pretty well."

Frosting flew as I retaliated, swiping another handful onto his arm. He dodged left, slipped on an errant glob of orange and fig filling, and nearly took me down with him. I shrieked, laughing so hard I doubled over.

The kitchen looked like a crime scene—cream cheese frosting on the walls, cake chunks on the floor, fig filling dripping from the counter.

"Ceasefire!" I declared, holding up my hands in surrender,

frosting dripping from my fingers. Even as a gob of frosting dripped down my arm, I couldn't help noticing how close he was, how his playful smirk morphed into something warmer. Sexier.

Grayson stepped closer, his smirk softening into something warmer. "Ceasefire? You sure about that?"

I met his gaze, my heart pounding as the playful energy shifted. "Positive," I whispered, grabbing his shirt and pulling him in for a kiss.

His lips were sweet in every sense—sugar, citrus, and laughter mingling in a kiss that felt indulgent and intoxicating. The chaos around us faded, leaving only the warmth of his touch and the steady thrum of my heart.

When we finally pulled apart, his eyes sparkled with amusement. "Best cake I've ever tasted."

I laughed, swiping frosting from his jawline. "Not bad for a disaster."

His grin softened, his voice quieter. "Courtney, disaster or not, I'd bake a thousand cakes with you just for moments like this."

I felt the same, though words didn't seem enough. So instead, I leaned into him again, my smirk returning. "Next time, I'm wearing a hazmat suit."

"Deal," he said, capturing my lips in another frosting-laden kiss, this one slower, deeper. His hands slid to my waist, pulling me closer as laughter gave way to something quieter, more electric.

"Courtney," he murmured, his voice low and rough, "I want you."

His words sent a ripple of heat through me, erasing any lingering self-consciousness. I slipped my arms around his neck, threading my messy fingers through his hair. "Excellent instincts," I teased, though my voice betrayed the anticipation humming beneath. "But we're going to need a shower after this."

"Later," he said, his lips trailing along my jaw, leaving a path of fire in their wake. His hands explored my sides, grounding me even as my pulse raced. He tilted his head and kissed me again, harder this time.

The marble counter felt cool as he lifted me effortlessly, the contrast sharpening every sensation. "You have frosting in your hair," he murmured, reaching for a towel.

I laughed softly, wiping my hands and swiping at my hair. "So do you. This is happens to be part of my new beauty routine."

His grin returned, sly and full of promise. "It works for you," he said, kissing me again, harder this time, his hands steadying me as if anchoring us in this messy, perfect moment.

He stripped away my apron. My shorts. My underthings. Leaving me naked on my counter. Yeah, I'd be scouring this spot with countertop spray.

As his touch grew bolder, I found myself spreading my legs for him, ready to let go and see where he'd take us.

He pulled out a condom he'd tucked into his wallet, ever the optimist. I loved that he came prepared. Within moments he was buried inside me, thumbing my clit, making me writhe on the granite, grinding into him.

This was happening fast. From zero to orgasm in—oh, my.

"Grayson," I whispered. Or moaned. Or cried. I had no sense of volume control in that moment. Everything else had disappeared, and was only us. His thumb. His cock. His kisses.

I shattered under his touch, a cascade of sensations that left me breathless. Instinctively, I pulled him closer, the motion so sudden something toppled to the floor with a metallic clank. The spatula? The frosting bowl? None of it mattered. There was only this— Grayson, us, and the heat igniting every inch of my being.

Grayson moved with a deliberate rhythm, his body a perfect counterpoint to mine, until I broke apart all over again. Trembling, I clung to him, his satisfied smile grounding me in the aftermath.

"Was that everything you could've hoped for?" he asked, his tone warm and teasing.

"You know it was," I murmured, still catching my breath. "Fast, hot, perfect." Then I hesitated, biting my lip.

"I'm sensing a 'but,'" he said, arching an eyebrow.

I laughed, leaning into him. "But… we still have this mess to clean up. That part's gonna suck."

He grinned, pressing a kiss to my temple. "Let's just say we've earned dessert first."

19

OFFICIAL COUPLEDOM

GRAYSON

It was a beautiful September Sunday, and the Sewickley Bridge arched over the Ohio River like a gateway. I reached for Courtney's hand, and when our fingers interlaced, it felt right.

Courtney sat beside me, smoothing her white capris like she was trying to iron out her nerves by hand. Her movements were small but telling.

"Feeling jittery about dinner with my sister?" I asked, squeezing her hand.

She smiled wryly. "A little. Stepping out as a couple feels... big."

"Don't worry," I said. "Mara's thrilled. She'd throw a parade if she could."

Her laugh eased my nerves. "Good to know she's on board." She traced her thumb over mine in slow, deliberate strokes. "Even if this goes south, it's not like we're stuck together in a lab. We'd survive. Amicably, even."

I tried to shrug off the tightness in my chest. "Right. Hypothetical heartbreak. Sounds fun."

Courtney tilted her head, her smile fading a bit. "How about we table the breakup talk and move on to my Tuesday presentation instead? Hypothetically less depressing."

I nodded, grateful for the pivot. "Tell me more, you intellectual diva."

"I've got a big pitch to a biotech group I met in Florence. The meeting's virtual, first thing in the morning. Tomorrow's all about perfecting the PowerPoint."

"Cinderella trading her pumpkin for a laptop," I mused. "I'm assuming the glass slipper is now a perfectly aligned slide deck?"

Her grin widened. "If all goes well, I'll be free for dinner after."

"Done." The light turned green, and I reluctantly let go of her hand to take the wheel. "I've got a mentoring session tomorrow. Dinner after that?"

"Perfect." Her grin turned playful. "Besides, the more time I spend with you, the more my appetite grows. We do have a certain knack for burning off calories, after all."

"Ah, the classic 'sex burns calories' line," I teased, loving the way her cheeks flushed even as her laughter spilled out. "You know that data's faulty, right?"

"Bad science or not, our version has to qualify as a high-intensity workout," she said, a playful edge of pride in her voice. "I mean, our sessions rarely clock in under an hour—unless we're sidetracked by kitchen cleanup. That's gotta burn some calories, right?"

As we pulled into Max and Sonya's driveway, Courtney lifted her chin toward the elegant house. "I was here last fall helping Emma rehearse for her school play. You'd be amazed what theater kids can accomplish when there's a deadline."

Before we even reached the door, three kids burst out like cannonballs. Emma led the charge, flanked by two friends I didn't recognize.

Courtney greeted them warmly. "Hey, Emma, Marley, Liam! How's sixth grade treating you?"

Their answers came in a rapid-fire chorus, overlapping so

quickly I could barely keep up. As they led us inside, the bright, lemon-scented foyer welcomed us, mingling with the smoky aroma of charcoal drifting in from the backyard.

Max stepped in from outside, his cheeks flushed from the grill, and tossed us a wave. "Hey, kiddo," he said, ruffling Emma's hair. "Where's the preteen brigade off to tonight?"

"Marley's place," Emma said, hoisting her backpack.

"*Ferris Bueller's Day Off*," Marley added proudly.

Max smirked. "Just don't take it as a manual for skipping school."

Emma grinned. "No promises!"

Max chuckled as the kids bolted for the door.

Mara and Sonya breezed into the kitchen, Zephyr trotting behind them like a canine chaperone. Mara's grin was sharp. "Well, well, well. Finally giving my matchmaking skills their due?"

Courtney raised an eyebrow. "Do you already have our couple name picked out?"

"Graytney," Mara declared with a triumphant grin.

I groaned. "Absolutely not."

Sonya pulled Courtney into a hug. "Hold on to him. He's as cute as a Hallmark movie lead."

Mara rolled her eyes, her protectiveness laced with humor. "Can we not objectify my brother in front of him? There's an unspoken sibling code here."

I grinned. "Objectify away. It's doing wonders for my ego."

Three sets of eyes turned toward me, amusement and exasperation battling for dominance.

Mara wagged a finger at me. "Time for you to disappear. Don't you have a grill to supervise? Maybe a beer to nurse?"

I raised my hands in mock surrender. "Message received. Exiting stage left."

Max handed me a chilled Yuengling and led the way to the patio, his grin laced with teasing. "You and Courtney are the talk of the barbecue."

Outside, the garden stretched in vibrant greens, the neatly trimmed hedges providing a serene backdrop.

"Why does that not surprise me?" I took a sip, a fond memory surfacing of Courtney laughing during the aftermath of Great Carrot Cake Disaster during a very memorable shower. I shook it off, focusing back on the present. "What's on the menu? Smells amazing."

"Ford's grilling steak and chicken," Max said. "Come see."

At the grill, Ford lifted the lid, releasing a smoky plume. "Steaks are almost ready."

"Speaking of well-done efforts," I said, shifting gears, "how was the honeymoon?"

Ford's smile softened as he checked the steaks. "Paris was amazing. Mara loved the museums, especially the *Musée Marmottan Monet*. Turns out Chance taught her a lot about art when they were kids."

"She's always had layers," I said with a grin. "From Monet to Marvel."

Ford chuckled. "My nerd queen, forever and always."

The sound of soft footsteps drew my attention and I spotted Mara with Zephyr at her side. "Eavesdropping, Sis?"

"Just that 'nerd queen' comment," she said, folding her arms with mock sternness. "What embarrassing truths are you spilling?"

"Just praising your art expertise," Ford said, pulling her close for a quick kiss.

Before Mara could retort, Sonya stepped onto the patio, the sunlight catching the salad bowl in her hands, while Courtney followed with a pitcher of lemonade. They placed everything on the table with the coordination of a practiced team.

I slipped an arm around Courtney, pulling her into a side-hug. She melted into me like we'd been this comfortable forever, and it took everything in me not to beam like a lovesick fool.

Ford, attention on the grill, called out, "Steak preferences, anyone?"

A chorus of "medium" and "medium-rare" filled the air, accompanied by Zephyr's enthusiastic bark, which earned him an indulgent pat from Mara.

As we took our seats and lifted our wine glasses, Max raised his for a toast. "To phenomenal company and excellent food."

"Hear, hear," Ford echoed, clinking his glass against Max's with a flourish.

I turned my attention to Sonya, who sat across from me. "How's the upcoming school year shaping up? Same classroom, different chaos?"

She sipped her wine thoughtfully. "Same classroom, yes, but this year's roster is full of energetic, competitive high-achievers. It's going to be an interesting mix to manage."

I nodded, thinking about the contrast between her job and mine. She wasn't just an educator; she was a mentor, a counselor, and sometimes even a referee. Meanwhile, I had the luxury of focusing solely on content delivery and letting the students sink or swim.

Courtney leaned in, her attention shifting to Max. "Sorry to hear you and Sonya only had a short honeymoon. School in-service days wait for no one, right?"

Max winked. "We're making up for it over Christmas. One week in the Virgin Islands, and Emma gets her own Disney adventure with Aunt Mara and Uncle Ford."

"Sounds like a win-win," Courtney said, her smile lighting up the conversation.

Max chuckled, but his tone shifted as he shot me a pointed look. "That is, as long as the production schedule stays on track."

The weight of his words settled in the air. I knew exactly what he was referring to—my concerns about the portrayal of one of the characters in Chance's film. It wasn't a minor issue, and apparently, it wouldn't be easy to fix.

Ford shifted uncomfortably in his chair. "After hearing back from Grayson, we watched the rough cut of the scenes with Ghost's girlfriend, and it's clear something's missing," he admitted. "Grayson's right. She's too one-dimensional. I think Chance would've hated that, and we need to fix it."

Mara's expression sharpened. "Her name is Maris, by the way."

Ford blinked, momentarily thrown. "Right. Maris."

"Referring to her as 'Ghost's girlfriend' doesn't exactly scream respect," Mara said, her tone growing pointed. "That attitude probably explains why she's so flat. Ever heard of the Bechdel test?"

Ford winced, recognizing the implication. "Damn, you're right. I didn't think about it like that."

"Obviously," Mara shot back. "The way Maris has been pared down in the script directly affects how she's portrayed on screen. It's like she's not even a full character."

I raised a hand. "Hold on—what's the Bechdel test?"

Mara's jaw dropped in mock offense. "How do you not know this? Were you selectively deaf during my feminist rants back in the day?"

I smirked. "Selective sibling hearing, remember? It's an art form."

Mara rolled her eyes. "How unfortunate. You missed out on the Bechdel test—a measure of representation. It has comic strip origins, from the eighties—Alison Bechdel. A movie passes the test if two women talk to each other about something other than a man. It's not perfect, but it's a start."

I rubbed my chin theatrically. "Feminist litmus test. Got it."

"Right now, Maris fails it hard," Mara said, crossing her arms.

Ford raised his hands in surrender. "Fair point. I'll make sure her character gets the depth she deserves. Honestly, I should've pushed for more in the script, but with so much focus on Ghost's story, Maris got sidelined. It wasn't intentional, but we need to fix it now."

I couldn't help but feel vindicated. "That echoes my notes. Maris felt like wallpaper in the script and the rough cut." I thought for a moment, wondering if Mara's social justice streak had influenced me more than I realized. "So, what's the plan? Reshoots? Script revisions?"

Ford ran a hand through his hair, his frustration evident. "I know it's late in the game, but we're at a crossroads. Either we fix this now and do it right, or we risk releasing something that doesn't hold up to Chance's standards. First, let's revisit the footage we already have. If necessary, we'll schedule reshoots. Whatever it takes to do Chance's work justice."

I felt a wave of relief that Mara, Ford, and I were on the same page. This wasn't just about fixing the script—it was about honoring Chance, the brother who had always believed in his graphic novel *Ghost*. No shortcuts, no compromises, just an gripping story.

As the conversation shifted to lighter topics, I caught Courtney's small, encouraging smile. Her quiet support grounded me. We'd figure this out together.

Still, my gut churned at the thought of poring over film clips when I should be catching up on research—or better yet, holding Courtney close. "Dinner in a screening room? What's next, a walk down the red carpet?" I quipped, trying to mask my hesitation. "Alright, I'll make it work. *Ghost* waits for no one."

Ford perked up. "How about tomorrow night? I'll even throw in dinner."

I glanced at Courtney, guilt tugging at me. We'd planned a quiet evening together, a rare moment just for us. But instead of frustration, she gave me a small shrug. "This is important," she said softly. "You should go."

I nodded, forcing a grin. "A date with celluloid and my brother-in-law? Who could resist?"

Ford grinned, visibly relieved. "Thanks. It'll help to work with someone who understands Chance's vision so we can get this right."

2 0

A SEWICKLEY DATE

Courtney

Saturday

> Conner: My new guitar came scratched, so I "fixed" it with a furniture marker. It looks like a bruise. Advice?

> Me: Maybe call it "artistic distressing"? Get Kincaid to fix it.

> Conner: Good call. He'll probably show up in a hard hat. Safety first, even for guitars.

A full week of *Ghost* reshoots slipped by before Grayson and I finally found ourselves in the same zip code again, with a rare weekend to ourselves.

Saturday morning, he pulled up to my place, a grin stretching across his face like a cartoon character come to life. I half-expected hearts to burst from the car vents.

. . .

Belt latched, I settled into the passenger seat. "So, what's on the agenda? I just want to relax—no strenuous activities."

"Today's all about indulgence," he said warmly. "Good food, comic books, and ice cream. I'm calling it the Sewickley Odyssey: Culinary Edition."

Laughter bubbled up, already chasing away residual stress. "You know me too well."

A sheepish smile flickered across his face. "I finally watched Ford's footage. Found out Chris Pitt was at the wedding. Had no clue who he was until I saw him on-screen."

"You didn't recognize the lead in *Ghost*?" I teased.

He lifted a shoulder, still grinning. "Oblivious charm is my specialty."

Lunch at In Vino Veritas set the tone over wine and appetizers in the crisp September air. Birds flitted near a small fountain—our first stop on this "odyssey."

Leaning back in his chair, Grayson savored a fresh strawberry. "You and your brothers seem close. But I recall you mentioning your dad right after Florence. Still wrestling with that issue?"

A twinge of guilt pulsed through me as I lowered my glass. Dad's email hovered in my mind like a neon sign I couldn't dim. Twice, I'd drafted a reply. Twice, I'd deleted it. Not ready. "Still no decision. He's not really in the picture. Neither is my mom. It's just me, Christopher, Conner, and Kincaid." Keeping my voice even was harder than I wanted to admit.

Quiet concern dimmed the light in his eyes. "Is it something you want to talk about?"

I shook my head, pushing a half-smile. "I will, someday. Just… not today." The weight lingered, but I shoved it aside. "Anyway, Christopher—my oldest brother. He lives in London, running a company with a spreadsheet for a life."

He steered the topic along. "Intense."

A wry grin tugged at my lips. "You have no idea. Last time he visited, he had an itinerary mapped down to the minute. I took him to a no-reservation taco truck just to watch him squirm."

He chuckled, leaning forward as if to catch every detail. "And here I thought my schedule was tough."

A shrug carried me to safer ground. "When we were kids, he practically ran the house. Then he got that scholarship to Penn State, and he was gone. I don't blame him, though. He needed the escape."

"And you stayed," Grayson observed quietly.

"Someone had to," I answered with another shrug. "Our grandparents helped, but Christopher and I took on most of it—he handled logistics while I refereed Conner and Kincaid's endless wrestling matches. Then he moved on, and I stayed behind."

A flicker of concern deepened his expression. "Do you miss him?"

I speared a piece of bruschetta, shaking off a faint flicker of longing. I admired how Christopher had built his new life in London, but sometimes I envied how far he'd gotten from our old chaos. Some wounds still throbbed.

I set down my fork and offered a tight-lipped smile. "We keep in touch. Christopher's busy, I'm busy. It works." The guilt about my avoidance of Dad's email still lingered, but I wasn't ready to unwrap that knot. Not yet.

His gaze lingered before he raised his glass, an easy grin returning. "To the Taco Truck Queen. Long may she reign."

My own glass clinked his, relief washing over me. "And may her sovereignty never be questioned."

After a sip, I let the mood settle. "So, how's the piano going? Still aiming for a comeback tour?"

He flashed a confident smile. "Teacher says I hesitate too much, so I'm working on that. You're welcome to a half-decent recital anytime—just promise not to laugh at my slip-ups."

"Deal," I teased, lips curving into a smirk. "But if it's 'Chopsticks,' I can't guarantee a poker face."

After paying the bill, we strolled through Sewickley's postcard-worthy streets toward *Ghost of a Chance Comics*. Mara had turned Chance's dream into a thriving store and vibrant tribute his *Ghost* series.

Inside, color and chaos reigned: comics, figurines, and Magic: The Gathering cards. A framed sketch of Chance's handwriting— *"Dreams aren't just for sleeping"*—stood proudly behind the register.

"Grayson, Courtney!" Mara called as she emerged from behind a curtain alongside her manager, Sam. "Are you early or am I late?"

"One o'clock, on the dot," Grayson teased. "What's up with you working in the back room? Isn't that Sam's job?"

She rolled her eyes. "Inventory day, and it's all hands on deck." She flicked a playful salute at Sam as he disappeared.

Grayson admired the shop. "You've done Chance proud. The place looks fantastic."

Mara's grin softened. "Thanks. It's a labor of love." Then her expression shifted to business. "I reviewed Ford's latest reshoots —Marin's finally a fleshed-out character. You did well on those notes, Grayson."

He exhaled, relief evident. "Good to hear. I'm meeting Ford soon to finalize things."

"Should've brought you in sooner," Mara admitted. "I owe you an apology for not looping you in."

Grayson gave a small, reassuring smile. "Sure, there were extra reshoots—but I'd rather fix it now than let mistakes slip by. It's all about doing right by Chance, right?"

Mara nodded. "We'll make him proud."

Before the moment got heavy, the door chimed. Gertrude, Sewickley's unflappable septuagenarian style icon, breezed in wearing sleek Lululemon yoga gear.

"Ah, my luminous ladies of book club," Gertrude announced. She focused on Grayson immediately. "You must be Mara's brother—the one with the dance moves! Rose showed me the video she took. You were remarkable."

Grayson's ears went pink. "My sisters did most of the work, trust me."

Gertrude let out a delighted laugh. "Don't be modest. You were the highlight of the show. Your comic timing was impeccable."

Mara grinned, clearly enjoying his discomfort. "She's right. You were fantastic, Grayson. I didn't know you had it in you."

Gertrude checked her Apple Watch. "Hot yoga calls. See you at book club, ladies!" And off she went, all composure and grace.

Mara smirked. "So, Fred Astaire, how's life post-dance sensation?"

"I was going for Justin Timberlake on SNL," Grayson countered lightly, though I saw the pride in his eyes.

Mara's teasing grin fell away. "Ignore Dad's post-performance comments. He wouldn't recognize talent if it danced across his coffee table."

Grayson shrugged, his tone light. "Some critics are impossible to please."

Watching them, I felt a protective surge. Grayson was finding his way back to music—and to himself.

He slid his hand into mine. "Having you both stand up for me...it means a lot."

Mara's attention shifted to me, her voice softened by genuine gratitude. "Word from the family grapevine is, you told Dad exactly what he needed to hear. Thank you. It's about time someone set him straight."

Grayson nodded slowly, regret underscoring his voice as he locked eyes with me. "I didn't want to face him down and make a scene at your wedding, but you're right that I've been letting him steer for too long. I've started making changes—script consulting, piano lessons, and..." He trailed off, turning to me with a warm smile. "You."

My heart fluttered at how simple and certain he sounded.

Mara's eyes gleamed with approval. "Finally. You've been Dad's 'Little Drummer Boy' for too long. Compose your own symphony—and maybe Courtney can be your muse?" She shot me a playful wink.

He turned to me, mischief brightening his features. "I'd like that."

"Good," Mara said with finality. "Being the oldest doesn't mean you have to carry the heaviest burdens. Remember: Dad's no different than a difficult grad student. Boundaries, boundaries, boundaries."

Except grad students don't come with all that emotional baggage.

Sam emerged balancing a clipboard and a calculator, summoning Mara back to her duties. She waved us off. "Inventory calls. Go frolic, you two."

Grayson offered his arm with a flourish. I looped mine through, and we stepped into the sunlit street.

My phone buzzed, interrupting the relaxed rhythm of the afternoon. A quick glance showed a message from Mercy:

> Mercy: Weird glitch in the lab server. Some files went offline, then popped back. Nothing urgent. Enjoy your day off!

I sighed, typing a quick reply.

> Me: Got it. Pete and his IT team can wrangle it. Server's mirrored, so no data loss. I'll check Monday if it keeps acting up.

"Lab gremlins," I said, tucking my phone away.

Grayson nudged me. "Off duty. No gremlins until Monday."

I smiled wholeheartedly and nodded—today wasn't for troubleshooting.

"Sweet Scoops, then your place to grab whatever you need, then mine," he declared. "An entire weekend to ourselves."

The weight of the last hectic weeks melted away. "Sounds decadent."

He lowered his voice. "Decadence is precisely the plan."

I leaned into him, letting his warmth anchor me. This

moment, this bubble of quiet belonging, felt like an oasis in the midst of our chaotic lives. Conner and Kincaid still buzzed my phone every few days—firing off texts about everything from business hiccups to last-minute baby prep—but neither had hit me with the usual crisis call lately. Kincaid and Lianna seemed blissful, busy picking out nursery themes, and he was renovating a couple of second-floor apartments downtown. He'd even sent me photos, asking for my "expert" input on paint swatches. Maybe they'd finally realized I needed breathing room, or maybe they were just getting better at standing on their own two feet. Either way, I wasn't complaining as I savored the quiet—for once, I wasn't in full-on ringmaster mode.

"I have to admit," he said, "the thought of waking up next to you and bringing you breakfast in bed is my favorite daydream. You in?"

"Ah, the sheer indulgence of it all," I teased, flashing him a deliberately dramatic smile. "You're going to spoil me beyond repair."

His eyebrows shot up with mock seriousness. "My mission is to spoil you in the most decadent ways possible." He chuckled, his voice dropping just enough to send a shiver down my spine. "How about we add some relaxation to our list of activities? Maybe a massage?"

"Are you offering?"

His fingers brushed lightly against the small of my back before settling at my waist, sending a ripple of warmth through me. "Of course. I never miss an opportunity to get my hands on you."

The slight possessiveness in his touch was enough to make me consider skipping the ice cream entirely and heading straight to his place. Almost.

On our way to Sweet Scoops, the sound of a public piano under the gazebo stopped us. The pianist's fingers danced through a lively melody, drawing a small crowd.

"That's James Booker's take on *Sunny Side of the Street,*"

Grayson said, coming to a stop. "It's a tricky piece, but he's pulling it off."

"Listen to you, Mr. Jazz Man. Didn't peg you as a lover of old standards."

Grayson's expression softened. "Booker's arrangements are like a Rubik's Cube of chords and trills. When I was a kid, I tried learning this, but it was way beyond my abilities. Dad insisted piano was a waste of time—if I'd never reach Carnegie Hall, what was the point? Mom said music was about joy, not perfection, but Dad's opinion always ruled."

The music wrapped around us, each note like a dusting of joy in the air. The man, probably in his fifties, seemed lost in his own world. A small crowd began to gather, drawn in by his impromptu concert.

Grayson gestured toward the pianist, admiration softening his voice. "Chance would've loved this. He always said art wasn't about impressing others—it was about finding yourself." He turned to me, eyes thoughtful. "We could all learn from that."

For a while, we let the music wash over us, enjoying a rare moment of quiet and contentment. When the last note ended, the crowd broke into applause. The pianist glanced up with a grateful grin.

Grayson's hand tightened around mine, and I savored the lingering chords and the warmth of his touch. Ice cream. A lazy weekend. Maybe a massage. It was enough to carry us through the heavier days ahead.

"Thanks, everyone!" the pianist called over the applause, transitioning to another tune.

I tugged Grayson gently toward the ice cream shop. "So, about that massage," I said, grinning. "Shall we head for dessert first?"

"Whatever you say," he murmured, leaning in for a quick kiss on my cheek. "But I have one condition: the Chocolate Decadence gets split fifty-fifty."

Later that evening, after we finished dinner at his place,

Grayson retreated to his spare room, giving me a moment to check work emails. Andrew's message popped up first—someone from MedcoVax had contacted him, and he wasn't sure how to respond. I told him we'd handle it Monday and come to a decision together. Pete messaged me next, confirming no data was lost in that odd server glitch, but he planned to run more tests.

Then my mail app highlighted a message from Dad, nudging me with "Do you want to follow up?" My stomach twisted. I opened the thread and realized I'd rather draft a note to her than face him directly. It felt easier, somehow, to reach out to the sister I'd never met rather than the father who'd let me down so many times.

The words came surprisingly fast—a brief introduction and a gentle invitation to connect. Nothing final, just a draft. After rereading it, I exhaled, saved the message, and closed my phone. Baby steps.

I set my phone aside. No more obsessing tonight—I was here with Grayson. A faint melody led me to the spare room he jokingly called "the studio."

I found him hunched over a keyboard in the dim light, wrestling with a jazzy riff from *Sunny Side of the Street*. The tune sputtered, fell out-of-rhythm, and died in a flat chord.

"Come on, Booker," he muttered, trying again. Another rogue note made him stop.

I cleared my throat softly so I wouldn't startle him. He turned, looking a bit sheepish.

"Sorry—didn't mean to sneak up on you," I said.

"Guess I was too busy butchering James Booker." He gave a crooked grin, half embarrassed, half relieved.

I gestured to the spare chair he'd pulled closer. "Mind if I listen? I promise no critiques."

He exhaled, nodding. "Sure. But it's still rough—like wrestling an octopus."

I settled in, my gaze on his hands as he cautiously started

again. The Booker-style progression unfolded, syncopations popping in and out. He stumbled once, paused to recalibrate, then kept going. Even with the slips, the raw passion behind each chord was impossible to miss.

When he finished, the final note lingered, sweet despite its imperfection.

"That sounded great," I said, warmth rising in my chest.

He laughed softly. "Liar. I'm not at Booker's level, but it feels good to try. The mistakes don't crush me anymore."

I rested my hand gently over his on the keys. "Maybe that's because you've decided it's okay to love something just for its own sake."

He glanced at our hands, then at me, eyes reflecting the lamplight. "It's weird how we work ourselves to the bone but never make time for what sets our souls on fire. Not that cancer research doesn't fire me up, because it does."

I nodded. "I get it. We're more than labs and deadlines. And for the record, I'm enjoying this side of you."

His fingers threaded through mine. "Thanks for putting up with my not-quite-Carnegie-Hall practice. You won't add this to our 'romance spreadsheet,' will you?"

I grinned. "Nope. This one's off the books—just for us."

A comfortable hush filled the room, broken only by the distant hum of passing cars. Finally, Grayson swiveled to face me.

"I'm still determined to crack Booker, but I do have a couple of pieces I can actually play start-to-finish—ones I don't totally fumble." He looked at me, hopeful. "Maybe tomorrow, I'll show off something that won't make you cringe."

"I'd love that."

He reached over and flicked off the keyboard, its faint hum fading into silence. Then he turned to me, a small, contented smile tracing his lips.

"For now," he said softly, "I'd rather end the night on a good note."

"With me?" I teased, rising from my chair.

He stood, closing the distance between us. In the lamplight, we lingered, breathing in each other's closeness—one step, one note, at a time.

21

DAD-SPLAINING

> Me: Hypothetically, if I burned garlic bread to a crisp while trying to impress Courtney, what would you suggest?

> Kincaid: Store-bought baguette and garlic butter. No one has to know.

> Me: Genius. Hypothetically, can I also blame the oven?

> Kincaid: Always. Ovens can't defend themselves.

"Carter, I swear, understanding this piece is like trying to untangle Christmas lights—what's the secret sauce?" I quipped during our virtual piano lesson.

He chuckled. "Chopin's secret sauce? It's not about the lights in themselves, but the shadows they cast. Let's hear what you've got."

My fingers hovered over the keys, poised like a diver at the edge of a board. This *Prelude in E Minor* had become my nemesis,

166

demanding more than technical prowess. I played through it, aware something was missing.

Carter's voice cut in. "Hold on. You're hitting the notes, but there's no breath. This piece isn't a sprint—it's a confession. Every pause, every dynamic shift, should feel like a sigh or a memory."

I paused, realizing I'd been solving a puzzle rather than telling a story. Carter demonstrated, each note suspended in a hush that spoke as loudly as the melody. The spaces weren't dead air; they were oxygen, giving the music a heartbeat.

Adjusting my approach, I coaxed the notes rather than forcing them. It finally clicked. This was what Courtney kept telling me— slow down, let life breathe. Taking time off for Mara's wedding had reminded me that the rests in life are as important as the action. Maybe breakthroughs only happen when we stop forcing them.

Those moments of hush weren't just in music, they shaped my days, too: a quiet Sunday morning, the electrifying seconds before Courtney and I first kissed. Letting the silence speak made the tune—and my life—feel richer.

When we finished, I thanked Carter and ended the call. My next mission: prepare for Courtney's arrival. A week apart felt like forever.

My home office—cozy but cluttered—became ground zero. I tucked away rogue papers, cleared half-written notes from the desk, and lit a sandalwood candle. Its subtle glow helped transform the chaos into something more welcoming.

In the kitchen, I frowned at my wine selection. Red or white? I couldn't decide, so I set out both, complete with glasses, on the island. The clock nudged me, raising my pulse. She'd be here soon.

Tonight was about letting her see more of who I really was— not just the bullet points on my CV. I reminded myself that each awkward note or pause was a step forward, not a stumble.

I assembled a cheese plate for the living room, the lamp in the corner casting a soft glow over the space. Why was I so on edge?

"Come on, Grayson," I muttered. "You've lectured halls filled with future Einsteins as well as future dropouts. You can play a little piano for one special woman."

My gaze caught a binder of lecture notes from years ago now standing neatly on a shelf I'd installed, and I drifted back to my first day teaching. I'd over-prepared to the point of scripting my jokes, convinced I needed absolute control. Then a student raised a hand, asked something off-script—and I improvised. Right there, I felt the classroom shift from a monologue to a conversation. It was magic. And all I'd done was let myself breathe in the moment.

A buzzing phone pulled me back. Dad. He rarely called outside business hours, so my heart kicked up.

"Hey, Dad. Everything okay?"

"Why wouldn't it be?" His rhetorical lilt instantly put me on alert.

Conversations with Dad were like verbal gymnastics, always leaving me off-balance. "Just surprised you're calling at the start of the weekend, that's all."

A knock at my front door saved me from dwelling on my irritation. Courtney stood there, radiant. I mouthed, *My dad*. She nodded, sliding inside with a supportive smile.

Dad continued, "Weekends might be leisure for most, but you could be burning the midnight oil on your next groundbreaking paper. Unless you've already pivoted and neglected to inform me?"

A flicker of annoyance tightened my grip on the phone. "Actually, I was about to play piano. For a guest."

"You? Piano?" He scoffed as if I'd joined a traveling circus. "Don't let it distract you from real work. If you lose focus, you'll never find your next research direction. Perhaps this explains why you're stalled. You'll never get anywhere if you don't stay laser focused."

His words oozed a specific kind of condescension that should have its own entry in the dictionary, under "Dad-splaining." My jaw clenched. Courtney's gentle touch on my arm grounded me. "Dad," I said evenly, "I'm capable of balancing more than one passion."

Courtney lightly brushed her fingers against my arm, her calm assurance anchoring me.

And suddenly, it hit me—were these insecurities even mine? Or had Dad planted them long ago? The thought settled like a revelation. So much of the pressure I felt wasn't self-inflicted; it was inherited.

"Don't get too comfortable," Dad pressed. "Distractions are steppingstones to mediocrity. Have you even identified a direction for your research yet? Focus is key, now more than ever. You can't risk falling behind in such a ruthlessly competitive field."

His words stung, but they also sparked a memory of a similar remark he'd said weeks ago about the biotech industry's cutthroat nature. "Dad, I've been managing my career pretty well on my own," I said firmly. "I don't need a lecture."

"Don't you?" he pressed, his voice heavy with implication. "Do you really want to follow the same path as your sisters? Mara with her 'quaint' comic book shop that nearly derailed her career, and Rachael and Aubrey off living *la dolce vita* on stage instead of settling into real lives and doing something that matters? Saving lives? Be careful you don't catch their careless ways."

I froze, disbelief washing over me. His words landed like an uninvited guest, their impact louder than anything else in the room. Courtney's hand tightened slightly on my arm. She didn't say a word, but her silent support nudged me forward.

I had to take a stand, not just in defending myself but also my siblings, whose achievements he'd just trivialized. "Dad, do you even hear yourself? Rachael is a shining star on Broadway, Aubrey is a member of the Houston Ballet, and Mara's built a successful video game company. Even Chance left behind a legacy —a thriving store and a graphic novel that's about to become a film. None of us followed your playbook, but we're still thriving. Maybe it's time you adjusted your definition of success."

A pause on the line. "I—Grayson, I—"

"Look, success isn't a one-size-fits-all formula. I'm proud of where I am, and I'm proud of my siblings. If you can't be proud too, then that's on you, not us."

I ended the call, letting the weight of the moment settle.

When I turned, Courtney's warm smile met me. Her presence eased the tension, and for the first time in what felt like forever, I allowed myself to breathe.

GRAYSON UNPLUGGED

COURTNEY

Grayson looked as if he'd gone twelve rounds against a foe who knew every one of his weak spots. The tension in his jaw and furrowed brow said his dad's words had landed hard, yet I caught a flicker in his eyes—relief, maybe, or determination. I tightened my grip on his arm, wanting him to feel I was there, fully on his side.

"That was tough." I met his gaze. "But standing up for your sisters and Chance like that? Incredible."

He exhaled, tension draining from his shoulders. "Thanks. After another round of Dad's critiques, I needed to say it."

I brushed my fingers over his arm, offering a small smile. "We don't have to follow the scripts our parents hand us. You're not just a character in one of Ford's movies—you're in charge of your own life."

A thoughtful glint lit his eyes. "It hit me mid-call. Most of these anxieties… they're not even mine. Dad's fears have been echoing in my head for years."

"Like you've been singing his song," I said quietly. "But now you're finding your own lyrics. I never had the weight of parental expectations, but I can see how hard it's been when it's disguised as love."

He nodded. "Exactly. I'm done carrying his baggage."

"I like the sound of that." I grinned. "Front-row seat when you unveil the new Grayson?"

His smile turned mischievous. "Speaking of front-row seats, are you ready for that personal mini-concert I promised?"

I feigned shock. "My private concert? Does that come with a backstage pass?"

"Complete with VIP treatment." He led me to the "studio," a keyboard against the wall of his office lit by sandalwood candles. "Welcome to Grayson's Recital," he said with an exaggerated flourish.

I settled into the desk chair, eyeing the wine. "Scented candles and two bottles? Who knew you were such a romantic?"

"Your choice, leading lady—red or white?"

"White," I said, flashing a grin. "Simple yet sophisticated."

He laughed, pouring me a glass. "White it is. Cheers to taking a breath."

As his hands moved over the keys, the room filled with the rich, haunting notes of Chopin's *Prelude in E Minor*. I was spellbound. Each pause, each deliberate movement, felt like a conversation between him and the music. When he reached a tricky section, I saw his focus sharpen, his breathing slow, and his expression soften. It was mesmerizing.

When the final note faded, I broke into a smile. "That was incredible—so emotional. Hard to believe you came back to this so recently. You're practically a musical genius."

He stood, collecting his glass with a modest laugh. "Genius might be pushing it, but getting back to music feels like reconnecting with a part of myself I'd forgotten. Carter, says the pauses are as important as the notes. He started drilling that into me, and I think it's finally sinking in."

I followed him to the living room, sinking onto the sectional.

The lamp's warm glow made everything feel cozy. I nibbled a piece of cheddar, sipping my wine.

"So, next weekend—chocolate soufflé?" he asked, breaking a comfortable silence. "Time to step up our baking game."

"From cookies and smashed cakes to soufflés. You'll be my sous-chef, right?"

He pretended to consider. "I should probably brush up on my emergency cake-catching skills. I vow to protect the soufflé at all costs."

I laughed, leaning into him. "After our last misadventure, I think it's only fair to keep you away from smashing activities. You can still be the official taste tester—just in case."

His arm curled around me. "Deal. Taste tester, emergency helper, whatever you need."

The soft hush between us felt charged, like we both recognized something shifting.

"Grayson..." I murmured, turning toward him.

His head tilted, voice quiet. "Yes, Chef?"

I closed the space between us, brushing my lips to his. In that moment, all the noise around us faded—leaving only the warmth we shared, and the promise of what came next.

23

A DEEPER CONNECTION

Grayson

Courtney tilted her face up to mine, her green eyes pulling me in until the world shrank to just us. Her lips brushed mine, soft and teasing, sending a spark through every nerve. The kiss deepened, a slow burn we'd been building toward all night. I wanted more—wanted to sweep her off her feet, carry her to the bedroom, and let the rest of the world disappear.

And why wasn't I doing just that?

Grinning, I pulled her onto my lap so she was straddling me, then stood.

She emitted a surprised giggle, hastily kicking off her shoes, which landed with soft thumps on the floor, and then secured her ankles behind my back. "Grayson, what are you up to?"

"I'm taking you to my room to have my way with you, m'lady."

She tossed her head back and laughed. "Then get on with it, my good sir. This lady is eager to be had."

I didn't need more encouragement than that. A moment later, I tossed her on my bed, her auburn hair a trail of fire against the charcoal-gray coverlet. As I stripped off my shirt, she propped herself up on her elbows to take me in, her appreciative gaze

174

trailing down my chest. I paused with my hands on my belt buckle, simply taking her in.

She raised one eyebrow. "Get on with it, Professor Stellar. You mentioned having your way with me a moment ago. That's a promise in my book, and I plan to hold you to it."

"Your wish is my command, m'lady." I stripped, my cock springing free, and the look of delighted appreciation on Courtney's face made me go even harder. "Your turn," I said, pulling her to her feet.

We both quickly removed her clothing. Once she was completely naked, she pressed her entire body against mine, all softness and curves. Velvety skin and heat. This woman drove me wild with want and need. We touched, kissed. In a mere heartbeat, we were both on fire. My brain stopped working and we were nothing but sensation. All hands and fingers and lips and tongues. All liquid and heat and passion and desire.

I pressed her against the wall by the door, and she let out a small groan of excitement and desire as she raised one leg and wrapped it around my waist, pulling my hardness closer so it pressed against her slick core.

"Reminds me of our first time," I said, pulling away slightly and trailing kisses down her neck. "Except we had a palm tree instead of a wall." I let out a shuddering sigh. I wanted this woman. Needed her. To be inside her would be glorious, but I didn't want to rush it. My goal tonight: to take my time with Courtney.

I grazed her mound with the back of my hand, knowing exactly how to drive her wild with a featherlight touch. She let out a whimper. "Grayson. Yes."

I kept my touch light, teasing, causing her to shudder in unmet need. "More, please," she managed to murmur as she reached down and pressed my hand more firmly against her.

I let out a soft laugh and complied, sliding a finger inside her. She was so incredibly wet. So ready for me. I used that molten liquid to coat her entrance as I carefully and meticulously drove her wild with my hand. She squirmed against the wall, panting and moaning.

"Now. I want you inside me, now." She grabbed hold of my cock, directing it exactly where she wanted it, and of course I did as she wanted, quickly and easily sliding inside her.

As I grabbed hold of her ass, pressing her against the wall, she lifted the other leg and wrapped it around my waist. I drove into her, and she sank onto my cock. We fit together perfectly, but in that moment, I remembered something crucial. I wasn't wearing a condom.

I didn't want to stop. Couldn't. But without a condom, I could only let things go so far. I'd have to keep myself reined in until I could manage to break away and get to the box in my nightstand.

Courtney arched her back in that moment, the back of her head pressed hard against the wall and her perfect breasts thrust toward me. She let out a moan as her pussy tightened around my cock and pulsed as wave after wave of pleasure coursed through her. It was all I could do to hold back and not join her as she crashed over that precipice of ecstasy, but babies weren't part of my life plan.

I took her in—losing herself in the moment. I couldn't help but revel in my own power. This incredible woman I'd fantasized about for years was currently wrapped around my cock, having the time of her life. This was a dream come true. A dream I hadn't believed would become a reality until—suddenly—it had. In one weekend on Turks and Caicos when we'd decided to give this thing between us a try.

Her eyelids fluttered. I recognized the signs after having been with her for weeks now. She was coming down from that amazing, orgasmic high of a moment ago.

She'd almost stopped breathing, but now those breaths came back hard and fast. Her heartbeat pulsed in her throat, fast and steady. A moment later, she opened her fathomless green eyes and I fell in, lost in those gorgeous depths.

"That was…unexpected," she declared, a smile dancing across

her lips. "And amazing." She lowered a foot to the floor, and I withdrew, steadying her as she stood in front of me and found her balance.

"Some of the best parts of life are," I said, recognizing a great truth even as I spoke it. "Ready for round two? I asked, drawing her over to the bed.

She gave a sexy smile that slayed me. "Always, with you."

Exactly the words I wanted to hear.

I hesitated. "Are you using any birth control? I didn't cum, but there's always a risk."

"I have an IUD, so we should be fine," she said, her tone reassuring. "But just to be safe, I'll take something as a backup."

Relieved, I pulled the box of condoms from the drawer and quickly sheathed myself. When I looked up, I found her kneeling on the bed with her backside to me, grinning saucily over her shoulder. The bedside lamp bathed her skin in a gentle, inviting glow that sent my pulse pounding.

"Oh, hell yeah," I said, moving to stand behind her. I slid my hands over her round hips, then reached around her and teased her wet pussy with my finger, flicking the nub as I nestled myself against her. She let out a moan of satisfaction as I slid inside, right back where I'd been only moments ago. I echoed her with a deep, guttural moan of my own.

She pressed her hips back against mine, grinding on me as I kept teasing and swirling with my fingers, driving her wild. She dug her hands into my charcoal-gray coverlet, holding tight as I drove into her, making her buck and moan and whimper with desire.

This. This moment with her. This connection. This was everything I'd been missing, needing, wanting in my life. Courtney, with her effervescence and intellectual fire and sexy surrender. Her understanding and compassion and level-headed logic. She was perfection.

I surrendered myself to the now. This gap in time. This space between the notes. This perfect silence of peace.

Finally, I felt her tighten around me again, and this time, I didn't need to hold back. I could let go without fear of consequences, ones I was certain neither of us wanted right now in our lives. As she came, so did I, pulsing with a liquid hot fire that tore through me.

The moment. The woman. Us. We were incendiary. I let go, releasing into her. Filling her. Filling us. Achieving our climaxes together.

My head exploded, and my entire world was us. This.

I finally blinked my eyes open, my hands still gripping her hips.

As soon as I released her, Courtney's knees gave out and she rolled onto her side, her head coming to rest on a pillow as she curled into a satiated ball of femininity.

After disposing of the condom and turning out the lights, I managed to move her under the covers and curled up behind her, my body wrapping around her as I held her against my chest.

She let out a sigh that morphed into a contented moan. "That was amazing," she breathed.

We lay there, entangled in one another, the world around us fading into a serene afterglow. I found myself tracing gentle patterns on her shoulder, each touch a silent acknowledgement of the depth of what we'd just shared. Her head was tucked under my chin, resting on my upper arm as I held her close, and I could feel the softness of her breath, rhythmic and soothing, in sync with my own slowing heartbeat.

Moonlight spilled through the curtains, bathing us in its soft luminescence. In this tranquil moment, words were unnecessary; the silence between us was filled with unspoken understanding and a shared sense of completeness.

I pressed a soft kiss to the top of her head. We stayed wrapped around each other, soaking in the shared warmth. Before long, sleep pulled us under, our tangled limbs promising more than just rest. Knowing us, we'd be ready for another round of lovemaking the moment we stirred in a few hours.

WHEN I WOKE UP, Courtney's alarm still hadn't pierced the silence. The faint scent of last night's sandalwood candle lingered, mingling with almond oil. For late October, the morning felt surprisingly warm, the ceiling fan lazily spinning overhead as though it, too, was reluctant to greet the day.

I rolled over, careful not to disturb her. Courtney lay there, skin still glowing from the massage, auburn curls a halo around her face. She looked serene, unburdened by last night's clash with my dad—or by our second round of very thorough appreciation.

Then the alarm kicked in: a cheery, instrumental *Bibbidi-Bobbidi-Boo*, the perfect embodiment of Courtney: playful, sweet, and unapologetically her.

She groaned, squeezing her eyes shut as though sheer willpower could silence the song. "Nooo," she mumbled, her voice thick with sleep. "I was having the best dream. My ridiculously hot, genius boyfriend played the piano for me, gave me mind-blowing orgasms, and finished with a massage. It was spectacular."

A grin stretched across my face. "He sounds like a keeper." I slid an arm beneath her and pulled her close.

She snuggled against me, her words muffled against my chest. "The best. Hope I don't wake up and realize it's too good to be true."

"Definitely a dream." I dropped a kiss to her forehead. "Because the real guy is just here to make you coffee and complain about the weather."

Her groggy laugh vibrated against me. "Mmm, you're not off to a bad start."

As I held her tighter, feeling the rhythm of her breath against me. If this was her version of a dream, I'd spend every day trying to make it her reality.

She giggled and snuggled closer. "Oh, my! Did my dream just

come true?" She wriggled against me, making my morning erection take notice.

"Care to make my dreams come true too?"

She slid her warm, firm hand around my shaft. "Is this for me?"

"All yours. No one else's."

She turned to face me. "That's good to know. That's one thing I refuse to share with anyone else."

I glided my hands down her back, then between us, teasing the cleft between her legs. Gently brushing back and forth as her breathing quickened, I had her trembling with desire in less than a minute. "Is this what you want?"

She gave a sigh of pleasure. "I want more. Grayson, I need you inside me."

Those words had me moving to sheathe myself in a condom. I nestled between her thighs and slid my fingers along her slippery cleft. I loved that about her. Always eager for me. Always longing for my touch.

Quickly putting on a condom, I eased my way inside her, slowly at first, then faster, harder, as her urgent hands on my back communicated her desire. I was tempted to draw out our lovemaking session the way we normally did, but we didn't have the luxury of time this morning. She had a schedule to keep if she wanted to arrive at the lab at seven-thirty sharp.

As I moved inside her, I slid my hand between us, pressing that tempting, erotic bud. I knew this would take her over the edge, and moments later, she found her bliss. With a deep thrust, I joined her and we both reached our pinnacle, shuddering a perfect release.

The shared rhythm of our labored breathing gradually slowed, the air around us thick with intimacy and the earthy scent of sex. My sheets had captured the warm aroma of almond oil, making our little bubble feel like a sanctuary.

A chuckle escaped Courtney's lips, warm and light, like the

first breeze of fall teasing the leaves. "I can't believe we were so fast." Her eyes sparkling with mischief.

I swept an errant auburn curl from her forehead, letting my fingers linger just long enough to earn a smile. "Making you late for work would be a crime against science. Possibly humanity. I'm not ready to be listed as an accomplice in the downfall of innovation."

"Priorities," she quipped, her voice a melody of humor and affection.

After she disappeared into the bathroom, I set about stripping the bed, the almond-scented sheets conjuring vivid flashes of last night. As she showered, I replaced them with fresh, crisp linens. Our laboratory of love—reset and ready for the next experiment.

Fifteen minutes later, Courtney emerged in a sleek, tailored dress that practically screamed "brilliant scientist." I placed a steaming omelet on the bar—ham, sautéed onions, and plenty of cheese.

"Breakfast of champions," I said with a grin.

She arched an eyebrow. "Or of scientific pioneers?"

"Why not both?" I handed her a thermal coffee mug. Its bold lettering read, "Caffeine: It's Elemental, My Dear Watson."

Her eyes lit up. "A portable lab assistant—always on task, always keeping my coffee warm."

I leaned in conspiratorially. "Speaking of experiments, want to join me for a dinner one tonight? Results may vary, but satisfaction's guaranteed."

She tapped her chin as if considering. "More 'welcome home, honey' vibes from Florence, or a 'smashed cake spectacular' repeat?"

"Why not both? A dash of spontaneity, a sprinkle of dessert—"

"And plenty of cleanup," she finished, laughing.

"Cleanup's half the fun," I teased. "You can't have chaos without chemistry."

She leaned in for a quick, espresso-shot kiss, then grabbed her coffee and headed for the door, heels echoing on the tile. As I watched her go, I realized this experiment of ours might be my greatest discovery yet.

24

THE CROSSROADS OF LOVE AND LAB COATS

COURTNEY

Navigating morning rush hour, I pulled into the lab's parking lot only slightly later than planned. Inside, the familiar scent of sterility and "mad scientist chic" greeted me. I set Grayson's punny thermal mug on my desk, where neon sticky notes and chocolate wrappers testified to my work-life balance—or lack thereof.

Mercy, Queen of Lab Snark, cast a withering glance my way. "Why do you look like a unicorn kissed you? It's offensive to the rest of us who've barely survived the morning."

I took a quick sip from the thermal mug serving as my shield. "Seven-thirty isn't exactly the crack of dawn."

Mercy adjusted her oversized glasses like she was prepping for a verbal duel. "Seven-thirty is the crack of dawn for anyone who doesn't face it with your level of cheer. Spill—what's your secret? Did you stumble on the elixir of eternal happiness in one of those test tubes?"

"Caffeine," I said solemnly, raising my mug. "Better than any elixir—though not quite unicorn-level."

She scribbled something on her notepad, the corners of her mouth quirking up. I glanced at the page, catching a cryptic

183

formula among the doodles, but Mercy flipped the paper before I could figure it out. Her skeptical glare softened, replaced by her signature smirk. "Coffee? No way. Pretty sure my unicorn theory is closer to the truth."

Laughter escaped me, letting her wit ease some of my tension. Mercy's humor was as much a part of my mornings as caffeine. Still, a tiny voice wondered why I was dodging her question. Grayson wasn't a secret, but tying him to my suspiciously good mood felt too much like confessing a crush.

Shaking off the thought, I threw on my white lab coat with a flourish. I had rapidly multiplying cancer cells awaiting my attention. "Alright, my little cellular miscreants. Let's dance."

Once I'd completed that task, I logged into the lab computer, spreadsheets and graphs bursting onto the screen in a swirl of data. With a detective's precision, I double-checked every label and culture. One mistake here could cost more than a cake missing baking soda—I refused to even consider it.

An hour later, the lab hummed with its usual symphony of machines and fans. Kitty and Andrew were busy with their own cultures as I found my groove, every motion—pipetting, labeling, analyzing—feeling like second nature.

Andrew caught my eye over the eyepiece of his microscope, brow arched in judgment. "You're humming again. It's unnerving."

I slid a fresh batch of cells under the lens. "Better than scowling at the universe."

Andrew chuckled, scribbling in his notebook. "Touché." Suddenly, he seemed to relax, his entire mood altering.

My thoughts drifted to a different performance—Grayson at the piano last night, fingers gliding over the keys like each note was a love letter. A smile tugged at my lips, momentarily hitching my pipetting rhythm. Distractions in the lab were like glitter: no place for them, and they made a mess of everything.

A gloved hand waved in front of my face. Mercy again. "Earth to Courtney. You spaced out. Was it the unicorn? Please say it was the unicorn."

I clinked the pipette into its stand as my grin surfaced. "No unicorns. Just thinking about how some people freak out about our work, like we're creating the next Jurassic Park."

Mercy snorted. "Please. My ex practically fled the country when he found out I worked with viruses. Men like that? Not worth the petri dishes they freak out over."

"I couldn't agree more," I said, thinking back to Stephan, the ex who'd run screaming the moment he saw a biohazard sticker.

As I moved to my station, I noticed Kitty darting between workbenches, her scuffed sneakers squeaking on the tile. She fumbled slightly with a pipette, but fatigue could fray anyone's nerves. "Everything okay?" I asked casually, glancing up from my own setup.

She nodded once, smile tight but polite. "Yeah, just tired. Stayed here too late last night."

Her tone was easy, and while I noted the tension in her movements, I didn't dwell on it. Everyone had off days, and mine had included enough caffeine-fueled blunders to sympathize. I let it go, refocusing on my task and the steady rhythm of pipetting.

Mercy adjusted her glasses with her trademark flair. "Alright, Courtney, time to spill. Why oncology? And don't act like it's just because you love petri dishes."

A quiet laugh slipped out while I labeled the last of my samples. "My grandmother. She passed away from ovarian cancer when I was in high school. Watching her suffer... it pushed me to fight back somehow."

The teasing glint in Mercy's eyes dimmed. "That's... actually kind of touching."

"Kind of?" I teased, trying to lighten the mood.

Andrew hovered near the PCR machine, his tone softer than usual when he chimed in. "Kitty's mom was diagnosed with breast cancer recently. Early stages, but it's still tough."

My gaze flicked toward Kitty, who was quietly measuring

reagents at the far workstation. Her head was bent low, and her focus looked unshakable. "I didn't know that," I said softly, my stomach tightening as I thought about how she'd worked late last night. That was a lot of stress.

Andrew nodded. "She hasn't talked much, but it's weighing on her."

Mercy cleared her throat, breaking the brief pause. "What about you, Andrew? Why oncology?"

He hesitated, then smiled faintly. "My older brother. Leukemia. It's why I switched to cancer research. It feels like... a way to keep fighting for him." He cleared his throat. "Left behind a wife and two kids. It's been tough on them."

Another beat of silence settled, the hum of equipment filling the gap as we all turned back to our tasks. Moments like these reminded us why we did this work—much bigger than charts and deadlines.

Kitty busied herself at the centrifuge, movements steady but almost too controlled. Andrew was right; she was wrestling with more than she let on. Weren't we all?

The rest of the day blurred past in data points and microscopic revelations. By the time I left for the day, I felt both exhilarated and exhausted. Yet driving to Grayson's place, the fatigue melted away, replaced by excitement.

I let myself in with the key he'd given me—a tiny, metal symbol of trust. Stepping inside to the aroma of something delicious and soft jazz in the background, I channeled my best *I Love Lucy*. "Gray-son, I'm home."

He appeared in the kitchen doorway, wineglass in hand and a smile bright enough to power half the city. "Ah, the prodigal scientist returns."

For the next few hours, we settled into a cozy bubble where work stress dissolved and laughter took over. I told him about Mercy's "unicorn glow" comment, and he recounted a debate with his students regarding the accuracy of the movie *The Martian*.

Being with him like this was why I made time for him—for us —in my life. He made everything better.

He cleared his throat, and when he spoke, a low, thoughtful rumble colored his voice. "Courtney... I have something important to share. Something... significant."

He paused for a beat, letting the hush settle around us, and I sensed he was working up to a leap he couldn't undo. "Go on. Spill the significant beans."

He held my gaze, his blue eyes locking on mine like he was decoding the universe—or at least me. "I'm not just falling for you, Courtney. I'm in freefall—no safety nets, no harness."

Time stopped. My heart skipped, then sprinted ahead like a sprinter at the starting gun. "I'm right there with you, in this freefall," I whispered, my voice softer than I'd intended. Saying it out loud felt like discovering a hidden variable that suddenly made my entire life equation click.

My phone buzzed, slicing through the moment like a dropped beaker. I pulled it from the couch cushion. The word "URGENT" flashed on the screen, followed by a message that hit me like a sucker punch: "Corporate espionage suspected—critical breach. Need your input ASAP."

Grayson's concern surfaced immediately. "Is something wrong?"

I stared at the screen as dread coiled in my chest. Years of work compromised? My throat tightened. "I need to read this."

Larry: Security breach involves key findings. Meet me here in 20 minutes. The security team locked down the building. Pete's on his way in.

MY FOCUS NARROWED as I started moving, already halfway off the sofa. Scenarios raced through my mind, each worse than the last. I didn't have time to process the emotional whiplash. This wasn't a crisis I could delegate. And yet, just as urgency pulled me toward the door, a sharp tug of longing made me pause.

Memories flickered—past relationships where my ambition had been seen as a rejection. A part of me braced for Grayson to object, to question why I had to leave after what we'd just shared.

"What can I do?" he asked, his voice steady and grounding, like an anchor.

Relief loosened the knot in my chest. Of course, Grayson wasn't like the others. His quiet acceptance reminded me that this wasn't a choice between him and my work—just terrible timing. Moments like these tested more than logistics; they tested our foundation.

Our eyes met, his calm dissolving any guilt. "Thank you." Two words carrying far more meaning than he probably realized.

Life wasn't a controlled experiment. Sometimes you had to trust your gut and hope for the best. This was a real-world test of our connection. Would this challenge strengthen us or expose cracks we couldn't see yet? A strange mix of dread and excitement swirled in me at the thought of finding out.

My phone buzzed again, jolting me back.

> Kincaid: Family dinner tomorrow night with Conner. He's finally starting to warm to Grayson. Lianna's making her famous lasagna. You two in?

The timing felt cruel. On one side, a cozy dinner promising laughter and warmth. On the other, a crisis threatening years of work. I exhaled slowly. "Kincaid wants us over for dinner tomorrow—Lianna's cooking, Conner will be there. I really want you to come, but this mess at work... I'm not sure I'll have the time or focus."

Grayson's smile dimmed, but only slightly. "This work crisis sounds serious, Court. It's probably best to postpone any family get-togethers."

His understanding twisted my heart. I wanted him in my world, laughing with Kincaid, trading sarcastic remarks with Conner, and bonding with Lianna. But this crisis loomed too large, swallowing everything else.

I grabbed my coat, guilt flickering with each step toward the door—not because I doubted my priorities, but because I could already see how this might play out over time. My work had always taken first place. Now I saw the weight that could put on someone who wanted more from me.

Still, our little bubble didn't burst. It wavered, but held. At the door, I checked him for signs of frustration; he stood there, quiet and composed.

"I get it," he said, his voice sure. "Don't worry about me. Go do what you have to do."

"Thank you." A small phrase wrapped in enormous feeling.

Stepping into the cool night air, I clung to his words. With Grayson, it wasn't about perfect execution or controlled outcomes. It was about embracing the mess, trusting the process, and figuring it out together. Somehow, life felt less like a problem to solve and more like something rich and imperfectly wonderful.

25

MUSIC AND SCIENCE

GRAYSON

> Me: Hypothetically, if I tried to make homemade pasta to take to Courtney and it turned into a sticky blob, what should I do?

> Kincaid: Dump the blob, order takeout, and pass it off as your own. Is this becoming a habit with you?

> Me: Switch out the takeout containers?

> Kincaid: That hides the evidence. Grayson, is there anything in your life that isn't hypothetical?

Alone again the following Thursday, I stepped into the quiet sanctuary of my home office. The familiar view of Oakland's rooftops through my window didn't feel as grounding as usual. Courtney had been burning the midnight oil at the lab all week, throwing herself into the security crisis with the single-minded intensity of Sherlock Holmes in a lab coat, determined to catch her own Moriarty.

I'd offered to bring her food, help her with internal audits, or even rub her feet if it meant easing her burden, but she'd waved me off with a grateful smile, insisting I'd be more of a distraction than a help. She wasn't wrong—Courtney's focus could cut glass when she was in problem-solving mode, and I admired that about her. Still, the days stretched on, and the unexpected pang of missing her began to creep in, a rookie sensation for someone who used to call solitude his "power hour."

Not that I could blame her. If I were in her shoes, I'd be running down every lead too. But knowing that didn't make the silence any easier.

Last night, I'd promised to bring her dinner. After ruining the meal and replacing it with restaurant fare, I'd carefully packed up everything and set out, only to get delayed an accident in the Fort Pitt Tunnel that left me marooned on the wrong side of Mount Washington for an hour. By the time I'd made it to her place, her car was already gone and the condo was dark. I'd left the food in her fridge with a note, a lost evening that only deepened the ache of wanting to do more.

I surveyed my cluttered desk—a battlefield of academia. Piles of research papers teetered precariously, and the blinking cursor on my laptop seemed to mock me like a cartoon villain. "Not tonight, you blinking menace," I muttered. "Tonight is about me-time."

My gaze shifted to the black-and-white keyboard against the far wall, its glossy surface winking at me like a seductress.

Sinking onto the piano bench, my fingers hovered over the keys. The cool, weighted feel of them was like a reset button for my soul. The lingering scent of sandalwood drifted through the room—a fragrant ghost of my impromptu concert for Courtney.

I began to play. The first notes of a simple melody flowed like water. The rhythm was grounding, each keypress like an exhale for my overworked brain.

But then my fingers started to wander, improvising beyond the sheet music. Carter, my piano instructor, had nudged me into exploring the unpredictable joy of riffing. It was freeing—like jumping into a conversation without rehearsing your lines. The patterns unfolded like mathematical progressions, each chord resolving into the next with a logic that felt both precise and creative. It was structure meeting spontaneity, a creative outlet I hadn't realized I craved.

As the melody twisted and turned, it began to reflect pieces of my life: taking a stand with my father, Ford's movie, my post-doc students, and then... a discordant note.

Joaquin.

My promising grad student had recently started interning at MedcoVax Pharmaceuticals—the same company where Courtney's academic nemesis from Florence had worked. My fingers froze mid-chord, my stomach tightening as unease coiled around my thoughts. What were the odds? Cue the suspense music.

I shook off my discord, refocusing on the keyboard. But the flow was gone, replaced by a jangling riff of anxiety. Joaquin was a rookie, bright-eyed and eager, but untested. I made a mental note to check in with him soon, just to make sure he wasn't wading into waters too deep for his boots.

For now, though, my focus returned to the keys, teasing out a new melody. It felt familiar, but not musically—more like the patterns in my research data. The rising harmonies and occasional dissonances mirrored the slippery puzzle I'd been coming back to for months, trying to corner a solution that always seemed one step ahead.

As the crescendo built, my thoughts aligned in a surprising flash of clarity. It hit me like the bass drop in a great song: music theory. Harmony and dissonance. Could I apply the same principles to my research?

I paused mid-note, my mind racing. Just as music had rules—chords that worked together and notes that created tension—cancer cells operated in patterns. They disrupted the harmony of their environment, creating cellular "dissonance."

What if I could map those patterns using bioinformatics, identifying the genetic and molecular "notes" that made cancer cells stand out? Like predicting a song's melody based on its structure, I might be able to forecast cancer cell behavior with unprecedented accuracy.

Eureka.

I hit the final note with dramatic flair, the sound ringing through the room like a victory bell. Leaping from the bench, I darted to my desk and opened my laptop. My fingers flew over the keyboard, adrenaline spiking as I translated the spark of an idea into something concrete. Algorithms, pattern recognition, predictive modeling—it was all there, waiting to be pieced together.

The model I envisioned wasn't just about crunching data. It was about finding the motifs—the cellular equivalents of a musical theme—that signaled a shift toward cancerous behavior. It was like composing a symphony, only this time, the goal was to rewrite the notes before the melody turned dark.

I leaned back, breathless, staring at my screen. My heart thudded a triumphant rhythm, the pieces clicking together with breathtaking precision. This was the breakthrough I'd been chasing—a way to predict cancer before it even started.

Still buzzing, I returned to the piano, my fingers striking a new melody, one lighter and freer, bubbling over with the joy of discovery. Music had always been my reset button, my translator when words fell short. And right now, it was the only way to express what was surging through me—excitement, relief, and a profound sense of *rightness.*

Halfway through, another thought struck me—a tweak to the algorithm that could refine the model further. I spun around, grabbed the nearest notepad, and scribbled furiously, diagrams and equations spilling across the page.

When I finally leaned back again, I couldn't help but grin. The puzzle pieces were clicking into place, and the picture they formed was breathtaking. This wasn't just a scientific breakthrough—it was a symphony, a harmony of logic and intuition coming together.

I turned back to the keyboard, and as the notes soared, my thoughts turned to Courtney. She was never far from my mind, but tonight, her presence felt especially vivid. She'd helped nudge me back to the keys, to remind me that music wasn't just a hobby —it was part of who I was. The idea, the spark, the melody… it all felt tied to her, like she'd unlocked something I hadn't even realized I'd lost.

The music trailed off, leaving the room in a gentle hush. I reached for my phone, eager to share the moment with her. But as I stared at the empty text screen, my thumbs hovered, the words tangling in my head. How do you capture a moment like this in a message? Science and music, discovery and joy—it felt too big for a simple text.

I ran my hand through my hair, glancing back at the piano keys as if they might help me find the right rhythm for my words. Music could say everything I couldn't, but this time, it was up to me to put it into words.

Okay. Just say it.

> Me: Hey Court! I just had the kind of aha moment that feels like I finally cracked a code. Can't wait to tell you all about it—it's like Einstein jamming with Mozart. Missing your smile and hoping your day's going great.

I hit send, my grin lingering as I leaned back, the energy still thrumming through me. The science gods had smiled, and so had the music. Tonight, for the first time in weeks, it felt like everything was in tune.

And I couldn't wait to share the harmony with her.

26

OF LOVE STORIES AND BOOK CLUB TALES

Courtney

The past two weeks had been a whirlwind—a blur of late-night calls, data dives, meetings with the IT department and the higher-ups, and the kind of exhaustion that clings to you like static. I'd spent hours combing through server logs searching for unauthorized activity, trying to pinpoint anomalies, coordinating with our IT team to tighten digital security, and holding tense meetings where every question seemed to echo with unspoken accusations. We'd implemented temporary measures—resetting passwords, enabling two-factor authentication for all team members, and increasing the overnight security presence at the lab—but nothing concrete had emerged to confirm the breach or its scope. I'd also spoken one-on-one with each of my team members, carefully framing it as a routine check-in, but more to gauge reactions and look for cracks in the façade. Everyone seemed just as baffled as I was.

Still, the gnawing uncertainty lingered. Ever since the security alert derailed my evening with Grayson, I'd been locked in a relentless search for answers. Every email from our main offices in San Francisco seemed to carry an unspoken warning: brace yourself. It was enough to leave me constantly on edge, caught between wanting to believe we were in the clear and fearing we were one step from catastrophe.

Tonight, though, I was determined to reclaim a slice of normalcy. Grayson and I had plans, and I was clinging to that like a lifeline. First, a quick stop at Sonya's in Sewickley for book club —a chance to catch my breath with friends before diving into what I hoped would be a relaxing evening with Grayson. Lately, our relationship felt like it existed in snippets—late-night texts, quick calls, missed connections, and fleeting visits. It wasn't enough, and I could feel the strain creeping in. A quiet voice in the back of my mind whispered: *how much longer can we hold on like this before something gives?*

My phone buzzed as I crossed the Sewickley Bridge, its surface glinting in the fading sunlight. A new email notification flashed across my dashboard screen, the sender's name hitting me like a weight in my chest: *Dad.*

As I drove down Sonya's street, fall leaves greeted me. I parked in front of her house, hesitating before opening the email. The words felt heavy, like they didn't want to be read.

Subject: *Adele*

Courtney,

I wanted to share this photo of Adele. She's been calling and asking questions about you. I told her you're busy with work, but she still hopes to meet you one day.

Also, I thought you should know Adele's mom and I are divorced. That's a long story for another time, but I don't see her very often.

Best Wishes,

Your Father

Attached was a photo: a bright-eyed girl with the same chin and eyes as me, her smile both warm and unfamiliar. My heart twisted. I hadn't expected to feel... this. The resemblance made her suddenly real in a way no email ever could, and the mention of the divorce left me unsettled. *Why now?*

When Dad had divorced my mom, I'd been at college, but Kincaid had been a senior in high school, and the change had been hardest for him. I wondered how Adele was handling it. Mom? She'd disappeared to the Florida Keys. I'd hear from her every Christmas when she sent a card.

I tucked my phone in my bag, shaking my head like it would clear the thoughts rattling around. Tonight wasn't the time to unpack this. Not here, not yet.

The picturesque charm of Sonya's neighborhood, with its stately Victorian homes and tidy rows of gardens, usually lifted my mood, especially during the fall with the trees in their glory. But tonight, it only reminded me of how far away I felt from that kind of settled life. Max and Sonya made it seem effortless—balancing work, family, and love with the kind of grace I couldn't imagine pulling off.

Inside, the familiar hum of voices greeted me, along with the rich aroma of something delicious wafting from the kitchen. "Courtney, you made it!" Sonya's voice rang out as I stepped inside, her face lighting up like I was the guest of honor.

"I was afraid I'd be late," I said, shedding my coat. "San Francisco kept me on a call until the last possible second. Security paranoia—it's never-ending."

Sonya handed me a glass of red wine, her expression a mix of sympathy and warmth. "Sounds like you need this more than anyone."

"You have no idea. This whole month's been a rollercoaster. I hit a research milestone, and then, bam—corporate espionage scare. It's been endless calls and barely any answers."

My sister-in-law, Lianna, glowing in her pregnancy, nodded sympathetically. "That sounds intense. Corporate espionage is no joke. One of our clients was hacked recently and had to pay a ransom. Scary stuff."

I raised my glass in a toast. "Here's to living on the edge of a data breach." Then added, "Brace yourselves, I've got even worse news."

A hush descended on the room, thick with anticipation.

With dramatic flair, I admitted, "I didn't read the book this month. Didn't even crack the cover."

Relief and laughter erupted around me. Gertrude fanned herself theatrically. "My heart, child! You can't spring news like that on someone my age. I'm seventy-nine, not twenty-nine!"

Lianna, still chuckling, waved me toward the sofa. "I usually wear the 'haven't read the book' crown. Thanks for stealing my thunder this time."

"I was so embarrassed I didn't read it that I almost didn't come," I admitted as I sat.

Sonya patted the spot next to her. "Well, I'm glad you're here. We've missed catching up with you—and hearing all the updates about you and Grayson. How are you two getting along?"

I forced a smile, feeling the warmth of their curiosity but also the faint sting of guilt. "We're great. He's incredible—smart, funny, and he can cook. What's not to love?"

Sonya swirled her wine, her gaze thoughtful. "Sounds like you've found a keeper. Meanwhile, I'm living in what I'm pretty sure is the pilot episode of a sitcom. Newlywed life, plus Kendra moving in, plus Emma and her rotating cast of friends constantly raiding the pantry—it's chaos, but the good kind. I gotta admit, I love it."

I grinned. "Sounds like you need a doormat that says 'Welcome to the Party.'"

Sonya chuckled, her earlier levity dimming. "Honestly, I love having Kendra here. She's a huge help. But then Dad contacted me, and... well, that threw me. We've been estranged from him for years, and now he suddenly wants to reconnect. I can't help worrying."

That hit home. *Déjà vu* much? Her words were a pebble dropped into a still pond, each ripple carrying truths I already sensed. I stayed quiet as she swirled her wine again, her gaze going distant. "Family doesn't always come back because they care. Sometimes it's because they want something."

The comment echoed my own fear, and I froze, my fingers tightening around the stem of my glass. Sonya's tone softened, but the wariness lingered in her expression.

"Especially when they suddenly pop back into your life," she added.

I mustered a neutral smile, deflecting with a quick joke. "Sounds like you've got stories, Sonya."

Her expression sharpened, a bitter edge creeping into her smile. "Don't we all? Some people will take as much as you're willing to give—and more."

Sonya moved on to another topic, but her words lingered in my mind, brushing uncomfortably close to truths I wasn't ready to face. I brushed it off, refusing to let it consume me. But Adele's face—her chin, her eyes, so much like my own—lingered like the after burn of a flash, leaving me with questions I wasn't ready to answer.

Mara's arrival sparked a flurry of chatter about her trip to Boston, but my thoughts kept wandering. Work stress and barely seeing Grayson these past two weeks weighed on me, an uneasy feeling creeping in that something had to give.

Before I could dwell further, Rose swept into the dining room, her energy as bright as her smile. "Hey, everyone! Sorry I'm late."

Sonya greeted her with mock sternness. "Perfect timing, Rose. We're about to dive into the book discussion."

As the group launched into conversation, my focus wavered. My father's email lingered in the back of my mind, mingling with the buzz of another message from San Francisco demanding my attention. I glanced at my phone, half-listening, until Lianna's gentle touch on my arm drew me back.

"Hey," she said softly, "want to lend me and Sonya a hand with dinner? It's almost ready."

Grateful for the distraction, I followed them into the kitchen, where the rich aroma of lasagna filled the air. Sonya, ever efficient, pulled the bubbling dish from the oven and slid in a tray of garlic bread. The room was warm and inviting, filled with cozy autumnal touches that made it feel like the perfect November evening.

Lianna closed her eyes and breathed deeply, a serene smile on her face. "This smells heavenly."

"You're eating for two, remember?" I teased. "How's the baby bump treating you?"

She beamed, resting a hand on her belly. "Wonderful. We had a check-up yesterday—everything's perfect."

I grinned. "Is my brother keeping up? Just say the word, and I'll remind him who's really in charge."

Lianna laughed, her joy palpable. "Kincaid's been amazing. It's so comforting having him beside me every night. And work's slowed down now that my project's in a new phase."

Her words sparked a quiet ache—a longing for the kind of steady connection she described. That deep, day-in-and-day-out bond I wasn't sure I'd ever let myself hope for.

We turned Sonya's kitchen into a carb-lover's paradise, piling plates with steaming lasagna and slices of garlic bread. The delicious smells drew everyone in like a beacon, and soon we were seated around the dining table, the conversation flowing as freely as the wine. I found it hard to keep up with the chatter about the book.

I found myself half-listening, my thoughts drifting to Grayson. The promise of seeing him later tugged at my attention like a magnet. My mind flitted between the demands of my work and the growing need to reconnect with him. The tension in my shoulders eased slightly at the thought of being in his arms again, even if just for a few stolen hours.

When we were done, I helped clear the table, the kitchen humming with the sounds of laughter and dishes clinking. My hands moved on autopilot while my brain replayed snippets of imagined conversations with Grayson. What would we talk about? Should I tell show him Adele's photo? Get his opinion? Or did we already have enough drama with the security scare? Maybe tonight we could finally relax and enjoy a quiet evening together without interruptions.

Mara joined me at the sink, drying dishes with her usual flair. She glanced at me out of the corner of her eye, her tone light but probing. "You've been a little off tonight. What's going on? Is it the work stuff?"

I hesitated, my fingers tightening on the edge of a plate. "That, plus something extra," I admitted, then exhaled. "He emailed me. After twelve years. Out of nowhere."

Mara stopped mid-dry, startled. "Who? Your father?"

I nodded, my voice tighter than I intended. "Yeah. And it wasn't to apologize. He wants me to meet someone—his daughter. My half-sister."

Mara's brow furrowed as she set the towel down. "That's... a lot." She paused, choosing her words carefully. "You don't have to let him back in, you know."

I looked down, fiddling with the edge of the dish towel. "It's not about him. It's her. She didn't ask for this estrangement any more than I did."

Mara leaned against the counter, her gaze steady and soft. "And now you feel responsible."

My voice cracked just slightly, betraying the emotion I'd been trying to swallow all night. "I don't know what I feel. Maybe rejected. Like she got the best of him—what he couldn't give me and my brothers."

Mara reached out, her hand covering mine in a firm but gentle grip. "That's not on you, Courtney. You don't owe anyone more than you're ready to give. But... maybe this half-sister of yours changes things. Maybe it's okay to feel something about her, while still keeping him at a distance."

Her words landed softly, like a reassuring nudge in the right direction. I forced a small smile, feeling a bit lighter but still sorting through the jumble of emotions. "Thanks, Mara. I needed to hear that."

She squeezed my hand one last time before returning to the dishes, her voice lightening again. "Anytime. And if you ever decide to throw a welcome-to-the-family party, I'll bring the wine."

I laughed despite myself, the tension in my chest loosening just a fraction. "She's twelve, so make it soda instead." Maybe she was right. Maybe it was okay to feel something about Adele. Just... not tonight.

My phone buzzed with an incoming call and I glanced at the screen, bracing myself for yet another work problem, but relief swept over me when I saw Grayson's name.

"Grayson. Hi!" I said, my voice coming out a little too bright.

"Hey. Got a minute?"

I glanced at Sonya and Lianna, both absorbed in their conversation at the sink. "Of course. Just tidying up here at Sonya's, but I'll be heading out soon. Can't wait to see you tonight," I added, forcing a smile into my tone.

But his next words made my stomach twist. "There's something we need to talk about. I'll be at your place soon."

The ripple of unease that followed felt too familiar, like the moment before a beaker tips off the edge of a lab bench. "Everything okay?" I asked, my voice tightening with worry.

Grayson let out a soft sigh, a sound that only made the knot in my stomach tighten. "No, it's nothing bad. I just... I really miss you."

His words landed like a sharp tug at an already fraying thread. And there it was—the other shoe, dropping right on cue. Guilt flared hot and insistent, but it wasn't new. I'd been bracing for this moment, knowing how little time we'd had together and how stretched thin I'd been. He wasn't saying anything I hadn't already told myself, but hearing it out loud made it feel more real, more precarious. How much longer could I keep asking him to wait before the thread snapped?

"Me too. Let's sit down tonight," I said, trying to sound optimistic. "Maybe we can go over our schedules or something. Make a plan. I know I have that trip, but after that things should get better." I hoped.

As soon as the call ended, my gaze landed on his text I'd all but forgotten about from earlier in the week. Grayson's break-through—the moment he'd poured his excitement into a message I'd barely registered. My stomach twisted as the memory hit. I'd been so buried in lab drama that my response had been lukewarm at best: a quick "congrats-that's-great" text. That scored about a one out of ten on the girlfriend scale. Maybe zero.

What kind of partner does that? The question pressed against my chest, an uncomfortable weight growing heavier with each breath. Grayson deserved someone who could match his enthusi-asm, someone present—not someone always playing catch-up or too distracted by her own chaos to celebrate his breakthroughs.

Lianna's voice cut through my spiraling thoughts. "What's up, Buttercup? You've gone from smiling to storm-cloud in record time."

I forced a laugh, weak and unconvincing. "Just realizing how tricky it is to juggle work and romance."

Lianna's eyes softened, but her words were firm. "It's not easy," she said, wiping her hands on a dish towel. "But the right person is worth the effort. Don't fall into the trap of thinking you'll have time later. Sometimes later never comes." Her voice wavered, and she added with a sheepish laugh, "Sorry. Pregnancy hormones. I get emotional about everything these days."

Her words struck a nerve I wasn't ready to face. My dad had always promised "later," too. Later had turned into years of missed games, unfinished puzzles, and cold family dinners. I'd spent my childhood waiting for something more than "quality time"—whatever that even meant. And now, here I was, offering Grayson the same empty promises.

The realization gnawed at me. Was I doing to Grayson what my dad had done to us? Offering him scraps of my attention while I poured the best of me into my work, convincing myself he'd wait forever?

Lianna gave me a knowing look, her voice softer this time. "If you're serious about him, don't let work rule you. Life's too short to leave the people you love waiting."

Her advice lingered, stirring guilt instead of clarity. Was I even capable of that kind of balance? My work wasn't just a job; it was a part of me. How could I make room for someone else without losing myself in the process?

The crisp November breeze whispered against the windows, soothing and unsettling all at once. My thoughts turned to Grayson's words: *"There's something we need to talk about."* The knot in my stomach tightened. What if tonight wasn't about making plans or finding balance? What if this was the beginning of the end?

As I pulled on my coat and stepped into the cool night air, the chill pricked my skin—a reminder of the choices looming ahead. Life didn't wait. And tonight, neither would Grayson.

2 7

A PROPOSITION

GRAYSON

Two hours earlier

The cool autumn air nipped at my face as I stepped out of the Biology building at six sharp, heading for my meeting with Ford. The scent of damp leaves and the faint glow of streetlights meant fall was here in full force, bringing fleeting thoughts of thanksgiving and pumpkin pie. Would Courtney and I spend the holiday together, juggling meals with both our families? I could only hope.

Even our attempts to steal moments together these past few couple of weeks had become minor logistical triumphs. I'd driven out to her place last Friday, only to find she'd been called back to the lab before I arrived. She'd sent me a quick text—*Sorry-have to go back to work. Miss you! Eat the tiramisu!*—but the absence of her smile stung more than I cared to admit. And just yesterday, we'd tried to meet for coffee in Oakland, only to have a last-minute meeting with her boss derail our plans.

Still, I smiled at the thought of seeing her tonight. One quiet evening together wasn't much to ask, was it?

My phone buzzed, its old-fashioned ringtone slicing through

the quiet. I grabbed it, hoping it was Courtney. Instead, Ford's name lit the screen.

"Hey, Ford. Sorry for the radio silence. It's been a hectic day."

"Glad I caught you. We're having a problem on set, and I'll need to cancel tonight. I still need your okay on those scenes, though, so we'll have to reschedule."

Frustration slowed my steps. Courtney and I had coordinated this evening around this meeting and her book club. If he'd cancelled sooner, she and I could've spent more time together.

"Alright," I said, masking my irritation. "Let's aim for tomorrow evening?" Although, even the best-laid plans could unravel.

"Thanks, Grayson. Our film editor's on edge, so the sooner, the better."

The call ended, leaving me standing in the chill, missing Courtney. The memory of her head resting against my shoulder, the warmth of her arms around me—those simple joys felt frustratingly out of reach.

All work and no Courtney, I thought, *is turning me into one hell of a dull boy.*

I'd head home first, then drive to Courtney's place. Too bad she lived so far away. How much were our commutes costing us —time we could never get back?

Stuck in the slow crawl of cars during rush hour, my thoughts ran at a marathon pace, leading me to a sudden realization: we had meticulously measured every aspect of our relationship, yet we had never considered the tangible cost of our commutes. What was the true toll, in time and emotion, of the *physical* distance between us?

In my home office, I opened my notes app and stared at the relationship metrics Courtney and I had started tracking as a joke. A new column, "Commute Time," tugged at me. I added the hours lost to traffic as well as the missed connections, each entry highlighting moments we could've spent together. Moments like the excitement of my breakthrough or the night Courtney had called to say her research was intact—moments better shared in person.

The more recent gaps in the data—gaps when we hadn't seen each other—felt like glaring voids. On a whim, I changed the data points into hearts. Cheesy? Maybe. But the image struck me: the rising pattern of hearts showed how strong we were, yet these recent empty gaps loomed, demanding to be filled.

A solution crystallized in my mind. *We needed to live together.*

I reached for my phone, my heart quickening. "Hey," I said when she picked up.

"Can't wait to see you tonight" she replied, her words mirroring my own thoughts.

"I'll be at your place soon. There's something we need to talk about."

As I ended the call, a flicker of excitement bubbled up in my chest. I hit print on the heart-filled chart, watching it emerge from the printer before carefully sliding it into a folder. I could already picture Courtney's reaction—sharp wit first, maybe, but followed by that rare, unguarded smile I couldn't get enough of.

On the drive over, I sat at a red light, tapping my thumb on the wheel when a text message buzzed from the dash. I glanced over, and my pulse jumped. Courtney?.

> Dad: Saw your article in The Lancet. Your work's good, Grayson. Always knew you'd get there.

I blinked at the words, waiting for his second text to drop. The one where he'd point out where I could've improved or launch into a speech about legacy and expectations. But nothing else came. Just the unadorned acknowledgment.

It wasn't an apology. It wasn't even close to a real conversation. But it was… something. A step—small, wobbly, but in the right direction.

I exhaled, long and slow, pocketing the phone. The knot that usually tightened in my chest after anything involving him wasn't there this time. Instead, I felt... lighter. Like I'd finally started to shift the weight I'd been carrying for far too long.

The light turned green, and I eased forward, the folder secure on the passenger seat. By the time I pulled into Courtney's neighborhood, the thought had settled: progress didn't have to be perfect to count. My father could keep his quiet compliments and grudging approval. I had bigger things to fight for now, and for the first time in a long time, I felt like I might actually win.

When I pulled up to her townhouse, she was stepping out of her car, still in her work clothes. She fumbled with her keys, dropping them and scooping them back up. The glow of the porch light gave her an almost ethereal look, but her usual spark seemed dulled, her shoulders heavy with a weariness I hadn't heard in her voice.

She waited for me as I approached, and I couldn't resist pulling her into my arms. For a moment, we simply held each other, our breaths syncing as the tension of the past two weeks melted away. When her lips met mine, it was like rediscovering something precious.

"Come in," she whispered, her voice soft and tired.

Inside, she filled two glasses of water and handed me one, her movements efficient but tinged with exhaustion. I downed a sip, too eager to wait. "I've been looking at the data," I began, flipping open the folder.

I'll confess, my focus was all over the place. My head was buzzing with all these conclusions I'd come to, but somehow, I completely missed Courtney's growing anxiety. I guess I was too caught up in my own whirlwind of excitement, which was fizzing inside me like an overenthusiastic champagne toast.

"The data?" Her brow furrowed as she took the papers. The folder slipped slightly in her grip, and when her gaze rose to mine, uncertainty clouded her eyes. "Is this about our relationship metrics?"

"Yes," I said quickly, realizing I'd skipped the preamble. "I crunched some numbers and found something important. See, all our relationship indicators are up—except for these recent gaps—"

"Wait." She cut me off, her voice tight. "Are you saying... are we breaking up? Is this not working out?"

Breaking up? Her words hit like a gut punch—I'd fumbled this so badly that she thought I was ending things. How had I turned a solution into a problem? Panic surged through me, and I scrambled for the right words.

"No!" I said, setting the folder aside and reaching for her hands. "It's the opposite. Everything else about us is amazing. But the commute? It's the only real issue, and I think I've found a solution."

Her brow remained furrowed, her hands trembling slightly in mine. "What kind of solution?"

"What if we moved in together?" I asked, my voice softening. "A place halfway for both of us. Somewhere fresh. Your townhouse is noisy, and you haven't even finished unpacking from your last move. You've said you don't love it here."

She froze, her lips parting as if she wanted to say something but couldn't find the words. Had I asked for too much, too soon?

"Grayson, I can't think about something this big right now," she finally said. "I'm stretched thin, and the idea of making another huge change in my life..." She trailed off, shaking her head. "It's overwhelming."

Silence stretched between us, each ticking second amplifying my anxiety. I'd hoped this would bring us closer together, but now I wondered if I'd made a tone-deaf move that was pushing us further apart.

Disappointment settled over me, heavy and unwelcome. "Of course. We can table it for now."

Her arms encircled me, her embrace weary but warm. "Please don't see this as rejection. I just... I need time to process."

Her words stung, a reminder of the distance between intention and impact. I nodded, kissing her forehead gently. "Let's get some rest," I murmured. "Maybe a glass of wine? A massage?"

She clung tighter, her head burrowing into my chest. "You're the best. That sounds perfect."

Later, as we lay in bed together, the room blanketed in silence, my thoughts churned. Had I misjudged what she needed? My excitement had blinded me to her exhaustion, and now regret filled the silence between us, a progression of missteps I didn't know how to rewrite. I just hoped we'd find our rhythm again before the gaps became too wide to bridge.

I wanted more with her—more time, more connection—but for now, I'd have to accept the spaces between us, hoping the next notes would bring us closer rather than leave our melody unfinished.

CONFRONTING THE PAST

COURTNEY

My alarm's chirping shattered my dreams of becoming the first scientist to discover a sleep-through-your-alarm gene. Groaning, I groped for my phone, dreading the usual flood of red-flag emails. Instead, my inbox was blessedly quiet, except for a text from Grayson that managed to be both sweet and vaguely stalkerish.

> Grayson: Woke up early and watched you sleep —but not in a creepy way 😄. You looked so peaceful, I couldn't bear to wake you. Off to an early department meeting. Catch you later. 😘

Memories of last night's "let's move in together" conversation jolted me awake faster than any alarm. Sure, life with Grayson was a dream, but the thought of merging households was drama on a soap opera scale. I was already maxed out emotionally, and jumping into cohabitation would require processing power I just didn't have at the moment.

This kind of decision-making warranted a deep dive into data. Scratch that—I already had the data. What I really needed was the mental CPU to analyze it. And caffeine. Definitely caffeine.

I shambled toward the kitchen, passing never-unpacked moving boxes that laughed at me, and started my Keurig while longing for one of Grayson's morning cups of coffee. I sipped my java as I headed back upstairs to shower and dress.

Once back downstairs, I brewed a second cup and cradled my morning elixir while I peered through the patio window. Overnight fog had blanketed the landscape, now lifting to reveal a trio of deer grazing in the dawn light. I quickly snapped a few photos to share with Grayson, but hesitated with my thumb hovering over the send button. Was I ready to initiate any sort of a dialogue right now? I had a world of thinking to do, and a quick drive to work probably wouldn't cut it.

Sure enough, twenty minutes later, I walked through the doors of the Cates Foundation, my mind as muddled as before. That's the downside of a short commute—barely any time for mental decluttering.

I strolled into the lab, ready to check on my cell culture, only to find Kitty deeply engrossed in pipetting a sample into a vial. Her scuffed sneakers peeked out from beneath the counter, and the roots of her dark hair, peppered with white, made me wonder how long it had been since she'd indulged in a salon trip. The image struck me as quintessential Kitty—dedicated to a fault, always putting the work above appearances.

"Good morning," I announced in a fake-cheerful tone. Fake it till you make it, right?

Kitty spun around so fast, she nearly sent the sample flying. "Courtney! Give a girl some warning, will you? I don't need a side of cardiac arrest with my pipetting!"

"Sorry," I said, holding up my hands. "Next time, I'll stomp in like Frankenstein."

"Please do. Lab safety first." She pressed a hand to her chest, her mock-exasperation softening into a grin that was both frazzled and genuine.

Relieved to find my cell line in good shape, I retreated to my office. Now was a prime moment to sift through the relationship metrics I'd accumulated since dating Grayson. Our initial honeymoon phase had been spectacular, but our recent schedules had stretched us thin, leaving me expecting diminishing returns. My eyes scanned the analytics, prepared to see the signs: romantic distractions bleeding into my work life.

Instead, the data revealed something I hadn't expected. Efficiency was up, stress levels steady, and productivity untouched. Our relationship wasn't a distraction—it was a balance.

As I leaned back, my thoughts drifted to the folder Grayson had handed me last night. I'd been so frazzled, I hadn't paid much attention beyond the initial misunderstanding. Now, his excitement replayed in my mind, along with the chart itself—heart-shaped data points replacing the usual black dots, each one carefully plotted like some whimsical map of his feelings for me.

It was such a Grayson move—a perfect mix of playful and sweet, the kind of thing that should have made me feel like a priority even when I'd been running on fumes. But when I told him I couldn't process his suggestion, I caught the briefest flicker of disappointment in his eyes. He'd smiled, of course, because that's who he was, but it left me with a tiny pang of guilt that stuck like a popcorn kernel in my teeth.

My gaze traced over my graph. Unlike his hearts, it was clinical, emotionless. Yet the message was the same. We worked—not just on paper, but in ways I hadn't fully appreciated. Maybe it was time to step back from the data and focus on the story we were building together.

My phone buzzed with a reminder—time for my daily check-in with Larry, the Director of R&D. Since the corporate espionage scare, he'd insisted on these debriefings, and honestly, I didn't mind. It was reassuring to know I wasn't the only one treating lab security like a full-time job.

As I eased into a chair across from his desk, I couldn't help but notice the way the overhead lighting caught the silver in his hair, giving him an air of weary authority. Larry was a veteran of the field, his career forged in the glow of fluorescent labs. "Another day, another battle against the invisible forces of doom." I gave a wry smile. "Ever feel like all this security is just a glorified game of 'Where's Waldo'?"

Larry chuckled, a sound both tired and genuine. "Only if Waldo's holding a USB drive full of proprietary data." He leaned back, the lines around his eyes deepening as his humor faded. "My wife says I've taken to pacing at midnight. Claims I'm strategizing security protocols in my sleep."

I raised an eyebrow. "Midnight pacing? Sounds like the glamorous life of R&D leadership."

"Glamorous, right. And now the board is micromanaging everything I do, which doesn't exactly help the insomnia." He gestured to a stack of reports on his desk, neat but slightly dog-eared, a testament to endless revisions. "They're in full-blown damage-control mode, and I need you to smooth things over when you're in San Francisco. Ease their paranoia, Courtney, because it's slowing me down."

I nodded, making a mental note to add "corporate diplomacy" to my growing to-do list. "I'll do my best, but you know how it goes—once paranoia sets in, it's like a weed. Hard to get rid of."

He gave a tired smile. "Just remind them why we're the best at what we do. They need to see results, not just reports."

Heading back to the lab, my eyes were on automatic high alert, scanning for anything out of the ordinary. Oddly enough, snippets from my college psychology classes started popping into my mind. Those lessons, seemingly unrelated to my life as a cancer researcher, were suddenly feeling pretty relevant.

The idea of a 'schema' resurfaced in my thoughts – those mental frameworks we all use to make sense of the world, shaped by our upbringing, values, and experiences. It made me ponder how my own schema, the lens through which I viewed life, was influencing my relationship with Grayson.

My mind wandered further, testing the edges of my own schema. The walls I'd built to protect myself from disappointment weren't just affecting my relationship with Grayson—they extended to everything, including family. Especially family.

Those emails from my father flickered in my thoughts, uninvited. Adele. How could I let someone so new, so unexpected, into my life without also opening a door to someone I'd fought so hard to forget about? Dad's attention had always been fleeting, and the scars of his emotional distance had taken years to heal. Letting Adele in felt like tempting fate—inviting vulnerability when I'd spent so long building my defenses.

Am I on autopilot? I wondered, reaching the lab's workbench and slipping into my lab coat. *Just going through the motions of being in a relationship without truly understanding my own reactions?*

I had always valued being logical and rational, carefully balancing my career and personal life to avoid emotional overwhelm. But as I snapped on my gloves, I found myself questioning the strict rules I had set for myself.

Standing there, poised to begin my work, a thought flickered through my mind. Maybe it was time to reevaluate those rules, to consider a different perspective on my relationship with Grayson. Could I be a bit more adaptable, more open to unpredictability?

I sighed, the weight of my thoughts pressing heavier with each passing moment. After work, I owed it to myself—and to Grayson—to take a step back and really reflect on my priorities. Maybe it was time to start questioning some of the self-imposed rules I'd clung to for so long, rules that might no longer fit the life I was building. What were these doubts about our relationship trying to tell me? Were they genuine concerns or just knee-jerk reactions rooted in fear? I needed clarity, not assumptions. What if a small shift—a willingness to let go of old habits—could lead us to something extraordinary? Or worse, what if I came to realize we were doomed?

A couple of hours later, my phone chimed with a text. My heart dipped slightly, filled with apprehension about the sender. I wasn't ready to face Grayson yet. I was still untangling what I wanted, and the thought of diving into that conversation before I was ready twisted my stomach into knots.

I checked the message and let out a sigh of relief when I saw it was from Rose.

Rose: I'm near your office. Want to hit the street taco place for lunch with me?

Me: Sure. I need a break.

Fifteen minutes later, we found ourselves in front of the outdoor taco stand, the chilly, clear November air adding a crisp freshness to the day. As Rose and I added toppings to our tacos, the aroma of cooking meat and spices wafted around us, making my mouth water. The cold air contrasted pleasantly with the warmth radiating from the stand, creating a cozy atmosphere perfect for enjoying our meal.

"Do you think we're overloading the tacos?" I asked, eyeing the precarious mountain of toppings on mine.

Rose smirked. "If it's not structurally unsound, is it even a good taco?"

"Fair point. Let's just hope I don't need a fork halfway through."

As Rose talked about a plot problem with the book she was writing, my mind still kept wandering back to my earlier thoughts. What if some parts of my schema were holding me back —like old software that needs an update?

"Hey, Earth to Courtney," Rose said, snapping me out of my thoughts. "You okay?"

"Yeah, sorry. Just thinking about some things," I replied.

"Like what? You look like you're debugging some complex code in that head of yours."

I chuckled. "Funny you should say that. I was thinking about schemas—those mental frameworks we live by. How sometimes they're like cybersecurity for the soul, constantly needing updates to protect against vulnerabilities, and maybe even to improve performance."

Rose's eyes sparkled, clearly intrigued. "That's deep, but it's accurate too. What brought this on?"

"Everything with Grayson is making me question if some parts of my schema are outdated. Like, am I setting up unnecessary barriers because of past experiences that no longer serve me well?"

"I'm all for change. Adaptation is key in life, but those lessons we learned…they came from lived experience. They're deeply ingrained."

"Sometimes, I think I've built my whole life around avoiding past pain," I admitted, thinking back to the emails I couldn't quite bring myself to delete. "It's like… I've put up all these walls to keep myself safe, but now I'm wondering if they're just keeping me stuck."

Rose tilted her head, curiosity sparking in her eyes. "Walls can keep the bad stuff out, sure. But they keep out the good stuff too."

The image of Adele's bright, curious eyes flashed in my mind. I wasn't sure which category she fell into—good or bad. Letting her in meant risking the kind of disappointment I'd vowed never to feel again. But not letting her in… that didn't sit right either.

Rose took a bite of her taco, pondering my question. "You know, in the novels I write, my main characters always have to confront unresolved issues from their past in order to move forward. It's part of their personal growth arc. Your real-life dilemma sounds like something right out of one of my stories."

I smiled, taking a bite of my own taco. "Time to debug the system," I said, more to myself than to her.

Rose chuckled warmly. "Just like the characters in my novels, it seems you have to earn your happily ever after. No 'click here to update' button for emotional growth, huh?"

"Wouldn't that be a lifesaver?" I returned the laughter, but internally, a fresh resolve was taking root. I needed to update my mental schema to better match the life I was actually living.

Work. Family. Responsibilities. Each word piled on like a weight, adding to a heavy load I'd carried since childhood. I loved my brothers fiercely, would always do so, but love wasn't the issue. It was the responsibility, the mantle of adulthood thrust upon me way too early. My parents had been physically present but emotionally absent, leaving me to pick up the slack.

"Thanks for the impromptu therapy," I joked, standing up. "I'll return the favor when you hit a writer's block."

As I stepped back into the office building and into the elevator, my hand automatically reached for the button to my floor. The elevator started humming as it lifted me upward, but suddenly lurched, coming to an abrupt halt.

"What the hell?" Frustrated, I jammed the button a few more times, half expecting a magic fix.

Trapped between floors, I jabbed the buttons like a woman fighting for her life—or at least her lunch break. "Seriously, universe? You had to pick today for a cosmic metaphor?"

As if on cue, the elevator began its ascent again. I slumped against the wall, the realization hitting me as sharply as the lurch had moments ago. I'd done the same thing to Grayson's eureka moment as I'd done to so many other connections in my life— pushed it aside in favor of work. He'd poured his excitement into that text, and I'd reduced it to a quick "congrats," like checking a box.

It wasn't that I didn't care—I just hadn't made the time or space to care fully. His discovery had clearly meant the world to him, and I'd barely paused to acknowledge it. That was dismissive, whether he said so or not. Worse? It wasn't the first time I'd let something like that slide.

Gripping the railing, my chest tightened as I replayed every missed moment: the dinner I'd written off when traffic delayed him, the late-night calls I'd cut short for emails, the small things I'd dismissed as trivial but that added up like ticks in the debit column of our relationship.

When the elevator doors finally opened, I stepped out, my

gaze falling to my phone. Grayson wasn't just offering solutions to our distance—he was reminding me how much he wanted this to work. His gestures, his music, his heart-shaped data points—everything he did felt like the opposite of my father's half-hearted efforts. Dad had always been the master of half-measures, swooping in just long enough to leave me wanting before disappearing again. Grayson? He wanted to build something real. Something lasting.

And Adele? She was the wild card. A new player in a game I hadn't agreed to join. But unlike Dad, she hadn't chosen any of this. If I let her into my life, it wouldn't be for him—it would be for her.

I'd been distancing myself from Grayson all day. The fact that I'd been avoiding his texts was proof enough. Maybe before we dove into the 'moving in' talk, I needed to debug my own mental programming. Rose had nailed it; how much simpler life would be with a 'software update' button.

I sat at my desk, staring at my phone like it held the answers to every unasked question. A new resolve sparked in my chest. I couldn't undo the past, but I could damn well make sure Grayson knew how much he mattered going forward. Starting with celebrating his breakthrough the way I should have from the beginning.

Grayson had said to take my time, and that's exactly what I intended to do, but that didn't mean I couldn't text him. I had a flight to catch tomorrow morning, and roughly a week before I returned from San Francisco. Seven days to untangle years of emotional knots. No big deal, right? Who needed a therapist when you had tacos, an elevator epiphany, and a boyfriend patient enough to wait out your existential crises?

Before I could talk myself out of it, I pulled up our text thread and started typing:

Me: Hey, I owe you a proper congratulations on your big eureka moment. How about we celebrate when I get back from San Francisco? You pick the place, and I'll bring the champagne. Your work deserves to be recognized properly, and I'd love to hear every detail about your discovery—preferably over dessert.

I hit send and leaned back, the knot in my chest loosening ever so slightly. It wasn't a perfect fix, but it was a start.

A COMPROMISING PHOTO

GRAYSON

Five days had passed since Courtney boarded her flight to San Francisco, leaving me to soldier on in my corner of academia at the University of Pittsburgh. November 10th might be just a date —but it was also the day when the late-season warm spell gave way and fall fully staked its claim on campus life, wrapping everything in a chill and the faint scent of damp leaves.

Clapp Hall's lecture hall, with its amphitheater seating and distinct vibe of *academic grandeur*, had become my second home. As I wrapped up today's lecture, the room felt electric with the buzz of students scrambling to pack up. Laptops clicked shut with the precision of a military drill, and backpacks were zipped with gusto that suggested Friday was so close they could taste it.

I flicked the lights back on, banishing the intimate dimness that had cocooned us in the depths of molecular biology. The large projection screen blinked to black behind me like a curtain falling on a play. I watched the students file out, their laughter and footsteps blending into a campus symphony of ambition and caffeine dependency.

Clapp Hall wasn't just a building. It was a portal to the future. Each seat held a story—a student who might one day cure cancer or design a drug that made *Viagra* look quaint. It was humbling, really, standing in the middle of it all, though less humbling when I caught myself checking my phone for messages from Courtney instead of basking in professional fulfillment.

My phone buzzed with a timely text from Susan, one of my Ph.D. candidates.

Susan: Just confirming our meeting tomorrow at noon.

Me: Still on. Looking forward to discussing your progress.

The life of an academic—a symphony of meetings, deadlines, and furtive glances at your phone to see if your girlfriend has texted.

Stepping outside, I felt the brisk air nip at my cheeks. My phone buzzed again. This time, it wasn't Susan but the realtor I'd been in touch with. Even though Courtney hadn't exactly *jumped* at the idea of moving in together, I hadn't given up hope. I figured it was like a science experiment: you needed the right conditions for a hypothesis to work.

Back in my office, Joaquin was waiting for me, leaning against the wall in that effortlessly casual way that only grad students seemed to pull off. His dark, slightly messy hair and wire-rim glasses gave him the look of someone who had thoughts deep enough to get lost in but was still approachable enough to discuss the latest Netflix series.

"Hi, Dr. Stellar,." Joaquin pushed his glasses up the bridge of his nose with the eagerness of someone about to drop an academic bombshell.

"How's the internship going?" I asked, fumbling for my office keys.

"Fantastic. Beyond expectations." His grin was wide enough to light up the hallway. Joaquin always brought a sort of relentless enthusiasm to his work, like a puppy who had just discovered tennis balls.

Once settled in my office, he leaned forward, producing a photograph with the careful deliberateness of someone unveiling a masterpiece. He slid it across the desk with the flair of a magician revealing the ace of spades.

"They have me working on a new set of markers for a particular cancer line. It looks really promising," he said, his voice vibrating with excitement.

I froze. The photo was eerily familiar—stark, clinical, and hauntingly similar to one Courtney had shown me just weeks ago amidst the flour and frosting of her cake-baking fiasco. Was it the same? The coincidence was too striking to ignore. My stomach dropped like I'd just missed a step on Cathedral of Learning's grand staircase.

Keeping my tone neutral, I casually snapped a photo of the image with my phone. "Did you take this?"

Joaquin shook his head, oblivious to the storm brewing inside me. "No, it was handed to me."

"And who took it?"

He hesitated. "I'm not sure. It was in the files they gave me on my first day."

An identical photo was no coincidence. The odds were astronomically slim. The hairs on the back of my neck stood up. If this was Courtney's research—and I was almost certain it was—then Joaquin had unwittingly stumbled into something big.

"Joaquin, you signed a non-disclosure agreement with Medco-Vax, right?" I asked, my tone carefully neutral.

His brow furrowed, and his earlier confidence gave way to unease. "Uh, yeah. That doesn't include talking to you, does it?"

"It does," I said simply. "And this isn't just about NDAs. That photo? It might be connected to stolen research."

His face paled. "Stolen? Are you serious?"

I leaned forward, lowering my voice. "Joaquin, listen to me. That image matches work I've seen before—work that never should've left its original lab. If MedcoVax has it, it's a huge problem."

He swallowed hard, his eyes darting toward the door. "I didn't—"

"I know," I interrupted. "I believe you had no idea. But this is bigger than both of us. You need to be careful—don't share this with anyone else. Let me look into it."

Joaquin nodded stiffly, his movements robotic as he gathered his things. "Okay. But... what happens now?"

I gave him a reassuring look, though my mind was already racing. "Now? We handle it. Quietly."

As the door clicked shut, the weight of the photo settled over me. This wasn't just an overlap. It was a breach, one that could unravel Courtney's career—and Joaquin's future—if I didn't tread carefully.

I texted Susan to reschedule tomorrow's meeting and then reached for my phone to call the university's legal department. As the phone rang, my mind was already racing ahead, juggling the immediate need for damage control with the far trickier question of how to tell Courtney.

How could I approach her without setting off alarm bells? How could we protect her research without creating a nightmare for both of us? Most of all, how could I make her see that this wasn't just about the work—it was about us and the future I was starting to envision more clearly than ever?

In moments like these, Clapp Hall felt less like a place of academic discovery and more like a chessboard, with every move carrying stakes higher than I'd anticipated.

Courtney had once described science as equal parts passion and patience. Now, I realized, that description fit relationships too.

I just hoped we had enough of both to weather what was coming.

TANGLED IN THE WEB

Courtney

> Conner: I need a name for a new appetizer. Dante's making goat cheese-stuffed jalapeños wrapped in prosciutto. What about Fancy Pigs in a Blanket?

> Me: That's terrible. How about "Devilish Piggies"?

> Conner: Now you're just making it worse.

> Me: You asked. I'm sticking to research. Marketing's not my thing.

Stepping into the Cates Foundation's law offices in San Francisco felt like walking onto the set of a legal drama—all corporate chic. The rich aroma of freshly brewed coffee mingled with the faint, lemony scent of polished wood. Everything screamed sophistication, from the sleek glass tables with legs that looked like they belonged in a museum, to the abstract art on the walls that likely cost more than my car. Even the lawyers looked like they moonlit as catalog models, striding purposefully, murmuring into their Bluetooth earpieces like they were negotiating world peace.

I trailed behind Evelyn, who navigated the labyrinth of cubicles with the precision of a guided missile in stilettos. The paralegals typed furiously, their concentration so intense it could probably power the entire Bay Area grid. We stopped at a corner office, where a shiny gold plaque announced: **Evelyn Tandris, Director of Legal Affairs, Intellectual Property.**

Evelyn's office was the crown jewel—a shrine to order and authority. Rows of law books lined the walls, an antique gavel rested on a pedestal like an Oscar for Legal Badassery, and her leather chair creaked ominously as she settled into it. She gestured for me to sit, fixing me with a look sharp enough to cut glass.

"We have a problem," she said, her voice so calm it sent a shiver down my spine.

"Define 'problem,'" I replied, trying to channel confidence but sounding more like someone who'd just been told their car warranty had expired.

"A week ago, someone else filed a patent for the exact method you developed to create your virus."

My jaw dropped. "What? That's impossible! I've never shared my research with anyone."

Evelyn raised a single eyebrow, the international sign for *Welcome to the Real World.* "Looks like someone played dirty, corporate-spy style."

My brain was doing somersaults. The security alert—of course. Someone must've gotten their hands on our work. "So, what's our next move?"

Evelyn opened a folder with the kind of flourish that could have used its own soundtrack. She slid a photo across the desk. "They included this when they filed."

"That's *ours!*" I lurched forward in my chair, grabbing for the image that had once lived safely in my lab.

Evelyn nodded, her expression serious but with a hint of triumph. "This photo might just be our ace in the hole when we push for a patent reexamination."

I frowned. "Reexamination?".

"They filed first." Evelyn leaned back in her chair. "And in the patent world, 'first come, first served' is the rule. But if we can prove idea theft, we can challenge their claim. This could be our smoking gun."

"So, we're David against Goliath?"

"More like David with a very good lawyer." Evelyn's smirk carried the confidence of someone who made Goliaths nervous. "In cases of alleged idea theft, we can present our evidence for a reexamination of the patent application. That's our game plan, and you're going to be our star player."

I straightened in my chair, summoning my determination like a magic trick. "I'm ready. Just point me at the bad guys."

Evelyn leaned forward, her lawyer instincts sharpening like a hawk circling its prey. "Do you know who took that photo?"

"Andrew. He texted me a copy right after he took it so we could discuss it."

Her eyes sparkled, and for a moment, I thought she might break into an actual fist pump. "Perfect! The original photo will have metadata—digital breadcrumbs like timestamps and camera details. We'll match it with your lab records. That text message gives us an additional layer of proof. It's like leaving a neon sign that says, 'This is ours.'"

"That sounds... almost too easy." Some of my anxiety eased.

Evelyn winced, as if my optimism were a slightly expired yogurt. "It should be, in a perfect world. But in my experience, nothing about patents and intellectual property ever is."

"You're not exactly filling me with confidence." I crossed my arms.

She shrugged, her lawyerly wisdom shining through. "Let's just say this isn't my first corporate skullduggery rodeo. We've got a strong case, but you'd better believe the other side will come out swinging."

"Do we know who filed the competing patent?"

Evelyn's lips twitched in a dry smile. "That's the twist—they filed under a fictitious name. The company's about as real as a unicorn running for public office. No records, no digital trail. It's a ghost."

"They can just do that?"

"Oh, absolutely," she replied with a knowing nod. "It's like the corporate version of wearing a fake mustache and calling yourself 'Mr. E. Nigma.' Keeps everyone guessing."

I frowned, trying to process this. "But why? What's the point of all the smoke and mirrors?"

She leaned back, her chair creaking ominously. "Think about it. Say a tech giant like Google files a patent under their name—it's like putting up a billboard announcing their next big thing. Competitors could swoop in, stock prices could wobble, and corporate spies would have a field day. Filing under a dummy company lets them play their cards close to the vest."

I blinked, feeling like I'd just peeked behind a curtain I wasn't supposed to know existed. "I'm suddenly feeling very naive. And here I thought my biggest problem would be keeping my coffee cup from tipping over during experiments."

Evelyn glanced at her antique clock, the ticking suddenly feeling like a countdown to chaos. "How's your schedule? This is going to take more than a quick chat."

I checked my phone. "I've got a board meeting coming up. Should I...?"

"Cancel it," she said firmly. "You live in Pittsburgh, but you're here now. Let's untangle as much of this mess as we can while we're in the same time zone."

Two hours later, leaving Evelyn's office felt like stepping off a particularly intense amusement park ride—the kind where you're not entirely sure you should've eaten beforehand. My head spun with legal jargon and strategic plans, but one thing was clear: this wasn't going to be resolved anytime soon.

Back at my hotel room, I cranked the shower to near-scalding, hoping the steam would evaporate the tension from my shoulders. Wrapped in my nerdiest comfort pajamas—chemistry equations and colorful beakers—I ordered room service and settled in for an evening of sushi, fruit, and, hopefully, some Grayson time.

By the time my video call with Grayson connected, his tousled hair and warm smile felt like a lifeline. "Hey, you," I said, sinking into the comfort of seeing him.

"Hey," he replied, adjusting his laptop. "How's California?"

"Let's just say I've earned every bite of this sushi," I quipped, holding up a chopstick for emphasis.

His laugh was soft and steady, grounding me in a way nothing else had all day. "I miss you. Let me make you dinner tomorrow night."

"You've got yourself a deal," I replied, smiling despite the chaos still swirling in my mind.

Just then, his phone buzzed off-screen, and his expression darkened. "Something's up?" I asked.

He sighed, running a hand through his hair. "Today's been like piecing together a puzzle with half the pieces missing. I stumbled into something with one of my students."

"I know the feeling," I said, stifling a yawn. "Do you want to unpack it now? Maybe I can help." Then I held up my hand. "Actually. Nevermind. As much as I want to be your person, I don't know if I have the mental capacity right now."

Grayson grimaced, his expression turning thoughtful. "That's okay. I should talk to you in person. It can wait. Tomorrow?"

"It's a date." Being in wrapped his arms sounded like bliss.

Just as I was about to end the call, my phone buzzed again, this time with an email notification. The subject line—Urgent: New Development in Patent Case—flashed ominously.

"Grayson, I have to sign off," I said reluctantly, my eyes fixed on the screen.

He nodded. "Hang in there, Court. We've got this."

"Fingers crossed we don't drop any balls," I replied with a half-hearted chuckle.

As his face disappeared from the screen, the weight of the email loomed large. Bracing myself, I clicked it open, the glow of my laptop reflecting a battle far from over.

SHELL GAME

Subject: Urgent: New Development in Patent Case

Courtney,

I wish this email brought better news, but a concerning development has emerged regarding the ongoing patent dispute.

During my investigation of the patent application mirroring your research, I uncovered troubling details about the filing entity, Biotech Innovations LLC. The company was created just one month prior to submitting the patent, and its financial transactions, registrations, and documentation are meticulously obscured. This level of professional obfuscation is rare, suggesting significant resources and expertise at work.

Additionally, I've received two anonymous tips via our legal hotline, hinting that a major pharmaceutical player may be backing Biotech Innovations LLC. While these leads remain unverified, they underline the urgency of our situation.

We need to convene as soon as possible to reassess our strategy. This isn't just about protecting your patent—it's potentially a battle against an entity with deep pockets and substantial influence. I've escalated the matter to our senior legal team, and we're preparing for what could be a significant legal challenge.

Please confirm your availability for an early morning meeting before you depart for Pittsburgh so we can move forward.

Evelyn Tandris

Director of Legal Affairs, Intellectual Property - Cates Foundation

3 2

CONFLICTING LOYALTIES

Grayson

The airport buzzed with its usual symphony of car horns, rolling luggage, and half-shouted goodbyes. I pulled up to Door 4, my eyes scanning the crowd. I spotted her weaving through the throng, water bottle in one hand and carry-on in the other. Her hair, normally vibrant, had lost its bounce, and the weariness in her step tugged at my chest. My news about Joaquin would add to her burden, and I dreaded it.

As she approached, I jumped out of the car. Her mouth quirked into an exhausted smile as I pulled her into a hug.

"Missed you," I said, planting a kiss on her forehead.

She exhaled against my chest, her shoulders sagging. "Missed you too. Thanks so much for picking me up. But if you don't get me horizontal in the next thirty minutes, I might collapse right here."

"Noted," I said, opening her door with a flourish. "Your chariot awaits."

She slid inside with a grateful sigh, and I stowed her luggage before climbing behind the wheel. On the drive to her condo, I stole a few glances her way. She looked ready to curl up and sleep

233

for a week, but when our eyes met, she offered a small, reassuring smile.

"Thanks for picking me up."

"Always." My stomach churned at the news I had to share. The photo. Joaquin. MedcoVax. I'd waited until now to tell her, thinking face-to-face was the better option, but now it felt like a weight I was struggling to carry alone.

At her place, she kicked off her shoes in the foyer and collapsed onto the couch while I hauled everything inside. I set her suitcase by the stairs and returned to find her curled up like a cat, hugging a throw pillow to her chest.

"Rough week?" I eased down next to her.

She nodded, her head falling back against the cushions. "Understatement. Evelyn dropped a bombshell. Someone filed a patent for my research. Using a photo Andrew took."

My stomach did a somersault. She already knew? "The same photo you showed me?"

"The very one." She met my gaze, her exhaustion giving way to simmering anger. "It's the only real evidence we have right now that our work was stolen, and it's all hidden behind a shell company. We don't even know the real culprit."

I hesitated, weighing my words. "Courtney, the issue I mentioned last night... it's connected to this."

Her brow furrowed as she straightened, suddenly alert. "What are you talking about?"

I drew a deep breath, then spilled everything—how Joaquin had shown me the photo, how I'd snapped a picture of it, how he'd broken his NDA, prompting me to contact the university's legal department. As I spoke, I pulled up the photo to show her, and as she took it from me, her expression shifted from confusion to shock to something dangerously close to fury.

"You're telling me your postdoc student has access to my work?" Her voice wavered, caught between disbelief and anger. "Grayson, who is Joaquin even working for?"

"MedcoVax Pharmaceuticals." I said the words softly, but they landed like a bombshell.

Her face went pale as her grip tightened on my phone, but her eyes burned with barely contained rage. "MedcoVax," she repeated. "The company that sent someone to torpedo my talk in Florence? And you've known this since yesterday?"

I opened my mouth to explain, but she didn't give me the chance.

"And instead of telling me immediately, you... what? Sat on it? Protected your postdoc while my research is at risk?" She stood abruptly, dropping my phone to the table.

"Courtney, I didn't mean—"

"Didn't mean to what?" she cut in, her voice cold. "Didn't mean to prioritize Joaquin over me? Over my work? My career?"

"That's not what I was doing," I insisted, crossing the room to her. "I wanted to handle this carefully. Make sure I wasn't hallucinating about that photo. He's a student, Courtney. He made a mistake."

"And I'm just supposed to be okay with you keeping this from me? With you deciding when is the best time to tell me?" Her arms crossed, a fortress around the hurt in her eyes. "And to be clear, the only right answer to that was 'immediately.' Do you even understand what's at stake here?"

"I do," I said firmly. "Which is why I told you as soon as we could talk in person. I thought—"

"You thought wrong," she snapped, her voice edged with frustration. "Timing matters, Grayson. You waited, and now I'm playing catch-up. Evelyn needed this information yesterday—we wasted the past twenty-four hours trying to figure out what you already knew. You didn't just wait—you withheld something vital."

Her words hit like punches, each one knocking the wind out of me. I'd thought I was protecting her, but I'd been wrong. I could hear something beneath her her words. Something that told me all

I'd done was echo betrayals she'd suffered before. She was right to be angry.

"I'm sorry," I said quietly. "It wasn't about taking sides or choosing Joaquin over you. I was trying to do the best thing for everyone involved, but I see how I hurt you."

She shook her head, her jaw tightening. "This isn't just about hurting me, Grayson. This is about trust. And right now, I don't know if I can trust you."

But her expression was set, the hurt in her eyes deepening. Abruptly, she crossed to the coffee table her movements sharp. "Your actions speak louder than words. I can't do this, Grayson." She picked up her phone, her voice firm. "You should leave."

The finality in her tone felt like a door slamming shut. She turned away, already lifting the phone to her ear. "Evelyn, it's Courtney. I know who filed the patent."

Her voice faded as I scooped up my phone and stepped toward the door, each footstep heavier than the last. I paused, hoping for a chance to fix this, but she didn't look back.

"I'm sorry," I whispered, the words swallowed by the closing door behind me. Outside, the evening air felt colder than it should have. As I walked to my car, the weight of my choices pressed down on me, and for the first time in a long while, I wasn't sure how to move forward.

33

ECHOES OF BETRAYAL

Courtney

"It's MedcoVax Pharmaceuticals," I said the moment Evelyn answered. "We need to brainstorm, ASAP."

The finality of the door closing behind Grayson still echoed in my ears, leaving the room colder and too quiet. Great. Now I had a corporate thief and an emotional train wreck to handle. Maybe I should've thrown a pillow at Grayson on his way out—it would've been more satisfying than this gnawing sense of disappointment.

A storm of feelings whirled inside me: confusion, hurt, and a sharp sense of betrayal. Grayson keeping something so important from me felt like a lie by omission, hitting a nerve I'd hoped was long buried. Dad's secrets had taught me that withholding the truth under the guise of "protection" only makes the hurt linger. How could Grayson not see that?

Now, with Grayson, those same feelings surged back. Good intentions or not, it felt like arrogance disguised as nobility. Why do men think avoiding honesty spares us the pain? It doesn't. It just makes the hurt linger longer.

The room seemed to shrink around me. I sank onto the couch, my legs too heavy with the weight of memories and new disappointments. Maybe I'd been wrong to think about changing my approach to life; clinging to my old defenses suddenly felt safer.

Evelyn's voice crackled through the phone, crisp and urgent. "MedcoVax? They're behind this? Spill everything."

"Here's the scoop." I relayed the details as best I could, trying not to let my lingering frustration with Grayson bleed into my tone. Evelyn didn't need to know about that train wreck.

She didn't miss a beat, her keyboard clattering in the background. "This throws us a curveball. Have you noticed any odd behavior on your team? Financial troubles? Anything suspicious?"

The thought that someone on my team could be involved was like a punch to the gut, but I knew she was right. There was no other explanation that made sense. "My team is more like a family. It's hard to believe it's any of them. But you're right—someone's betrayed us. It has to be internal, but we checked everyone out after the scare a couple of weeks ago and didn't find any red flags."

Evelyn's response was brisk. "Then we need to dig deeper. Keep me updated."

As the call ended, I felt both relief and frustration. Somewhere in the halls of Cates, trust had been breached. And I had to figure out who'd shattered it. Trust, once so dependable, now seemed fragile, like thin ice.

With a newfound sense of purpose, I picked up the phone, dialing Larry, the VP of R&D. His voice, laced with concern, greeted me. "Courtney, you're top of my 'urgent' list. Evelyn filled me in after your meeting this morning. What's your take on all this?"

Glad to skip the long-winded explanations, I launched into the new revelations. "Turns out, MedcoVax Pharmaceuticals is behind this mess." I ran him through what I'd learned and finished with, "Now, we've got to figure out who's behind the leak."

Larry let out a heavy sigh. "I'm already on it. I've arranged for an undercover pro to blend in with your team. The company assures me they'll bring in someone who knows the science, inside and out. We'll catch this mole. Whoever it is won't even see it coming."

I pinched the bridge of my nose, tension flaring. "Larry, you know the first thing everyone will think when a new person shows up is that we suspect a mole. My people aren't stupid."

Larry's tone didn't waver. "We've been interviewing for months. This hire won't be out of the ordinary. If anything, it'll look like we're finally moving forward. Business as usual."

I paused, grudgingly acknowledging the logic. "Fine. But whoever you bring in better be convincing. If they're out of their depth, the team will sniff them out in a heartbeat."

"They'll be believable," Larry assured me. "The company I hired is top notch. You'll be impressed."

I exhaled slowly, uneasy but willing to concede. "Let's hope so."

Larry's voice grew heavy with guilt. "I should've seen this coming. This breach happened on my watch."

"It's my project." My own guilt prodded at me like an insistent little sibling. "I should've been more paranoid."

Larry chuckled dryly. "Paranoia is my department, Courtney. Don't worry—we'll fix this."

34

HER LINGERING PERFUME

GRAYSON

Leaving Courtney's place, the door's click felt like a gavel, final and unforgiving. My feet moved on autopilot while my mind spun. An hour ago, I'd been picking out curtains in my head. Now? I was the lead in a drama I didn't audition for.

Slumping into my car, the faint trace of her perfume twisted in my chest. That scent used to soothe me; now it felt like a bitter-sweet jab, each inhale replaying our greatest hits—our first kiss, that wedding-reception dance, our infamous cake catastrophe. I rolled down the window, hoping fresh air might clear my head. The perfume faded, but her voice lingered, sharp and unrelenting.

Tonight was supposed to be the turning point: I'd planned to share my MedcoVax findings and brainstorm solutions like two mystery-solving detectives. Instead, she'd shown me the door.

Merging onto the expressway, I let James Booker's *Classified* wash over me, the intricate piano mirroring the complexity of what we'd built. With Courtney, life felt like a duet—challenging yet profoundly moving. I couldn't bear the thought of going solo again.

As the city lights blurred by, a surge of resolve took hold. Misunderstandings and hurt feelings weren't the end of our story;

they were just plot twists. Jazz, not tragedy. We knew how to improvise, and I refused to let our music fade. Sometimes you need the rests—to catch your breath—before hitting the next crescendo.

The door of my apartment clicked shut behind me, the evening's dimming light casting elongated shadows across the room. The wall clock ticked in the background, its steady rhythm a stark contrast to the silence enveloping me.

How had I gotten to this point? Where had I gone wrong? And, more importantly, how could I make sure I never made the same mistake again?

Without realizing what I was about to do, I called Mara—my sounding board since we were kids. We were always there for each other, and if anyone could help me navigate my way through this, she could.

"Grayson, how's it going?" she asked, her tone light but ready for whatever I threw at her.

"Honestly? Today's been a rough one." I leaned against the counter, the cool granite grounding me.

"Talk to me. What's going on?"

I exhaled slowly, spilling the story: the withheld information, the fallout with Courtney, and the trust that now lay shattered between us. The words tumbled out, each one heavy with regret.

Mara's silence spoke volumes before she finally said, "That's rough. I'm sorry. But have you considered what Courtney must be going through?"

"What do you mean? I thought that's exactly what I'd been doing."

She sighed, her tone shifting to one of gentle reproach. "Remember back in college when I was dealing with that breakup? You were ready to confront the guy, but instead, you sat with me and helped me sort through my emotions. That's what Courtney needs from you now."

Her words hit home, but I hesitated. "I think I'm the last person she wants to confide in right now. She's angry with me."

"She's been through a lot with both her parents, but her dad..." Mara said. "What has she shared with you about him?"

Bits and pieces surfaced. "She's mentioned he was mostly absent. They've been estranged since the divorce, but she mentioned him a while back. She never wanted to talk about it though."

Mara sighed, her frustration barely masked. "There's more to it, Grayson. More than just an absent father."

A knot of uncertainty tightened in my chest. "Is it really my place to know this if she hasn't chosen to tell me?"

"Look, I might be crossing a line by oversharing, but you're family. Sometimes, you have to trust your gut. Dad would've overanalyzed this too, but you can't fix everything by waiting for certainty."

A pang of guilt shot through me at the thought of mirroring our dad's habit of second-guessing people. "What are you trying to say?"

"Courtney's father had a secret relationship for years. After the divorce, he married the woman, had a daughter, and didn't bother to tell Courtney she had a half-sister until months later—over the phone, no less. After the divorce, he disappeared from her life. Just... erased her and her brothers."

I struggled to process this. "I knew they weren't part of her life, but I never knew things were that bad. She didn't tell me."

"She's trying to leave it behind. Some wounds cut too deep to unpack, even with someone you trust."

The parallels to my own actions hit me like a gut punch. "So when she accused me of prioritizing Joaquin over her..."

Mara interjected, "It's the echo of her dad's choices—choosing his new wife and baby over her and her brothers."

I leaned back in my chair, the picture becoming clearer. The parallels were painfully clear. In trying to protect Joaquin, I had inadvertently mirrored the actions of the man who had hurt her most. I'd repeated a pattern of secrecy and exclusion she'd known all too well.

But another, sharper realization hit me like a punch to the gut: I hadn't just prioritized Joaquin. By holding the information back for a day, I'd taken it upon myself to decide what Courtney should know and when, managing her the way her father had controlled what she knew. My intentions had been good—I'd wanted to shield her while she was exhausted, to make sure I was right before I worried her—but in doing so, I'd taken away her agency, her right to the truth. It was a boneheaded decision, one I'd always regret.

Mara's voice pulled me back. "You see it now, don't you?"

"Yeah." The weight of my mistake settled heavily. "I thought I was protecting her, but I was controlling her. That's not love—it's arrogance."

"Exactly," Mara said, her tone softening. "Start with owning up to your mistake. A heartfelt apology can sometimes crack the hardest shells."

Apologies alone wouldn't cut it, though. I needed to act. "I've been thinking about the patent filing. I need to help her fix this mess."

"I like the way you're thinking." Her approval threaded through her voice.

"Yeah, but I'm stuck on what to do next. Emotional support's a given, but it isn't enough. She needs more."

Mara's voice broke the silence, sharp with purpose. "Remember when the university hired Soren Security for that data corruption issue? They specialize in corporate espionage, too. You could use that connection to help her."

A couple of years ago, the university had brought in Soren Security after a major research project hit a sudden roadblock— over a year's worth of data, corrupted out of nowhere. At first, it looked like a tech glitch, but the stakes had been too high to shrug it off as a random fluke.

Soren's team had uncovered the truth: it wasn't an accident. It was a calculated cyber-attack, orchestrated by a bitter ex-student aiming to sabotage our cutting-edge biological research. I'd been the liaison, translating our science for their tech experts and decoding their findings for our team. Long days, late nights—working with Soren had been an eye-opener, and they'd not only nailed the culprit but also helped us lock down our systems to prevent another attack.

A flicker of hope sparked. "I'll reach out to Soren tonight."

"That's the spirit. Show her, don't just tell her," Mara said.

As I hung up, resolve settled over me. Fixing this wasn't just about the patent or my mistake—it was about proving to Courtney that I trusted her to decide what she could handle. And this time, I'd act, not just apologize.

35

HEARTS AT STAKE

An hour later, I walked into my quiet kitchen to find a bottle of wine and a bag of groceries—classic Grayson. His thoughtfulness, once comforting, now felt like a bittersweet jab. The California Cabernet Sauvignon, my favorite, sat there like an unspoken promise of a night that would never happen. Returning it felt melodramatic—straight out of a bad soap opera—but the idea lingered.

My phone pinged with an incoming text.

> Grayson: Thought you should have a copy of this.

Attached was the photo he'd taken of Joaquin's cell. *Our* cell.

I didn't reply, but just sighed and put the groceries away, hand hovering a moment over the corkscrew before giving in. Pouring a glass felt oddly soothing, as if I could uncork clarity along with the wine. Was I built for relationship complications? My track record suggested otherwise. Career-focused, too stubborn, maybe just scared—the questions swirled faster than the Cabernet, and the wine offered no answers.

I needed advice—someone to cut through the noise, mixing reason with humor. Mara crossed my mind, but spilling my guts to Grayson's sister felt risky. One slip, and I'd create more problems than I solved. No, this was a Lianna conversation.

Cocooned in a white blanket on my sofa, I tapped my sister-in-law's contact, searching for the right words.

"Hi, Court. How was sunny California?"

My rehearsed intro vanished. "Just got in. Lianna, I… I think Grayson and I are on the outs." The words spilled unfiltered, raw.

A small pause crackled through the line. "Courtney, what happened?"

I gripped my wineglass, trying to gather my thoughts. "It's all too much. Work is one thing, but layering relationship drama on top? Like juggling fire. And now with the research theft, it feels like life's throwing curveballs faster than I can catch them."

"Wait, your research was stolen?"

"A competitor stole my research and filed a patent. Grayson found out who was behind it before I did, and instead of telling me, he shielded his student. Like I didn't factor in."

She latched onto the first part. "Corporate espionage is real. At Rainforest, our security's crazy—passwords, surveillance, you name it. It's just how things are these days."

I let out a soft laugh, swirling my wine. "Fort Knox-level security is exactly what I need. But I'm afraid it's not some faceless stranger behind this, Lianna. It might be someone on my team—someone I trusted."

Dad's betrayals crept into my thoughts, his secret family and tangled lies twisting the knife. "I let my guard down, and here I am, reliving everything Dad taught me about betrayal."

Lianna's voice grew gentle. "I get it, Courtney. After catching my ex with someone else, trust isn't my strong suit either. But what did Grayson do?"

A heavy exhale drained from me. "He recognized a photo of my cell when one of his grad students showed it to him. The student said it came from a pharma company he was working with. Grayson waited until tonight to tell me."

"Did he say why he held back?"

Pulling the blanket tighter, I let my frustration show. "I didn't give him much of a chance. I'd only learned about the patent theft yesterday and told him when we met. I was still reeling, and I couldn't see why he wouldn't tell me right away. He knows how much my work means to me."

Lianna waited a moment. "But you only told him about the patent tonight? It's ironic. You're upset he didn't share immediately, but you did the same thing. Sounds like you two are playing by different rules."

The realization struck like a slap. I hated how right she was. I'd kept my patent issue to myself for an entire day; Grayson's withholding mirrored my own.

"You have a point," I admitted, voice low. It felt like pulling teeth. I pushed off the sofa and set my wine down. Pacing the room let me match restless thoughts with restless feet—until a sharper jab hit me: *What about you, Courtney? Haven't you been doing the same thing by not telling him about Dad's email? About Adele?*

I sank onto the couch, the blanket a protective barrier. Keeping Adele a secret wasn't the same—my choice was tangled in fear and avoidance. It had everything to do with me, and nothing to do with him. But the hypocrisy settled in like an unwanted guest. How could I demand total honesty when I couldn't share my twelve-year-old half-sister?

Secrets always leave cracks.

"But it's not the same," I insisted, more to myself than Lianna. "The patent news doesn't alter Grayson's future. What he kept from me directly affects my career, my life. He protected Joaquin at my expense. I wasn't even part of the equation." Bitterness edged my voice. "I get he didn't mean it as betrayal, but that's how it feels."

Lianna offered me the space I needed. When she finally spoke, her voice held gentle truth. "Part of his job is to look out for his students, right?"

I huddled further into the blanket, as if it could shield me from the growing weight of everything left unsaid. "He should've trusted our relationship and told me right away. This only confirms my biggest fear. We're both dealing with our own crises —him with his student, me with my stolen research. I can't pull him into my chaos It's all just too much."

Had I just made a decision? Was I really planning to break things off with Grayson?

Lianna's determination broke through. "He's been your anchor. Doesn't he deserve to share his feelings too? He's earned your support. Don't make unilateral decisions about your relationship. Talk to him before you decide."

Tears blurred my vision. "Lianna, I just... I can't. I've made up my mind. It's better this way. I'm not the partner he needs. He deserves better than what I can give right now. I'm too broken, too afraid I'll never trust anyone fully."

Clutching the blanket, I tried to articulate the storm in my chest. "My whole life has been about finding a cure. That's my north star. Grayson is... everything I've wanted, but that doesn't mean we're meant to be."

Lianna's voice broke through my self-pity, filled with empathy and a hint of challenge. "Do you really think love's not worth the effort because of one rough patch?"

Curled up, knees drawn in, I spoke so quietly my words nearly vanished. "I've always believed happiness comes from within. That I don't need a man to find it. My emotions are a labyrinth right now, and dragging Grayson in feels unfair. I'm not even sure I have the bandwidth for it."

A pause while Lianna gathered her thoughts. "But isn't love all about navigating those labyrinths together?"

Her words struck a chord. "I used to think I could handle anything. Now I'm struggling to keep a houseplant alive, let alone figure out love."

Lianna's tone was tinged with sadness. "Courtney, what are you saying? That you think you don't deserve happiness?"

Tucking a loose strand of hair behind my ear, I felt the weight of everything. "I'm not saying happiness is impossible. It's just... chaos right now."

Her voice stayed warm yet firm. "Everyone, including you, deserves happiness. Don't sell yourself short."

A hint of vulnerability crept into my words. "Happiness?" I whispered. "I didn't mean—this isn't about love or happiness."

Lianna, always perceptive, pressed gently. "You mentioned 'love.' At least twice. Maybe there's something to that?"

I fumbled for a denial. "It's not that. I didn't mean—" But the truth lingered, unspoken.

Her sympathetic tone held understanding. "Sometimes our hearts speak through slips of the tongue. Think about what yours might be saying."

A deep breath steadied me. "I need time, Lianna. Can we talk tomorrow?"

She didn't hesitate. "Take all the time you need, Court. I love you and I'm here, no matter what."

I exhaled gratitude. "Thanks. I appreciate it."

Hanging up, my mind spun like a centrifuge, separating each emotion. Fear, doubt, and reluctant hope crystallized. The unknown variables—my feelings about love and worth—were the toughest to quantify.

Refilling my glass, I half-laughed at my own ignorance. I could decode genetic sequences in my sleep, but my heart? Still an enigma. If only love came with a user manual.

36

GRAYSON UNRAVELS THE KNOT

Grayson

The next day, the campus buzzed with its usual morning energy, but my footsteps fell heavier than usual. With each stride, I felt less like a professor on his way to work and more like a detective chasing down a lead—minus the trench coat and dramatic flair. If only solving this patent mess, or mending things with Courtney, could be as straightforward as getting from point A to B.

As I arrived at the legal services office, a cocktail of nerves and resolve churned in my stomach. Inside, standing at the receptionist's desk, I found my lawyer, Holly, staring at a calendar on the computer screen.

"Holly?" She pivoted with an elegant startle, her face quickly shifting from surprise to recognition. "Grayson? My calendar's all over the place today. You're my eight o'clock appointment, aren't you?"

"And I even managed to make it here on time."

She gestured towards her office. "Let's chat in here. Away from any prying eyes and ears."

Stepping into Holly's office was like entering a shrine to academic bureaucracy. Shelves groaned under the weight of legal

250

tomes, and her desk was a battlefield of files and Post-it notes. The chair across from her, with its slightly frayed armrests, told the story of countless tense meetings. I was about to add another chapter to its well-worn saga.

"So, any updates since we spoke yesterday?" Holly's tone was all business.

Taking a deep breath, I explained what I'd learned from Courtney about the shell corporation's patent application and the Cates Foundation scrambling to respond.

"That does put a new spin on things." Holly tapped her pen against the desk in a measured rhythm. "If her lawyers are already aware their research has been compromised, Joaquin's accidental slip might stay under the radar. For now, let's keep this contained."

Her words landed with the weight of a discordant note, pulling at the edges of my resolve. A silent tug-of-war played out inside me, between her cautious strategy and the truth I'd already laid bare.

"Actually..." I cleared my throat. There was no point in delaying. "I already told Courtney about the photo—about Joaquin showing me MedcoVax's image of her research. She's looped in her patent attorney."

Holly stilled, her pen halting mid-tap as she frowned. The pause was heavy, loaded with questions she didn't need to ask.

I met her gaze. "She deserved to know. I couldn't keep it from her."

For a moment, Holly studied me, her expression unreadable. Then she leaned back, letting out a sigh that carried equal parts resignation and reluctant approval. "Fair enough. You're right— she had a right to know. Let's just hope this doesn't complicate things for you and Joaquin. Lawyers tend to turn clear waters into a murky mess."

Her words lingered, but I couldn't shake the sense that I'd made the right move, even if it had thrown a wrench into her so-called "strategy." The silence stretched, awkward enough to push me to break it.

"So, we just… wait?" I asked, frustration nipping at my tone.

Holly's lips quirked into something between a smirk and a reprimand. "Think of it as strategic patience. Like chess, Grayson. Timing is everything."

I groaned softly, scrubbing a hand over my face. "I've always been more of a checkers guy."

Holly's raised brow turned razor-sharp, the kind of look that said she wasn't about to let me off easy. "Not a strategy kind of man? Maybe it's time you start learning."

The remark stung just enough to land, mostly because she was right. Strategy wasn't my strong suit, but I couldn't let that be an excuse—not now.

"As long as the Cates lawyers don't entangle you and Joaquin in this, you should be okay," she continued, her tone sliding back to businesslike. "Patent attorneys rely on concrete evidence. They'll need more than a professor's gut instinct to take on a company like MedcoVax."

Stepping back into the bustle of the city campus, my phone vibrated with the urgency of a chess clock ticking down. Glancing at the caller ID, I saw it was Soren Security.

"Hello?"

"Dr. Stellar? Soren Security here. Thanks for reaching out—it's like you've been studying the chess board. The Cates Foundation brought us on to track down their mole, but we need someone with your expertise to help strategize the next moves. You're our queen's gambit."

"Secret weapon?" I leaned against a storefront, trying to sound calm while mentally high-fiving myself. "I like the sound of that."

"Good, because this isn't a solo gig. You'll be teaming up with one of our specialists. Think of it as a buddy-cop situation—minus the car chases. Probably."

A partner. Some of my tension eased at the thought of having an expert guide the way. I was out of my element here. This wasn't a collaborative research paper or a departmental committee; this was about tracking down corporate espionage. Real-world consequences, high-stakes pressure, and the potential to make things worse if I didn't measure up.

Still, Courtney's research was on the line, and sitting this out wasn't an option. If Soren believed in me, I'd rise to the occasion.

"Count me in. Whatever it takes." I willed my voice to sound steadier than I felt.

"There's more," Soren added, his tone dropping into something more conspiratorial. "This gig's not just a feather in your cap. We're talking a week's salary for a day's work. Two at the most."

The incentive made my eyebrows shoot up. I leaned against the storefront for support, half-wondering if I'd misheard. "Well, that's a nice perk, but honestly, I'd do it for free."

Soren's laugh crackled through the phone. "That's noble of you, but we insist on compensating our consultants fairly. You'll be earning every penny."

Fair pay for what, exactly? My background in oncology? The idea of working alongside seasoned pros in combating corporate espionage felt surreal. I'd spent years analyzing data, not chasing down moles. But if someone had stolen Courtney's work, I wanted to help bring them to light.

"Great." I firmed my grip on the phone as determination replaced my nerves. "I'm all in. Just tell me when and where."

"Clear your calendar for the next forty-eight hours starting now. Welcome aboard, Detective Stellar."

37

SHADOWS AND SUSPECTS

COURTNEY

I walked into my office, coffee in one hand, phone in the other, the brisk fall air still clinging to my skin. Normally, the hum of Cates felt like stepping into a reliable routine—a bubble of familiarity. Today, it felt more like a crime scene, and I was the detective fumbling for a flashlight.

My eyes drifted to the thermal mug. Grayson's mug. The one I hadn't gotten around to returning. The one with the smug, geeky caption: *Caffeine: It's Elemental, My Dear Watson.* Between my chaotic schedule and the whirlwind trip to California, it had slipped my mind.

Maybe it was time to stop using it. Return it. Draw a line. And yet... I didn't move. The thought of giving it back felt heavier than it should, underscoring the nagging doubt that last night's decision might not have been my finest moment.

My gaze shifted to a neon-yellow Post-it stuck to my laptop. Larry's unmistakable scrawl—big, bold, and brimming with the confidence of a man who made delegating an art form—stared back at me.

Meet us in the conference room

Larry

"'Us?' Since when did Larry start using the royal we?" I tossed my bag onto the chair and shooting off a quick email to my team.

The mug stared at me from its perch on my desk. I grabbed it and headed to the conference room. Maybe I'd use it today and think about returning it tomorrow.

I pushed open the door, and Larry's booming laugh hit me like a cymbal crash, startling enough that I nearly dropped my coffee. "Please, not the shoes," I muttered, dancing back in my new gray suede pumps just in time to avoid a splash zone.

And that's when I saw him.

Grayson.

My stomach plummeted as my heart launched into an unsanctioned marathon. Grayson turned toward me, his expression calm, composed—like he had every reason to be here, which he absolutely didn't. His tailored pants and rolled-up sleeves said "approachable," but the way he carried himself screamed "mission-critical." Of course, he had to look annoyingly good while being annoyingly unexpected. Why was he here? And why, of all places, did it have to be this conference room, with *my* boss?

"Grayson?" The word came out strangled, like my vocal cords couldn't quite decide on the tone.

He didn't smile. No half-smirk. No familiar spark. Just business.

Larry, on the other hand, seemed oblivious to my tension. "Courtney, great timing! Dr. Stellar's joining our team for the investigation." He said it like he was announcing the arrival of free pizza in the break room.

"Grayson… is joining the team?" My voice pitched up at the end, somewhere between disbelief and mild panic.

Larry glanced between us, his brows lifting. "Wait—hold on. You two know each other?"

Grayson finally spoke, his tone cool and measured. "We've met."

Larry chuckled, oblivious to the undercurrent. "Small world, huh? Well, that makes this even better. No need for awkward introductions! Grayson is going to help us identify the mole. His buddy from Soren Security will handle the tech side."

My brain felt like a Wi-Fi connection on the fritz. Grayson. Here. At *my* job. With *my* team. Why the secrecy? Why hadn't he given me a heads-up?

"Courtney? You alright?" Larry peered at me like I might keel over.

"Fine! Things are just… moving a bit fast."

Grayson's lips twitched—just barely—but he stayed silent.

Larry forged ahead, blissfully unaware of the tension filling the room. "We're on a tight schedule. Grayson will start shadowing your team immediately. Courtney, you'll work with Christian from Soren to dive into the digital side of things. Between the two of you, I expect progress by day's end."

"By today?" I asked, incredulous. "Larry, finding a mole isn't like flipping a switch. It's not something we can just wrap up neatly in a day."

Larry grinned. "I have faith in you. Grayson's knowledge and Soren's resources will give us the edge we need. I'm counting on you two to get it done."

And just like that, he left, leaving me alone with Grayson.

The silence was deafening.

I turned to him, unsure whether to laugh, cry, or demand answers. "So," I said, keeping my voice even, "how did you end up... moonlighting with Soren Security?"

Grayson's expression softened, just a fraction. "I worked with them a couple years ago. When I heard about your situation, I reached out. Turns out, Cates had already hired them."

"You reached out?" My fingers tightened around the mug, the ceramic cool against my skin.

"I wanted to help."

I nodded, unsure what to say. "Thanks."

His gaze met mine, steady and unflinching. "Courtney, I'll always have your back. You know that, right?"

The lump in my throat threatened to choke me. "About the other night..." I started, the words faltering.

He shook his head. "We'll find the right time to talk—really talk—I promise. Just not here, not now. Let's focus on the work first."

I nodded, swallowing hard. "Right. Work first. Let's head to Conference Room A. I'll introduce you to the team."

38

MEET THE TEAM

GRAYSON

Courtney ushered me into the conference room, her confident stride a sharp contrast to the cautious pace I'd adopted. It felt like stepping onto a stage without knowing my lines, despite the hours I'd spent reading up on the cast. My pulse quickened as I tightened my grip on the file folder. This was it.

The lively hum of conversation filled the room, punctuated by the squeak of a marker on a whiteboard. A middle-aged woman with scuffed shoes gestured emphatically, her tired eyes flashing with determination. She had to be Kitty—her bio mentioned she was the team's veteran researcher and the glue holding things together.

Next to her, a man with his arms crossed and a furrowed brow nodded along. That had to be Andrew, the group's data analyst, known for his meticulous attention to detail. He looked every bit the part—focused, deliberate, and about two seconds away from launching into a statistical argument. In other circumstances, I bet we'd be great friends.

In a chair toward the back, another woman leaned against the table, her posture almost casual if not for the skeptical scowl aimed at the whiteboard. Mercy, I decided. The notes on her described her as a no-nonsense biochemist with a reputation for cutting through fluff to get to the heart of a problem. Judging by her expression, someone had clearly failed to impress her.

A younger woman sat at the conference table, taking notes. Roz the intern, I assumed.

I tried to keep my breathing steady as I took in the group, but the weight of the room's collective energy pressed down on me. The people I'd studied in bios were now fully in motion, their dynamics already on display. Time to see if I could fit into this ensemble—or at least not trip over my own feet during the first act.

I hadn't expected my entrance to interrupt their debate so abruptly. Their heads turned in unison, the silence that followed sharp enough to cut through steel. If this were a movie, there'd be a dramatic record scratch right about now.

Courtney's voice, warm and confident, cut through the tension. "Sorry to interrupt," she began, her tone smooth as glass. "I've got exciting news. Everyone, this is Dr. Grayson Stellar, our newest team member. You might know him by reputation."

Reputation. The word hung in the air like a neon sign. My stomach churned. Sure, my name was attached to a few note-worthy papers, but being "that guy" in a room full of brilliant researchers wasn't exactly comforting. Especially not when I was here under false pretenses.

Andrew's eyes lit up, his grin wide. "Dr. Stellar? This is awesome for our team!" His excitement was genuine, forcing a startled smile from me.

Beside him, Roz's jaw dropped. "You're THE Dr. Stellar?" she blurted out, her voice squeaking with enthusiasm. "I cite your research all the time!" Her cheeks flushed as she quickly added, "Sorry—geeking out a little."

I relaxed just a bit. "Always happy to meet someone who's read my work."

Courtney jumped in with a warm smile. "See, Grayson? You've got fans everywhere. No pressure or anything." The comment earned a few chuckles, breaking the tension and easing Rozalia's visible nerves.

Mercy raised an eyebrow. "So, when did this hiring happen?" Her no-nonsense tone reminded me of a particular skeptical professor during my grad school days. I wondered if they might be related.

"Looks like Larry's been pulling strings behind the scenes." Courtney grinned, keeping the mood light. "Grayson's here to help us make a push for the finish line with our research while looking for any errors we might have overlooked in our process." Her gaze swept the room, steady and confident. "We need to get him up to speed, fast. I'm relying on all of you to welcome him in. Share your knowledge, show him how we do things here. We're shooting for quick integration."

Andrew grinned. "We'll get Dr. Stellar in the groove in no time!" The room buzzed with laughter, the ice finally cracking.

I offered a nervous half-smile. "Thanks in advance for the deep dive."

Courtney's confidence radiated as she gave a playful wink. "I know it's a tall order, but I believe in this team." She turned to me, her expression neutral and professional. "Once you're done here, come find me. If I'm not in my office, my assistant will point you in the right direction."

39

PETE'S DISCOVERY

COURTNEY

"Courtney! Perfect timing!" Pete, our IT director, sprang to his feet as I stepped into his office, his usual energy practically bouncing off the walls. "Let me take you to the digital detective from Soren Security."

I matched his enthusiasm with a smile. "Looking forward to it. Lead the way."

As we walked down the hall, Pete's animated demeanor dimmed just slightly, replaced by something more measured. "Just a heads-up, Christian's a bit... unique."

"Unique how?"

Pete's smirk turned sly, the kind of expression that said he was holding back something good. "Let's just say he's more about results than charm. But you'll see."

He pushed open the door to the IT security room, revealing a space that hummed with a quiet intensity. Rows of monitors cast a blue glow over the room, reflecting off sleek servers in what looked like a high-tech command center. A faint tang of solder and plastic lingered in the air, completing the scene.

At the heart of it all sat Christian, a wiry young man with messy dark hair and an intensity that radiated from his hunched frame. His fingers danced across the keyboard, his focus so absolute it was almost tangible.

Without even looking up, he spoke, his voice clipped but steady. "Dr. Courtney Gillette?"

I blinked at the abrupt tone, glancing at Pete, who leaned casually against the doorframe with a knowing grin.

"That's me." I stepped fully into the room.

Christian waved vaguely toward a nearby chair, still staring at the screen. "Sit," he said, his tone more directive than inviting.

My eyebrows shot up. "Excuse me?"

Pete shot me an exaggerated wink, clearly enjoying the spectacle. "*Told you,*" he mouthed silently.

"Sit," Christian repeated, this time adding, "We need to optimize your footprint."

I turned to Pete, who was clearly biting back a laugh. He gave me a thumbs-up and made a quick exit, leaving me with this charming enigma.

I perched on the edge of the chair, feeling more like I was entering a particularly challenging level of a video game than starting a professional collaboration. "So, you're Christian?" I ventured.

"Christian," he confirmed flatly, his eyes still glued to the screen. His fingers moved with the speed and precision of someone inputting launch codes.

Without warning, he stopped typing and turned to face me. His intense gaze was like a spotlight, scanning me from head to toe as if I were a program he needed to debug. "You have a posture that suggests skepticism," he observed, his tone almost clinical.

I blinked, thrown. "I... beg your pardon?"

He nodded, as if confirming his own hypothesis. "People who sit on the edge of their chairs usually don't trust the process. You can lean back. I'm good at my job."

Suppressing a laugh, I leaned back just enough to be polite. "Thanks for the reassurance."

Christian's setup caught my eye—a cluster of monitors surrounded by cables, and a jar of jellybeans that seemed wildly out of place. He noticed my glance and, with surprising solemnity, plucked a few from the jar. "Brain food," he explained, holding up a green one. "Green for inspiration." He paused, picking out a black one and setting it aside with a disdainful flick of his wrist. "Black licorice is the devil's work."

I let out a surprised laugh, unable to help myself. "Noted."

Seemingly satisfied that I had passed some kind of test, he handed me a freshly printed sheet, his tone shifting to professional urgency. "Review this. The highlighted lines are items we should prioritize."

Scanning the list, I frowned. "Attached USB drives, printed documents, communications with external entities around the theft timeframe… Are we building a digital detective kit here?"

Christian tilted his head, a flicker of amusement crossing his face. "In a way. This will identify your thief's digital breadcrumb trail. I've set my software to comb through your data, but narrowing the parameters will save time. Focus is key."

I nodded, already making notes. "Our big breakthrough was shortly after I returned from a trip to Turks and Caicos in mid-August."

He scribbled a note with startling efficiency and handed me a sticky note in return. "Shoot me the file names ASAP. Time is a resource in short supply."

His abruptness was beginning to feel oddly endearing. "Roger that, jellybean commander." I rose from my chair.

Christian didn't react to the nickname but returned to his keyboard as though I'd already left.

Back at my desk, I sifted through the pertinent files, meticulously indicating the ones most likely to have appealed to the thief, then sent the information in spreadsheet form to Christian. I tried to focus on some of my regular tasks. The unease from the morning lingered, but I pushed it aside, focusing instead on salvaging what I could from the chaos.

Post-lunch at my desk, I was halfway through the latest round of fire-fighting when a familiar knock broke my concentration. "Can we chat?" Grayson asked.

Leaning back in my chair, I turned to face him, my pulse instantly jumping into overdrive. He looked good. Too good. A few strands of hair fell over his forehead, tempting me to brush them back just for the excuse to touch him. Not a great idea. I needed to distract myself—fast—before I did something monumentally stupid.

Still, seeing him here stirred something unexpected in me. Maybe it was the fact that he'd thrown himself into this investigation, doing everything in his power to help me, despite how poorly I'd handled our conversation two nights ago. A flicker of guilt threatened to rise, but I tamped it down. He could have told me about the theft sooner—but he was here now. That had to count for something.

"Back from playing detective already?" My words tumbled out in a rapid-fire burst, one question piling on top of the next. "Are you up to speed yet? Was your technique successful? Casual interrogations over coffee, I presume?"

Grayson's soft chuckle cut through my whirlwind of words, grounding me in the moment. "Something like that. I'm no Hercule Poirot, but I did my best to keep things friendly yet probing."

I couldn't help but smirk. "Let me guess—your charm worked its magic?"

"More like careful observation." He took the seat across from me. Despite his calm demeanor, he looked slightly out of place, like a spy dropped into an academic conference. It was distracting, to say the least.

"How did things go with Rozalia?" Her over-the-top hero worship earlier still lingered in my mind, like an unresolved subplot. Definitely not jealousy. That would be unprofessional.

Grayson leaned forward, resting his elbows on his knees, his fingers laced together in thought. "She was jittery, kept glancing at her watch, fidgeting. I couldn't tell if it was nerves about the investigation or something else. But her reaction stood out."

I tapped my pen against my desk, thinking aloud. "Rozalia is usually the epitome of cool. She's acting off, so that's worth noting."

Grayson nodded, his brow furrowing. "I'll keep shadowing the team, see if anyone else stands out…or can be eliminated."

Before we could dig further into our theories, my office door creaked open, revealing Pete. Normally cheerful, he looked unusually tense, his energy subdued.

"Courtney, can I… can I have a moment?" He shifted his weight awkwardly from side to side.

"Of course." I motioned for him to come in. "What's going on?"

Pete swallowed hard and reached into his pocket, producing a flash drive. His hand trembled slightly as he handed it to me. "I just found this in the server room. Under the raised flooring. I had lifted a floor panel to run a new ethernet line when I spotted it."

My stomach knotted as I took the small device from him. It felt deceptively light in my hand. "What's on it?"

Pete hesitated, his expression taut. "Your entire project, Courtney. Everything. From the earliest drafts to your most recent discoveries. Even your correspondence with the team."

The room seemed to tilt for a moment as his words sank in. My fingers clenched around the flash drive as a wave of unease swept over me. "Everything?" My voice barely rose above a whisper.

Pete nodded grimly. "Every byte, Courtney. It's a digital blueprint of all your research. It even includes information from two days ago." He shuffled uncomfortably, the weight of the revelation clearly taking a toll on him.

I turned the flash drive over in my hand. The brazenness of it was staggering. Someone had stolen everything and hidden it right here, within the sanctity of our labs. "And you found this stashed under a floorboard?" My voice was tight, incredulous. "That's like finding a needle in a haystack."

Grayson's voice broke the tense silence, his tone sharp with curiosity. "Or more like a carefully hidden needle. Why there? Were they afraid of being caught with the evidence?" He turned to Pete, his expression focused. "Did they only steal the data, or destroy the original work as well? Did you check if any files are missing from the main servers?"

Pete shook his head. "I checked just before I came here, and everything seems intact. But whoever did this... they had a high level of access, knowledge, and a plan."

The room lapsed into a heavy silence as Pete left, and I slumped into my chair, gripping the drive. My thoughts spun like gears trying to mesh, frantic but unproductive. Across from me, Grayson shifted in his seat, his elbow propped on the armrest as his fingers began drumming lightly on the edge of my desk. The rhythm was soft, steady—almost soothing—a series of quick taps followed by a longer pause, like the faint outline of a melody.

I looked up, my brow furrowing slightly. "You always do that?"

"Do what?" Grayson blinked, his fingers freezing mid-tap, as if he'd just become aware of what he was doing.

"That." I waved a hand toward his desk drumming. "The... rhythm thing."

His lips twitched, caught between a grin and a sheepish smile. "I guess I do. It's a habit—music's always there, somewhere in the back of my head."

For a moment, it distracted me—how effortless it was for him, like breathing. A small, grounding detail in the middle of this chaos. I turned the drive over one more time, refocusing. "Well, let's hope the rhythm gods have your back because we need a foolproof plan."

Grayson's expression shifted back to sharp focus, his fingers stilling as he straightened in his seat. "Let's update Christian. He can help us set a trap. The mole can't stay hidden for long."

40

HOLMES, WATSON, AND HEARTSTRINGS

GRAYSON

After leaving Christian to do his techno-wizardry on the USB drive, I followed Courtney back to her office, where a stack of papers and a determined gleam in her eyes signaled that our next phase of detective work was about to begin.

"Let's go through the employee list and discuss your impressions." She handed me a freshly printed spreadsheet, still warm from the printer. "I also want to look at non-team members and decide if any of them are potential suspects."

As I flipped through the papers, my attention snagged on a familiar thermal mug perched beside her monitor. Its inscription, *"Caffeine: It's Elemental, My Dear Watson,"* was like a breadcrumb trail leading straight back to those easy, laughter-filled mornings.

She caught my gaze lingering and reached for the mug, holding it up like it was evidence in our ongoing investigation. "This is yours."

I waved her off, keeping my tone light. "Keep it. You've earned it—Watson always deserves the best."

Her lips twitched, the faintest shadow of a smile breaking through the guarded exterior. "Are you saying I'm Watson in this scenario?" she teased, leaning back slightly. "Because if you're claiming Sherlock, I expect a deerstalker hat and a British accent. Go big or go home."

"Well, I'm no Benedict Cumberbatch, but I think I could pull it off." It was good to see her crack a joke, even if it was just a sliver of the Courtney I missed.

She rolled her eyes but didn't hide her smirk. "Let's not get ahead of ourselves. The last thing I need is you monologuing about 'the game being afoot.'"

I chuckled softly and leaned closer to her desk. The faintest hint of her perfume wrapped around me, both comforting and bittersweet. "Alright, Watson." I gestured to the spreadsheet. "Let's dive into this case before Larry accuses us of being a comedy duo instead of solving his problems."

Courtney grinned, then turned away focusing on the list. As she slid her finger down the first page, her focus was impossible to ignore. She scanned each name like a human lie detector, her pen tapping against the desk with rhythmic deliberation. My gaze flicked to her necklace—the silver cancer awareness pendant I'd returned to her after our trip. She touched it absently, her fingers brushing the small charm as if grounding herself.

After an hour or so, I gave a sigh. "The data on that drive was too coordinated—too targeted and specific. It has to be someone with deep project understanding and access, not just some IT person who doesn't understand the science. That means it can only be one of the researchers." I scanned the files again. "Kitty, Andrew, or Mercy." I shook my head as I reviewed Roz's hire date and security details. "It can't be Roz. She doesn't have the access or the technical knowledge to piece everything together. Plus, the timeline doesn't fit with when she started."

"Any other explanation?"

I shrugged. "Someone not on your team with the specialized knowledge requited? I suppose your spy could pose as a security guard or a cleaning person. That person would be a lot harder to identify because I'd assume their CV or resume would have been entirely fabricated." I shook my head. "I think it makes more sense to focus on your team."

Courtney bit her lip, her brow furrowing in a way that made her look both brilliant and heartbreakingly vulnerable. "I hate this part," she admitted softly, tucking a loose strand of hair behind her ear. "Suspecting one of my people feels... awful."

Her voice faltered for a moment, and I instinctively reached out, my hand hovering inches from hers before I caught myself. Touching her now—after everything—felt too complicated, too weighted with meanings I wasn't ready to unpack.

"I get it." I kept my tone steady. "But if we don't figure this out, someone's going to get away with sabotaging you and stealing your work. That's not fair to you or your team."

She nodded, but her expression remained clouded. Her pen twirled absently between her fingers, a small tell that she was wrestling with more than just the spreadsheet in front of her.

"Can you talk to them again?" she asked after a pause. "See if you can... I don't know, sense anything off?"

"Consider it done." I rose from my chair. The urge to say something more—something reassuring—nagged at me, but I kept it simple. "We'll find the mole."

As I left her office, the weight of everything—this investigation, her guardedness, the unsaid things between us—pressed down on me. Solving the mystery of who betrayed her team was important, but it wasn't the only puzzle I needed to solve.

On my way to see Kitty, I spotted her alone inside a small, glass-walled conference room. I watched her for a moment as she worked, her head bent over a stack of papers. My soft knock on the doorframe made her glance up, her expression brightening with recognition—though there was something else there too, a flicker of unease.

"Hey, Kitty. Can you spare a few minutes for the newest recruit?"

"Grayson, hi!" Her cheerful tone felt a little forced. "Come in. Welcome to the team."

"Thanks." I slid into the chair across from her.. "I'm still getting my bearings, but I've been hearing good things about how secure everything is around here. Cates seems to run a tight ship."

Kitty nodded, her shoulders relaxing slightly. "We had a scare a couple of weeks ago and things have tightened up a lot. We have different levels of access for different roles. It's all about safeguarding our data."

I leaned back in my chair, aiming for casual curiosity, like someone trying to suss out lab culture more than anything else. "Good to know. I've been looking at some of the workflow logs to get a sense of the pace here. Everyone seems to put in a lot of late nights. Is that normal, or am I just looking at a particularly busy month?"

Her hand hovered briefly over a pen before she answered, her tone light but cautious. "Oh, it happens when deadlines are tight or when experiments need monitoring. Cell cultures don't care what time it is."

I chuckled, offering a self-deprecating smile. "I guess I'll need to get used to after-hours paperwork for requesting accessing project files. That's standard for most labs I've worked in."

Kitty blinked, her brows pulling together slightly. "Oh—no, not here. Your access level includes 24/7 permissions. That's standard for anyone in your role."

I let my eyebrows lift, like that was a pleasant surprise. "Really? That's a relief. One less form to file at midnight. It's always tricky coming into a new place and learning the rules."

Her smile returned, less forced this time. "Happy to help. If you need anything else, just ask."

I stood, offering a friendly smile as I tucked my hands into my pockets. "Thanks, Kitty. I appreciate your time."

As I stepped out into the hallway, I couldn't shake the subtle tension lingering in the room. Kitty's bubbly demeanor felt genuine on the surface, but there'd been a hitch—something beneath it that made me wonder.

Not that I had any right to pat myself on the back. I wasn't exactly Hercule Poirot, deducing grand conspiracies with a twirl of my metaphorical mustache or subtly guiding a suspect into confessing all. I'd stumbled through that conversation like a guy fumbling in the dark for a light switch, half-hoping I'd find something useful and half-afraid I'd break something instead. If there was a mole, they were more likely to trip over me than I was to outsmart them.

Still, I'd gotten one small clue: 24/7 access. The question was whether that was normal. If so, it was certainly a place where they should tighten security.

Next stop: the break room.

The scent of scorched coffee greeted me as I stepped in, along with the sight of Andrew pouring himself a cup from the ancient machine in the corner. With his neat blond hair and easygoing air, he gave off golden-retriever energy in human form.

"Hey there." He greeted with a wide grin, raising his mug in a friendly salute. "Need a caffeine boost?"

"Always." I shot him a matching his grin. "But right now, I'm just trying to figure out where everything is—and everyone."

Andrew chuckled, taking a sip of his coffee. "You'll get the lay of the land in no time. This place is like a big puzzle, but once you know the pieces, it all clicks." He set down his mug, his voice dropping to a mock-conspiratorial tone. "And if you're looking for the best coffee hacks, I'm your guy."

"Noted." I leaned against the counter. "I'll take you up on that lesson sometime. For now, I'm just trying to get to know the team. I hear there was some kind of security issue recently?"

Andrew's face darkened, concern flickering in his eyes. "Yeah, about a month ago. But honestly, it couldn't have been anyone here. This team's as solid as they come. I'd vouch for every single one of them. I think we must have been hacked."

I tilted my head, studying him. "So, no suspicions at all? Nobody who seems... off?" This would be the prefect chance for him to throw someone under the bus and deflect attention from himself.

"Nope." He shook his head emphatically. "We're a tight-knit group. If something shady went down, it wasn't from inside."

It was hard to tell if Andrew's confidence was genuine or just a polished façade. Either way, he was good at playing the loyal teammate.

"Good to know."

As I headed for the door, his voice followed me. "Don't forget—coffee hacks. Anytime!"

His optimism was contagious, but it didn't dispel the gnawing suspicion in my gut. One of these three teammates was our mole. But which one?

Mercy's office was a world unto itself.

The green glow from her thriving collection of plants bathed the room in a calming light, and the gentle trickle of a water fountain provided a soothing backdrop. Mercy herself was seated at her desk, typing away with the kind of precision that suggested she could probably hack the Pentagon if she wanted to.

Her dark clothes and calm, deliberate movements gave her an air of quiet authority, like she had the whole world under control from her botanical command center—like a spider lying in wait.

"Dr. Grayson Stellar," she said without looking up, her voice smooth and devoid of any particular emotion.

"That's me." I stepped into the room and took a seat. "Nice setup. Not what I expected."

A faint smile played at the edges of her lips. "Why? Did you think I'd be surrounded by spreadsheets and soul-crushing fluorescent lighting?"

"Maybe a little." I took in the jungle-like atmosphere. "It's impressive. Like a rainforest, but, you know, without poison dart frogs or things that want to kill you."

Her eyes flicked up, amusement briefly breaking through her usual calm. "For now. But the plants have their moments."

I let out a soft laugh, trying to gauge if that was humor or an actual warning. "I'm still learning the ropes here. Thought I'd check in about data access protocols. Seems like everyone's really dialed in."

Her fingers paused on the keyboard as she studied me, her gaze sharp and assessing. "The protocols are standard. Is there something specific you're concerned about?"

I chose my words carefully. "I've noticed some after-hours file access. Just trying to understand the work patterns here. Does everyone burn the midnight oil?"

Mercy sat back, folding her hands in her lap. "I do what's necessary for my position, whether that means late nights or early mornings. My access is routine, and I follow protocol to the letter."

Her tone was calm, but there was an edge to her words that suggested I'd hit a nerve.

"I'm sure you do," I said evenly. "I'm just trying to get a sense of things."

She leaned forward, lifting a small watering can and soaking a nearby plant with deliberate precision. "If you're looking for insight into security, I suggest speaking with Courtney. She's more familiar with the team's routines."

She set down the watering can and gave me a pointed look. "She's also a lot more patient with people asking obvious questions."

I might as well have walked in here with a neon sign blinking: *Here to snoop!* Mercy had seen right through me, and she wasn't even trying to hide it. I sucked at this. Stealth and subtlety clearly weren't my strong suits. If I'd been aiming for undercover cool, I'd landed somewhere closer to awkward intern who asks too many questions.

Clearly, Mercy had figured out why I was really here—or at least suspected something—and her suggestion to "speak with Courtney" wasn't just a redirection. It was a warning, wrapped in polite professionalism and perfectly watered ferns.

I stood, trying to exit with whatever dignity I had left. "Thanks, Mercy. I'll let you get back to it."

She gave a curt nod, her focus already drifting back to her keyboard, but I didn't miss the subtle shift in her expression—like someone who'd filed my visit away as another piece of a puzzle.

As I walked out, her voice followed me, smooth as ever. "And Grayson? Next time, maybe come with better camouflage. You stick out in this jungle."

Mercy one, Grayson zero.

Back in Courtney's office, I sank into the chair across from her desk. The familiar scent of coffee mingled with the faint trace of her perfume, grounding me in the moment. For all my big ideas about "playing detective," it was clear I wasn't cut out for cloak-and-dagger games. I was no James Bond. Heck, I wasn't even a Hardy Boy.

If anything, I was an amateur actor flubbing my lines, and the audience was starting to notice.

Courtney glanced up from her laptop, her tone light but her eyes sharp. "So, tell me. Did you manage to solve the case in one afternoon, Sherlock?"

"Not quite." I ran running a hand through my hair, feeling as flat-footed and underprepared as I had that night I'd challenged Courtney to a chess match. "Kitty's bright and cheerful, but there's something beneath the surface—nerves, maybe, or something else entirely. Andrew's... well, Andrew. He's an open book, loyal to a fault—or he's putting on an Oscar-worthy performance." I paused, letting out a long sigh. "And Mercy? She's sharp. I'm pretty sure she clocked me the second I walked into her botanical fortress. Her office might look like a spa retreat, but she's got the vibe of someone who could spot a mole from a mile away—and let you know it with a smile."

Courtney's brow arched, amusement tugging at her lips. "Did you at least water her plants while you were there?"

"I would've if it bought me some goodwill." I leaned back with a rueful smile. "But let's just say I wasn't stealthy enough to win any awards. If there's a mole in this group, they're doing a much better job playing their part than I am mine."

Her expression softened, though the wheels were clearly still turning behind her eyes. "Well, you didn't promise me espionage mastery, so I guess I can't be too disappointed."

"Good, because I'm pretty sure Mercy's already filing a mental report about me under 'suspicious behavior'."

Courtney chuckled softly, but her focus returned to her screen as she mulled over my feedback. "It's progress," she said, almost to herself. "You've given me something to think about." Her gaze softened, a flicker of gratitude shining through. "Thanks for helping with this, Grayson. It means a lot that you're here."

I leaned forward, resting my elbows on my knees. "We'll need to coordinate with Christian. Maybe he's up on something we've missed."

Courtney nodded, the determined gleam returning to her eyes. "If anyone can find a digital breadcrumb, it's Christian."

For a moment, the tension between us felt less like a wall and more like a bridge—fragile, but possible to cross. Despite the weight of everything unsaid between us, the urgency of the case held us together, like two halves of a puzzle waiting for the right pieces to connect.

As she stood, she added, "Grayson—thanks. Not just for the investigation, but for..." She paused, searching for the words. "For being here."

I offered her a nod, swallowing back the mix of emotions her words stirred. "We'll figure this out, Courtney. All of it."

41

RED-HANDED

Courtney

The clock ticked toward three o'clock as Grayson and I stepped into the almost otherworldly realm of the security room. Bathed in the dim glow of flickering monitors, the space felt timeless, insulated from the chaos outside. Christian, hunched over his command center of screens, didn't bother looking up as we approached.

"Got names?" he asked, his voice clipped and efficient.

I handed over the list of three names, and his fingers flew across the keyboard, a blur of motion. "Cloning their drives now," he muttered. "If there's dirt to dig up, it's already quaking in fear." He tossed a handful of jellybeans into his mouth, his gaze never leaving the screens. "Gotta move fast before someone thinks to start scrubbing."

Christian was already lost in his digital world, his intensity filling the room. Grayson and I exchanged a glance—silent acknowledgment of his brilliance and the tension coursing through us both—before we slipped back into the hallway.

As I pressed the button for the elevator, Grayson broke the silence. "Christian's got the digital side covered, but what about non-electronic clues? Paper trails, physical files—stuff a computer can't pick up?"

I tilted my head, considering. "It's not a bad idea. We might turn up a clue that points to someone outside the team. Sometimes people forget that the simplest evidence can be the hardest to hide. A misplaced receipt, a printout, even handwritten notes—those things don't vanish with a hard drive wipe."

"Exactly," Grayson said, his lips twitching into a faint smile. "Good, old-fashioned sleuthing. Let Christian handle the high-tech forensics, and we'll hit the lab to see if anyone left behind something they shouldn't have."

We stepped into the elevator and I pressed the button for the floor with the labs. "You think our suspect got sloppy?"

"Maybe not sloppy," he admitted, leaning back against the elevator wall, "but people are creatures of habit. Even the smartest ones make mistakes. And right now, we're looking for anything that doesn't belong."

The sterile brightness of the lab greeted us as I slid into my white coat, the fabric cool against my arms. I motioned toward the corner desk. "I'll check the handwritten notes. You take the access logs. Let's see if we can figure out who's been stealing my life's work."

Grayson nodded, grabbing a clipboard from its hook and diving straight in. As he scanned the pages, his brow furrowed with laser-sharp focus. I busied myself with the logbooks, flipping through the pages in search of anything that seemed off. Any handwriting that seemed out of place or timestamp that didn't make sense.

The lab hummed with a quiet intensity, broken only by the sound of fluttering pages and the occasional beep from the equipment. I was just starting to feel the weight of doubt creep in when Grayson's voice broke through the silence.

"Courtney, come see this."

Something in his tone made my stomach twist. I abandoned the logbook and hurried over, nearly knocking heads with him as I leaned in to see the clipboard he was holding. Our shoulders brushed, and for a brief second, my focus wavered. His scent—clean, warm, and distinctly Grayson—hit me like a rogue wave of nostalgia.

"Here." He pointed to an entry. "Why did Kitty check the cell line just an hour after you did? And on a Saturday, no less. This was last month."

I leaned in closer, my hair brushing against his arm as I squinted at the entry. "That's... not normal. There's no reason for her to double-check my work unless—" I trailed off, the implications sinking in.

Grayson stepped back, his jaw tightening. "Let's cross-reference with the handwritten logs." He moved with the kind of focus that said this wasn't just about solving a case; it was about keeping me steady.

I followed, flipping to the same date in the logbook. "This is my entry." I tapped the page with my pen. "But look—just underneath..." My voice trailed off as I noticed faint, erased writing beneath my notes. I leaned closer, tilting the page to catch the faint pencil impressions.

Grayson stood at my side, his expression darkening. "Kitty must've written it down out of habit—she probably panicked and erased it later, hoping no one would check."

"That's sloppy," I muttered, my voice tinged with disbelief. "She should've known better."

He tilted his head, a wry smile tugging at his lips. "You sound almost offended."

I arched a brow. "I'm a perfectionist, Grayson. If someone's going to tamper with my logs, they could at least do a decent job." I froze, noticing something off, flipping forward in the log book, then back again, confirming my suspicions. "There's a page missing. Check the page numbers."

The small bubble of humor burst as reality settled back in. Kitty. Someone I'd worked with, trusted, and even defended at times. Now, it felt like every note, every text I'd ever shared with her had been a blueprint for her betrayal. My chest tightened, anger rising like a hot tide. What else had she tampered with? "Sabotage is bad enough, but this?" I slammed the logbook shut. "This is personal."

Before he could respond, my phone vibrated loudly against the lab counter, its screen lighting up with Christian's name. A video call. I answered quickly, holding it out so Grayson could be seen on camera as well. "Christian, we've got something."

"Same here." His voice was sharp and urgent. "Watch this. I've got a live feed from the server room. Someone's tearing it apart—literally."

He flipped the camera to point at a security monitor with a grainy video feed. Kitty's figure filled the screen, her movements frantic as she yanked up floor panels and pulled on cables like a thief in a heist movie gone wrong.

"She's looking for the USB drive." Grayson voice was laced with quiet intensity.

"She's doing more than that," Christian cut in. "She's pulling power plugs. It's messy, but if she gets lucky, she could do some real damage—maybe even destroy your data."

My stomach twisted as alarms blared, the red light casting a frantic glow over Kitty's wild, desperate movements. It was like watching my worst nightmare unfold in real time. At the noise, she froze for a moment, then dove across the floor, yanking another panel loose.

"We need to stop her. That room is just down the hall." I was already moving toward the door, Grayson close behind, his long strides easily keeping pace.

"Christian, can you lock her in?" Grayson asked.

"Not from here." Christian's clipped response came through the phone. "Get to her before she destroys something."

The blaring alarms seemed to echo louder as we sprinted down the hallway, our footsteps pounding against the tile. By the time we reached the server room, the siren was deafening, the red lights casting eerie shadows across the walls.

Grayson shoved the door open, and we burst inside—only to find chaos.

The floor panels were askew, cables spilled out in a tangle, and the faint scent of burned electronics clung to the air. But Kitty? She was gone.

"Damn it," Grayson muttered, his jaw tightening as he surveyed the wreckage.

"She can't have gotten far." My words sounded hollow, even to me. My stomach twisted. We had proof of her betrayal, but she'd slipped through our fingers, leaving us with more questions than answers.

Before I could decide what to do next, Pete skidded into the room, his face a mix of panic and determination. "What the hell happened here?" His gaze darted from the mess to me and Grayson.

"Kitty," Grayson said sharply. "She was here tearing everything apart. Christian saw her on the security cameras."

As if on cue, Christian's voice came through the phone I still clutched in my hand. "You're not gonna believe this. Security just radioed. They're tracking her through the building."

My stomach twisted, adrenaline surging through me as I lifted the phone to look at him. "Where's she heading?"

"Toward the east stairwell," Christian said, his voice clipped. "You might still catch her if you move."

Grayson and I exchanged a quick glance and bolted for the door, the off-putting silence of the server room giving way to the pounding of our footsteps down the hallway. My mind raced as we turned the corner, the alarm system blaring overhead like a war cry.

KITTY-CATCH

Grayson

As tore down the hall, the fading wail of the alarms was replaced by the rhythmic slap of our footsteps against the tile. At the south exit, the harsh afternoon sunlight illuminated a knot of security guards standing just beyond the glass doors.

They had her.

Kitty was a mess—hair tangled, lab coat slipping off one shoulder, her expression a cocktail of panic and defiance. "This is a misunderstanding!" she shouted, her voice cracking. "I was just making sure the alarms worked!"

Courtney and I slowed as we approached. Kitty's wide, tear-filled eyes locked onto Courtney, her voice shifting to something closer to a plea. "Courtney, please, you know me! I wouldn't sabotage the project! This is all a setup!"

"The cameras don't lie, Kitty." I stepped forward, my tone cutting through her performance. "You weren't checking the alarms. You were tearing out cables and ripping up floor tiles. You didn't get set up—you got caught."

For a moment, her face froze, her brain scrambling for its next move. Then, like a dam breaking, she crumpled to her knees, clutching at her lab coat. "I was desperate! You don't understand —I didn't mean to—what about my kids?"

Beside me, Courtney's silence was deafening. Her face was composed, but I could see the storm brewing beneath the surface. Hurt and anger clashed in her eyes, but she held herself steady.

"She's only sorry because she got caught," I murmured, leaning closer to Courtney.

She gave a small nod, her jaw tightening as the guards cuffed Kitty and led her away. Kitty's protests faded into the distance, leaving behind an air of finality that didn't feel remotely like relief.

As we stood there, watching them disappear, it hit me: catching Kitty changed everything. Joaquin was off the hook. The photo he'd shown me—Courtney's stolen research—now had a trail leading directly to Kitty, and Joaquin's accidental role was no longer relevant. We had the real thief.

I turned to Courtney. Her shoulders were squared, her face a mask of calm resolve.

"Grayson, we need to wrap things up." Christian's voice buzzed from Courtney's phone, loud enough for both of us to hear. "Meet me in the security room."

Courtney lifted her phone to face him. "Send the security footage to Larry as soon as possible. I'll handle the next steps with him."

Christian's voice crackled back. "Already in progress. I've got everything logged and ready to hand over. It's clean—Kitty didn't cover her tracks."

"Thanks, Christian." She ended the call with a quick tap and slid the phone into her pocket.

"Meet me in my office when you're done with Christian," she said over her shoulder, not breaking stride as she headed down the hallway.

I watched her disappear around the corner with purpose. Whatever she was feeling, she wasn't about to let it show. Not yet.

Back in the security room, Christian was already packing up, his movements brisk and methodical. The room still hummed with the quiet buzz of servers and monitors, their blue glow softening the edges of the space.

"That was dramatic," Christian said without looking up, shoving cables into his bag with a precision that matched his demeanor. "Kitty's in custody and I already sent the evidence to Courtney and Larry. My part's done."

"You're leaving?" I asked, surprised.

He slung his bag over his shoulder, his expression unapologetic. "Catch an earlier flight or stick around for tomorrow's drama? No contest." He paused by the door, glancing back at me with a knowing smirk. "But you? Figure out your priorities with that woman before you regret it."

I raised an eyebrow. "What's that supposed to mean?"

"You know exactly what it means," he said, his smirk widening. "Don't screw things up with her."

And with that, he was gone, the door clicking shut behind him. The quiet that followed felt louder than the alarms had.

My phone buzzed, the sharp vibration breaking the silence. Pulling it from my pocket, I saw the notification—a reminder about meeting Kincaid later this evening.

I tapped to confirm, letting out a measured breath. There were still things to handle here, but this meeting was non-negotiable— important enough to stay on my radar no matter the chaos. A glance at the clock reassured me I still had plenty of time, but first, I needed to check on Courtney. After everything we'd been through today, I couldn't shake the need to see how she was holding up—and figure out if there was anything I could do to help.

My gaze drifted to the glowing monitors, the weight of the day pressing heavily on my chest. Kitty's betrayal, the investigation, the quiet tension that lingered between Courtney and me—it all swirled in my head. But it wasn't just the day's events; it was the look on Courtney's face when Kitty crumbled. Composed on the outside, but I knew better. This had cut deep, and the thought of her carrying that alone was unbearable.

I turned and headed for her office. We'd agreed to talk about us when this was over, and I owed her the space to decide what that meant. But this wasn't about answers—it was about showing up. Because no matter how strong she seemed, Courtney didn't have to weather this storm on her own. Not while I was here.

TIED ENDS, LOOSE THREADS

Courtney

I stared at my phone, my thumb hovering over Larry's name. Knowing the truth about Kitty wasn't enough. We needed her to admit it, to point the finger at MedcoVax, and help us prove the theft beyond any doubt.

A thank-you note from her sat on the corner of my desk, mocking me with its hollow sentiment. *"Courtney-You're the best boss ever. I love being on this team."* Last spring, it had felt like camaraderie, a token of trust. Now I knew it was just a lie, a relic of betrayal that made my stomach churn.

I took a steadying breath and dialed. The line connected on the second ring.

"Courtney," Larry said, his tone brisk and sharp. "What's happening? I heard the alarms going off. Did you find the mole?"

"We did." My voice sounded firmer than I felt. "It's Kitty. We caught her tearing apart the server room looking for a flash drive she'd hidden there. Christian compiled everything—security footage, data transfers, her access logs. It's ironclad. She tried lying her way out of it, but when she learned we'd caught her on camera, she broke down in tears and admitted to everything."

Larry let out a low exhale, the kind that spoke volumes. "I

knew it would be someone close, but... Kitty? Damn it. Evelyn's already called twice, wanting answers. MedcoVax is doubling down on its patent filing, and unless we move fast, they're going to bury us."

I closed my eyes briefly, letting his words settle. "We have the evidence, Larry. We can prove Kitty stole it. But if we want to tie this to MedcoVax, we need her to talk. She's the only one who can give us the connection we need. She has to name names."

"Then we make her flip," he said, his voice sharp. "Do whatever it takes. MedcoVax filed first, and our only shot is proving they stole from us."

"I understand." I gripped the edge of my desk to steady myself. "I'll be in your office in twenty minutes. We can plan our next move then."

"Good. I'll loop Evelyn in on this. And Courtney?"

"Yes?"

"Good work. I know this isn't easy, but you handled it."

The line went dead, leaving me in the heavy silence of my office. Relief mingled with anger, twisting in my chest like a knot. Kitty hadn't just jeopardized the project—she'd betrayed us all. Every late night, every breakthrough, every ounce of sweat and hope my team had poured into this work was now tangled in MedcoVax's sticky hands. And I'd trusted her to keep it safe.

A knock at the door cut through my rising nausea, pulling me back to the present.

Grayson stepped inside, his hair disheveled, his sleeves rolled up. He looked like he'd walked through the same storm I had, but instead of frazzled, he carried that quiet steadiness I hadn't realized I needed.

"Hey," he said, his voice soft, as he closed the door behind him. "How are you holding up?"

I managed a nod, though I wasn't sure why. I was far from being okay. "Larry's taking it well enough, but this is going to gut the team. Roz, Andrew, Mercy... they're going to take this personally. I know I do."

Grayson pulled up a chair across from me, his expression serious. "What Kitty did? That's on her, Courtney, not you. Not them. Don't carry the weight of her choices."

I wanted to believe him, but the guilt clawed at me. "She was my responsibility, Grayson. I trusted her when I shouldn't have. This is my failure."

"No," he said firmly, leaning forward. "It's not on you. You handled this better than most people would've—faced the possibility of a mole with determination and grit. For the record, I'm impressed."

His words eased the sting of doubt, though the ache lingered. "Thanks," I said quietly. "That means a lot."

Grayson's gaze softened, and his voice lowered, threading sincerity through every word. "Courtney, listen to me. I'm here—whatever you need. Navigating a course forward with Larry, cleaning up this mess, or just holding steady when it feels like the ground's shifting—I've got your back."

The words hit like a wave, cracking the walls I'd held up so carefully. Before I could stop myself, I started to explain. "Do you know why I reacted the way I did? Why I pushed you away?"

His brow furrowed slightly, but he didn't interrupt.

"It's my dad," I said finally, the words heavy but necessary. "He didn't just leave—he built a whole second life. A boat, hidden bank accounts, even a half-sister I didn't know existed until she was six months old. It felt like every part of my family was a lie, like I'd been living in someone else's story without realizing it. Finding out... it shattered everything I thought I knew about trust. Even now, years later, the cracks remain—fragile, invisible until someone presses too hard, and suddenly, everything splinters again." My voice wavered, the words heavier than I'd anticipated. Grayson stayed silent, his hand resting lightly over mine in quiet support. His steady presence made it easier to keep going.

When I fell silent, he didn't rush to fill the space. Instead, he tilted his head slightly, his gaze thoughtful. "You know, when trust breaks, it can feel like nothing's solid anymore. Like you're walking on thin ice—one wrong step, and you crash through." His thumb brushed the back of my hand, a small, grounding gesture. "But you're stronger than you give yourself credit for. You've built something incredible—not just your work, but the way you lead your team, the way you push forward even when everything feels impossible."

I blinked, his words catching me off guard. "That's... a different perspective," I admitted. "I've had to be strong because there wasn't another choice."

"And that's why I admire you," he said, his voice steady. "But you don't always have to carry everything on your own. Trusting someone again—it's terrifying. I get that. But if you're willing to take that step, even a small one, you don't have to carry this weight alone."

His words arrowed straight into me, cracking through my armor. I nodded, the ache in my chest sharp and unrelenting. "When you waited before telling me about the theft..." My voice wavered. "It felt like history repeating itself. Like I'd been blind-sided again. I've been so scared of letting anyone in, only to have it all fall apart."

Grayson's hand tightened gently around mine. "Courtney, I get it. What your dad did—it's left a mark. But you're not him, and neither am I. Trust isn't easy, especially when it's been broken before. But if you're willing to give this a shot—to work through the messy parts together—I'm all in."

His words lit a small flame of hope in my chest. "I want to try," I said quietly, meeting his gaze. "I'm scared, but I do want to give this a chance."

"That's all I needed to hear." Grayson reached for my hand, threading his fingers through mine, his smile soft and unwaver-ing. "Whatever comes next, we can handle it."

My desktop computer chimed with a reminder, breaking the moment. I glanced at it reluctantly, the weight of reality creeping back in. "I need to get to Larry's office," I said, standing.

Grayson rose with me, his steady presence grounding. "Let's

talk later tonight. After this is over, we'll figure out the rest. How about if we celebrate over ice cream."

That made me smile. "It's a date." My voice sounded a little steadier, the weight on my shoulders just a bit lighter.

As I turned to leave, I glanced back at him. His steady gaze met mine, full of reassurance and something deeper, something I hadn't dared to hope for. And in that moment, I knew—this wasn't the end. Not for us. Not by a long shot.

###

I rubbed my temples, the day still not over. I stood in Larry's office, where the hum of overhead lights made the silence feel uncomfortably loud.

He flipped through a small stack of notes, eyebrows drawn together. "She's talking, you know. Kitty, I mean." His voice was low, as if we were conspiring, and my chest tightened, a mix of anger, disbelief, and betrayal bubbling under the surface, threatening to spill over. "Security's holding her, and she's giving them a statement."

My heart twisted. "A statement? So... she's really admitting it?"

Larry nodded and handed me a single page covered in Kitty's uneven scrawl. "She says MedcoVax offered her more money than she'd seen in her entire career. Claimed her mother's medical bills were drowning her, and she figured nobody here would step in to help. Told herself it was a onetime deal—said nobody would get hurt."

I stared at the page, my anger and pity tangling up inside. I understood desperation—family medical bills, feeling overwhelmed—but it didn't dull the sting of betrayal. She'd had options. She could have come to me. Instead, she'd chosen to cut corners, leaving our trust in tatters. "She actually wrote all this?"

Larry sighed, handing me the paper. "She claims she felt overshadowed—like you were the 'obvious star,' and nobody would give her a second glance. She admits she panicked, took the deal, and then everything spiraled."

A hollow ache settled in my chest. "I would have helped her," I whispered, my throat tightening. "She never gave me the chance."

"That's the tragedy of it," Larry said quietly. "But she's cooperating now, which means we have enough to nail MedcoVax for stealing your work."

My eyes flicked over Kitty's confession, each sentence a reminder of her desperation—and her betrayal. "It's like a punch in the gut, finding out someone you trusted believed no one here would lift a finger to help her."

Larry placed a hand on my shoulder, his tone gentler than usual. "Kitty's choices are on her, not on you. Don't carry this guilt. Focus on the upside: with this, we can undo MedcoVax's patent and get your research back on track."

44

HEARTFELT CONFESSIONS

Grayson

> Kincaid: Good luck tonight, man. Hope it works out.

> Me: Thanks. I think I'll need it.

Despite the cool autumn air, adrenaline kept me warm as I arrived early at Sweet Scoops. I settled near the window, hyper-aware of two keys in my pocket—and the weight of their meaning.

The door chime jingled, and Courtney stepped in. Light seemed to cling to her. Our eyes met, and a shiver of anticipation ran down my spine.

"Hey," she greeted softly, her tone tentative but warm.

I rose, heart pounding. "Dr. Watson. You look oddly composed after the day we've had."

She let out a quick laugh. "Maybe it's the thrill of cracking the case, Sherlock. Finally pinpointing Kitty as the mole is a huge relief. Definitely calls for celebration."

I nodded at the counter. "One scoop at a time."

We picked our favorites—Cider House Rules for her, Choco-

291

late Sinsation for me—and wandered outside into the crisp air. The streetlights bathed the sidewalk in a golden glow.

"How about a walk?"

Courtney's posture eased. "Sounds good. I need to unwind."

Side by side, we strolled toward the town center, the crunch of leaves punctuating our steps.

"So," I ventured, "what happens next with your stolen research?"

She hesitated. "With Kitty's confession and Andrew's photo, we have the evidence to petition to revoke MedcoVax's patent. Legal stuff takes forever, but at least we're moving forward. Our lawyer thinks the threat of a lawsuit will get MedcoVax to withdraw their claim."

"That's a big step."

Her smile faded. "Hard to be relieved when someone I trusted sold me out. I get why she did it, but she never gave any of us a chance to help. I'm really struggling to come to terms with it."

I touched her arm gently. "She made her choice. At least she's helping fix things now."

Courtney nodded, a faint smile tugging at her lips. "With Evelyn leading the charge, I think we've got this."

Courtney nodded, though her eyes stayed clouded. We turned a corner toward the old gazebo, and she spoke more quietly. "I've been thinking a lot about my half-sister lately."

My steps slowed. "Your dad's... surprise baby?" Was Courtney finally going to open up?

She nodded. "The one and only. Her name's Adele. He emailed me recently—twice, actually—saying she wants to meet me." She slowed her pace, brushing her fingers against mine until they intertwined.

"What will you do?"

Her lips pressed into a thin line as we resumed walking. "I've decided I want us to meet—but on my terms, without involving my father. I don't want to let him back into my life...not that he's asking for himself. But my relationship with him has nothing to do with her. She's twelve...just a kid. Not her fault she got dragged into Dad's mess."

I squeezed her hand. "Any idea what you'll say?"

She let out a shaky laugh. "I keep picturing a Disney Channel sitcom scenario: 'Hi, Adele, surprise! I'm your sister—ice cream?' But maybe it's a start."

"Ice cream is universal," I teased, lifting my cone..

Her expression turned thoughtful. "I just want her to know she's not alone, no matter how messed up Dad can be."

Her smile grew a little, and she nudged me with her elbow. "Maybe I'll take that under advisement."

"What your doing is huge," I said softly. "You're giving her a family."

Her fingers tightened around mine. "My brothers have complicated feelings about Dad. It's easier talking to you— someone who listens, who doesn't have a stake in the old drama."

Warmth spread through me. "You're stronger than you realize, Courtney. Whatever you decide, you'll handle it."

She gazed at me, relief flickering in her eyes. "Thank you. For being here, for everything."

We reached the gazebo, the wooden posts framed with string lights giving the piano prominence. With our ice cream eaten, we both tossed our napkins in the trash can.

"Those metrics we discussed," she said, a teasing lilt in her tone, "and those creatively embellished charts of yours? Impressive positive trends."

I arched a brow. "Ah, the heart-shaped data points truly groundbreaking work. I accept your admiration."

She laughed again, the sound lighting up the cool night. "Groundbreaking. Working with you today reminded me of what a great team we make."

I smiled, warmth spreading through me. "Uncanny, isn't it? How well we click?"

Her expression turned softer, introspective. "Isn't it ironic? We can crack a corporate espionage case in less than a day, yet figuring out our own relationship? So much harder."

"Life's messy," I said, stepping closer. "And the heart... well, the heart's the most complex puzzle of all."

I took her hand, leading her to the piano bench—the same spot where the musician had played James Booker a few weeks ago. When we sat, our hips touched, and our shoulders brushed, the contact grounding me in a way I hadn't felt in weeks. The air between us hummed, full of unspoken words and lingering tension.

Finally, Courtney drew a breath. "There's something I need to say."

My heart lurched. "Yeah?"

She exhaled, voice trembling with courage. "I've fallen for you —hard. Tripped over my shoelaces, tumbled headfirst down the rabbit hole, and landed smack-dab in love with you."

Her confession stole my breath. She'd beaten me to it. "Courtney Gillette, I fell down that rabbit hole a long time ago. And it's the easiest terrifying thing I've ever done. I love you too."

Her eyes shimmered, a laugh escaping as she wiped at a tear. "I'm hopeless," she said with a sniffle. "Getting all emotional when you're so composed."

"Composed?" I tucked a curl behind her ear. "You have no idea. I'm barely keeping it together." I had so much I wanted to say, but I wasn't sure where to begin.

Inspiration struck, and her laugh was soft, brushing over me like a breeze as I lifted my hands to the piano's keys. I'd let the music thrumming through my veins tell her how I felt. "Let me show you something."

She stayed next to me, our hips touching, as she leaned to one side so I could play. My fingers drifted over the keys, launching into Ray Charles' *Hallelujah I Love Her So*. When I swapped a few lyrics for playful a reference—*I bring her coffee in her Sherlock mug* —she burst out laughing. By the final chord, her cheeks were flushed, eyes bright.

"No drama, huh?" She wiped at her cheeks again. "You just serenaded me in the middle of town."

"Worked, didn't it?"

She laced her fingers with mine. "Completely."

I dropped my voice. "Maybe the ending makes all the heartbreak and chaos worth it."

Her smile turned tender. "You know, I'm so completely crazy about you."

"The feeling's mutual."

She shot to her feet, brushing off imaginary dust. "Can we walk? This is a little too public for more waterworks."

Standing, I slipped a key from my pocket, glinting under the lamplight. "If it's privacy you want, consider this your golden ticket."

Her brows arched, curiosity igniting. "What's that, Mr. Holmes?"

45

ENVISIONING A LIFE IN HARMONY

COURTNEY

Grayson led me across the street to a door tucked between a couple of boutiques. His key turned with a soft click, though the flicker of nerves in his eyes betrayed him. He glanced back, his expression a mix of hope and teasing confidence. "Ready for a little adventure?" He held the key out to me.

I hesitated, curiosity tugging at me. His voice carried the promise of something unexpected, something I couldn't resist. With a small nod, I took the key from his hand and stepped inside.

A staircase stretched ahead, each step echoing softly as I climbed. Whatever waited at the top felt significant. The faint scent of fresh paint greeted me as I pushed open the upstairs door, revealing an empty apartment both elegant and welcoming.

At least no one jumped out shouting, "surprise!"

Light from streetlamps came in through the wide windows. The apartment was newly renovated, untouched—a blank slate brimming with possibility. When Grayson flicked on the lights, golden warmth filled every corner. My eyes were drawn to an archway at the far end, hinting at the kitchen beyond like an invitation.

I wandered toward it, my steps automatic, though my heart thrummed with anticipation. The polished countertops gleamed under the soft light, every detail crafted with care. This was Kincaid's work—my brother's signature craftsmanship evident in the sleek finishes and thoughtful design. I could feel the weight of what was coming, the way Grayson's energy shifted as he watched me take it all in. He wasn't just showing me around; this was leading to something bigger. Leaning against the counter, I turned to him with a playful smile, trying to mask my fluttering nerves. "So, what's the big reveal here? This isn't just a casual tour."

He took a steadying breath, his gaze meeting mine. "I want this to be our home." His voice was soft, but there was conviction behind it. "Kincaid handed me the keys tonight. He just finished renovating it, and we're the first to see it. With the proximity to both our jobs... I thought this could be the perfect place for us."

I let the words settle over me. Living in Sewickley wasn't unfamiliar—I'd only moved away a few months ago. There were drawbacks: the rush-hour traffic I'd face on the bridge, Grayson's longer commute time to Pitt. But the advantages were hard to ignore: the charm of the walkable streets, the absence of constant airplane noise humming overhead, the quiet that let you hear your own thoughts. But mostly, there was Grayson. It all added up to a better life. A happier life.

Still, the question lingered—was I ready for this? Were *we* ready for this?

My heart screamed, *Yes, what are you waiting for?* But reason tugged at me, urging caution. Big decisions shouldn't be rushed, right? I turned my focus back to the apartment, letting it speak to me. The kitchen sparked visions of us baking together, filling the air with the scent of chocolate and vanilla. Beyond it, the bedroom promised peace, and the bathroom, with its pristine tiles, hinted at long, indulgent baths. It was perfect—undeniably perfect.

But when I looked at Grayson, standing there with hope in his eyes, the perfection of the space faded into the background. His expression, open and vulnerable, felt heavier than the key I still clutched. He seemed to hold his breath, waiting for me to speak.

"It's beautiful, Gray," I said finally, my voice quiet but firm. "But... we've been on a rollercoaster lately. Twists, turns, and barely catching our breath."

His body tensed, and he took a step closer. "Rollercoasters are more fun when you've got someone holding your hand."

The corner of my mouth tugged into a reluctant smile. "Fair point. But before we jump into this, we need to talk—really talk. About what we want and where we're headed. We've never done that—not on a personal level."

Grayson nodded, moving to lean casually against the window. Moonlight framed him, his posture open and inviting. "Then let's talk."

"We've escalated from 'I love you' to 'let's live together' in minutes," I said, half-laughing to cover the knot forming in my chest. "It's... a lot to process. Give a girl a second, okay?" I took a steadying breath, forcing myself to start with the basics. "First, I need to make something clear: my work isn't just a job—it's a part of me. That's not changing."

Grayson's expression softened, his nod immediate and sincere. "I respect that. It's one of the reasons we fit. Our careers aren't just jobs—they're callings. And that commitment? I have it too"

His reassurance settled me, but I knew this was only the beginning. I paused, the weight of what I needed to say next making my chest feel tight. Our gazes locked, his steady and patient, encouraging me to continue. I exhaled slowly, searching for the right words. "There's something else," I began, the confession forming carefully. "Something I've known in my heart for a while but haven't said out loud."

He waited, silent, his presence grounding me.

"I don't want children, Grayson," I said finally, my voice a mix of determination and vulnerability. "Balancing motherhood with the dedication my work demands—it wouldn't be fair. Not to me, not to a child, and not to the dream I've poured everything into. I want to be at the forefront of cancer research, to make a real impact. The last thing I want is to turn into my dad... someone who had kids but was never around to raise them."

Grayson lifted his hands in a calming gesture, his voice as steady as his gaze. "Courtney, you're not alone in this. I'm with you, completely. Mentoring students? Rewarding, sure. Parenting? It's just not part of the life I see for myself. Sharing this dream with you, though—that feels exactly right."

Relief washed over me, unexpected and profound. "You don't want kids either?" My voice softened as the realization settled in, uncoiling a tension I hadn't fully acknowledged. "That's... a huge relief."

He smiled, his tone as warm as his words. "I value what you're aiming for, and I'm with you. We're a team," he said, his gaze holding mine with quiet intensity. "Anything else we need to talk about?"

I hesitated, knowing there was more to share—pieces of myself I needed him to understand. "There's one more thing," I said, my voice steady but weighted with significance. "I might not want kids, but my family? They're non-negotiable. Adele's still a bit of an unknown and Christopher's in London, but Kincaid and Conner are here in Sewickley, and Lianna's expecting—my niece or nephew is on the way. Staying close to them, being part of their lives, matters to me. It always will."

Grayson's smile deepened, his warmth wrapping around me like a favorite blanket. "That works perfectly for me. Mara and my parents are here too. Our roots are planted in the same soil. Anything else on your mind?"

I smirked, the tension easing. "A few things. You already know about my trust issues—and let's not forget my abandonment issues. But here's the real bombshell..." I leaned in, lowering my voice as if revealing a state secret. "I think I might be allergic to cats. After spending any time with my brother's cat Mick, I sneeze like crazy."

His laughter rang out, warm and unrestrained. "No cats?

That's the dealbreaker?" His eyes gleamed with amusement. "Alright, guess we'll have to forgo the furry companions. Maybe we'll really push the envelope and get a hairless cat someday."

"That has potential," I said, fighting a grin. "They're so ugly, they circle back to adorable."

"And you could knit it tiny sweaters."

"You've got knitting on the brain today," I teased. "Maybe it's time you picked up some needles and yarn for your next passion project." Then, with a playful tilt of my head, I added, "Speaking of non-negotiables, my book club meets monthly. It's sacred—books, laughter, and an amount of wine that would make Hemingway jealous."

Grayson chuckled, leaning in conspiratorially. "Hemingway. Cats. It's all coming together. And book club is sacrosanct? Got it. Sounds like your version of a secret society. I can see it now—part literary analysis, part world-saving strategies." He paused, a playful glint in his eye. "Or is it world domination?"

My gaze drifted to the window, where the gazebo below shimmered under the soft glow of moonlight. "The gazebo," I said, my voice quiet, reverent. "It's special to me. Especially after tonight. It's where we reconnected, where music spoke when words alone wouldn't do." Warmth spread through me, a quiet tide of contentment and anticipation. "This view overlooking it... it feels like living here with you is meant to be."

Grayson followed my gaze, his expression softening. "As it should," he teased lightly, then his tone turned serious. "It's like our own personal landmark. A place that's ours."

An idea began to take shape, one that felt as natural as breathing. I turned to him with a spark of excitement. "How about this? We start a weekend tradition. Something that anchors us. I'll bake something new every Saturday—like when we made my Orange Fig Carrot Cake or the chocolate mousse. There's an entire world of desserts you haven't tasted yet." I paused, letting the thought settle before continuing. "And in return, every Saturday evening, you play the piano for me at the gazebo. R&B, classical, pop—

whatever you're in the mood for. My baking, your music. A rhythm to our lives."

Grayson cocked an eyebrow, feigning deep thought, though the smile tugging at his lips gave him away. "Sweet treats paired with sweet beats? I like it. Sounds like the perfect plan." He stepped closer, his hand finding mine, our fingers intertwining as naturally as the moonlight spilling through the windows. "If I were to add a demand, though, it'd be this: we agree to always make space for the things that bring us joy. Right now, it's baking for you and piano for me. In the future? Whatever new passions come our way."

"Like knitting?" I gave a playful wink. "Deal. I think we might have this whole coupledom thing figured out."

Grayson stepped back theatrically, clutching his chest as though mortally wounded. "Wait! Does this mean we have to pick a couple name? Gray-Court? Court-son? That might be a deal-breaker for me."

Laughing, I jabbed him lightly in the ribs. "Alright, your high-ness. No cutesy couple names. Not even 'Grayt-ney'—although, I have to admit, that one's the least offensive."

The weight of the day felt miles away, and in this moment, we were just two people trying to find our rhythm. My gaze was drawn back to the window and the gazebo below. Bathed in moonlight, it glowed softly, like a promise waiting to unfold. He stepped closer, his hand finding mine.

"Since we're skipping the couple names," he said, his tone teasing, "should we move straight to matching sweaters? Maybe something with cats and chemistry beakers?"

I raised an eyebrow. "Cats and chemistry? You really know how to sweep a girl off her feet."

"Stick with me," he said, his grin widening. "I'll knit you a sweater so romantic it'll be banned in seven states."

I rolled my eyes, but my cheeks hurt from smiling. "Careful, or I'll hold you to that. It might be easier to start with a scarf, you know."

"Noted," he said, leaning in with a glint in his eye. "But if I knit it for you, you're wearing it proudly."

"As long as you're modeling it for Instagram," I shot back just before his lips met mine, sealing the deal in a kiss that was as ridiculous and perfect as we were.

As far as endings went, this one was pretty solid—messy, warm, and entirely us.

46

COUNTDOWN TO FIREWORKS

GRAYSON

The following summer

The July sun spilled into our bedroom, casting a warm, golden glow across Courtney as she slept, her auburn hair sprawled across her face in a makeshift sleep mask—her resourceful solution to the sun's sneak attack. Even asleep, she radiated the kind of energy that made me smile.

Life with Courtney was a mix of surprises and routines that never got old. Our apartment kitchen had turned into a stage for flour-dusted dance-offs, and I'd somehow become her book club's tech wizard, keeping Mara connected from Boston or L.A. or wherever she might be traveling to. Even on the busiest days, Courtney had a way of turning the mundane into something worth remembering.

This past year had been a whirlwind of milestones and challenges. Professionally, my research into cancer prediction was on the brink of breakthroughs that could revolutionize early detection. My dad, once a relentless critic, had eased off, finally recognizing I had more interests than just my work. And yes, I had successfully knitted my first ever scarf. But I still hadn't added a hairless cats to our family. Yet.

The corporate espionage saga had tested all of us, but in the end, Kitty's whistle-blower testimony had let Joaquin off the hook and exposed a MedcoVax insider, leading to a settlement. Courtney's research could finally move forward to human trials—a victory that mattered most.

Today, though, wasn't about work or past battles. Today carried a new kind of anticipation. Courtney's thirteen-year-old half-sister, Adele, was arriving from Texas where she lived with her mom on, of all things, a goat farm. She'd radiated excitement at finally meeting her siblings over last week's video chat, and Courtney had been counting down the days too.

Beside me, Courtney stirred, brushing her hair back with a groggy swipe. "Morning," she mumbled, looking adorably disheveled.

"Big day." I leaned in to kiss her forehead.

She stretched, letting out a contented sigh. "You nervous?"

"Me? Not at all. You and Adele have already clicked on video calls. She's going to fit right in. Besides, Sinan's party is the perfect icebreaker. She's Emma's age, isn't she? They'll find plenty to talk about."

Courtney's face softened, but a flicker of doubt lingered in her eyes. "I hope so. I just want her to feel welcome."

I grinned, ready to lighten the mood. "What if we put her to work in the kitchen? We could make those chocolate eclairs together. I might have picked up everything we need already. Surprise!"

Courtney's eyes lit up at the prospect of baking. "You're full of surprises, aren't you? That's a perfect idea. A shared project will help her settle in—and I know the crew will devour the eclairs."

If only she knew just how many surprises I had planned for her today.

An hour later, we were on our way to the airport to pick up Adele. At the airline counter, we secured passes to meet her right at the gate. Our anticipation only grew as we stood near the jet bridge, each passing moment building a quiet sense of excitement.

When Adele appeared, her strawberry-blond hair catching the overhead lights, I recognized her instantly. With her school back-pack slung over one shoulder, she looked every bit the seasoned traveler—though the slight tension in her expression told me she was a bit nervous about today.

Courtney waved with her trademark enthusiasm, and Adele's shoulders relaxed as she spotted us. The moment she reached us, Courtney pulled her into a hug, breaking through her shyness in an instant.

"Finally!" Courtney exclaimed, her voice full of energy. "I've been so excited to meet you in person!"

"Me too." Adele's reply came less enthusiastically, but just as heartfelt. Her voice carried a faint trace of something unspoken behind the Texas twang, a hint of sadness that tugged at the edges of her words. "I've wanted to ever since I found out about y'all."

Courtney's expression softened, her hand lightly brushing Adele's shoulder. "I wish we'd reached out sooner. We've missed so much, but you're here now, and that's what matters."

With her luggage collected and safely stowed, we settled into the car. Courtney rattled off details about Sinan's party and who Adele would meet there—her brothers, sister-in-law, and niece Harper—her excitement spilling over like it always did.

Adele's voice carried a mix of hesitation and curiosity. "Being an aunt at my age is... weird."

I caught her thoughtful expression in the rearview mirror and smiled. "At least you'll have Emma to hang out with tonight. She's my niece and your age—I think you two will hit it off."

Courtney turned in her seat to face Adele. "We've got a chill day planned—some baking before the party. Chocolate eclairs. What do you think?"

Adele hesitated, then shrugged. "Baking's cool. Mom and I cook together sometimes. She's really good at it. We've even made cheese from goat's milk."

Courtney's jaw dropped. "Wait, you're a cheesemaker? How

did you not lead with that? You're officially the coolest member of this family."

Adele's cheeks flushed, and she gave a small, almost shy smile. "It's not that exciting. Mostly I just help with the milking. The cheese-making part is messy and smells bad."

I smirked, flicking on my turn signal. "You know, if the eclairs flop, you two could pivot to goat cheese tarts and convince everyone it's the next big thing in French cuisine."

Adele's lips twitched into the faintest of smiles, but she didn't quite laugh. The earlier tension in her shoulders remained, though it had loosened slightly under the casual banter. She glanced out the window, her expression thoughtful, as if trying to take it all in without giving too much away. "I can't believe how green this place is. Everywhere you look, something's growing."

Courtney followed her gaze. "I never really thought about it, but I get that's because we get so much rain here."

As I drove, I couldn't help but think about what today meant for Adele, for Courtney, for the entire fractured family. She wasn't just meeting new faces; she was stepping into a new chapter of her life. No pressure, right?

Courtney turned to me, her voice low enough that only I could hear. "Today's going to be a good day." Her words were simple, but confident.

I reached over, giving her hand a quick squeeze. "The best."

47

SISTER TIME

COURTNEY

> Me: Adele's officially here and settling in. She's been quiet but super sweet. I think she's warming up.

> Kincaid: Quiet now… just wait until Conner starts telling his infamous "I burned down mom's kitchen" story.

> Conner: Hey, that story's a classic! Everyone loves it.

> Me: She'll love it, but let's aim for "cool uncles" today, not "overwhelming." Pace yourselves.

After settling Adele into the guest room, I steered her toward the kitchen—the heart of any proper family bonding experience. Humming an off-key rendition of *Fly Me to the Moon* (Frank Sinatra would've wept), I tried to infuse the moment with light-hearted energy. But for all her teenage awkwardness, Adele tackled the choux pastry like a pro.

I leaned over to inspect her progress and whistled low. "Look at you, pastry queen. This batter is a glossy masterpiece. Mommy Julie would've framed it."

Adele's lips twitched into the faintest smile, her focus unwavering as she stirred. "Sounds messy."

When it came time to pipe the dough onto trays, I handed her the piping bag like I was bestowing a family heirloom. "Your turn, Sis. Show me what you've got."

She hesitated at the nickname but then grinned, accepting the challenge. With a steady hand, she piped perfect, ruler-straight lines onto the baking sheet. My "artistic" approach, on the other hand, left squiggles resembling panicked earthworms.

"Not. A. Word," I warned, brandishing the piping bag.

"I didn't say anything," she replied, her face solemn but her shoulders shook with silent laughter.

By the time the eclairs were baking, we perched on stools, the room filled with the kind of anticipation only a kitchen project can create. "They're going to be perfect," I declared, determined to will it into existence.

They were—golden, crisp, and practically begging for custard filling and chocolate glaze. "You get the honors. I don't trust myself not to eat one," I said.

We were halfway through whisking the cream when Adele set the bowl down with a slight sigh, her smile faltering. A flicker of uncertainty passed over her face.

"Do you think Dad even realizes I'm here?" she asked quietly. "He hasn't called or anything lately. He hates texts, so I email him, but he almost never answers."

I nudged the mixing bowl closer, a familiar pang stirring in my chest. "Honestly, probably not," I told her. The admission tasted bitter, but I refused to sugarcoat the truth. "From what I've seen— and lived—our father's best skill is being absent."

She gave a short, humorless laugh, her shoulders sagging. "Figured. Mom says I shouldn't wait for him, but I keep hoping he'll wake up and remember he has another daughter."

"I get it." I measured out the sugar. "But some people never learn to be there for anyone else. Believe me—I wish it were different, too."

Adele let out a short laugh that didn't reach her eyes. "Yeah, it's mostly Mom and me running the place. Goats included. We haven't really needed him in a while."

I reached over and gave her shoulder a quick squeeze. "I know exactly how that feels. But I'm here whenever you need a sister— whether it's venting or baking or just sitting on the couch binge-watching a series. Whatever you want."

She cracked a more genuine smile at that. "Definitely an upgrade. Besides, I'm way more excited about this party and meeting more of my family than hearing from him."

"Good." I picked up the whisk again, deliberately shifting the mood back to playful. "He's had his chances. Not our fault he blew them. Right now, your only job is making sure these eclairs put all my past baking fails to shame. Deal?"

"Deal," she said, stirring with renewed focus.

"Now, whisk that cream—no tears in my eclairs!"

She laughed, tension fading. "Back home, the goats would be all over this. They'd probably climb onto the kitchen counter just to see what we were doing."

I raised an eyebrow. "Goats on the counter?"

She nodded, a wry smile creeping in. "They love climbing everything—fence rails, tree branches, random trucks. And they hate being alone. They'll stand outside the house, staring at the door like little stalker ninjas."

I laughed, letting the ludicrous image of goats wearing ninja suits chase away the last hints of awkwardness. "Okay, you've convinced me—our life is missing goats."

She smiled—an actual, full-on smile—and glazed each pastry with the precision of someone defusing a bomb. By the time we boxed them up, the kitchen felt lighter, warmer, like we'd baked more than dessert.

Later, upstairs, Adele held up a summery outfit of shorts and a flowy top. "Does this work for the party?" she asked, her tone hopeful yet uncertain.

"It's perfect," I said, already envisioning how great she'd look. "Do you have a sweater? Sin's patio can get chilly after sunset."

Her brows shot up. "But it's summer."

"Welcome to Pittsburgh," I replied with a shrug. "Sixties at night. You'll thank me later."

She shuddered theatrically. "Sixty degrees in summer is just wrong."

Laughing, I headed to my closet. "Borrow one of mine. Come pick while I figure out what to wear."

Adele followed, muttering about freezing summers. A few minutes later, she emerged with a cozy white sweater while I stood holding up a floral dress and a sleek jumpsuit.

"Grayson," I called, summoning my boyfriend like he was my personal fashion consultant. "Bohemian Rhapsody or Downtown Diva?"

He studied both with the gravity of a runway judge. "Hmm… The floral dress screams book-club-picnic-gone-wrong."

I groaned. "The Great Grape Heist?"

"The one and only," he confirmed. He glanced at Adele. "That was the day Gertrude commandeered everyone's wine glasses, claiming she was rescuing the 'neglected reds.'"

Adele snorted softly as I shook my head, grinning. "Don't forget the part where she 'redistributed' the wine so no glass went unappreciated. Max still insists his merlot was mostly chardonnay by the end."

Grayson laughed. "The woman's a legend in chaos management. But this jumpsuit?" he added, tilting his head in thoughtful appraisal. "It says *Runway Rebel,* and I like it."

I tossed the dress aside. "Rebel it is."

Adele, observing with quiet amusement, finally spoke. "You guys have the weirdest stories. I can't wait to hear more."

I pulled her into a side hug. "Oh, don't worry. You'll have your own weird stories soon enough."

The drive to Sinan's house was short, the eclairs nestled in the backseat like culinary crown jewels. Once we arrived, they were an instant hit, with everyone swooping in to snatch them up.

Kincaid spotted Adele the moment we stepped onto the huge patio. His face lit up as he made a beeline toward her, arms open like he'd known her forever. "So, this is the legendary Adele?"

With an overly theatrical flourish, I gestured toward her. "Allow me to introduce Adele Gillette—the newest star in our ever-expanding family galaxy!"

Kincaid swept her into a bear hug. "Welcome, baby sister. Come meet the family." He gestured to Lianna, cradling their baby. "This is my wife, Lianna, and our daughter Harper."

Lianna's smile was instant and welcoming. "My new sister-in-law! It's so great to meet you." She shifted Harper so Adele could see her. Of course, Harper chose that moment to wave her chubby hands, drawing a tentative but genuine smile from Adele.

"Connection achieved," Grayson whispered in my ear, and we exchanged a grin.

Conner appeared next, his smirking smile as irrepressible as ever. "Hi, Adele. I'm your brother Conner. The only one you haven't met is Christopher, but he's stuck in London, doing London things."

"Three brothers and a sister," Adele murmured, looking overwhelmed. "This is all so crazy."

"And don't forget your sister-in-law and niece," Lianna added with a wink. "We count."

Conner, ever the entertainer, launched into one of his favorite tales. "We were just talking about Courtney's famous kitchen disaster—"

"Conner, stop," I groaned.

"Oh no, this is a classic," Kincaid said, backing him up. "Salt instead of sugar. Mommy Julie's birthday cake. Truly unforgettable."

"And truly inedible," Conner confirmed. "Leave it to Courtney to turn it into an inspirational speech about resilience."

Adele let out a laugh. "That sounds just like you," she teased, flashing a grin at me. "You always have a way of turning every video call into a teachable moment."

"Always," I said with mock seriousness. "Turning disasters into life lessons is my superpower."

The patio filled with chatter and laughter until Mara clinked her glass, drawing everyone's attention. She stood, radiant, with Ford at her side. But before she could speak, Kincaid—ever the organizer—called out, "Sean's missing. Anyone know where he is?"

Rose looked up, blinking as though recalling Sean's existence from her mental writer's cave. "Sean's in Mexico, hanging off some cliff, I think."

Adele's gasp was equal parts amusement and alarm, her eyes going wide.

Rose waved it off with a casual flick of her hand. "He's fine, really. Just stunt work for a film. He'll be back next week."

Just then, Rose's phone buzzed in her hand. She glanced at the screen and stepped away, pressing it to her ear.

"What do you mean you're halfway down a cliff? You couldn't wait to call me until you were safe on the ground?" she hissed, shooting me a half-exasperated, half-amused glance as she turned away to continue the conversation in private.

I caught only that snippet—and couldn't help grinning at the sheer chaos of it. Who knew what Rose and Sean's relationship had in store next?

Grayson cleared his throat, redirecting everyone's attention. "So, you were about to drop some news, Mara?"

Mara exchanged a meaningful look with Ford, a beaming smile lighting up her face. "We have some exciting news..." His hand rested on her belly in a way that practically telegraphed their announcement .

I gasped, already guessing. "No way! Are you—?"

"Pregnant!" Mara announced. The single word sent a ripple of cheers through the group.

Sonya wasn't far behind, standing with Max. "Guess what? So are we!"

"Seriously?" Rose cried out, feigning exasperation. "Double weddings, double babies. You two are exhausting!"

313

48

A DANCE AT DUSK

GRAYSON

I leaned on the deck's railing, the city below shimmering like it was in on my big secret. The lights along Pittsburgh's rivers glowed in the deepening dusk, their reflections rippling across the water. Fireworks barges drifted idly, oblivious to the weight of my plans. Tonight's fireworks weren't just a spectacle—they were the backdrop for something monumental. No pressure, right? Everything had to be perfect. Absolutely perfect.

I glanced over at Courtney, laughing with Adele and Sonya on the other side of the patio. The velvet box in my pocket felt heavier than it had any right to be. As the sky grew darker, my heart pounded like a drummer gone rogue. This wasn't just about the ring—it was about us, our future, and hoping I'd chosen the right moment to ask her to make it forever.

"Thought I'd find you here," Sinan said, sidling up next to me. His smirk was so knowing, I half-expected him to start narrating my inner monologue. "Big night, huh?"

Feigning nonchalance, I shrugged. "The biggest." My voice was steady—my pulse, not so much.

Sinan clapped me on the back. "Don't choke. We're all rooting for you."

Kendra's voice cut through from her perch where she was surveying the three rivers. "Grayson! Stop brooding and come bask in my dominion over Pittsburgh's bridges. Someone's gotta keep these beauties safe, and spoiler alert—it's me."

Grateful for the distraction, I laughed. "You're the reason I trust every bridge in this town. Thanks for keeping us safe."

"Bridges are my day job," she said, flipping her hair dramatically. "But the real engineering marvel? Both of our sisters announcing they're pregnant. Talk about miracles of timing and biological precision."

I chuckled but couldn't resist glancing at Courtney again. She was glowing—partly from the string lights, mostly from being her incredible self.

Kendra followed my gaze and raised an eyebrow. "Word on the patio is, you've got some personal fireworks planned."

"Perhaps," I replied, the word heavy with the weight of everything I had planned for tonight.

She leaned closer, her grin sly. "Better stick the landing. We're all counting on you to deliver."

As the last rays of sunlight slipped below the horizon, Sinan switched off his playlist and shot me a glance—letting me know everything was on track. Everyone's chatter quieted, anticipation spreading like an electric current as they all avoided looking at me and giving away the moment. This was it.

The first burst of fireworks illuminated the night sky in a cascade of vibrant color, just as my cooking class friends spilled onto the patio through the sliding glass doors. Conner's guitar sounded first, the chords smooth and deliberate, followed by Max's rich, Sinatra-esque voice, crooning *Fly me to the moon.*

Courtney's head turned, her eyes lighting up as recognition dawned. She'd been singing it just this afternoon. That smile—it was everything I could ever hope for. Every jittery nerve in my body hummed in harmony with the melody.

Max's voice was the cue for our organized chaos to begin. My makeshift dance crew sprang into action, spinning, snapping, and channeling the Rat Pack with varying levels of success. I led the charge, throwing in a finger snap and a spin, feeling more like a flailing penguin than a suave crooner. But Courtney's laughter—pure and bright—was all the encouragement I needed.

When Sinan tossed a fedora my way, I caught it with an exaggerated flourish, tipping it with mock bravado. Courtney's laughter rang out as she wiped tears from her eyes. "You're absolutely ridiculous," she said, grinning through the giggles.

"Ridiculously in love," I shot back, taking hold of her hand and twirling her into an impromptu spin and keeping her with me as I danced her around the deck.

Adele and Emma joined the fray, their initial hesitance melting into full-blown giggles as Kincaid and Max guided them through the moves. Even Dante—Mr. I'm-a-Chef-Not-a-Dancer—joined in, his grin widening with every clumsy step.

As the final notes of the song swelled, Max crooned, "I love you," and my backup dance crew retreated, their laughter and applause fading into the crackle of fireworks overhead. For a moment, time seemed to still, the fireworks casting Courtney's face in a glow of shifting gold and crimson. It was just us now, held in a perfect frame of starlight and celebration.

My knees hit the deck, the velvet box trembling in my hands as I opened it to reveal the vintage Irish Claddagh ring. Its heart-shaped diamond caught the light, winking like it shared my secret.

"Courtney," I began, my voice steady despite the riot of nerves inside me. "From the moment we flew to that double wedding together, my life has been filled with new experiences and unexpected adventures. You're the melody to my harmony. I want every sunset, every sunrise—with you. Will you marry me?"

Her eyes filled with tears, but her smile didn't waver for a second. "Yes, yes! Of course I will."

She dropped to her knees in front of me, her hands cupping my face as she whispered, "You stole my heart the day you outwitted Zephyr and that snaggle-beaked seagull, produced the wedding rings from your pocket like a true hero, and offered me a tissue when I was a mascara-smudged mess. You're my knight in shining armor, Gray. Always."

Sliding the ring onto her finger, the fireworks overhead blurred into the background, their explosions no match for the light in her eyes. All I could see was her—radiant, laughing, and mine.

Somewhere in the crowd, a cheer went up, voices mingling with the celebratory pop of a champagne bottle. Glasses clinked and laughter rippled through the night, but it all felt distant. The world had narrowed to just us.

"Here's to Courtney and Grayson!" my sister shouted. "Our dynamic duo of romance and science. May your love story be more epic than any comic book."

I kissed her then—a kiss full of promises, possibilities, and everything we hadn't yet put into words. The fireworks might've painted the sky, but it was the way she kissed me back that made the moment unforgettable.

EPILOGUE

Courtney

One year later

> Conner: Adele cheated at Scrabble last night. She made up a word: "Zebraloo."

> Adele: I did not! It's a legit term. Ask Kincaid.

> Kincaid: …It's from a nursery theme Courtney vetoed. But honestly? Great word.

> Me: I still stand by that veto!

> Grayson: Hypothetically, if "Zebraloo" isn't a word, how can it be used in Scrabble?

> Adele: It is so a word. You're all just jealous I won.

The hum of the airplane's engines was oddly soothing as Grayson and I lounged in business class, a definite upgrade from economy's sardine-can aesthetic. Outside, the night sky stretched endlessly, stars winking as they accompanied us on our journey.

It was impossible not to think of Turks and Caicos, where this love story of ours had first taken flight—pun intended. This commercial flight lacked Ford's exotic mojitos and the in-flight chocolate assortments, but the connection between us? Still as vibrant as ever, even if we now carried more baggage—literal and metaphorical.

Grayson, always tuned in, caught me frowning at the snorer two rows ahead. His fingers laced with mine, sending a familiar flutter through me. "Deep in thought or planning that guy's wake-up call?"

"Both," I said, sighing dramatically.

The anticipation of co-presenting at the conference crackled between us, but it was his new Cates Foundation venture that truly had us flying high. Grayson had his own research team there now, working right alongside mine. Life was in sync—professionally, personally, and everything in between.

I glanced at the silver bracelet on my wrist, with its seaglass charm we'd found on the beach the first night we'd spent together. To anyone else, it was just jewelry; to me, it was a piece of moonlit beaches and whispered promises.

The flight attendant's arrival with Screwdrivers stole my focus. I raised my cup to Grayson. "To us—and to the Cates Foundation for business-class tickets."

Grayson tapped his cup to mine. "To you—for proving brilliance and wit are unstoppable."

The banter had me smiling, but as I reclined my seat, Grayson leaned closer, his grin pure mischief. "By the way, I've got something special planned in Amsterdam."

I narrowed my eyes, my rusty detective instincts kicking in. "Do I need to be worried?"

His smirk was pure Grayson, a mix of charm and mischief. "I took inspiration from our baking adventures—especially the infamous Carrot Cake Debacle—and your story about making *cantucci* in Florence. I've signed us up for a cooking class."

"Dutch apple pie?" I guessed, laughing.

Grayson grinned. "Something like that. Just no repeat of the Great Carrot Cake Debacle, okay?"

"As long as I'm not the one cleaning frosting out of weird places, I'm in."

He reached for my hand beneath the blanket, his touch grounding me. "You know, stepping into this role at Cates has been monumental. It feels like I've tapped into something bigger."

"You have, Gray," I said softly. "Our work might be separate, but it feels connected, like two pieces of the same puzzle."

The rhythmic hum of the engines mixed with the comfortable silence between us, and my eyelids grew heavy. As I drifted off, Grayson's hand stayed wrapped in mine, a steady presence anchoring me through the flight.

When the seatbelt sign chimed hours later, it jolted me awake. Below, Amsterdam shimmered like a glittering map, its canals promising adventure. Grayson stretched beside me, his smile relaxed and filled with anticipation. "Good morning, my love."

His hand found mine as the plane began its descent. Fingers intertwined, we shared a moment of silent anticipation, our excitement bubbling under the surface.

I turned toward the window, taking in the view. Crooked houses and winding waterways came into focus. With a judder that felt more like a polite hiccup than a proper landing, the plane touched down. Tomorrow, the conference would be our stage, a chance to shine together, but today? Today was for exploring. And, apparently, for baking.

I glanced at my wrist, where my bracelet caught the light. Beside it, my Claddagh ring gleamed—a simple, perfect choice for a scientist who regularly wore gloves in the lab, its heart-shaped diamond reflecting the vows we'd exchanged at the Allegheny County Courthouse.

Grayson's thumb brushed over my ring, his eyes meeting mine with that familiar spark. "Ready for the next adventure?"

"With you? Always," I replied, grinning.

And as we stepped into the cool Amsterdam morning, I thought, *Bring it on.*

THE END

ACKNOWLEDGMENTS

A heartfelt thank you to Rose Pletcher for brainstorming with me in the early stages of this book. When I was struggling to figure out how Courtney would discover her research had been stolen, Rose suggested the idea of the cell image—a stroke of brilliance I never would've thought of on my own. That pivotal detail is entirely thanks to her insight, and I'm deeply grateful for her contribution.

Thank you, Doug Donaldson, for your invaluable insights into the complexities of inter-pharmaceutical collaborations and the risks of corporate espionage. Your expertise added depth and authenticity to this story.

DANTE'S EASY ITALIAN MEATBALLS

Level: Moderate
  Prep: 15 minutes
  Refrigeration Time: 1 hour
  Cooking Time: 25 minutes
  Total Time: 1 hour and 40 minutes

Ingredients

- 1/3 cup plain bread crumbs
- 1/2 cup milk (water or beef broth work as substitutes)
- 2 tbsps olive oil
- 1 onion, diced
- 1 lb. ground beef
- 1 lb. ground pork
- 2 eggs
- 1/4 bunch fresh parsley, chopped
- 3 cloves garlic, crushed
- 2 tsps salt
- 1 tsp ground black pepper
- 1.5 tsps dried Italian herb seasoning
- 2 tbsps grated Parmesan cheese

Directions:

1. Cover a baking sheet with foil and spray lightly with cooking spray or use a silicone mat.
2. Soak the bread crumbs in your liquid of choice (milk, water, or beef broth) in a small bowl for 10 minutes.
3. Heat olive oil in a skillet over medium-high heat. Cook and stir onions in hot oil until translucent, about 5 minutes.
4. Mix the beef and pork together in a large bowl. Stir the onions, bread crumb mixture, eggs, garlic, parsley, salt, black pepper, Italian herb seasoning, and Parmesan cheese into meat mixture with a rubber spatula until combined. Cover and refrigerate for about one hour (or use a rapid cooler!)
5. Preheat an oven to 425°F.
6. Using wet hands, form meat mixture into balls about 1 1/2 inches in diameter. Arrange onto your prepared baking sheet.
7. Bake until browned and cooked through, about 15 to 20 minutes.

CANTUCCI RECIPE (ALMOND BISCOTTI)

Level: Moderate
Serving size: 30 cookies
Prep time: 10 mins
Cook time: 45 mins

Ingredients

- 2 cups+1 tablespoon (250 g) all-purpose flour (sifted)
- 1 cup minus 1 tablespoon (185 g) granulated sugar
- 1 teaspoon baking powder
- 2 large eggs
- 1 teaspoon grated orange zest
- 1 teaspoon pure vanilla extract
- 4.4 oz (125 g) raw unpeeled almonds (you can replace the almonds with pistachios, hazelnuts, pecans, or walnuts)

- *Variations:*
- Chocolate Covered Cherry version: add 1/4 cup of dried cherries + 1/4 cup of chocolate bits + 1/4 cup of cocoa powder + 2 teaspoons of the "juice" from a jar of Maraschino cherries (I love Luxardo cherries, so choose the juice from them).
- Mint chocolate chip version: add 5 drops peppermint oil or 1/2 teaspoon extract (the oil is better) + 1/4 cup chocolate bits.
- Glazed version: Drizzle the cantucci with glaze after you remove it from the oven.
- Chocolate version: Add 1/4 cup cocoa powder to the cookies when you make the dough, or melt some chocolate and coat the bottom of the cantucci with it.
- Additional versions: experiment with lemon zest, candied ginger, dried cherries, white chocolate chips, coconut and coconut extract, dried cranberries, cinnamon chips, toffee bits with instant coffee, or semi-sweet chocolate chips.

Directions:

1. Preheat the oven to 350°F (180°C).
2. In a large bowl, combine the flour, sugar, and baking powder.
3. Add the eggs, orange zest, vanilla extract, and mix all the ingredients.
4. Put the dough on a lightly floured surface and knead it until the dough is slightly sticky and smooth.
5. Add the almonds and knead the dough until they are well combined.
6. Wet your hands and divide the dough in half and shape

each piece into a 12 inches (30 cm) log that's about 2 inches (5 cm) wide.

7. Line a baking sheet with parchment paper or a silicone mat. Place the logs on a baking sheet. Make sure there is enough room between the logs.
8. Bake for 30 minutes. The loaves will be golden brown.
9. Remove the logs from the oven and let them cool for 10 minutes. Using a sharp, serrated knife, cut diagonally into ½ inch (1.5 cm) slices.
10. Put the cantucci slices on the baking sheet and bake an additional 10-15 minutes.
11. Cool the cantucci on a wire rack.

COURTNEY'S (AND SHERI'S) ORANGE FIG CARROT CAKE

Serving size: Serves 12–16

Prep time: 2 hours 30 mins

Cook time: 35 mins

Difficulty: High

This cake requires quite a few tools, so make sure you have them all!

Ingredients

Cake:

(Calls for 7.9 inch pans greased and lined with parchment paper. I used 9 inch pans)

- 4 large eggs
- 1.5 cups light brown sugar
- 1 tsp vanilla extract
- ⅔ cup light cooking oil such as sunflower oil
- 3 cups carrots, grated
- finely grated zest of 2 unwaxed oranges
- 2¼ cups of '00' cake flour or pizza flour

- 1½ tbsp baking powder (Don't forger this!)
- 1 tbsp ground cinnamon
- ½ tsp ground ginger
- ¼ tsp salt
- 1 cup almond flour
- 1 cup or about 2.5 oranges fresh orange juice

Jam:

Seriously. Buy fig jam and add some orange zest and chopped walnuts. You'll thank me. But, if you insist, make it from scratch as follows:

- 1-1/3 lbs figs, quartered
- finely grated zest of 1 unwaxed orange
- ½ cup honey
- 1 tbsp corn starch
- ¼ cup walnuts, chopped

Cream cheese filling and decoration

- 2 sticks unsalted butter, softened
- 3-1/2 cups powdered sugar
- 2 tsps vanilla paste or vanilla extract
- finely grated zest of 2 unwaxed oranges
- 12 ozs. full-fat cream cheese
- 1/2 cup walnuts
- 2 tbsp maple syrup
- 1 fig, cut into 8 wedges

Equipment:

- 3 - 8" cake pans, greased Dand lined with parchment paper
- 1 lined baking sheet (for the walnuts)
- Palette knife (some people call it a long metal spatula)

- large piping bag
- medium piping bag fitted with a small star nozzle
- medium piping bag fitted with a large star nozzle
- medium piping bag fitted with a medium plain nozzle

Directions:

1. Heat the oven to 350°F
2. **Make the cakes**: Whisk the eggs, sugar and vanilla extract together in a stand mixer fitted with the whisk attachment until tripled in volume.
3. With the mixer running, pour in the oil. Add the grated carrots and orange zest and whisk to incorporate.
4. Switch to the beater attachment. Add the flour, baking powder, spices, salt and ground almonds to the egg mixture and set the mixer running on its the lowest speed, mixing until all the ingredients are just incorporated.
5. Slowly pour in the orange juice, mixing until all the liquid is fully incorporated.
6. Divide the cake batter between the three prepared pans. Bake for 30–35 minutes for 7.9" pans, or until a skewer inserted into the center of each cake comes out clean. Leave the cakes to cool in the pan for 5 minutes, then turn them out onto a wire rack. Turn the cakes the right way up and leave them to *cool completely*.
7. **Make the Jam**: Meanwhile, make the fig and walnut jam. Tip the figs, orange zest, sugar and pectin into a heavy-based saucepan set over a medium heat. Bring the mixture to a simmer and cook until the sugar has dissolved. Increase the heat and boil the mixture for 10 minutes, until thick. Remove the pan from the heat and set the jam aside to cool – it will set as it cools. Once

cool, stir through the chopped walnuts. **Note:** if using store-bought jam, simply warm the jam in a saucepan and add the orange zest and chopped walnuts.)

8. **Make the cream-cheese frosting.** Beat the butter and icing sugar in a stand mixer fitted with the beater, on medium speed for 3–5 minutes, until pale and creamy. Add the vanilla and orange zest, and beat again to incorporate.

9. Add the cream cheese and beat to incorporate, being careful not to overmix. Transfer three quarters of the frosting into the large piping bag. Divide the remaining frosting between the three piping bags fitted with a nozzle and chill until required.

10. **Make the candied walnuts.** Toss the walnuts in the maple syrup and put them on the lined baking sheet. Bake for 20–25 minutes, until golden. Leave the walnuts to cool completely.

11. **Assemble:** Snip the end of the large piping bag. Pipe dots of the cream-cheese frosting onto a cake plate or stand. Place one of the cakes on the stand or plate and pipe frosting on top, spreading it evenly to the edges with a palette knife. Pipe a ring of frosting around the edge of the sponge and fill the middle with half the fig and walnut jam. Place a second cake on top and repeat. Check for leaks. Repair if necessary.

12. Add the final cake and pipe a generous layer of frosting on top. Smooth it out with a palette knife to an even layer.

13. Pipe thick stripes of frosting around the side of the cake and scrape away the excess with a cake scraper to give a semi-naked effect.

14. To decorate, using the icing in the piping bags fitted with nozzles, pipe differently shaped kisses of icing to create a crescent shape on the top of the cake. Decorate with the fresh fig pieces, and candied walnuts.

BIBLIOGRAPHY

Contemporary Romances
By Sheri Tyler
The Way to a Woman's Heart series - the **Coming Home** trilogy
Slow Simmer
Here's the Scoop
From Bitter to Sweet

The Way to a Woman's Heart series - the **Destination Wedding** trilogy
One Cup of Chemistry
Say Cheese!
Kebabs and Kisses

Historical romances
By Sheridan Jeane
Gambling On a Scoundrel

Secrets and Seduction series:
** Lady Cecilia Is Cordially Disinvited for Christmas*
**(only available via Sheridan's VIP club)
It Takes a Spy…
Lady Catherine's Secret
Once Upon a Spy
My Lady, My Spy
Along Came a Spy

Duke By Dawn (Novella, part of the anthology *Dukes All Night Long*)
Coming August 2025

The Rose and the Spy - a Victorian-era Romantic Suspense trilogy
Coming 2026
Whispers and Spies
The Spy In Disguise
A Spy For All Seasons

ABOUT THE AUTHOR

I'm Sheri Tyler, and I write the **Way to a Woman's Heart** series of romcoms set in Sewickley, a small town near Pittsburgh. These books all feature my favorite things: food, books, family, and friends.

More about me?
My alter-ego in writing is Sheridan Jeane. I publish my Victorian-era historical romance and romantic suspense novels under that name.
I'm the daughter of an artist/art-therapist/professor mother and an opera-loving/computer engineer/do-it-yourself father. Growing up, I assumed parents routinely converted their garages into well-stocked art studios complete with potter's wheels, kilns, and every color of paint under the sun. Didn't every second-grader learn how to weld or nail shingles on the roof of the 2-car garage their dad built? And what about all those after-opera cast parties? Weren't they run-of-the-mill too?
No?
Go figure!
That probably explains my quirky outlook on life.

Visit me at www.SheridanJeane.com
Or
www.SheriTyler.com